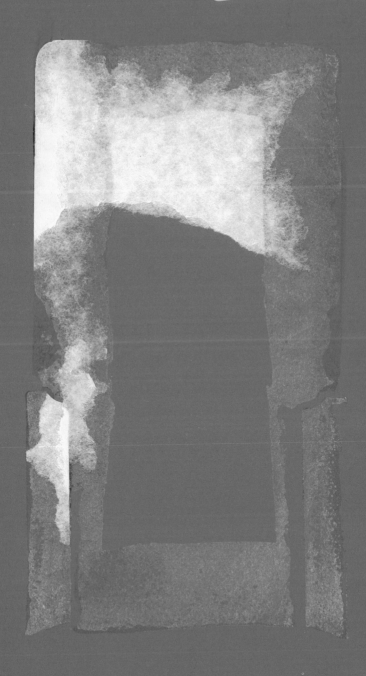

Hard on the Road

Hard on the Road

By Barbara Moore

Doubleday & Company, Inc.
Garden City, New York
1974

Library of Congress Cataloging in Publication Data

Moore, Barbara, 1934–
    Hard on the road.

    I. Title.
PZ4.M8186Har [PS3563.057]   813'.5'4
ISBN 0-385-08191-X
Library of Congress Catalog Card Number 73-13091

For Joy, with sorrow

Part One

One

If Otis Wasum had done the proper thing by crying out, "Defend yourself!" instead of just mumbling at me, "You little Fairchild sonofabitch," I maintain that I would have known instantly how to deal with him, and the whole thing would have ended right there. Mr. Stein wouldn't have been shot down in the street; Otis's brother Shirley wouldn't have been arrested; everything that happened to my Cousin Calvin and me and the people we met on our trip to the West would never have happened. But that's what Otis did, only mumbled, looking startled, and I left him alone, and the clock on the courthouse hadn't even clicked off a minute before he poked his brother's rifle through the window and opened up. He wasn't shooting at me. He was shooting at my father. He hit him, too, just a little groove on the hand, but in the process Otis also got Mr. Stein, the right heel of Mr. Harmon A. Berry's boot, and a four-layer lemon cake that Grandmother had made as a surprise for Calvin and me for the trip.

It was far from funny. The cake, yes, and perhaps Mr. Harmon A. Berry, a big talker about his feats in both peace and war, who yelped aloud when struck and withdrew into Veeder's Livery without making a single effort to revenge himself. But Mr. Stein had stepped out into the street with my father, and Otis's wild firing hit the old gentleman directly in the throat. Mr. Stein raised his hands to the wound with a look of surprise such as I had never seen. I regret that I have seen it since.

Of course there was hell to pay. Fairchild men came running. From where I was, still halfway down the outside staircase of Uncle Dawkins Fairchild's store, I could see Calvin leave the big camera he was so proud of and run to Mr. Stein. Someone's horse was screaming, and Cousin Wash Fairchild's mules became frantic and tried to run off with his wagon. It was seconds before I moved, and when I did it was to my father and Calvin and Mr. Stein. I swear to God that, because of the unsanctioned way he'd done things, it never once crossed my mind to go back up the stairs and confront Otis Wasum. It wasn't at all that I was afraid.

Mr. Stein was leaning against Calvin when I got to them, with Calvin's arms around him, and my father kneeling on the other side. Mr. Stein's blood spurted out over Calvin's good suit, bought for traveling. His throat was making a sound. I started shouting, I think just at Cousin Wash Fairchild's mules, until my father said, "That will do, Pepper." He sounded just as cold and calm and polite as he always did. He mostly went on sounding that way until we left, that same afternoon, as he insisted we must. He did not come to the stage to say good-bye. I thought it was because he was so mad at me, as I was mad at him, but to tell the truth, it probably just didn't occur to him.

But that was my father's way. He refused to show that anything could ruffle him, not even the grief that Otis Wasum brought to us that day, by impropriety and poor shooting, in the county seat of Claiborne Parish where we Fairchilds mostly lived and which Calvin and I were leaving that day, first by stage, then by catching the V.S. & P. Railroad in Shreveport. I had never been on either a stage or a railroad before, but I'd seen the town just about every day of my life, and before the trouble started I had been saying farewell to it in my thoughts, figuring it would be the whole summer before I saw it again.

Naturally, I should have been enjoying myself. Farewell to Homer, Louisiana, which I felt would probably find a place in history only as my birth site. Farewell to the family, just about all of whom had come to town to see us off, and to Mr. Stein, down for his annual visit from New York. Farewell to a boy I saw on the street, Timmy McClanahan, who at fourteen was younger than I, so I ordinarily didn't associate with him much, but who shared my passion for base ball and once traded me a card I coveted of Michael J. "King" Kelly of the Chicago White Stockings for one which pictured the world's most famous long-distance hitter, Roger Connor of the Troys.

I had stopped to talk to Timmy for a minute, and the reason wasn't nice: as close as I felt to my Cousin Calvin, I was feeling peevish about an errand he had sent me on, and was getting even by dawdling. It was bad enough to have everyone in the parish watching him try to take a photograph and being ready to laugh at him, as they always did, and, therefore, getting a snicker or two ready for anyone who happened to be associated with him in public, which was me. Having to run the errand, which was to tell a Wasum that Calvin asked him please to stay out of the picture, seemed just one straw too many.

And I had to be associated in public with Calvin. I was being sent by the family to look after him during our travels, which were to take Calvin and me to Denison City, Texas, to pick up a photographer's wagon that was to be equipment for Calvin's new profession in San Diego, California. I was to drive the mules for him and deliver him to a Mr. John Swiss Parker in California, who was some kin to the Spinkses, which was Grandmother's family. Since my duty was generally to help him, I'd already been helping him all I could to take a photograph that Uncle Dawkins wanted of his mercantile store with the family all lined up in front of it. But though Calvin and I were good friends, it was beginning to shame me to be seen so much in his company, particularly since a bunch of tiny kids were hanging around, jostling the legs of the tripod and trying to get a peek through the camera and giggling, as they always did, every time Calvin spoke.

Everyone said Calvin stuttered, but he didn't really. He was born with a harelip, which Grandmother said hadn't been basted in time, so he couldn't always speak too plainly. But what the main trouble looked like was, when he was troubled or nervous or maybe had some difficult word to say, the word got stuck in his mouth. His torn upper lip and his good lower lip clamped shut while he worked on it, and finally it came out nasally and with a kind of pop, like, ". . . Pepper, there's someone in the top of the picture." If he really stuttered, as the people in the parish did when they mocked him, it would have been "Puh-Puh-Puh-Pepper" or "puh-puh-puh-picture."

That was when I first saw Otis Wasum in the window. At that particular moment I was ducked in under the focusing cloth. I peered into the ground glass of the big view camera the family had bought Cousin Calvin, and sure enough, upside down at the bottom of the glass, there was someone in the second-story window of Uncle Dawkins's store.

"It looks like one of the Wasums," I said.

"Oh lord," Calvin sighed.

He sounded worried, and I ducked back out from under the cloth. Calvin was sweating. It was late May, so the weather was already good and hot, and Calvin was working hard to take the photograph before his plate dried. But I knew he was also sweating because my father had already called to him once to hurry up.

"Go ahead," I said. "He won't show. He's too far up."

"Yes he will," Cousin Calvin said. "And he's not Fairchild kin."

Of course, a Wasum wasn't. Fairchilds and Wasums never went hunting together and never even married, because twenty years ago, right after the war, there had been trouble between us, and there had been new trouble between us over a court case that very spring. Until today, the only new fighting was just a fistfight between me and Otis Wasum, but the feelings between us Fairchilds and the Wasums remained uneasy.

Well, so there was a Wasum in the window of Uncle Dawkins's store, and that would never do in a Fairchild family portrait, and Calvin was worried about it.

I said, "Can't you shoot the picture without the top story showing?"

Calvin's face got more worried-looking, as it always did when he was having a hard time saying something, and his jaw and neck muscles tightened, and there was this little silence before he managed to get out, "Please, Pepper. Just go tell him I asked him to stay out of sight until after the picture."

The bunch of little kids giggled at him again, and I walked away quickly. There was a good crowd in town. No doubt a lot of the parish people were just attending to everyday business

6

and trading, but there was also plenty of talk about my and Calvin's trip as well. So there was Timmy McClanahan, and I stopped to tell him farewell for the whole summer, hoping that whoever was in the window above the store would maybe get out of the picture on his own. Then I went on up the outside staircase to the second story of Uncle Dawkins's store, not very fast and not liking it.

The store loft was loaded to the brim with cartons of cigars, sacks of onions, old furniture that Grandmother wanted him to keep for her, an occasional bale of cotton that Uncle Dawkins had taken in trade and such, and I wended my way through dim stacks and bales, and I could hardly believe my eyes when I saw that it was Otis Wasum who was sitting in the window.

Otis was slight-built and fair, like all the Wasums. We weren't friends even before the new trouble; Otis didn't seem to care for friends. But of course I knew him a little, especially because he had been working at Uncle Dawkins's store until his father got mad at my father over the court case, and Otis quit. Then we'd had our fistfight, and it seemed highly inappropriate to me for Otis Wasum to be sitting in a Fairchild store on a Fairchild rice sack, staring vacantly out the window. I saw that he was eating an apple, a rifle leaning against the wall beside him, and an empty gunnysack near his feet, but I attended first to the thing I'd come about, the window. I said belligerently, "Otis Wasum, you get away from that window. You're spoiling the picture."

"Oh," he said, startled. He jerked back away from the window, looking apologetic. Then he recovered himself and mumbled, as I have said, "You little Fairchild sonofabitch." He added, "You got no right to tell me what to do."

I said, "And you got no right to be in my Uncle Dawkins's loft eating his apples." I doubled up my fists and prepared to resume our fight, if that's what he wanted. As an afterthought, I also added, "You Wasum sonofabitch."

"You better be careful," he said. "You just remember that your daddy and my daddy is on the edge of a blood feud, and if you get too smart, you're just likely to be right in the middle of it."

"That's silly talk," I said. "There ain't going to be no feud unless your daddy goes clean out of his mind. There's more of us

7

Fairchilds than there ever will be Wasums, and your daddy surely knows enough arithmetic to know when he's well off. Us Fairchilds would swamp you in a week."

"Numbers wouldn't make no difference if the head was cut off," he said.

"The head?" I said. "Whatever are you talking about?"

Otis stared at me, and his pale blue eyes were motionless as stones. After a second, he shook his head two or three times and mumbled, "What's the matter with you, Pepper Fairchild? Your Uncle Dawkins don't care if I sit in his loft, he lets me come up here."

"You're lying," I said. "My Uncle Dawkins don't want nothing to do with the Wasums since your daddy went so hog-wild about his hogs. What's more, you stole them apples, and furthermore, what are you doing with that rifle? I'll bet you stole that rifle, too." I looked at it closer. "Why, that's your brother's rifle. Shirley will skin you alive for swiping his rifle."

Otis never spoke very loudly, and he had a good case of the mumbles that day. He said something about ". . . my brother knows" and ". . . going squirrel hunting" and then his voice came up a little and his washed-out eyes began to move about, and he said, "Be careful what you say, Pepper Fairchild, or I'll give you a taste of what I gave you two weeks ago."

All right, I admit it, maybe I backed away a step or two. It was because of the way Otis's eyes looked. But I said, "You never whipped me. Maybe that's what you've been telling people, but you never did."

"You just watch out," he said.

"Well, you just stay away from that window and stop ruining other people's photographs," I said.

He started mumbling again, and I turned on my heel and left, feeling I'd told him off pretty stoutly, but worrying about that fistfight. The way it looked to me, it had been a pretty even fight. No, more than that. I won. Otis and I were about of a size, but he was older, and I stood up to him for a full twenty minutes, down by Dr. Paul McDade's cow lot, and it was Otis who backed down, or I felt I'd have still been there fighting.

I shoved through the bales and boxes and to the top of the outside stairs, and I got there just in time to hear my father call out, "Calvin, if you're going to take this photograph, you'd better take it right now."

I think my father was thinking about my new stepmother standing out there in the sun, with two or three of the little nephews arranged in front of her. My father said it politely, as he said everything, but I could tell he meant it, and obviously my Cousin Calvin could too. Calvin said, "All right, everybody hold real still now."

So I was stuck. I couldn't run downstairs and through the picture, or that would have ruined it. I couldn't see the family, lined up in front of the store, but from the stairs I could see Calvin across the street, hurrying to arrange the focusing cloth on the back of the camera. He fumbled around, carefully removing the shield from the plateholder with the big glass plate we'd got ready earlier. Then he took off the lens cap and called again, "Now be still. Be real still."

I held my breath. He wanted it just right, you see. The family was all there watching Calvin, and he was leaving, and the family had spent a lot of time and money for his training and all the equipment and arranging for the photographer's wagon and arranging for him to have his new profession in California. So it was important to Calvin to get that photograph just right. He'd even loaded the new James Flash Lamp the family had bought him, because he had said the sun was so high it would cast dark shadows on all the faces unless he used flashlight powder to lighten them. I felt guilty when I saw him grab up the lamp. I was supposed to hold it for him. But I told myself that it was Calvin who had sent me away.

The flash powder went off, brighter than the sun. Calvin clamped the lens cap back on the camera and sang out, "All right. Everybody can move now." His voice was happy.

The family broke up then, and everybody started talking. My father and Mr. Stein walked out in the street to speak to Calvin. I started down the stairs, half thinking that I'd better rush down and join Calvin in our makeshift darkroom to help him develop the exposed plate, and half thinking that I should run tell Uncle Dawkins about his apples, and then tell Shirley Wasum, Otis's brother, about Otis swiping his . . .

Rifle.

That was when it finally came to me.

I gasped, "Oh my God." My lips were forming the words, "Father, Father," to call out to him.

And Otis Wasum started shooting.

Mr. Stein, who had chosen the wrong moment to walk in front of my father, fell with a bullet through his throat on the first shot. I believe it was the third or fourth shot that nicked my father in the hand. When the wild shooting stopped, my young stepmother ran out into the street to my father, but he turned her around and gave her a little nudge away from the mortally wounded Mr. Stein. Some said later that Mr. Stein's throat bled on the hem of her dress, but that wasn't so. What was so is that my father's blood soiled her, for I saw it.

But then there was blood everywhere, and spatters of that lemon layer cake. Grandmother was vain, in the nicest way, about her baking, and she had wanted the cake in the photograph.

So there was everything happening all at once, and it was happening fast. When I could make my legs move and run the rest of the way down the stairs, I pushed my way, mostly through Fairchilds, to my father and Calvin and Mr. Stein, as I have said. People were staring around, some up at the store windows, and my Uncle Raleigh, who was a Hillman and not a Fairchild and therefore had not been in the picture, boomed out, "It come from up there." A cluster of my uncles and some of the grown-up cousins and some of the men from the street followed his pointing arm and rushed up the stairs I had just come down. Others ran into the *Homer Iliad* building next door. I stayed where I was and watched Mr. Stein die.

The whole family took it hard. They were upset, of course, that my father had been shot at, but he was alive and Mr. Stein was killed, and, what's more, he was killed while he was our company. That any harm should come to him, a Fairchild guest, hit by a bullet aimed, badly, at a Fairchild, was scarcely to be borne. But I knew it was hardest on Calvin and my grandmother. Calvin had two special friends in the world, me and Mr. Stein, and he had just returned in early spring from spending six months with Mr. Stein in New York, learning how to take views and portraits under a fine photographic artist Mr. Stein knew there and persuaded to teach Calvin, so Calvin could have his profession.

My grandmother's grief came from the fact that Mr. Stein had saved my grandfather's life in the war. Mr. Stein was a Jew from Bad Ocheim, in Bavaria, Germany. He was a back-peddler through the Carolinas and around when he first came over, and he told good stories of those times, but he stopped peddling and started soldiering when the war came. Rightly or wrongly, he chose the North. He was a prison guard at Rock Island, Illinois, when my grandfather was captured and taken there. Rock Island for a southern prisoner was like Andersonville for a northern prisoner: a grave for living men.

Things being the way they had been, there was little Mr. Stein or other well-intentioned men could do, and as Mr. Stein used to tell it, saying "I'm sorry" doesn't feed someone who's starving. It was Grandmother who decided more or less independently that Mr. Stein had saved Grandfather's life, later after the war ended and he began to come down once a year to visit with Grandfather. When Grandfather died, he still kept coming to see the family. Of course we had all adopted Grandmother's view. Mr. Stein was a hero, and we treasured him.

He died in such pain that I could barely stand it. It didn't take more than a few minutes, but if I had had a gun with me I would have put it to his head and pulled the trigger and at least saved him those minutes of pain. No, that isn't necessarily correct; perhaps it's myself I would have saved from witnessing those few minutes of his pain. Instead, I finally stumbled away from Mr. Stein and got my arms around one of the posts by Uncle Dawkins's store and butted my forehead against its rough wood and panted to myself over and over, "Sonofabitch, sonofabitch, sonofabitch."

I was then fifteen, and I wasn't supposed to say that kind of thing. My stepmother, who was only nineteen herself, heard me and immediately started saying, "Why, Pepper Fairchild!" and, "Shame!" and things like that.

I told her, "Keep the hell away from me!"

She raised her hands to her bosom and blinked at me. Her eyes were a shade you rarely see, a clear, light green, clear and bright like some jewel, and she was very full in the blouse. Her hands raised that way showed the golden wedding ring my father had given her the previous fall. Soon, she would not be going out; her blouse was already even fuller, and her waist thickening, so that she had taken lately always to muffling herself in a shawl. Both the shawl and her skirts had the blood on them.

The sound from Mr. Stein's throat was growing fainter. I tried to collect myself. They called me Pepper not only because I had red hair but because of my temperament, and no one except perhaps Calvin knew the efforts I sometimes made to control myself. I said, "Beg pardon," and started to turn away, but she grabbed my arm.

She stared at me a second, then dropped her green eyes and looked flustered. Flustered myself, I said, "Something has got on your dress. Let me take you inside the store."

I touched her elbow and guided her into the leather and molasses and new-cloth smell of Uncle Dawkins's store, running through all the confusion of Fairchild uncles and aunts and cousins. Two aunts came hurrying, probably remembering why my young stepmother was hugging that shawl on a bright day in late May, and I turned her over to them. My place was not with her. Nor was it with my father; I thought he'd made that clear by that cold, calm way he'd spoken to me. If anywhere, it was with Calvin, and I started back to him. But directly in my path, walking along just as casually as you please from around back of the store, was Otis Wasum.

Otis didn't say anything. He stared at me with those pale blue eyes, and they said enough. His hands went to the back of his pants, brushing, brushing off dust, and then he leaned and dusted off his knees. His nostrils were trembling like a rabbit's.

But he still didn't say anything, and I said, low, trying to keep my voice from trembling as much as his nose, "May you be goddamned to the deepest hell, you stinking Wasum bastard."

"Bastard" was the worst thing anyone could call Otis Wasum, since many people thought he was. But Otis never blinked. He said softly, "This begins it. You open your mouth, and I'll kill you. If I have to chase you to hell, I'll kill you."

I believe in the next second I might have reached for his neck, or maybe those staring eyes. There is, of course, pleasure in rage, and I really believe I might have done that. But my father, at that moment, seeing me lean toward Otis, called one disgusted word, "Pepper!" And at that same moment my Uncle Raleigh came running down the store steps.

"Here's the rifle, Judge," my Uncle Raleigh yelled, holding it in the air. "It was jammed behind the rice sacks, upstairs." He ran, naturally, even being a·Hillman, to my father.

My Uncle Bentley Fairchild leaned over my father's shoulder and looked at it and said, "That's Shirley Wasum's rifle."

"Hell yes it is," Uncle Raleigh said.

By natural gravity, other men were drawing near my father where he was kneeling with Calvin beside Mr. Stein's body. Sam Spinks, one of the grown-up cousins, darted suddenly aside. When he came back into view he was drawing Shirley Wasum with him. Shirley, fair and blue-eyed just like Otis but a good ten or so pounds heavier, being maybe ten years older, was one of those wild, tough young fellows who like to do things only in their own way and in their own good time. He looked daggers at Sam Spinks for daring to touch him like that, but he certainly made no effort to run away.

"That ain't my rifle," Shirley said negligently but in a voice of tempered steel.

Uncle Raleigh held up the .38–40 Model 73 Winchester with "1 of 1,000" engraved on the barrel. The rifle was known well in the parish, which is how I had recognized it earlier, for Shirley claimed to have paid one hundred dollars for it back in '75, when the whole parish was eating pone instead of cornbread, as we couldn't afford leavening just at that time. Uncle Raleigh sputtered, "Why, man, you're telling me this ain't your rifle?"

Shirley inspected it and began to look puzzled. "It can't be," he said. "I left mine home."

Now came Mr. Wasum, Otis's and Shirley's daddy, pushing through the crowd. He had graying fair hair and the same blue eyes and he was snapping, "What's this, what's this, what's this?" but you had to be from Claiborne Parish to understand him, because he would never wear his teeth.

Shirley understood him, of course, and flinched like a puppy dog that fears a scolding. The older Wasum boys and their father helled around together, hunted possum together, and, the parish tsk-tsked, all drank together once each boy got to be twelve or so, but for all his easy camaraderie with his oldest sons Mr. Wasum never let them forget he ruled the roost.

Shirley said to Mr. Wasum placatingly, "Hell, Daddy, I guess it looks like my gun, but it can't be. I left mine home."

So Mr. Wasum said to the men around him, "Don't you go accusing my boy. He didn't shoot at Judge Fairchild. I taught my boys better than that. If Shirley had wanted to face down the judge, he would have called him out in the street."

More men had hurried up, filling in and widening the circle. I had to push hard to get through them, and I tugged my Uncle Raleigh's sleeve. "It wasn't Shirley," I said. "It was Otis."

Uncle Raleigh, distracted by all the noise, said to me, "What?"

Everyone was talking and pressing close to look at the rifle. I raised my voice. "It was Otis who shot the rifle. I saw him with it. Up there." I gestured to the top story of the store.

Mr. Wasum looked bewildered. He said, "Why that can't be!" Then he gazed over my shoulder, questioningly. I turned. Otis Wasum had followed along right behind me.

Now, although Otis struck the parish as indifferent and at times downright hostile to his older brothers, everyone knew he was at least enough like them to think Mr. Wasum made the sun rise every morning, and with his father's eyes on him Otis seemed to lose confidence. He mumbled to me, "You're crazy with the heat. I been right here, all the time."

Mr. Wasum said sternly to Otis, "Are you sure?" Otis nodded. So Mr. Wasum said to my father, "Judge, can't you control that whelp of yours any better? He's got no call to be making up a pack of lies just because Otis whipped him a couple of weeks ago."

"He didn't either whip me," I said. "Sir."

"Shhhh," my Uncle Raleigh said.

The whole crowd was muttering. Then the undertaker, Mr. Willis Blountley, moved in and grabbed Otis's arm.

Mr. Wasum's face got a troubled look. He glanced quickly at me, then at his youngest son, Otis, and lastly he looked at Shirley. He said, "Shirley, tell them. Otis couldn't have done it."

Shirley seemed fuddled. He said, "I don't know what happened, Daddy. I wasn't nowhere near. I was over to the blacksmith's, looking at them new mules."

"Ah, son," Mr. Wasum said. There was misery in his voice. "They're going to put your little brother in jail. You can't let them do that. Tell them the truth."

And Shirley's face seemed to snap to attention with understanding. He said, "Oh!" and then, "No, no, the Fairchild boy has made an error. It wasn't Otis. It was me did it."

The crowd muttered still more. I said, "But I *saw* him. He was in the way of Calvin's picture, and I went up there to tell him to move. It was Otis, and I marched right up to him, and I saw him with Shirley's rifle by the window. There's not a chance in the world I'm mistaken."

Everyone looked at me. Oddly. Everyone but Shirley. Shirley looked at his daddy, and he firmed his jaw, and he said, "He didn't do no such thing. I don't like to say it, but Judge Fairchild's boy is lying. It was me in that window, and the boy never came anywhere near it."

My Uncle Raleigh said, "If someone was in the way of Calvin's picture, then he would show, wouldn't he? What about it, Calvin?"

Calvin turned his eyes up from Mr. Stein. They had tears in them. He tried to speak, but his words got stuck. Finally he said, "Maybe. I got a glimpse of someone when I took the photograph. He might have come back after Pepper left."

Naturally, it was my father who took over. He'd been holding his fingers on Mr. Stein's wrist, where the pulse would have been. The throat is better, some say, for a weak pulse, but with poor Mr. Stein that was impossible. My father rose and wiped his hands absently with his handkerchief. "Is that so, Calvin? Was one of the Wasums in the photograph?" He spoke slowly and a little loudly, as he always did with Calvin. Maybe because he never spent much time with Calvin, my father seemed to figure both Calvin's mind and his ears were as defective as his speech.

"Yessir," Calvin said. "At least I think so."

"Was it Otis or Shirley?" my father said.

Calvin looked away, and his mouth started working. "I guess

I don't know, sir. I guess I was too busy to pay much attention."

"Is a photograph evidence, Judge?" Mr. Blountley asked.

"I don't know what the precedent might be," my father said, "but we'd better look at it. Go on, now, Calvin. Pepper, go help your cousin."

Calvin shook his head. He was dead white, and his eyes kept going to poor dead Mr. Stein. "The plate's probably spoiled," he said. "Collodion dries right fast."

Shirley Wasum said, "I don't know what all this fuss is about. It's my rifle, and I said I did it, and I did it."

"Sir," I said. "It was Otis. I *saw* him."

My father only nodded and said, "Go help Calvin develop that plate."

Blood was trickling down between my father's little finger and the ring finger, dripping on the dusty street. Stoically, he ignored it, and he seemed stoically determined to ignore me, too. I went. I was so mad that tears were in my own eyes by now, and my face was hot, and my ears felt bright red. Just because my father had been acting funny and testy with me ever since he'd remarried, and just because he'd been so touchy about my fistfight with Otis Wasum, didn't mean he shouldn't believe his own son. I was a witness. I was better than any photograph. I saw it.

Otis Wasum shouldered me hard when I walked by and whispered, "You're going to get it now. You'll see." His daddy grabbed him by the collar and held on, but Otis didn't do anything else. He just stared at me. I helped Calvin carry the big, heavy camera into the back of the store to the little room we had prepared, and got a fresh bucket of water before we closed the door.

We had done this before, practicing with the camera. Usually I just stood out of the way, so Calvin wouldn't run into me in the dark, but today I stuck close to him and felt for and found his shoulder and said, "You all right, Calvin?"

"I'm all right," he said.

"Poor Mr. Stein," I said.

"We'll talk about him later," he said.

I dropped my hand from Calvin's shoulder, but his hand came and found my arm. He pressed it quickly. "You're my partner, Pepper," he said. "There ain't no words for what a help that is."

Well, Calvin tried as hard as he could with that dried plate. He poured ferrous sulphate over it and said he was ready and I took away a rag we'd stuffed in a crack in the boards and held a piece of red glass over it, the way we'd figured things out, to give Calvin a small working light. The image usually jumped up right away on the plate and got brighter by the minute, but from what I could see this one was coming slowly. Calvin kept working with it, and I kept standing there holding the red glass.

To tell the truth, I didn't really pay close attention to what Calvin was doing. At that moment, I was mostly concerned with just being furious with Otis and Shirley Wasum for lying and with my father for apparently choosing to believe that I, rather than they, was the liar.

It was not as though I was surprised to think that, if my father had been shot at, it was a Wasum who did it. The bad feeling between us, as I have said, went back twenty years, when Mr. Wasum fought a duel with Grandfather. The duel took place by the courthouse square, and everybody in the world saw it, but it was a duel that the parish even twenty years ago had discussed only behind their hands, because both its cause and its effect were considered too indecent to speak on just in case women and children might be listening.

The cause was a Galloway bull that Mr. Wasum brought all the way from Scotland before the war. Mrs. Wasum and the whole tribe of older Wasum boys, then mostly just little boys, managed to keep the bull alive and healthy during the war. So the war ended, but in our parish things just seemed to get worse. A lot of good land lay fallow because of a want of field hands, and so did a lot of good cows because of a want of a seed bull. Times were so bad that the Wasums needed money, like everybody else in the parish, but nobody could afford the fee that Mr. Wasum wanted for that Galloway bull's service.

They argued about that, my grandfather and Mr. Wasum. My grandfather's position was: we all had to stick together until times got better, and then Mr. Wasum could collect all the back fees he wanted off the bull, because then folks could afford to pay. Mr. Wasum's position was: it was his bull, and he needed money now, and he hadn't heard of my grandfather just giving away his cotton.

So they compared their watches and met at two in the afternoon on the square. Our code duello wasn't fancy, but it was strict. Each man, as was prescribed, stepped out to the center of the street and started walking toward the other, carrying his gun in his hand, and it was fire at will. Mr. Wasum smoked a cigar all the way through it, which produced a lot of admiration for him in our parish, and he nearly killed Grandfather with a bullet in the stomach and one in the arm, once they got within fifteen or twenty feet and started hitting each other. But Grandfather hit Mr. Wasum, too, and what made the duel indecent was not only the seed bull that started it but that Grandfather shot Mr. Wasum in the crotch.

Grandfather was ashamed and mad as hell about it once he got well enough to think about such things, and by that time he had other things to be mad and ashamed and grieved about. Uncle Camden Fairchild, my father's brother and Calvin's father, shot the bull in revenge, then the Wasums had shot him, and an all-out feud had broken out between the families. Like war, feuds had no set rules in our part of the world. The practice was to shoot on sight, and there was plenty of shooting. Grandfather and Mr. Wasum both tried, but it took months and months to make peace, and of course we never truly forgave each other for the various killings.

I guess, in a way, Otis was among the casualties. He was born three years after the duel, and there was considerable doubt in the parish that Mr. Wasum, crotch-shot as he was, could have sired him. Mr. Wasum appeared to doubt it too, at least at first, and although Otis grew up looking like all the other Wasum boys, he never acted like them—standoffish where they were hail-fellow, a stay-at-home where they ranged like hounds throughout the parish, namby-pamby where they were unbridled rogues. Once Otis got to be of a fair size and the old man noticed he apparently had another son, Mr. Wasum seemed downright troubled by Otis, and baffled, too, as the parish knew, like a hen that's hatched a clutch of duck eggs and is straining itself to cope with the result.

So that was the old trouble.

The new trouble had almost started that spring, over land the Wasums held out on Dorcheat Bayou. Nowadays, the Wasums didn't do much with their land besides running a few hogs, and hunting, and fishing in the bayou, but the Long Bell Company came in right next to them and set up a sawmill, and got the V.S. & P. Railroad to set up a leg of track to take the timber to the mill. It looked to me like progress, a thing I was interested in, but Mr. Wasum claimed his land was ruined, what with hogs, game, and fish all scared into scarcity by the noise of the big saws. He went so far as to bring the quarrel to court, but my father sat on the case and nolle prossed it for lack of evidence. How could man communicate well enough with hogs, I heard him joke to my new stepmother once, to know whether they felt harassed by noise or just finally had deduced that if they stayed around their tribe would surely be decimated every fall?

What nearly happened this time was not a duel but an affray. That had its own set of rules and procedures, too, and Mr. Wasum embarked upon the affray properly enough by warning my father that he'd better go armed. Mr. Wasum then had the obligation, if they chanced to meet, to refrain from drawing his own gun until he cried out the usual warning, "Defend yourself!" And I maintain that there wasn't a soul in the parish, knowing the Wasums and the Fairchilds and the rules, who would have doubted that if a Wasum chanced to meet a Fairchild and didn't cry the warning, why, then, the Wasum had left his gun at home or just wasn't in the mood that day, and there would have been no shooting. That was the way we did things, or would have, if Mr. Wasum hadn't apparently cooled off and counted up on his fingers and realized that we Fairchilds outnumbered the Wasums by almost three to one, and finally called off the affray. I heard a little taunting by the boys around town telling Otis the Wasums sure had been quick to back down, but there wasn't any killing and there wasn't any trouble, except that a Wasum and a Fairchild maybe got in fistfights, if we were still boys and one boy said some nasty thing about the other boy's father and new young stepmother, which I never breathed one syllable of to anyone. But in Claiborne Parish we just did not skulk around in the top stories of mercantile stores and, without a single word of warning, shoot people down in the streets.

I guess the thing that was equally shocking to me was that it was Otis who committed such a violent, improper act, and not Mr. Wasum or even Shirley or one of the other full-grown Wasums. Yes, all right, we'd had the one fight, but Otis was the quiet Wasum, close-mouthed and steady like his ma, people said when they were trying to talk nice about him, and not boisterous and wild like the other boys and his daddy. And he was only seventeen, and I would be that in two years, and for all my temper it had never even crossed my mind to want to kill somebody.

Cousin Calvin was dipping fresh water from the water bucket. I could tell by the sound. In the dim light I thought I saw him reaching for the bottle of potassium cyanide to pour over the plate. "Did it do?" I said. "Can you see it's Otis?"

"The plate got awful dry," Calvin said.

He kept tinkering. I started wondering, if Otis Wasum had done the proper thing and had, when I walked into the second story of the store, cried out, "Defend yourself," instead of skulking and mumbling so he could sneak a later shot at my father, what would I have done? Tried to make the first grab for that .38–40 Winchester, and shot him? Dead?

There was another thing that I didn't think about. Or tried not to, anyway. That is, when I first heard those shots, and saw people falling, who did I think would end up dead? Surely not poor Mr. Stein. And there was the question in my mind: considering the way he'd tongue-whipped me after I had the fist-fight, and told me not to interfere in the affairs of my elders, which I thought I certainly hadn't, and sentenced me to a whole week in the smokehouse when the family was having barbecues and picnics and fish fries almost daily in honor of Mr. Stein's visit and my and Calvin's upcoming trip, and when I flared and told him plainly that he was being unfair because he had a new family and didn't care for me any more because of the baby on the way, and he said calmly that I was just a boy and didn't understand anything about fairness and would have to grow up before I understood adult problems; considering everything, then, when those shots blammed out: what if?

Calvin washed the plate again, dipping water over and over

it, and I judged it was all right to stop holding up the red glass and let just the crack of natural light come in. I poured water for Calvin to wash his hands.

"It got too dry, Pepper," Calvin said. "You can't make out much of anything. Even Mr. Stein. But I guess that's not the kind of portrait a person would want anyway, is it? Poor Mr. Stein, standing there smiling, not knowing that in five minutes he'd be dead?"

His voice was chokey, and he cleared his throat, and I said, "Let's take it out in the full light. Maybe it'll show better."

We did. The store was full of Fairchilds. Everybody stopped talking when we came out, and my Uncle Raleigh came to me, looking mad as though he'd been arguing, and banged me on the shoulder a few times. Everybody looked at me. Still very oddly.

Well, Uncle Dawkins got down a piece of black cloth, and we laid the glass negative on it so as to make a positive. Everybody came crowding around. Sure enough, in the very tip-top, there was something blurry in the window, something that could have been a face. But anything that dim, it could have been anybody. There was a big, collective sigh, and everybody started looking happier, although I couldn't for the life of me see why.

"It got too dry," Calvin said again, awkwardly.

My Uncle Raleigh said, "Don't you trouble yourself about it, Calvin. This business of photographing must be mighty tricky."

"It was because the plates have to be developed right away," Calvin said. "And the way things happened . . ."

"Not a soul in the world could have done more," Uncle Raleigh said.

My father came into the store. My stepmother moved over to speak to him, and she must have told him about the plate not coming out, for my father said to Calvin, "Calvin, you'd better get someone to help you clean off your suit, and get all your camera things packed now. The stage is due in not more than a half-hour. And both of you, be sure you get over to say good-bye to your grandmother before you go. They've taken her to Mrs. Idabelle Sealy's. She'll be even more upset if you don't go to say good-bye."

I suppose I just gaped at him. I said, "But sir, we can't go now. I'm a witness. So's Calvin."

My father glanced at the dim plate. "It would appear to be unnecessary," he said, "since Shirley Wasum confessed. They've taken him over to the jail."

"But Father!" I said. "It was Otis in the window! I saw him. I spoke to him."

The Fairchilds in the store didn't murmur. They didn't even seem to breathe. They all just turned away. I looked at them, confounded.

My father said to Uncle Dawkins, "Dawk, can we use your office for a minute?"

"Certainly, certainly," Uncle Dawkins said, and everyone drifted away from us, like fishing corks in a fast current. My father and I didn't even go to Uncle Dawkins's office. We just stood there by the yard goods and talked. My father's hand kept smoothing the piece of black cloth that Uncle Dawkins had spread out.

He said, "I think it will be best for you to go on with your Cousin Calvin, Pepper. As Calvin is incapable of looking after his own affairs, and as you're young but capable, and a summer away from home will give you a chance to reconsider our—"

I said, "But, my God—"

His face hardened, and he said, "Don't let me hear you talk that way."

I said, "But Father, I'm a witness."

He said, "I want no more of your back talk. Perhaps I'm wrong about you. Perhaps you're not even capable of a simple thing like helping your cousin get to where he's got to go. If you don't feel you're up to the obligation, just say so, and we'll get some other member of the family to do it."

I said, "It's not that, sir. It's Otis Wasum. I thought you'd want me to stay here and testify."

My father looked at me, and I was gradually coming to know the expression. It's the way the crowd of men around Shirley Wasum had looked at me, and the way the family had just looked at me. He said, "Regarding your quarrel with young Otis, whatever your reasons for resorting to falsehoods about him, I would prefer that we discuss it no further."

"Sir? You think I'm lying?"

"You leave me very little choice," he said. "I must either consider you a liar or a coward. Taking into consideration your blood and your rearing, do you really want me to believe that you saw Otis Wasum, and you didn't try to stop him?"

My insides turned over. I said haltingly, "But sir, you can't think I knew what he was going to do!"

"You've insisted on saying to everyone within hearing distance that you saw Otis in the window holding a rifle, that you even spoke to him. No wonder the others drew such an obvious conclusion. Pepper Fairchild. Judge Fairchild's son. Craven. Afraid to face the threat of a gun. Too afraid even to cry out a warning. Thank God Shirley Wasum had the decency to own up to his crime and thank God there's no photograph to give continued impetus to the murmuring. It's less onerous to be branded a liar than spineless. Perhaps by the time you return, some of the shame will have dissipated."

"But you can't really think—" And then I stopped. He did think it. That's what they all thought. I said, "Sir, I'm sorry. But if that's the way you feel, then I must bid you farewell forever, for I will not be returning at all."

"Don't be foolish, boy. In a few months this will all—"

"No sir, I'm not just a boy. I'm near to grown. And if my own people haven't got any more faith in me than that, then I wouldn't care to come back."

"Nonsense," he said. "You will do as you have been instructed, after which you will return home. And I trust you will keep in mind that until you *are* grown, obedience to—"

"No, I tell you, it's farewell."

"Be quiet," he said. "You've already made one opprobrious mistake today. Don't make another by speaking in anger words that you will later regret."

"I won't never regret it," I said. "I ain't never coming back, and I don't care if you all rot with the leprosy. You could beg me to come back, but I won't. I'll just keep going until I—"

He slapped me sharply across the face. It was not done in anger, for that was not his way, but just to stop my babbling. I winced and shut my mouth and didn't say another word. Neither did he.

The store was very quiet. My father looked at me for a while, then turned to call to Uncle Dawkins, giving him instructions about getting this and that member of the family dispersed to the various Fairchild homes. It was always complicated, because a few lived right in town, but most, like us, lived out.

After that, Uncle Raleigh came and banged me a few more times on the shoulder, looking even madder but saying nothing about my father's slapping me or anything else. Calvin came, looking bothered, but saying nothing either, and a few dozen uncles and cousins came and stood in the way, also saying very little and trying to act as though nothing had happened, while I helped Calvin wipe the blood off his suit and helped him pack the big view camera and all those little bottles of chemicals.

Among the uncles was Uncle Dawkins, and I finally opened my own mouth long enough to ask him to unlock the big store safe and give me the little sack that he held for me for safe-keeping.

"Your money sack?" said Uncle Dawkins, not very happily. "What do you want that for?"

All I said was, "A body that's traveling might need some extra money."

"Yes, but traveling, you never know what kind of unsavory company you might fall in with. It's tempting fate to carry money around."

"I expect I can look out for it all right," I said, and the way I said it must have convinced him there was no jollying me out of the idea, and he handed over my sack.

Then after that I went to Mrs. Idabelle Sealy's to say good-bye to my grandmother, who was lying down in the best bed-room and who kept asking if we'd kept ahold of the fried chickens and light bread she'd packed for our lunch and lament-ing that she had no dessert to send with us. Like Calvin, she didn't talk about Mr. Stein, and like the rest of the family, she didn't talk about what was foremost, by then, on my mind.

And finally, after all that, I even found smiles for the kin, mostly men who my father hadn't yet distributed to their homes, and who kept on trying to act just everyday. They said things like, "Now, Pepper, you look after Calvin, and then hurry right back home," and, "Pepper, don't you be bringing some Indian bride back with you, you got to finish school before you get married." Then the bugle blasted, signaling the stage's approach, and people started looking expectant, and odds and ends of non-family came, clustering around the post office for letters that they hoped would be arriving. My Uncle Raleigh drew me aside.

Uncle Raleigh was a big man, half a head above most of the Fairchilds, and we tended toward height. But then he was my dead mother's brother, and not a Fairchild at all. For a time he didn't say much. The stage came, and people got out, and all our baggage was put on. Uncle Raleigh and I watched everything, and we watched the Fairchild part of the family telling Calvin they'd come to California and kill him if he didn't write, and not to meet his own Indian bride along the way.

The bugle blew again, and it was time to get on. Uncle Raleigh said, "Now listen to me, Pepper, I won't have you go to worrying just because folks . . ."

I mumbled sullenly, "I ain't got nothing to worry about."

"Of course you ain't," Uncle Raleigh said. "Isn't that what I'm telling you? Whatever you did or didn't do, I know you had the best reasons in the world for it, and that's what I told the others. That's the important thing, the reasons a man has for hisself."

"Yessir," I said.

"Well, Pepper," he said. "Well. Well, I reckon you and me are enough alike for you to be able to take on the world at fifteen. I was."

"Yessir," I said again.

But he wouldn't let me go until he banged my shoulder some more, like getting hit by a bear, and hugged me. I hugged him back. Calvin was staring around, looking anxious, until I got through all the Fairchild back-thumping and got on.

That's how we left. Like the kinfolk had told me, the four horses dashed down the street at a rapid gait. They said it would feel like my first ride on a fast train, a feeling of awe and fascination.

I guess I was too numb to notice it. For my father's words had told me only too clearly what all those odd expressions were saying, when the family looked at me.

Poor Calvin. To think I'd been worrying about associating with him in public, and to think that he was now being seen in public with me, Pepper Fairchild, the parish coward.

Two

Our train was filled with a small bunch of drunken drovers and a big bunch of Swedish and Iranian immigrant families going West, and whereas people so new and strange ordinarily would have riveted my attention, I was so distracted that I could scarcely heed them, even when the train would get up speed on straight stretches and the Swedish and Iranian people would commence wedging in babies so they wouldn't fall, and trying to find the conductor, and hollering.

They hollered, opined a drummer for the Little O.K. Cast Iron Pig Trough, because in those times some people still had serious doubts whether the human body could withstand such high speed. By the time we parted with the drummer at Dallas, where Calvin and I changed to the Texas & Kansas Railways, I had my own serious doubts whether the human ear could have withstood much more of his chattering.

It wasn't the drummer's fault. He just liked to talk, and even though Calvin and I were both too inattentive to make a very good audience, we were about the only people he could find to talk English to. Calvin was preoccupied all through our three-day train trip, brooding about Mr. Stein I figured, and I was pre-occupied, running over and over again in my mind those lost moments when I had seen Otis Wasum with an apple and a rifle and had ruined my life.

With my broody thoughts still back in Claiborne Parish and

the loft of Uncle Dawkins's store, I worked and worked and worked on that, and here's what I worked out:

I felt that I was no coward, and I felt it was beneath me to try to defend myself from unjustified charges such as that. What I did charge myself with, and therefore wanted desperately to prove untrue, was stupidity.

I had done other stupid things before, jeopardizing my life, as all children will, but I and the other people had survived my stupidity, and this time others had not. I attributed my mistake wholly to stupidity—stupidity in assuming that all people follow the rules, because without rules and the willingness to follow them, there would be chaos.

Naturally, I had been making all the standard resolutions: I would never be a fool again, and I would prove that I was responsible. And ten years from now, when I was successful and respected and quite probably famous (not to mention a millionaire), everybody in Claiborne Parish (to which word would, of course, get back) would realize how sorely they had misjudged me.

But why make them wait ten years if I could help it? My first responsibility was to get Calvin to California, and by and by, while the immigrant people continued hollering and the drummer continued droning, I determined and resolved myself to the point that I could barely wait to get started on that chore, so the word could fly back to Claiborne Parish about how well I had done.

It looked easy enough. All I had to do was to drive the mules for Cousin Calvin, as I have said, and advise him and not let him get in trouble, and deliver him to San Diego and the arms of Mr. John Swiss Parker, as the family had arranged. In turn, Mr. John Swiss Parker was to deliver Calvin to a photographic artist he had written the family about who had assistants out beating around every town and settlement in southern California under the banner of "Phemister's Photographs." Once I got Calvin as far as San Diego, Mr. John Swiss Parker would take over the chore of advising him and helping him and keeping him out of trouble, and I would be free to turn my attention to the new life that, having ruined my old one, I was now embarking upon.

So the first step was picking up the photographer's wagon that had been arranged for Calvin in Denison City, Texas, en route to which I had learned, willy-nilly, that the Little O.K. Cast Iron Pig Trough could feed eight large hogs at a time, and that Denison City, which the drummer assured us he visited frequently, had two ice houses, a slaughterhouse, a cotton compressor, a Masonic Lodge, a Good Templar Lodge, a base ball club, four churches, five taverns, and an unknown number of faro banks. What it didn't have, almost, was a photographer's wagon, which was the one thing Calvin and I learned for ourselves.

The train got to Denison City in midafternoon, not more than about an hour late, and Calvin and I were quick to climb off. We'd accumulated a good coating of soot and cinders. The fried chickens Grandmother had sent with us had long since gone, and one of the two greasy meals they'd had the nerve to charge a dollar a person for at the train stops had given us both a good case of the trots. The first thing we did was look around the depot and find a privy. The second thing we did was start out seeking a certain Professor Beuhlman, who was selling the photographer's wagon. Where we ended up was the Ringer & Johnson Hardware Company, for Professor Beuhlman had sold the wagon twice.

This wagon part of Calvin's new profession had been arranged in Minden, Louisiana, where a man engaged in a thriving photographer's business had told one of the uncles he'd received word that one Professor Beuhlman was settling down permanently in Denison City and so was willing to sell at a bargain price his fully equipped, strictly high-grade portable studio and the mules that transported it. After the family had decided on Cousin Calvin's future, correspondence was entered into and twenty-five dollars was sent on account, the balance to be paid upon inspection and acceptance of wagon and mules by Calvin and me. My father tended to the papers and the cashier's check for the balance. He had made it clear that it was I who was to inspect and accept. I could advise with Calvin, but the responsibility was mine. I was glad to have this immediate, responsible deed to attend to. My spirits rose. I set about it almost cheerfully.

Denison City was still a rough town then, and despite all its businesses and churches, no one had yet dug out all the stumps in the avenues left and right of Main Street. We walked up and down, looking for Professor Beuhlman's place of business. Calvin also looked for Indians, for he was wild to see and perhaps photograph some, and we were right on the south edge of Indian Territory. But we didn't turn up much more than some stray cows wandering along and a slew of what I strongly suspected were gay women flaunting about the streets.

We finally asked at the marshal's office. He told us that there had been a Professor Beuhlman in town, but he had sold out his atelier to a portrait- and view-taker named Mr. Lewels. The marshal directed us to him. We asked Mr. Lewels where was our wagon, and the most he could think of was that Professor Beuhlman had sold a wagon to the Ringer & Johnson Hardware Company. He sent us there. By then, it was already coming clear to me what had happened, but Calvin wouldn't hear of going back to the city marshal. He was just anxious to find that wagon.

At the Ringer & Johnson Hardware Company, the first person we met was a Mr. Henry Ringer, a tall man in gray overalls and a blue-brimmed hat. He had the overalls pulled down and was inspecting a large bruise on his hip. He looked a little startled when I said, "Beg pardon." He pulled up the overalls and said, "I got a little careless. I just got too close when a bunch of them mules was playing. That wasn't a mean mule."

Well, we stated our business and he started looking grave. "Boys," he said, "I bought what you might call a wagon from that Beuhlman fellow, and paid him fifteen dollars cash and got a signed bill of sale."

I said, "I guess you got a better price than we did, Mr. Ringer, for we Fairchilds advanced twenty-five dollars, with balance due on inspection."

"Beuhlman was in a considerable hurry," said Mr. Ringer. "I've known that to affect price."

Cousin Calvin's face worked, and he said, "Pepper, can't we at least look at the wagon?"

Mr. Ringer stared at Calvin, but he didn't see much. Calvin had a way of keeping his head down. To boot, from the time he had been old enough to have a beard he had grown an uneven mustache to try to hide where the upper lip was split. But every time he spoke, he gave himself away, and Mr. Ringer asked me, "What's the matter with your friend?"

"Nothing," I said. "He's just fine. Mr. Ringer, would it put you out if we was to look at the wagon?"

"That wagon's in a back lot, boy," he said. "Come along and see."

He hollered to a little boy he called Roman to come point out the wagon's location. We all followed Roman past a shed filled with barbed wire and a pile of rusting windmill parts and a stock pen to a fenced lot jammed full of old buggies and carriages and market wagons. Roman threaded us through to the southeast corner and pointed.

The wagon was one of the strangest-looking vehicles I'd ever seen. The body was longer than the average. In front was a spring seat and in back of that a little bench, both covered with a kind of canopy you usually saw on a surrey. In the back half of the wagon was a kind of big wooden box or small wooden room, about the shape and size of a privy. The whole thing was painted blue, somewhat faded from standing out in the weather, and lettered in gold on the privy part was "S. J. Boldini, Artist." In smaller letters was "We Take Ranch Pictures. Family Groups a Specialty."

"Who in fire was S. J. Boldini?" I asked.

Mr. Ringer laughed. "Someone with a big family, I reckon. That wagon's got seating space for six, if you squeeze a little, and standing space for four more. That's the reason I bought it. It's an investment."

I said carefully, trying to say it as my father would, "Mr. Ringer, it looks to me like you didn't buy anything but a scrap of paper, for Professor Beuhlman already had contracted it to us, and our contract date is bound to precede your sales date."

Mr. Ringer stopped laughing. "I don't know what kind of contract you got, but a bill of sale is a bill of sale, and that's what I got," said he.

"Yessir," said I. "I wonder if you'd care to walk over to the city marshal's with us, for since you've got papers and we've got papers, this is for the law."

Calvin had scooted over to inspect the wagon. He succeeded

in getting the door of the privy part opened. A strong odor of chemicals floated out.

Mr. Ringer said, "Roman, I thought I told you to clean all that junk out of there."

"I started," Roman said, calm as you please. "I hauled out two wheelbarrow loads, but Mr. Johnson said stop before the air got poisoned and the trees all died."

"Did you dump it somewhere near?" Calvin said.

Roman looked puzzled and turned to me for interpretation. I repeated it.

"Out next to the manure pile," Roman said, gesturing to the rear of the lot. He grinned at me slyly. "That's some wagon," he said. "You know what they call it? People come a-running every time they see it driving down the street and they say, 'What is it? What is it?' So around here they call it the 'What's-It Wagon.'"

"That's supposed to be a fully equipped, traveling photographer's studio," I told him, a little stiffly. "And it looks to me like you've been dumping out all its equipment."

Mr. Ringer said, "Now look here, boy, I bought that for a plain wagon, and it's been occupying limited and much-needed space here in my lot for a wagon, and when the federal government finally gets off its ass and opens the country right there across the Red River for settlement, I am going to sell that wagon for a wagon." He stopped, then added as a kindly explanation to a stranger, "Boy, Denison City is the gateway to the Indian Territory, and when all of Denison is ready to move across the Red it's going to need something to move in. And I'm going to be ready for them."

As a business investment plan, it seemed to have its possibilities. Business investments were of considerable interest to me, and I looked impressed, which I was. But I said, "Mr. Ringer, if the federal government sends the word and those gates fly open, it would be a pity for you to be all tied up in court just then for selling a wagon on which a legally signed and sealed paper was drawn up by Judge Fairchild of Claiborne Parish, Louisiana, himself."

Mr. Ringer frowned. He said to Roman, "What you hanging

around here for, Roman? Get back up front, and get ready to holler the minute a customer comes in."

All this time Calvin had been poking around inside the studio part of that wagon, and now he jumped down and came over to us, looking as gloomy as an overcast Sunday.

I asked, "Have they broke up everything?"

Mr. Ringer said, "Now see here, that stuff was every which way and smelling to high heaven when that Professor Beuhlman came galloping in here with a wagon and mules he said he legal owned and legal was just dying to sell. Nobody here broke anything."

Calvin just looked sad. He was never one to argue. I said to Mr. Ringer, "I guess those mules would be the ones our paper covers. Two henny mules, one eight and one six years of age, near-black and with good dispositions."

"You can't hold paper on them mules," Mr. Ringer said. It was a groan. He tried to recover. He said, "If it's the same pair of mules, they've been eating me out of house and home. Not to mention a fee for storing that sorry excuse for a wagon. Boy, somebody owes me one hell of a lot of money."

Well, I could see I'd both made progress and slipped back. Mr. Ringer was a man who liked mules, that was plain, and henny mules have been known to endear themselves to more than one man. Old Mr. Buck in our parish had a henny mule once, and he swore that the difference between a henny mule, which is born of a jenny donkey and a stud horse, and a regular mule, born of a jack donkey and a mare, is the difference between sweet spring and black winter, the hennys getting all the good points of both blood lines, and the plain mule getting all the bad. But I had Calvin's face, turned to the ground to hide his split lip, before me, and it was clear to me that the wagon was all his main concern. So I tackled the wagon first.

I told Mr. Ringer, "I guess I'll talk to my cousin here a couple of minutes."

"Talk away," he said politely. "Talk about feed bills, while you're at it. I guess I've had those mules boarding out at my home place for nigh six weeks now. Oh, and you might talk about Mrs. Professor Beuhlman. She showed up not long back from some place in Kansas. They tell me that's the reason the professor and some yellow-haired gal with a store complexion he'd been hanging around with left town so rapid-like. I guess maybe Mrs. Beuhlman'd have some interest in the professor's property."

We withdrew to a big manure pile at the back of the lot. Calvin was anxious to see if any chemical bottles or glass plates remained intact after Roman's dumping. He got down in a ditch where we spotted glass, and I sat on the bank and tried to advise with him.

"Calvin," I said, "it looks to me like we'd better get you straight on to California by some other means. That wagon's a mess, and that Mr. Ringer's got his hands on the mules that were to carry it. We can try the law, which he obviously would just as soon avoid, but it's clear as day that he's going to counter with a whopping board bill. The way I see it, you could send the papers back to the judge, and I guess if anyone could retrieve that advance money, he could. Then I'll tell you what I think we ought to do. We'll move on down the road to someplace that don't think wagons is made of gold and buy a plain one cheap and be on our way. I'd say take the train, but you'd have to send home for more money, and I guess you wouldn't want to do that, now would you? Besides, this way we'll have our plain wagon to sell when we get to California. Maybe the judge will complain, but he ain't here and I am, and you just write him that I took the responsibility for it."

Working carefully, for some of those chemicals used by photographic artists were poisonous, Calvin was looking among the pile of glass in the ditch for that which might be unbroken. He found one vial. It was empty, but he laid it on the grassy bank.

Calvin said, "You're not really saying we should make the trip without a proper photographer's wagon, are you, Pepper?"

"Well, no, just for temporary," I said. "Phemister's Photographs expects you to show up with one, so we got to locate one for you. I'll bet the family can write Mr. John Swiss Parker and he can run down a *really* proper one for you in California, quick as a wink, and it'll be there waiting for you when you get there. You'll see."

He worked on a while, and didn't say anything.

I said finally, "If you ask me, that's what they should have done in the first place. Maybe this one sounded cheap, but they wasn't here to look at it, and I guess there's Claiborne Parish Fairchilds that still hasn't figured out that what you buy cheap can be just that—cheap and shoddy, not to mention sold twice over."

Maybe I sounded a little bitter. Calvin looked at me and I looked at him, and he climbed out of the ditch and sat on the bank with me. The manure pile smelled pretty high, and there were bluebottles buzzing all about. We sat there brushing them off.

After a while, Calvin said, "If you had three wishes, what would you really like to do in all the world, Pepper?"

"Make three million dollars," I said. I guess I was short with him. It made me impatient, having Cousin Calvin act so what-would-you-do-if-you-had-a-magic-wish with me, because I had always been about the only person in the family who hadn't seemed to switch back and forth between pitying and despising Calvin, and we usually got along fine, at least when we were in private together.

That's when Calvin opened up with me and finally told me what he'd been planning as his own secret all along. He said, "If I had three wishes, I'd like to see a lot of pretty countryside going through the West and take views of it with my camera and a photographer's wagon, and I'd like to sell the views to the illustrated magazines in New York, and I'd like to make enough money so I wouldn't have to go take charity from Granny's kin in California."

I stammered, "Why, Calvin, that's not charity to take help from kinfolk."

"Isn't it?" he said. He looked straight at me. Calvin's eyes were his one fine feature. They were shy and innocent, like a girl's, but even the shyest girl would have found more use than he did for eyes that were hazel, not just a dull, flat hazel like many, but deep and splendid, with rays in them of an even deeper hazel, and those rays were speckled with gold.

"Well, hell, Calvin," I said.

"Don't cuss," he said. "Pepper, if I had the nerve to try it without the family to back me up, maybe I could work just on my own, and not have to work for Phemister's Photographs. I bet

35

I could make ever so much more money just on my own, and then maybe I could help the family for a change. It's always been a case of them helping me. I thought I had it licked when I tried schoolmastering, but you know how that turned out."

"But Granny's kin is just going to help you get established," I said. "And Phemister's Photographs sounds a fine, steady job that you'll be just crazy about."

Calvin said, "Pepper, if you don't understand, there's not a Fairchild that could. You're like I'd like to be. You're independent."

Well, he had me there. But my responsibility was to deliver Calvin to California, and I knew clear as day what the parish would think if word got back to them that I'd started out my successful and respected and quite probably famous new life by failing in my very first responsibility. So I side-stepped and said, "California sounds a grand place to go. You do want to go there, don't you, Calvin?"

"Maybe for a time," he said. His eyes got dreamy. "Maybe to look at it, and say thanks anyway to Mr. John Swiss Parker, and maybe by then to have some money to send back to the family. But wouldn't it be fine to be all on your own, maybe out where there's still lots of open country and lots going on, like New Mexico or Arizona Territory? The way I'd thought it, if I could learn how to manage, I'd put you on the train in San Diego and then maybe double back. . . . Pepper, say, do you know what we could do? If there was still plenty of time before school starts, you could double back with me, and we could take views coming and going and sell them. The train's bound to stop somewhere in the territories, and you could head back from there. . . . Pepper, by then there'd be even more money, and you could be the one to take it to the family, and you'd say, 'Here's money sent by Calvin to start paying back what was spent on him, and when it's all paid back then he'll just send more as a present.' You'd take my message, wouldn't you, Pepper? After all, you and me, we're partners."

Now this was just like Cousin Calvin. He would step right in the middle of horse manure every time, the home folks said, because his eyes were always up on the clouds. I said, "I guess the only message anybody could send right now is, we got skinned, and we got no photographer's wagon and no mules and a sight less money than when we started."

"Oh," Calvin said. He drew in his breath.

I was sorry right away that I'd hurt his feelings. I apologized, but Calvin said, "No, you're right, Pepper. I guess I'll never be anything but a damned fool."

"Why there's not a word of that true, Calvin," I said. "You're as smart as anyone. As smart as me any day." Then I gulped, remembering that it could perhaps be figured that I was not as smart as I had always thought, and I muttered, "Smarter."

Calvin looked at me worriedly. He had been so wrapped up with grieving about his true friend, Mr. Stein, and, I could see now, maybe thinking some of his own secret aspirations to be independent and successful, that I didn't believe he'd realized fully what all had happened back in Claiborne Parish, and just how people looked at what had happened, and the spot that I'd put myself in. But I didn't want to start him to thinking about it. If the whole world considers you a fool, it's nice to have at least one person who hasn't yet caught on. So I said, maybe sounding somewhat toplofty, "A person's got to think of what he can do before he can do it, or he can't realize his ambition, Calvin. You've just got to make careful plans, that's all. You've got to be practical, and you've got to plan things all the way."

"I guess I thought I had planned," Calvin said wistfully.

"Careful planning means finding out all the facts first," I said.

"I investigated that wagon pretty thoroughly just now," said Calvin.

"Now, Calvin, people'd stare at you, riding along in a thing like that. You don't want that wagon."

"I guess not," he said.

Well, he wouldn't say anything else. He just sat there shooing away the flies. It was exasperating, but I'd already come down hard on him once and hurt his feelings, and I didn't want to do that again. I said, "Do you really want that wagon?"

"No, no," he said.

"Old Roman gutted it like a chicken," I said. "Just look at all those broken plates there in the ditch."

"Lots of the chemicals are still all right," he mumbled. "You should have looked inside, Pepper. It's got little shelves with shelf guards nailed all around the walls, and those bottles ride along just as snug as can be. And light-tight? Not a speck of light comes in when you close the door, except just enough from that little yellow-paned window. Did you notice that yellow-paned window?"

"I guess I was pretty busy listening to Mr. Ringer talk about feed bills and storage bills," I said.

Naturally, that shut Calvin up again, and I sat there, feeling worse and worse. Finally I said, "You know, Calvin, I guess it wouldn't really be such a bad idea to give your new profession kind of a trial run, so I'm thinking on a compromise."

"I don't want you to do anything you don't think's right," Calvin said shyly.

"No, what I'm saying is, a careful man who finds out everything and makes good plans might do just fine to take a few views for the New York magazines and begin to learn how it's done and all, and then maybe after a few years' seasoning with Phemister's Photographs in California he'd be in a lot better shape to set up all on his own. Now don't that sound more careful and practical?"

Calvin studied his hands. Without looking at me, he said, "I guess it sure does."

I watched him for a moment, feeling troubled, then said, "Listen, about Mr. Ringer, what do you think—we could put in fifteen dollars from our eating money, and sign over the check for the mules, and threaten him with the law if he says another word about board bills. There's a man that hates lawing. You can tell just by looking at him."

"It wouldn't work, Pepper. We'd still owe the balance on the wagon to Mrs. Professor Beuhlman. It wouldn't be right to cheat her."

That was Calvin for you. And that was the way it worked out. We had to pay a feed bill, too, though we got it down to seven dollars, and got skinned twice over on the mules, for Mr. Ringer couldn't bring himself to part with the hennys and insisted we take two other mules he raked up, one just rising three years old, charging us the full forty dollars apiece for them. He claimed that was dirt cheap for the then and the there, saying stock was at a premium because folks might be begging to buy at

38

any price at any minute, the minute being whenever the Indian Territory was opened. I took time out to ask around at two livery stables, and found Mr. Ringer was not necessarily cheating on the price; boomers were already making repeated attempts to colonize the Unassigned Lands, and stock prices were high. But this much is true: if it hadn't been for the way Calvin's poor ruined face looked when he told me he guessed he'd never be anything but a damned fool, I'd never have handed over that cashier's check signed by our banker back home for such a broken-down-looking outfit.

It all meant a lot of running about and looking all over the place for Mrs. Professor Beuhlman, and it took all day. We got our portmanteaus and the bundle of quilts and pots and Calvin's big camera from the railway depot and locked them in the studio part of the wagon. Then we took the bench out of the front and curled in as best we could and slept there. We didn't eat dinner. The trots we'd gotten back down the line were still telling on our stomachs.

The next morning, Calvin sprang the rest of it on me, and word came from home about another unexpected difficulty I might be encountering in delivering Calvin to California: that same stinking snake, Otis Wasum. We heard about Otis in a telegram from Uncle Raleigh. Here's how things went:

Calvin rolled out early, scrubbing and dusting and rattling bottles around in the back. I roused myself after a while and went to look for Roman, because, not anxious to spend money on another eating-house meal that just made you sick, I thought to get him to run home and give his momma twenty-five cents for enough buttermilk and fried bacon and cornbread to keep us going.

But what do I encounter first but the local postmaster, a be-whiskered, thin man with a lot of letters stuck in his hatband, some of them looking as though they'd already seen a season or two of rain. He was lost in Mr. Ringer's back-lot empire between the barbed wire and the windmill parts. He'd come to bring us the telegram, and that was as far as he'd managed to get.

When he saw me, he looked relieved and said, "Excuse me. I wonder if you could help me to locate a gentleman by the name of Mr. Pepper Fairchild? I understand he's living temporarily somewhere amidst this jumble of hardware items." I told him I was Pepper Fairchild, and he looked surprised and said, "Ah. Good morning to you. The telegraph office sent this around to me last night, in that Professor Beuhlman no longer lives here, and I thought I'd just drop it over to you." And he held it out.

Well, that was the first telegram ever sent to me, myself, in all my life, and it was all I could do to act casual when I said, "Oh, thank you." There were the words, written on the outside in a Spencerian hand, "Mr. Pepper Fairchild, care of Prof. A. B. Beuhlman, Denison City Township, Texas."

"How the devil does one get out of here?" the postmaster said.

"Uh, right up this way," I said.

Once he saw daylight through Mr. Ringer's front door, he seemed content for me to drop behind, and I unfolded the message to read:

Shirley escaped him and Otis has went keep eyes peeled

Raleigh W. Hillman

"My God," I gasped, though I wasn't sure why, for the sense of Uncle Raleigh's telegram wasn't fully apparent. But I turned and ran back to the wagon, and what does Calvin do just then but exit from the studio part of the vehicle wearing a clean shirt and his traveling suit all brushed and saying to me, "Pepper, it's been a long trip and you need to rest up, so you just take it easy and I'll be back around sundown."

"Whatever are you talking about?" I said. "Look here. Uncle Raleigh sent me this genuine telegram."

Calvin took it from my outstretched hand and read it, looking all at sea.

He studied it so long that I said, "It says Otis has went and,

'Keep eyes peeled.' Maybe Uncle Raleigh thinks Otis is going to follow us."

"What would Otis want to do that for?"

"Calvin, he's crazy. You should have heard the way he talked —keep quiet or I'll kill you, and stuff like that. That was later, after it was all done."

"And Shirley?"

"Well, I don't rightly understand the whole telegram. It says Shirley escaped him. I don't know who 'him' is."

"Maybe it means him and Otis has went. But why would Shirley follow us?"

"Hell, Calvin, I don't know everything. I just now got the telegram. Maybe the feud is on. Although surely Uncle Raleigh would have mentioned it. Or maybe Uncle Raleigh thinks they're going to follow us and engage us in a show of arms."

Calvin's mouth began to work, and after a while he got out, "I fear that would make sense. If they're dead set on some dark vendetta, the best way would be to come at the two weakest members of the family."

That riled me. "We aren't by any sense the weakest members," I said crossly.

"No, no, I just mean we're Fairchilds, and we're off alone. We're off where they can get at us, not back in the bosom of the family like the others. Besides, you're the judge's son, and since you licked Otis in that little fracas you had, maybe he's mad enough to think you'd be a tempting target to start a vendetta."

Well, that cooled me down some, Calvin's saying flat out that I had won that fistfight, but I said, "Just let Otis poke his nose around here and see what he gets. Shirley, too, if they're together." By that time I had noticed his suit. I said, "Where in fire are you going?"

"Uh, I'm going to find work for a day or two," he said. "I'm hoping that Mr. Lewels who bought Professor Beuhlman's atelier can use a hand."

The only time Calvin had ever worked, and not just at Uncle Dawkins's store or farming or helping others of the family, was the year he tried schoolmastering, and the way even the smallest kids cut up when he tried to teach them was something the parish still talked about. I said, "Now Calvin, that Mr. Lewels didn't look any too prosperous when we talked to him yesterday, and I didn't exactly see folks flocking in to sit for their portraits. He needs help just about as much as those bluebottles need more manure to buzz around."

"Well, then, I'll ask around for something else to work at," Calvin said.

"What in the world for? What did we spend all our money for yesterday but a traveling photographic studio? There's your work standing right there, painted pukey blue."

"Yes, well, there's a little problem in that," Calvin said.

I sat down on the edge of the wagon. I folded the telegram carefully. While I was very pleased with Uncle Raleigh for sending one to me, its contents seemed more puzzling than spectacular, and the Calvin problem took precedent. "Tell it to me quick," I said.

He mumbled so, I had to ask for it louder, and it came out: tin plate for ferrotypes and more glass plate for ambrotypes and nitrated cotton and potassium iodide and pyrogellic acid and albumen paper and a bunch of other stuff I couldn't even pronounce. Roman had done a fine job of dumping with his two wheelbarrows full, and what he hadn't gotten around to was in some cases too old and in other cases dried up, and the supplies Calvin brought with him would not stretch far, and I finally stuffed my fingers in my ears.

"Please, Pepper," Calvin said, trying to unstuff them. "Please, now. It'd take all our eats money and then some. And like you said, we can't send home for money. Not this soon, when we haven't even started yet." He looked around the wagon lot uneasily, maybe already keeping his eyes peeled, and went on, "Now, all I have to do is work awhile, and we'll find you a good safe place to stay, and pretty soon I can buy the things I need to make photographs. Then we can hit the trail and it'll be clear sailing, for I can make all the money we'll need by selling lots of views. We'll just hurry up a little on the way to California. Or Pepper, listen, you wouldn't even have to come with me all the way. If it gets near school time, we can just put you on the train wherever we are."

There he went again. But I tried to control myself. I said, "Calvin, didn't you listen to me about planning? Even if I was interested in catching some train, what would we use for money to buy the ticket? You know as well as I it's being sent to Mr. John Swiss Parker in San Diego so it wouldn't get robbed off us along the way."

"Well, by then I'll have made plenty of money for the train," Calvin said. "Pepper, listen. Pepper, don't you believe me? Pepper, you got to believe me. You're my partner."

"I ain't," I shouted. "I'm what was being sent to see that you got to California without doing some damn-fool thing to disgrace the family! And I don't need some damned train ticket, because I ain't going back to Claiborne Parish anyway! I'm going to look for me a sound business opportunity in the West, and when I find it I'm going to set to work and I'm going to make more money than any damned Fairchild has ever seen, and you or Grandmother can come visit me any time you want, but I don't care if I never see any other stay-at-home, let-the-world-run-over-you, hungry Fairchild, haughty Fairchild, damned Fairchild again!"

"Don't cuss," Calvin said. In a little while, he added, "No Fairchild's ever gone hungry."

I said sullenly, "In the seventies we did. Granny said so."

"Everybody was hungry then. Things were bad then, worse than the war. But the state's straightened up considerably."

"There's not a Fairchild still has anything," I said. "A little store. A little farm. Being county judge. What's that to be so proud about?"

"Fairchilds aren't proud. They're just settled," Calvin said.

"That's bad enough," I said. "They don't know things are changing. They don't even know there's money can be made in this country. I'll tell you something now. I'll tell you the truth— I don't think there was a single Fairchild in Claiborne Parish that even wanted the sawmills to come in."

Calvin sighed. "I guess they liked the trees," he said.

"So did Otis Wasum and his folks," I said.

That was about ninety things in a row I shouldn't have said. Certainly I hadn't meant to let anything slip about my private feud with my father until I had my future all set up and ready to go, much less tell it in a way that would hurt Calvin. But I'd said so much now that Calvin started looking sore-troubled.

He said, "Pepper, what's happened? A week in the smoke-house, now I know that's a lot, but the judge don't always see he's being too strict, and that's no reason in the world to run away."

"Who's running?" I said. "Going off on your own isn't running."

"Well, but then maybe he wasn't so wrong wanting to stay away from trouble with the Wasums. That Otis and Shirley. It worries me, your Uncle Raleigh's telegram. Maybe Otis is just a poor, crazy boy, but Shirley, now, Shirley could be downright tough to tangle with."

I growled, "I'm not scared of either of them for one minute, if that's what you think, and there ain't nothing at all to worry about."

"I know you ain't scared," Calvin said. He blinked at me, searching, trying to feel his way into things. He said, "Pepper, you got to go home in the fall. Just because the judge made you spend a week in the smokehouse—"

"Holy God," I said, so riled I felt ready to howl. "That's one little bitty thing, and I'm talking about lots and lots of things. Now the straight of it is, the judge and I have never got on, and I'll tell you, Calvin, I'm . . . I'm seceding. If we could secede from the Union over State's Rights, why then I guess I can secede from the family over Pepper Fairchild's Rights."

"I see," Calvin said. He turned his eyes full at me, seeing. "Then I guess this is the first time in my life I've ever been sorry I bear the name I do, for that must mean that you aim to secede from me, too."

And then we just sat there, silent. After a while I felt so bad that I did the only thing I could. I went around to the little wooden room on the back of the wagon and got my portman-teau and pulled out the heavy little sack I'd hidden carefully under my clean drawers. I said to Calvin, "I spoke things wrong just now. We've always been more than even kin, we're true friends, too, and I aim that we always will be. This here is to prove it."

And I reached the hat from his head and dumped the sack in it. It was money, mostly silver dollars, but more than one gleam-ing gold piece was there. It looked impressive to me just as it was, and I didn't bother to open the little package of greenbacks I'd wrapped in a piece of oilcloth.

Well, Cousin Calvin was flabbergasted. He said, "Pepper, what is this? Wherever did you get all that money?"

"It's mine, every nickel. That's what I meant by being practical and making a plan. See this big old silver dollar with the X mark? I sold a barrow to John Murphey that I raised from a little shoat Uncle Raleigh gave me. And this little yellow one—isn't he pretty looking?—I got him for milking for old Mr. Buck all one winter. This is money I saved."

"What did you save it for?"

"I told you, for a sound business opportunity. I used to think maybe as soon as I was grown I might invest my pile in getting the Dorcheat made navigable as far as Sike's Ferry, for surely a body who controlled such a waterway could make money galore. But now that I'm not going back to Claiborne Parish, I don't doubt that some fine opportunity in the West will be more profitable by far. Like I told you, a man's got to plan ahead if he wants to make things work. A man wants to make money, he's got to have money to invest when the right opportunities come along. Well, the way I see it, I've found my first opportunity. Whatever of this money we need for photographic stuff, Calvin, we'll just spend it. You're my investment, Calvin."

Calvin's face got red as a cardinal's tail. He said, "I can't tell you how proud you make me, Pepper. But we can't spend money you've worked and saved so hard for."

"Sure we can," I said. "Partner."

Cousin Calvin sat and looked at me so long that I got a little embarrassed. Then he stood up and reached for my hand and shook it up and down, up and down, just as if I'd been a grown man. His mouth worked so hard it looked like the words would never come out, but he made it at last:

"I promise I won't fail you. Partner."

Three

So we headed West, neither of us saying any more, in the Fairchild way, about either our private aspirations or about Uncle Raleigh's telegram, but both of us keeping our eyes peeled. My little sack was considerably lighter after Calvin bought the things he needed from Mr. Lewels's atelier, and our eating money that the family had figured would take us all the way to California barely got us out of Denison City. Calvin wasn't a bit worried. At first.

Leaving Denison City promptly was my idea, of course. A problem we both knew well, and which was why the family had decided on California for Calvin in the first place, was that around our parts any town big enough to support a full-time photographer already had one. In Denison City, for instance, there was already Mr. Lewels trying to scrape a living. So I told Calvin, Mr. Lewels just sits there in town, but what about the country folks? And I reminded him of Phemister's Photographs always out making rounds and about the lettering on the wagon, "We Take Ranch Pictures." So two mornings later, when we had everything as ready as it would ever be, I clucked up the mules, Old Jeb and Young Jeb, and we set off looking for ranches.

The first thing we found was a young tramp hoping for a ride. A bunch of little children, some white but mostly black, come down from slaves who'd belonged to the Indians, were chasing after us and staring in wonder, not at Calvin for a change, but at the strange appearance of the What's-It Wagon. One tiny little girl with peppercorn hair fell down and began crying so hard that Calvin finally told me I'd better stop so he might look at her. The tramp came out from among some live oak trees, on one of which he had just nailed up a big white reward notice that said in big black letters:

$1,000 REWARD

WHEREAS, in the vicinity of the municipality of Denton, Denton County, Texas, within the last seven weeks, three men have been murderously slain and robbed, and

WHEREAS, the names of these aforesaid three slain men are as follows:

JASON WALLER
JIM LONGINO
JOHN THOMAS BLANCHARD and

WHEREAS, I, Hamilcar B. Burr, Merchant and citizen of said municipality of Denton, Denton County, Texas, being in shame and hatred of these foul crimes, and wishing to help our fair town free itself of the malignant presence of these cursed and most abominable murderers and robbers, and wishing to do my duty to my town, my county, my state, and my God,

THEREFORE do I hereby offer a reward of $1,000 for the capture, alive, of the men, principal participants in the aforesaid crimes, said sum to be paid in addition to any rewards from county or state or others.

HAMILCAR B. BURR

First the tramp squatted down and spoke to Calvin, and they talked a minute, and then he came over to me.

"Beg pardon," said he, "but I don't believe I made myself understood to your friend there."

Well, I could see why. People who didn't know Calvin sometimes found him hard to understand, but there was nothing the matter with this young man's mouth and I still could barely make him out.

"What can we do for you?" I said when I thought I'd figured out the gist of it.

"Why, I see you're going toward Sherman, and I wondered if I might ride along with you."

That's how I knew he was a tramp. He not only talked peculiarly, but he was willing to ask for a ride in a wagon that, if we'd been back home, I would frankly have been ashamed to be seen in.

I said, "Sir, I fear we can't help you, as my cousin is a photographic artist, and we'll be stopping at every ranch along the way for him to take portraits."

"That's all right," the young man said. "I need to stop along the way myself. I'm supposed to nail those posters up." He pointed. "See?"

He waited until I looked at the poster again, then he said cheerfully, "Mr. Burr is paying me two pennies apiece to put them up, and there were a hundred posters. His agent provided the nails and a hammer. Do you suppose I could find a buyer for the hammer when I'm through? What do you suppose a good hammer's worth? It's quite a good hammer."

At least that's what I thought he said. I'd never encountered an accent so thick. Calvin joined us before I could make out enough of it to essay a reply, and the man turned to him and asked in his cheerful voice, "Well, sir, and did you get that little Zambo patched up?"

"She just skinned her knees a bit," Calvin said.

So there we were, with the tramp not able to understand Calvin's speech, and me hardly able to understand his, and by the time we got it all cleared up, Calvin was asking the man politely to take his seat in the wagon, up front on the spring seat, and Calvin would sit on the bench behind us. They wasted a lot of time jawing about that, neither quite understanding the other from the looks of it, and the tramp fetched a big bundle of posters and a pack from among the live oaks and jumped up, lively, to the wagon. He took the bench. At least he was mannerly.

He scrunched himself forward and said, "May I introduce myself? Gilmore Carmichael. Please consider me at your service."

"Mr. Calvin Fairchild," said I, nodding at Calvin, "and I'm Pepper Fairchild."

"Brothers?" the tramp said.

"No sir. Cousins."

"Well it's certainly a pleasure," he said. "I'm in your debt. Those posters are heavy as sin."

"How come they're wanting them posted way up here?" I asked. "Denton. That's sixty or eighty miles south, isn't it?"

"About fifty, I believe. Hamilcar B. Burr must be papering the countryside with them."

"You from these parts, Mr. Carmichael?" I asked.

He enjoyed a merry laugh over that. "Do I sound like a Texan?"

"We're only a short time in Texas, and I'm not sure I know yet just how they sound. Except they sound different from home."

"I'm British," the tramp said. "I've been in your country, oh, perhaps a little over a month."

So that explained why he sounded so funny. He began asking us where our home was and all about the photographic business. After a while, we could understand him a lot better, just as he got the hang of Calvin's speech, and they passed the time of day together. He popped questions like a string of firecrackers and soon had Calvin telling him about us being hard on the road to San Diego, California, and I was relieved to hear Calvin even go so far as to mention Mr. John Swiss Parker and Phemister's Photographs. In turn, the tramp told Calvin he was contemplating a "ramble to a town called Tombstone in the Arizona Territory, wherever that is," and Calvin schoolmastered him a little in geography, and they both seemed to enjoy themselves. I was busy mainly with the mules. Young Jeb didn't harmonize well yet, and Old Jeb was having to work hard keeping him in step.

Ordinarily, I guess not many things could be nicer than

traveling like we did along a strange road, through rolling land, with big groves of live oak turning up often enough to break sun glare and monotony, and the wagon rattling and the trace chain jingling and Mr. Carmichael, who put on no more airs than someone from back home and early asked us to call him Gil, jumping out every so often to nail up a poster and then running back to leap on the wagon. He was grown, of course, maybe even a little older than Calvin, who was twenty-six, but he ran like a boy. He would have looked like one, too, except for the kind of beard that results not from design but from not shaving often. He was light of build and short. He was probably an inch or two shorter than I was, and I intended to grow plenty more before I called it quits. For the rest, he was fair of hair, which could have used trimming, with gray eyes that had a lot of laughter in them. Why he was nailing up reward notices for two cents apiece he didn't say, and naturally we didn't ask.

But we didn't run across any ranches, and I began to get worried. There was just a poor-looking farm here and there. Calvin was obviously getting worried, too, for he finally asked the question of Gil.

"As you've been putting up posters around, mayhap you know this part of the country," Calvin said, "and could tell us when we start getting into the ranching area. It's ranches we're specializing in today."

"I'm afraid I couldn't say," Gil said. "The most I've heard in Denison City is that a lot of the niggers that came over the line from the Indian Territory grow garden vegetables for sale in the town. I imagine these are all just Chino or Zambo farms."

"What's the difference?" Calvin asked.

Gil looked at us quizzically, as though he thought we should know even better than he, but he said, "According to Tschudi's list of half-castes, a Chino is a cross between an Indian father and a Negro mother, and a Zambo between a Negro father and an Indian mother. Or is it the other way around? I read dozens of tour guides to your America. It all runs together in the mind."

I said, "Do they really come out different?"

"Well, naturally the male defines the bloodline," Gil said. "Isn't that so? Although, now that I think of it, I'm not sure what Mr. Darwin would say."

"Who's Mr. Darwin?" I asked.

"Well . . ." Gil said.

"A scientist," Calvin put in.

I said, trying to understand it all, "All right, but is it, say, like henny and plain mules?"

"What?" Gil said.

"Never mind for now," Calvin said. "What say we turn in at the next farm and try our luck?"

Gil laughed his hearty laugh. "Surely you're not planning to take portraits of niggers," he said.

"Oh, we have lots of niggers in our home parish," Calvin said, "and I imagine they might like portraits as well as anybody else."

Gil's face reflected a sort of mental blink. "You know, I think you're absolutely right. They'll probably like it immensely," he said, and he jumped down to tack up another reward notice.

So we tried the next farm. By chance it was white, though it looked as poor as the others. There was an old grandmother boiling the wash in the front yard, and she called off the dogs and a half-dozen children that came running out. The grandmother said, "Step down. I expect you're looking for Zwing."

Calvin gave me a pleading look. I handed him the lines and stepped down. Gil just sat on the bench in the wagon and looked on with lively interest.

"Ma'am," I said, "this is Mr. Calvin Fairchild, photographic artist, and we're here to offer you a special opportunity to have four permanent, lasting ferrotypes on tin at the rate of one dollar for all four, of you or your pretty grandchildren here or your husband's barn or any horses or cows your husband might especially prize."

"Don't you want to see Zwing?" the grandmother said uncertainly. "He's just gone out hunting with Hugh. He'll be back most any time."

"Well, no ma'am," I said. "It's you we wanted to see."

She eyed Calvin and Gil and the wagon. "Which one is S. J. Boldini, Artist?" she said. It turned out she could read.

Calvin seemed quite unable to bring himself to speak, so Gil jumped off the wagon. "Madame, I have that honor," he said. He bowed. "And this is my illustrious colleague, Mr. Fairchild."

She couldn't make out a word of it, I would have bet. But she commenced to patting her hair a bit. "A dollar," she said, at length. "A dollar, now, that seems mighty high."

"For four permanent photographs on tin?" Gil said. "Tintypes that you would treasure all your life? Tintypes that would occupy a place of honor in what I'm sure is a charming little parlor there in your charming home?"

Frankly, I felt that I should be doing the talking, because maybe if they were washed up the lady's grandchildren could be called pretty, but a two-room shack with a dogtrot in the middle of it is not what you could stretch to call a charming home. But, then, she couldn't understand that English accent. Maybe all she understood was that bow Gil made her when he claimed to be S. J. Boldini.

"Well, a dollar does seem high," she said. "You children, you come away from that wagon, now!"

"That's no ordinary wagon, ma'am," I said quickly, before Gil could horn in again. "That's a fully equipped, traveling photographer's studio."

"Just fancy," the grandmother said. She cast a glance at her boiling wash, and called to one of the children, "LaFay, come stir those shirts!"

I said, "Naturally, Mr. Fairchild produces the tintypes right on the spot, and you don't have to wait and wait before you can enjoy them."

"Well," she said.

We had her. I said, "Mr. Fairchild will just get out his fine fifty-dollar camera and get everything all prepared, and you can go get ready, for of course the first portrait will be made of you."

"I've got to change my dress," she said. "Do you think I want my portrait made in some old thing I put on to do the wash?"

"Mr. Fairchild wouldn't dream of rushing a lady," I said. "Now, I expect you'll want a fine portrait of your grandchildren here for the second tintype. What about the barn? Does your husband especially prize that barn?"

It took nearly an hour. Impossible to understand him or not, the grandmother had to consult with "Mr. Boldini" to decide what all she wanted four tintypes of, and I guess maybe she caught a word here and there. She settled on Hugh Junior standing holding a half-bred Jersey in front of the barn for one picture, and herself on the gallery in her black Sunday best for the second, and a young woman raked up from somewhere with a brand-new baby for the third, and the grandchildren and the young woman and her all together for the fourth. She wanted to wait for Zwing and Hugh to come back from hunting to get them in, too, but "Mr. Boldini" talked her out of it.

Calvin did fine. He prepared the tin plates and made the pictures and then popped into that little privy-looking room and popped back out later with the tintypes, not mounted or framed, but what did they expect for a dollar? The whole family waved until we were clear out of sight.

Down the road a little distance, I said to Gil, "Excuse me," and I handed Calvin the silver dollar the grandmother had handed me. He turned it over a time or two, just beaming, then handed it back. "You're the one with the business sense," he said. "You keep it for us, partner."

As treasurer, I was not exactly weighed down by the business we did during the rest of that day. Not that we didn't do any more business. We never did find a real ranch, but we turned in on a place owned by a Mr. Robert M. Burgess, who raised blooded cattle, and Calvin was kept as busy as you please taking portraits of a tribe of Polled Angus bulls and heifers. The catch was, Mr. Robert M. Burgess had no cash and paid us off in salt beef.

The lack of cash held pretty much through the day. Evening found us still a piece away from Sherman and rounding up, for the second time, three white Leghorn pullets that a recently married couple had exchanged for a portrait in their wedding clothes. We had locked up the chickens in the privy part of the wagon. Every time we opened the door, they flew out cackling.

The light would soon be failing. Old Jeb was tired from trying to keep the young mule in step all day, and I said to Calvin after we'd asked at the last farm and been turned away, "Maybe we should start thinking of stopping for the night."

He looked, longingly I thought, toward a line of trees that told us we were coming to a creek, but he said, "Oh, no, I reckon we could push on and get to Sherman tonight. Gil is probably anxious to get on in."

He could have added, "To get paid for nailing up posters," but of course he didn't.

But Gil mind-read Calvin as well as I did. He said, "There's nothing in Sherman I'm anxious to do. My paymaster, Hamilcar B. Burr, awaits me all the way down the route in Denton. Mr. Burr seems a careful businessman, and my wage depends on an agent due to ride from Denison City to Denton on Friday. Among the duties of the agent is to count the posters he sees along the way. Otherwise, I assure you I would have thrown them all in the nearest ditch."

Calvin laughed, no doubt thinking Gil didn't mean it, and said, "Then do you mind camping out overnight? If there's anything pretty enough ahead, I'd love to get set up and take some views while there's still enough light. *Harper's New Monthly Magazine* uses no end of western views."

I didn't comment, but it didn't seem to me we were West enough yet to start wasting plates. Texas looked different from our home parish, all right, but the main difference was oak instead of sweet gum, bois d'arc instead of cypress. And it didn't seem sensible to me that New York magazines would pay money for such as that.

The place I picked out for us on the creek was already occupied. A family with two big girls, one with black hair who looked about my age, had pulled a wagon in and were scouting out the site as though they were figuring on stopping early, just like us. Gil said, "Wait a minute." He jumped out of our wagon and ran to a tree and commenced nailing up one of his reward posters. The man of the family went and studied it.

The girl with black hair came over to me. I noticed she had her breasts well under way, not too big yet, but there. She said, "What in the ever-loving world do you call that kind of a wagon?"

"I guess you've never seen a high-grade traveling photographer's studio before," I said.

She giggled. "No, and I've never seen a chicken with two heads, either. But I saw a hog eat a just-born calf once."

They were from Missouri. The man called the black-haired

girl over to read the poster out loud to him, then he came and said, "Evening," to Calvin and me and had the girl read our wagon.

"Traveling, I see," the Missouri man said to us.

"Yessir," I said, "all the way to San Diego, California."

"You following the Butterfield?"

That was the old Butterfield Overland Mail route. Its stages hadn't run since early in the war, when the federal congress annulled its contract, but many travelers heading West still followed it or some other established route. I said to the Missouri man, "We plan to do so. Folks said that was about the easiest way."

"That's what folks said to us. We been passing lots of wagons going West, but not no wagons like this." He studied the gold lettering a bit more, then said, "What kind of artist?"

"My cousin, Mr. Calvin Fairchild, is a photographic artist," I said.

He nodded awhile. He jerked his thumb back toward Gil's poster and said, "What kind of robberies?"

"That I couldn't say," I said, "for we're new to this part of the world."

"Three men?" he said. "All killed?"

"That's what the poster says."

The Missouri man said, "Three men. I never saw a notice quite like that. They gave each of them a line to hisself."

"Yessir."

"Butchered and robbed and left to blowflies?"

"I hope it wasn't as bad as all that."

He nodded a bit more, then seemed to make up his mind. "Well, I guess we'll be going on in to Sherman for the night," he said. "I wish you good evening."

Of course we wished it in return. Then we exchanged the expectation of encountering one another along the Butterfield. Then they picked themselves up and were gone in five minutes. The black-haired girl craned her neck and looked back at us, but she didn't wave. So neither did I.

Gil looked about him, smiling.

I said, "I think you did that on purpose."

"What?" said he.

"Nailed up that murder poster right under those folks' noses. The agent that's coming Friday, he'll never be able to count a poster so far back in the trees."

"You think not? Then I suppose that will just have to be my contribution to our evening's comfort. Two cents that I won't be paid."

Calvin started clucking and saying of course Gil hadn't frightened people away on purpose, and Gil started teasing that I surely had looked a lot at the black-haired girl, and I stomped off and left both of them. I took the mules with me, to water them.

Well, there was good grass around, though we'd brought corn for the mules to carry along from Denison City. I let them roll, then wiped them down and staked them out to graze for a while. By the time I got through, Calvin was down by the bridge making squares with his fingers as if he was contemplating taking a view of just the plain old trees. Gil was getting up firewood, whistling and bustling around. He'd already dragged the barrel of salt beef from where I'd put it behind the bench, just as if it belonged to him, and he asked if we had matches, saying he seemed to have lost his from his pack. I opened the wagon's privy part, where we kept careful things, and those three damned chickens came flying out again.

"Catch them! Catch them!" Gil cried.

"I'd like to know how," I said. All three flapped into a tree. They were gabbling with wild excitement.

Gil climbed up the tree as lithe as a monkey and soon had them all shaken out. I captured them on the ground. Calvin came up from the creek bed and helped.

"I wonder," said Gil, when he was back on solid ground, "if the menu shouldn't read chicken tonight instead of salt beef."

Now, those were Calvin's chickens. I had some investment in them, too, it should be remembered. But there was Mr. Gilmore Carmichael, casually disposing of them. He did, too. Calvin readily agreed with him that chicken would be fine, just as if we were back home and Gil was a visitor that you tried to offer anything you could think of to please him. I'd certainly been taught manners enough to know that hospitality was a thing to regard seriously, but it was hard to see that it was something you killed yourself over for any tramp who asked for a ride and then stayed with you the entire day.

To make matters worse, Gil had never killed a chicken before and looked squeamish about starting, and Calvin was anxious to take a view by the creek that he thought would be pretty. It was Pepper Fairchild, of course, who ended up having to kill and scald and pluck those pullets.

By the time the sun went down and the mosquitoes came up, I'd fried those chickens as best I could. They didn't taste like Grandmother's, but they weren't bad. Gil ate hungrily. Then he rummaged in his pack and found cigarette makings, which he shared with Calvin and, I had to admit, politely enough offered me, and we settled back on our quilts and watched the stars come out. Gil showed me Jupiter, which he said had moons just like our moon and a big red patch on it that some scientist with a big telescope had recently discovered, and he wondered out loud for a while if it might be a real world, like ours. Then Gil sighed and said, "How marvelous. A marvelous meal and a marvelous day. This is the kind of day you can remember all your life."

"It's been a right fine day," Calvin agreed.

"It would have been a sight finer if we had more cash money to show for it," I said. "Salt beef and pullets isn't going to pay for all the photographic chemicals we've been running through."

"We'll soon be into real ranching country," Calvin said. "We'll make cash money there."

"I don't know that I'd count on that," Gil said. "If I were you, I believe I'd concentrate more on the small settlements and towns. That's where one would expect money in any region to accumulate."

"But ranch pictures, now," said Calvin, gesturing at the wagon, "Mr. S. J. Boldini must have made money at them or he wouldn't have specialized in them."

"I only know what happened to a friend of mine," Gil said. "Actually, I suppose that's why I'm here. His family owned a cattle run, you see."

We had to stop and work on that, and it finally turned out that a cattle run was British for cattle ranch, which Gil's family's friend, named Mr. Frederick Fassnidge, had somewhere near the upper reaches of the Brazos River. When Gil found himself short of funds in a foreign country it occurred to him that he could do worse than look up good old Freddie.

This required additional backing up, for I was naturally curious to know which foreign country, which turned out to be America, which I had certainly never heard called foreign before. Then, since he had brought up the subject himself, it seemed all right to ask, and I asked why was it he had gone traveling with no funds.

"Oh, I started with adequate funds. My aunt gives me little dribblings of money, you see, to stay out of Manchester. That's where my father lives."

"Where's Manchester?" I said. "I've only ever read of London."

"Then you have a rough idea of Manchester. It's a good bit northwest of London, but they're just alike. Great, dirty places with sprawling suburbs." He laughed his merry laugh. "I'm always glad to leave, but my aunt doesn't know that yet, and I assure you I'll never tell her."

Talking about his family like that with non-family like us made me uncomfortable, and I said, thinking to change the subject, "I guess you like traveling a good deal."

It turned out later he'd been just about everywhere, all over Europe and once even to India, but that night he only said, "Sometimes. I've enjoyed this trip."

"Where-all have you been here?" I said.

"Just New Orleans, and now Texas." Gil glanced at me and said, "How old are you, if you don't mind my asking, Pepper?"

"Fifteen," I said. "Why?"

"That's old enough," he said. "I'll tell you what I did. I took ship this time from Liverpool to New Orleans. I didn't want to go to New York City. I have an idea New York City is just like London, and I do believe I've concluded that the only fit life for a man is the rural life."

"Calvin here's been to New York City," I said. "He's also been to a nearby place named Coney Island, and they have a hotel there that's shaped like an elephant. Tell Gil about that hotel, Calvin."

"Another time," Calvin said politely. "Just now I'd like to hear Gil tell about New Orleans."

"But of course you've been there," Gil said.

"Not yet," I said. "The fartherest I've ever been before was to Bay Tree, Arkansas, where Calvin and I once sold two over-weight bales of cotton. Bay Tree looked pretty much like our home town. What's New Orleans like?"

"I hardly know. I was only there overnight. I went to a whore-house and got dosed down with laudanum in a whiskey smash. When I came to on the docks the next morning I didn't even have the money left to pay my hotel bill. So I smuggled my belongings out and left. Fortunately, I don't think I got dosed down with anything else. I'd been wondering."

"Uh," Calvin said, looking quickly at me, "and that's why you decided to look up Mr. Frederick Fassnidge?"

"Yes, my sisters said he had written last from a place called Dallas, and it didn't seem too far from New Orleans, so I thought I'd ramble over there."

"Kind of a far ways to ramble," I said.

"So it was. And then Freddie turned out to be as strapped for ready-money as I was, although I must say he's going to be im-mensely wealthy August eleventh."

"What's so special about August eleventh?" I said.

"Why, he's got in on this marvelous mining enterprise, the Arizona Consolidated Mining Company. I'm sure you'll keep this confidential, but you see, they've struck water in Tomb-stone!"

"Oh," I said.

"Water?" Calvin said.

"Yes, Freddie tells me the town has absolutely none of the stuff. It's filthy with silver and gold, but they haven't even enough water for a stamping mill and they have to haul the ore, oh, who knows how far to be worked."

He laughed, enjoying some private joke, and went on to tell us how Freddie had traded the ranch for shares in a company formed to sink a shaft in some mine called the Sulphuret and install big steam pumps every hundred feet to pump up water that had appeared at the Sulphuret's five-hundred-foot level. Then they'd mine the Sulphuret for silver, sell water for a stamp-ing mill, and sell any excess for irrigation, turning the desert into a garden.

"I had a chance to get in on it myself," Gil said cheerfully, "but I seem to have muffed it. You see, the pumps will arrive August tenth, and they won't be able to keep things quiet after that. The stock price will soar. One could make quite a nice little profit by buying on August ninth and selling on the eleventh. That's what Freddie recommends. I know I don't have to ask you not to repeat this, but Freddie has private information that the supply of water is not unlimited, you see? They've let the word get around that the water comes from a flowing underground stream, but it seems that it's really just a localized subterranean reservoir, and I suppose they'll use it all up in a year or two. Leave it to Freddie to know how to skin the natives. He's devilishly clever about financial things. I suppose I shouldn't repeat this either, but the ranch he's unloaded on his partners is rather useless. The ranch had all gone to hell since your Slave War, you see?"

Now, I felt a little rankled, partially because I suspected I was one of the "natives" that Freddie knew so well how to skin and partially because being devilishly clever about financial things was what I wanted to be, and I envied anyone who already was. So when Gil said, "Slave War," I said grouchily, "Our what?" although of course I knew what he meant.

Calvin said to Gil, "We don't call it just that."

"Oh," Gil said. "I beg your pardon."

"That's all right," Calvin said. "Some folks call it the War Between the States, and some say the War for Southern Independence. In the North they call it the Civil War or the Rebellion. I guess Rebellion fits pretty well. The South denied that the North had the right to curtail its freedom just for the sake of unity, so it seceded." Calvin never even looked at me, but Gil did, with a puzzled look that I was coming to be familiar with.

"Well," Gil said. "Well, the Fassnidges were rather slow in getting around to looking into their ranch after, er, your war, and Freddie found it absolutely oozing with interlopers when he came out to see to it. They wouldn't even let him on the place when he tried to inspect it. He received an order to return the way he came unless he wished to see strange sights, so away he went. Of course he stands to make ever so much more money, more quickly, from his stock in the mine. But you see, if Freddie's any sample, ranchers can't be counted upon to have any money at all. He'll be living on nothing a year until August eleventh. A pity. I had to look elsewhere for ready-money."

"Like Calvin," I said. "Calvin was going to go looking for work so we could buy photographic chemicals, but I said . . ." I stopped. Ready-money was a thing I now had considerably less of myself, and it wasn't a subject I cared to discuss with someone like Gilmore Carmichael.

"Me look for work? Good lord no," Gil said. "I came looking for another acquaintance, to see if he wouldn't like to lend me enough money to buy into Freddie's company." He laughed a long time over this. I couldn't see why, until he went on to tell how the joke was on him. Freddie's partners had offered Gil an opportunity to sell A.C.M. Company stock, with a share for him for each share he sold, but he turned the idea down because he thought it would be much easier to borrow from his other acquaintance, a Colonel Stevens, an Englishman who was engineer of the Texas & Kansas Railways, which Gil said was built with English gold and owned in England. Colonel Stevens was supposed to be somewhere between Denton and Denison City, but he wasn't. He was back in England.

"So there I was," Gil ended cheerfully. "Stranded."

"What are you going to do now?" I asked.

"Hammer my way to Denton and collect my eight shillings from Hamilcar B. Burr," Gil said. "My two dollars, I mean. That should take a day or two. There doesn't seem to be much point in planning beyond that."

Calvin looked at me, and even in the flicker of the fire I thought I could see the wish in his eyes to offer Gil the silver dollar we'd made, and I said quickly, "I guess you could write your aunt in Manchester, England, for some more money."

"Not for five more months," he said. "Unless I'm actually in Manchester and the old lady wants me out, she doesn't care to hear from me more often than that."

"What about your father?" I said. Calvin cleared his throat, and I said, "Beg pardon."

Gil only laughed. He said, "I no longer have a father. We never got along, for various reasons, and after a really fine row several years ago over my joining the Social Democratic Federation he, uh, 'ceased to consider me henceforth as a member of his family.' He did it up right, you know. My sisters say he obliterated my name from the family Bible. And of course he cut me out of his will. A pity. I was the only son, and my father had done quite well in the sherry trade. I suppose that's where the original trouble started. I didn't want to go into the sherry business. Or into any business."

I leaned back in my quilt and watched the night. Cicadas were unwinding somewhere. Gil and Calvin talked on about the Social Democratic Federation, which turned out to be some off-sounding group that aimed at overthrowing capitalistic society and substituting something called "ordered co-operation" in place of "anarchical competition." I didn't know what to think about that, but I soon relaxed when Gil said he had gotten disgusted with these people's factional strife and had quit them to work on his own for what he called democratic control of the economic resources of the community. If I had Gil pegged correctly, he didn't do much work of any kind for anything. After that I didn't listen much. I was thinking about the big, red-covered Bible at home, and wondering if, when I didn't come home, my father would take it out of the shelf where it was kept and take his pen and scratch out my name and blow on the page to dry it and then put the Bible back. But one thing about the Fairchilds, I somehow couldn't see my father scratching out the name of his only son. If the new baby my stepmother was carrying was a boy, well, maybe then. As if I gave a damn.

Calvin said, "Aren't we, Pepper?" and I said, "What?"

"Aren't we already in the prairies?" he said. He turned back to Gil. "I reckon we've seen the last of the piney woods. Then we'll be past the prairies and in the true plains. It's like the ocean, they say. They say the wind blows a thousand miles."

Calvin's voice was low and rapt. So was Gil's when he spoke: "A thousand miles."

"The last new land," Calvin said.

"We always look West," Gil said. He flopped over on his stomach and propped his chin in his hands. "Why is that? Because we were expelled from the Garden to the eastward? Then isn't eastward where we should look for our new life?"

"Men just always do seem to look West," Calvin said.

I thought they were both only dreaming out loud. But I listened. What Calvin had said about the wind and the sea had caught me. On the other side of a sea would be a shore. On a new shore, there could truly be a new life. I intended to look things over carefully and be practical and, hopefully, be devilishly clever about it, but that's exactly what I had in mind for myself.

"If it's the last new land," Gil said, "maybe it really would be worth taking a look at. By August ninth, preferably. You know, Freddie and his partners paint the most dreadful pictures of what their scheme is going to do to that mining town. Oh, they think it sounds lovely—a hundred smokestacks adorning the hills . . . the lulling music of the constantly dropping stamps at their stamping mill . . . steam whistles blasting."

Calvin said, a little sadly, "It sounds just like New York City."

"Indeed, one would want to grab one's money and run," Gil said. "You know, Calvin, you've really let us down a bit over here. I believe we all expected you to develop a whole new breed of men and a whole new society. Oh, I know that we keep exporting Freddies to help you ruin things, but what do you have in your New Yorks and Chicagos and Tombstones and thereabouts? Captains of industry. *Laissez faire*. Machines. It's England all over again."

"I don't like to be the one to say it, but if you'd bought the stock in the mining company, wouldn't you be a captain of industry yourself?" Calvin said.

Gil laughed softly. "My friend, you've trapped me. But I thought I might give my profits away. Help the cause back in England. Endow the Socialist League, perhaps, and educate towards revolution. We mustn't allow things to go on the way they are, must we?"

"Is that what you're looking for?" Calvin said. "Something better?"

"I don't know. Perhaps I only think there must be something better."

Calvin said, "Well, we've got to think that."

"Or at least hope," Gil said.

I sighed. "I'd better go bring in the mules for the night."

The fire was low, but I could see both of them look startled. Then Gil said, "We'll help." He jumped lightly to his feet. He gave Calvin a hand to help him up, then said to both of us, "I wonder, would it put us too far out of our way to detour through Denton? I'm told the road is excellent. Better than the cutoff from Sherman."

"Why no," Calvin said immediately, "t'would be no trouble at all. We'll probably find no end of ranches between here and Denton."

"Excellent," Gil said. "I imagine I've put up at least twenty-five or so posters today, and there's no point in wasting all that work. We can collect the two dollars as we go through."

Calvin said, "You can stay here and rest, Pepper. We'll get up the mules."

And I did stay there, dumbfounded. They'd never said a direct word about it. I'd listened enough for that. But it was as clear to me as spring water under noon sun what was going to happen: Calvin wasn't going to say a word to stop him, and that wandering tramp who wanted to be a captain of industry just so he could become some crazy sort of social revolutionary, who treated a pair of strangers' salt beef and pullets as his very own, who found no point in planning his life more than a couple of days in advance, who could no more be counted upon to look out for himself than dreamy-brained Calvin, whose total assets apparently amounted to the two dollars he'd get for putting up posters—minus two cents for one too far from the road—Gilmore Carmichael was obviously now planning to go all the way to the West. With us.

Four

I tried to head Gil off. I even invested in it. Naturally, I invested my own money, because Calvin wouldn't have thought it was right to try to get rid of even an uninvited guest, and so the way I figured it, it wouldn't have been right to invest what little money Calvin had made in trying to do just that. It was complicated. I figured it all out carefully.

First the opportunity had to arise, and it did when we hit one of the world's biggest chuckholes coming into Sherman and messed up a wheel. We had to stop over, getting it fixed, and Gil began to worry that he wouldn't get his posters nailed up all the way to Denton by the time the agent was to ride the route on Friday. That was the opportunity. Here's what I did:

I got out my sack and got out a greenback and gave it to Gil and sent him on ahead. I made it convincing. I pointed out to him and Calvin that the way things were going, we were making grub but too little money, and that the thing to do was advertise. We worked out a nice notice that told people Calvin Fairchild would be coming through, and they should get their portraits made.

Well, Calvin was so pleased that even if I'd considered confiding in him that the whole thing was just a scheme to get rid of a new burden of responsibility named Gilmore Carmichael, I would have changed my mind on the spot. Calvin said maybe our notice should say Mr. S. J. Boldini was coming through, to avoid confusing people about the wagon, but I could tell easily that he was tickled at the idea of seeing his own name printed in a newspaper.

I went and talked to the editor of one of Sherman's two newspapers, who was nice, and who told me that Denton had a photographer, as far as he knew, but he thought there was none in a thriving nearby community, Krum, with a thriving weekly newspaper, the *Krum Chronicle*. With that information in hand, I told Gil he should go to Krum and place our notice there. Naturally, I never expected to see him again. Not once he had Mr. Hamilcar B. Burr's two dollars and my greenback in his pocket. Calvin would be disappointed when our notice with his name wasn't in the *Chronicle*, but I promised myself I'd stake him to another advertisement sometime, and make it up to him.

Something that worried us happened in Sherman after Gil left. The wheelwright agreed to fix our wheel in exchange for portraits of his three little girls, and while Calvin and I were off at the wheelwright's house, someone must have come along and spotted our wagon sitting on the street and decided to play some kind of joke on us. Because when we came back out to develop the plate, we found a scrawled note tacked onto the dark-box door.

It said:

GOD HATH SENT
ME TO PROCLAME
A DAY OF VENGENCE,
PRAY,

I thought right away about Otis Wasum and his big brother,

Shirley. Not that I had any thought that Shirley might have written the note. Shirley might be a reckless hell-raiser, but he was straight and direct like his old daddy, and no churchgoer to boot. But Otis, when he wasn't busy starting fistfights and sneaking around in mercantile stores to lay for innocent people, was kind of Sunday-school prone and went to all the tent revival meetings with his momma. That note sounded like something he might have constructed slyly to put the fear into us, and it did succeed in making me pretty nervous. I wanted to start carrying my shotgun, a Greener 10-gauge that my Uncle Raleigh had given me for a fowling piece, but Calvin said no, it was just a coincidence that some passer-by had elected to put a Bible notice on our wagon. He said in the first place there wasn't much chance Otis and Shirley could have followed us or found us in such big country, and in the second place why wouldn't they have made a try for us if they had indeed found us, and in the third place that I was just being jumpy because of Uncle Raleigh's mysterious telegram. Personally, I figured I wasn't being jumpy, just careful. I couldn't fathom the whole thing, but at least I knew it wouldn't have been so hard for Otis and Shirley or anyone else to find us, since the folks back in Claiborne Parish knew we would have to head south from Denison City to reach the Butterfield. I put the shotgun near to hand in the wagon just in case I was right, but Calvin preferred to think it was just some wandering evangelist who had put the note there.

Before all that happened I had entertained the idea that we could maybe linger in Sherman awhile and make some money, for people were interested as could be in the What's-It Wagon. But Calvin, dreamy and quixotic as ever, thought we had to get on to Krum by Saturday, to meet Gil and to make photographs, as our advertisement supposedly said, and what with that note on the wagon and my worrying about Otis and Shirley and all, I decided not to argue. I knew well that we didn't even have to go through Denton County, since Gil would long be gone with my greenback, but I couldn't very well explain that to Calvin. So when we finally left Sherman we worked our way along the route to Denton, still keeping our eyes peeled as instructed by Uncle Raleigh and also looking for the turnoff to Krum.

We were late getting into Krum. This was cotton and wheat

country, and folks had a little money in their pockets here and there, despite the high railway freight charges that they complained about a lot. We camped by a nice pond Friday night, although, shades of home, I saw two water moccasins and we both got edgy and slept in the wagon bed. We started early Saturday morning, but a farmer stopped us right in the roadway and said he guessed his wife had a craving to have her portrait made. He insisted we come along to his house, or I swear Calvin would have hurried us on into Krum by the time the sun got strong. As it was, it was probably ten o'clock when we could begin seeing the town off ahead of us.

Meadowlarks were whistling. I'd spotted more than one covey of bobwhites. I've known men to shoot meadowlarks for quail, not noting the yellow in the wings or even the difference in how they fly, and I was telling this to Calvin, who didn't hunt, and watching hedgerows. Your bobwhite might be found in an open field, but you wouldn't find many meadowlarks hanging around hedgerows. Then:

"Good God almighty!" I said.

"Don't cuss," Calvin said.

"But good God! It's him!"

I pointed, for it was—Gilmore Carmichael, dozing in the shade of the hedgerow we were just passing.

"Well, well," Calvin said, and his damaged lip split wide in a big smile that he forgot to point downward. "Stop the mules, Pepper."

Gil sat up, sleepy-looking, and Calvin was out of the wagon and helping him before he had time to get to his feet.

"I was beginning to think you weren't coming," Gil said.

"We ran into business along the way this morning," Calvin said. "The man just wouldn't be turned down."

They commenced patting and pounding each other, happy as two pups. Gil said, "I have something you'll be interested to see." He dug into his pocket and reached out a newspaper. Calvin beamed and laughed over it, sounding shy.

Up Gil sprang to the wagon. He rumpled my hair, which, being red, seemed to attract people that way. "It should be a good day," he said to me. "A shop is raffling off a parlor suite at the stroke of noon, and they expect the town to fill up for the occasion. That's what the editor of the paper told me. She's a woman. Quite a young one." He laughed. "Have you ever heard of a woman running a newspaper? I want you to get a look at her. She's as peppery as you."

"Oh, red hair?" I said. I think that's what I said. I was still just so bowled over with surprise.

"No, just peppery inside. Calvin, give Pepper the newspaper. Here. That's quite an advertisement, isn't it?" He looked as proud as if he'd written it. Of course, he did help. The exclamation marks and changing "artist" to "artiste" were his idea. I must say it looked splendid. It said:

Mr. Calvin Fairchild!

Photographic Artiste
from
New York City and Homer, Louisiana! !
Will arrive in town Saturday
For a few days.

ELEGANT PORTRAITS!!!

and Views a Specialty.

We got Gil's pack loaded into the wagon and he settled himself on the bench, his head poked so far forward that it was just about on a line with ours, rattling away. He'd gone into Denton and collected his two dollars from Hamilcar B. Burr. The agent had miscounted and they only wanted to pay him a dollar and seventy-eight cents, but he'd insisted, and he had his way. No, he hadn't parted with the hammer. The two dollars in hand, he'd sworn he'd lost it. He had backed them down. Being somewhat smaller than most men, he'd early had to learn to stand up for himself, you see? He gave them back the leftover nails. Hamilcar B. Burr had made the agent count them.

There was laughter all through this, warm as sunshine, and despite myself I couldn't help but be sort of glad to see him. I tried to sort this feeling out, but it wasn't easy, for on he rattled all the rest of the way into town. Krum was just a crossroads hamlet but drew business from a large market area. He'd gotten our copy of the paper when it started off the press the night before, near nine o'clock, and spent the night in Krum with some fellow who'd been working in the slaughterhouse to get up a road-stake for going to Arizona Territory to go into mining, which gave him and Gil a common interest. Traded the hammer at the town's one hotel for a late supper for both of them. Had we ever before heard of a woman running a newspaper? Her brother-in-law was owner, but the woman took the advertisements and largely wrote it. And was she peppery? Listen to these editorials: Red Territory should be settled solely by the Indians, and the white trash hanging around North Texas hoping to grab somebody else's land should go back where they came from. And: If the slack and mush-headed cotton farmers of Denton County just sit on their hands and let Thos. Wilson & Co. continue to frighten off all potential competitors via the services of hired bullies, they would have only their own well-documented stupidity to blame if cotton-ginning charges rose to sky-high levels at picking season.

We went first to the newspaper office. That was Gil's idea. He'd seen how Calvin kept reading that notice of ours, and decided Calvin should have an additional copy. After that, he'd take us to the perfect spot he'd picked out to park the wagon and set up shop.

For a Saturday and a day when a parlor set was to be raffled off, that was the quietest town you could ever hope to see. There were some women and little children on the street, but few men. In front of the newspaper office, a little old man was sitting on the boardwalk drinking from a pint bottle of White Rye Whiskey. We stopped.

"Who're you looking for?" the old man promptly shouted out.

"Uh, a copy of today's newspaper," said I.

"Ain't none," he shouted.

Well, there seemed little point arguing with a man who would sit about drinking whiskey and shouting on the public street. I handed Calvin the lines and climbed down to go inside.

"Ain't nobody there," the little old man shouted.

I was patient. I said, "Well, when will somebody be back?"

"Ain't coming back," he shouted. "Leastwise she ain't. You'll have to look for her down by the cemetery."

This aroused Gil. "That young woman?" he said. "She died?"

The little old man cackled. He laughed so hard that he began to roll about on the boardwalk. Like most, it had been put up in sections by the individual merchants, and each had his own idea about the proper height, so there were steps up and steps down all along the line. The old man rolled off the nearest step and landed face down. He lay there sort of giggling to himself.

"What in fire is going on here?" I said to Gil.

"I can't imagine," he said. "Could she have died? Had we better find out?"

"We sure should," I said. After all, the way it had turned out, my greenback had been invested in that newspaper. I stepped to the door and looked inside. The newspaper office was all topsy-turvy, with things strewn about everywhere.

"Perhaps we should drive by the cemetery," Gil said.

It was all the way out of town, down a hill by a creek. We could see wagons and horses and folks milling around as we came down the hill. A man rode by us on a horse, going fast toward the cemetery, and Gil shouted to him:

"Mr. Desmond? Wait a minute, Mr. Desmond. What's happening?"

The man reined up a second. He may have been about the same age as my father, which was forty-five, but it was hard to tell. He sat his horse with a look of easy strength, but his face, sun-darkened just about to the color of his old, well-cared-for California saddle, was deep-lined and, at least at that moment, grim. His eyes flicked quickly over us and our wagon. He said to Gil, "Have you arms? I had to go back after my rifle. Hurry up, if you want to help."

"But, man, you've been ill," Gil said. He sounded bewildered, and it must have been a silly thing to say, for the man only grimaced and gave boot-heel to his horse. He was down the hill in a wink.

Gil said to us, "He's been ill. He shouldn't be rushing about that way."

"Is he a friend of yours?" I asked.

"I suppose so. That's the man I had supper with last night."

73

Calvin said, "Then we'd better hurry, Pepper."

We did. Gil's friend, Mr. Desmond, was nowhere in sight when I tied the mules, but there was shouting and angry voices from some big trees by the creek. I glanced at Calvin, and he nodded, and I took my shotgun out from under a piece of tow sacking where I had been keeping it handy since the note in Sherman. Calvin hadn't brought along an arm. He always said he was too poor a shot. Gil pulled a tiny pistol out of his pack and stuck it in his pocket.

We were all three excited and worried by then, and we ran across a cornfield toward the voices. The cemetery lay off to the side. I noticed even as I ran that people in these parts were pretty careless about letting weeds grow on their kin.

The voices belonged to a big bunch of men. In the middle of them was Gil's friend, Mr. Desmond. He was saying savagely, "Back off, now. I'm warning you."

We pushed through them. They moved aside for us easily enough, maybe at the sight of my shotgun. None of them seemed to be carrying much more than an occasional sidearm. In the middle of the circle with Mr. Desmond was a woman covered from skirt-hem to head-top with feathers. She was crying. Near her stood a man dabbed with oozy brown stuff and a feather or two here and there.

A little old man, about the age of the one who fancied White Rye Whiskey back at the newspaper office, said to me, "Who are you, boy? You just put that shotgun down and get out of here. This here is no concern of yours."

"I guess it is," I said loudly. "I guess where I come from we don't just stand around and let a bunch of sonsofbitches tar and feather a woman."

"Hell, boy, that's not tar," the man said. "That's just molasses."

But I moved into the center of the circle with Mr. Desmond. Calvin was right beside me, firm at my shoulder. I didn't know where Gil had gotten off to, but, turning, I spotted him. He had chosen what must have been the biggest man there, a tall, broad fellow, bald but young, and stationed himself in front of him, glaring at him as if at any minute he just might decide to eat the fellow alive.

Someone else in the crowd said, "What the hell, we're done anyway."

But still another man, with a big, black beard, said, "He's going to chew up that newspaper and swallow it. I'm not done until I see him swallow it."

The man with the dab of feathers said in a gloomy voice, "I'll be glad to. I've told you before and I'll tell you again, it's *my* newspaper and my responsibility."

There was an admiring murmur from the crowd. They liked that. But the woman sure as heck didn't. She couldn't stop sobbing, but she got out at the feathered man, "You half-bred, half-born, lickspittle sycophant. You trash."

"Let it be," Mr. Desmond said to her. "Never mind. Let it be."

"And let that be a lesson to you," the black-bearded man said to the feathered man. "You let her turn that newspaper into a piece of outhouse bung fodder. She—"

Mr. Desmond lowered his rifle on him. There was a sudden silence. It hung in the air so long that I could start hearing bird-sound and water-sound down by the creek. Then in the back of the crowd some of the men started to move away. Voices came again, men murmuring: ". . . through . . ." ". . . taught her a lesson . . ." ". . . says 'S. J. Boldini' on that wagon . . ." ". . . fear we tromped down a lot of Ordway's corn . . ." The man Gil had been glaring at was among those who left, and Gil came farther into the dissolving circle with us.

The little old man who had first spoken to me started away, then turned back. He said stoutly to Calvin and me, "You meddling whelps. You're not welcome in Krum, Texas. You stay out of our town."

"I expect it's not a town we'd care to be seen in," Calvin said, but the old man didn't understand him.

Well, they left. Ordway's young corn, if that's who it belonged to, underwent considerably more trampling. The feathered man said gloomily to us, "It was calling them mush-headed. I warned Emma it was going too far. She'd already gadflied everybody in the county."

The woman doubled up a dainty fist covered with feathers and sprang at him. She hit him square on the forehead. Down he went on his back, and she stood over him and cried, "Mush!

Slab-sided mush! You're the mushiest of all! You didn't even stand up to them! You let them spit on you!"

She sounded hysterical, that was sure. Mr. Desmond had done fine with the crowd, and maybe we'd helped, but it was Gil who was able to contend now. He touched her elbow. She jerked it away, but he took it again and turned her toward the creek. "I'm sorry we got here so late, Miss Prosser," he said. "Those contemptible cowards. I'm afraid there's molasses in your hair. There's water right here."

She was still sobbing, but trying not to. I guessed if they'd just used molasses she was probably crying as much from humiliation and fury as she was from hurt, although I noticed later the feathers had been well mixed with cockleburs. Gil got her started for the creek, with her still sobbing out, "Thieves," and "Blackguards," and things like that, but maybe also beginning to think about what she must look like with molasses in her hair.

Mr. Desmond took on the feathered man. But not to help. He gave him a hiding with several new words I'd never heard used just that way before, the gist of his message being the kind of creature the man was for standing by and letting a bunch of mangy dogs molasses-and-feather his sister-in-law.

"What could I do?" the feathered man said. "I told them the responsibility was mine. I told them to molasses-and-feather me instead. What else could I do?"

"I guess you're going to go slinking back there," Mr. Desmond said.

"My . . . my wife is there. My family. My newspaper."

"Get going," Mr. Desmond said.

"I . . . I think Emma should come back to town with me," the feathered man said.

"Stop thinking. Get going," Mr. Desmond said.

"But . . . Emma . . ."

Mr. Desmond took a step toward the feathered man.

Off he went. Across the cornfield, a few men were still standing about. We could see them talking for a minute, then one of the men gestured, and the feathered man climbed into a wagon. They all left. Mr. Desmond turned his back on them and moved off to the creek. We followed.

Gil had persuaded the woman to sit down on the creek bank

and was bringing her water in his hat. She'd gotten some of the feathers off her hands. She'd just about stopped crying.

Mr. Desmond said to her, "Are you all right?"

She said, "I'd like to kill them all."

"Um," Mr. Desmond said. "Gil, I don't think the lady knows your friends, and maybe they've earned an introduction."

Well, Gil named Calvin and me, and he renamed himself and Mr. Desmond, who said his first name was Hap, because their acquaintance with Miss Emma Prosser was apparently slight. She tried to collect herself and say the necessary how-d'you-do's. She thanked us for helping her, and so did Mr. Desmond.

During all this thanking, Gil fetched another hatful of water and poured a bit on her arm and began to try to help get off the feathers. Mr. Desmond said, "The creek would be best for that. And this boy here would be the best to help you, Miss Prosser." He eyed Calvin's split lip, distracted enough after all the excitement to do it openly, and said, "Him, too."

But Gil jumped into the creek, boots and everything on, and insisted on helping Calvin and me help her. When the feathers started coming off, I could see why. Miss Emma Prosser was a ripe woman. Ripe like a bursting fig in sunlight, with a ripe, moist mouth you'd think wasps would be quick to buzz around. She was somewhat disarrayed, with her hair out of its pins and her dress askew, and after a while so much skin was showing that she thanked Gil and Calvin and sent them back to Mr. Desmond on the bank and just kept me to help her. When I finished there were still molasses stains on her dress and my breath was coming a bit hard.

Mr. Desmond had leaned himself and his rifle against a giant pecan tree. He politely looked away, chewing a twig, until Emma spoke and thanked him all over again. When she wasn't mad and calling people names, she seemed to have nice manners.

"Tell me how I can best help you, Miss Prosser," Mr. Desmond said. "Do you want me to get a buggy? Do you want to go back into town?"

"I'll never set foot in that town again!" she cried.

"If you're worried about—"

"I'm not worried about those vile scavengers. I'd be worried *for* them. I couldn't trust myself if I ever saw a one of them again."

She was spirited all right. She began to stride back and forth and act it all out for us. They had come about an hour earlier that morning, once the newspaper had had time to be delivered, and at first they'd all just stood around and jawed about "editorials contrary to the community's interest." As if straight-spoken editorials didn't make people sit up and take notice. She'd learned that from her poppa, who had run newspapers all over Kentucky and Ohio. It was he who had staked her brother-in-law, time and time over, for starting dinky little newspapers, and staked him again, each time the last one failed, for the sake of her three-year-younger sister. This last newspaper, the *Krum Chronicle,* was failing again when her poppa, who had long been ailing, finally died, and she had come West to take over where her poppa's money had left off. The *Chronicle* was back on its feet in her first month and started showing a profit in her second. Naturally, she'd written plenty of editorials, to make people take notice of the *Chronicle,* and there wasn't a word in them that wasn't true, and what did we think of a bunch of blackguards who'd handed her such dirty service?

I thought that she'd probably jawed them into molasses-and-feathering her when they maybe just came to grumble. But I didn't say it. Instead, I said that, where we came from, we'd call them dirty curs for picking on a woman.

She said, "Good grief! It's not because I'm a woman. It's because they're a pack of . . . vile . . . the miserable little . . . mush-headed . . ." She'd started crying again.

It seemed to me it was my fault. I tried to make remedy. With Gil's help I coaxed her across the cornfield and to our wagon, and got her settled in the shade of the canopy on the spring seat. Gil dug into his pack and fetched out a flask quarter-full of brandy, which she waved away and then consented to sip about enough to make a hummingbird do headstands. After a while she settled down again. She said:

"Who's S. J. Boldini?"

"We don't know," I said. "We just bought this wagon. Calvin is a photographic artiste, and we're hard on the road west to San Diego, California."

"Oh," Emma said, wanly.

She didn't speak again for a while, and Mr. Desmond, who stayed on the ground but was leaning against the wagon, looked her over much as if she were a heifer for sale and he was toting up her good and bad points against her price. Pretty soon he said, apparently idly, to Calvin and me, "Gil tells me you're routing through the New Mexico and Arizona territories. Is that right?"

"Yessir," I said.

"I'm headed to Arizona Territory myself," he said. "Big Bug."

"Is that a town?" I said.

"No, Big Bug's a creek," he said. "They found a lot of placer there in '63, and while there ain't much placer left, they're doing good in those parts working lode." He pulled a few rough little rocks out of his pocket and exhibited them.

"Is that silver, sir?" I said.

"Of course not. Gold. A good friend of mine sent me these samples. His own claim got took by eastern capital, but I figure there's plenty of possibility left. I plan on gold for a while to get up a stake for ranching."

I said, "Gil's got a friend thinking on water in Tombstone."

Gil cast an uncomfortable glance at Miss Emma Prosser and said defensively, "Well, it's not just water. There's silver too. And the A.C.M. Company consulting engineers believe there's a huge body of copper underneath the silver."

"My," Mr. Desmond said mildly, "that batch of engineers seem to think they've got everything in the world in just that one mine."

Gil said, "But you said yourself some other mine in Tombstone has struck water. That shows there's definitely water there."

"Yes, the Grand Central and the Contention both, from what I hear. Maybe that means you're going to have some competition in the water-mining business."

Now Gil started looking more self-assured—in fact, downright smug—and he said, "*But*, my good fellow, do they know how to handle it? It will do them no good unless they can get it to the surface. The A.C.M. Company engineers have the trick all worked out—duplex, triple-expansion, condensing-type pumps with steam cylinders, ordered from England, of course."

I said, "What in the world kind of machinery is that?"

Gil smiled suddenly. "I haven't the least idea," he confessed. "But it sounds impressive, doesn't it?"

Our damp and dampened refugee was apparently coming back to life. She said, "What is that famous mining company planning to burn to make steam for its pumps? Cactus?"

"Oh no," Gil said. "Trees, I suppose."

"They're scarcer than water in those parts," Mr. Desmond said.

"Coal?" Gil offered, somewhat less certainly.

"Maybe there's coal," Mr. Desmond said. "I never paid much attention to such as that. What's below ground is not my usual line."

I said, "It sounds like you know the country above ground."

"I do," he said. "I know it well."

"Have you spent time there?"

"There and elsewhere."

"We'd thought to follow the Butterfield going through," I said.

"That's what Gil told me."

Gil's face took on an excited look. "Desmond knows the country, whereas we have the wagon and what-not. What do you think, Miss Prosser? There's nothing to stay here for. I think you should go with us. And Mr. Desmond, of course."

"Dear me, I couldn't put you out like that," she said.

"Well, it's a thought," Mr. Desmond said.

"You'd both be mighty welcome," Calvin said.

"Oh really, you must come," Gil said.

I said nothing at all. He had done it again—struck me dumb with surprise. Here he'd offered a wagon and mules and means that he had no share whatever in, that I could see, to a pair of perfect strangers, and invited them as nice as if we were in a parlor sipping tea to go west with us.

And they did.

Five

But first, Miss Emma Prosser did set foot in Krum, Texas, again. Nothing would serve but that she go straight down the main street of a town that had run her out and stare every passer-by straight in the eye. It took some time.

To begin with, she had to let her long brown hair dry and bun it up as best she could, she having lost most of her hairpins and we carrying nothing of that sort in our supplies. Next she had us drive her to the newspaper office. She went inside and looked around and refused to answer her brother-in-law. She left without taking anything. I had decided by that time she was just waiting to see if anybody wanted to fight.

Lastly, she had us drive her to her sister's house, which was out past a big feed mill on the edge of town. The sister rushed outside, eyes all red and scared, followed by three little children whose eyes looked much the same. She grabbed Emma and rushed her into the house. We could hear the sound of lots of crying and carrying on. The crying sounded sad, not angry, so I judged it was the sister doing it.

We waited. I got plenty hungry. Mr. Desmond waited on his horse at first, watching the road, then he finally got off and the horse started cropping the tall Johnson grass that grew along the roadside. Finally Mr. Desmond said to me, "Do you know how to use that shotgun?"

"Yessir," I said.

"Pepper's a dead shot," Calvin said. Mr. Desmond didn't catch it, but Gil did, and saved me the problem of having to repeat a compliment on myself.

"It's taking Miss Prosser a time to pack," Mr. Desmond said. "I'll go by and get my own traps. If anyone tries to come down that road, I want you to see that they don't come very far."

"What about you, sir?" I said. "From the way folks looked at us as we drove through, maybe you shouldn't go into town by yourself."

A very small smile, as though something tickled him but he was trying not to show it, flickered at the corners of his mouth. "I expect I won't have any trouble," he said.

"I can go with you," Gil offered.

"No need. You wait here and carry out Miss Prosser's things."

"What if she changes her mind?" I said. "What if she decides to stay?"

Mr. Desmond's face went grim. "Are you trying to say she's not welcome to ride along with you?" he said.

"Oh no, sir," I said.

"I can look out for Miss Prosser," Mr. Desmond said. He looked very firmly at Gil as he said this. "She won't be any trouble to you." A little less firmly, he added, "I can also be of considerable help to you along the way. I'm telling you this, it's rough country where you're going, and I've got good friends all along the route who'll be happy to repay past favors."

"Well, that's mighty fine," I said.

"We won't be a burden on you," Mr. Desmond said, looking firm again. "I was sick for a time, but I'm fine now. It was nothing catching, either, unless working too hard in the sun is catching. I thought my lungs had stopped, but I'm fine now."

"I'm glad to hear that, Mr. Desmond," I said.

"You can call me Hap," he said. But I never could. He was always Mr. Desmond to me.

He got on his horse, a nice-looking roan gelding with two white stockings, and left. Gil watched him. He said, "He doesn't look so fine to me. He looks ill."

"Maybe it's just age," I said.

"No, he looks ill. What if he becomes ill again along the way?"

"Well it was you that invited him," I said. I hadn't meant to say it. The words just came out.

Gil looked surprised. "Wasn't it all right?"

Calvin started in to say soothing things, like of course it was all right, and naturally we were happy to assist Miss Prosser in any way, and Mr. Desmond seemed a fine man, and along that line. Then there was movement down the road. One man on foot. I put the shotgun across my lap and was starting to feel a little edgy until I saw it was only Emma's brother-in-law from the newspaper. He stepped to the other side of the road and circled around us and headed for the front door.

"Do we allow him to enter?" Gil said.

"I guess so," I said. "It's his house."

He was no sooner in than Emma came out. She'd changed her stained dress to an all-over brown thing with a white collar and a white hat. It would have done for church. The sister and brother-in-law followed her. He was saying, ". . . must take some money."

She ignored him. "Good-bye, Alice," she said to the sister. "And remember, if you're ever in difficulties, get in touch with me immediately."

"You're going to be the one who's in difficulties," the brother-in-law said gloomily. "I know I haven't much money, but you must take—"

She stopped him with a steely look.

The sister apparently had never let up crying. She said weakly, "Emma, you must take the money. I know we can't pay it all back yet, but you can't just go off without a penny to your name."

"Tut," said Emma. I had the strong impression she was addressing her words to someone other than her sister. "I fear your household will need it worse than I. Besides, I'm far from penniless. Shall I leave you something extra? For when things begin to go . . . bad again?"

"Oh Emma," the sister wept.

"Things are going to go just fine here," the brother-in-law said, but he still sounded gloomy.

Emma said, "I fear some people may find out it's not so easy when they finally have to fish or cut bait all on their own. But remember, Alice dear, as soon as I'm settled you can always count on me."

The sister wept, "But Emma, what will you do? Where will you go?"

"Tut," said Emma. "Doesn't the *San Francisco Chronicle* have a lady reporter? Isn't Catharine Amanda Scott Coburn an editor on the *Portland Evening Telegram?* The real West is progressive, and there are ladies running newspapers all over it. I'll simply look around and make my choice. I don't need all the money our poor poppa threw down a rathole. I'll do very well on my own."

The brother-in-law looked gloomier than ever. The little children crowded to the door and began helping their mother cry. Emma told us that we could bring her trunks out now, please.

There was one middle-sized trunk and a scad of little boxes and bundles and things. "Where do we put them?" I said to Calvin.

"In back of the bench, I guess," he said. "Maybe I can make some room later in the dark-box."

We were still stowing stuff when Mr. Desmond came riding back. A big black dog with a skinny tail was trotting behind his horse's heels. Mr. Desmond was carrying not much new except a blanket roll and a couple of saddlebags on the back of his saddle, and a big paper parcel of something that smelled mighty meaty and good. He tipped his hat to Emma and her weeping sister and leaned over to set the parcel in the wagon. The dog flopped down under the wagon right below the parcel.

The brother-in-law watched all these various affairs with big sad eyes, which went from Calvin to me to Gil to Mr. Desmond. Finally he picked Calvin. He said to him, "I'm not saying she didn't try to help all she could. I'm not saying their daddy didn't help. What I'm saying is, it's hard to go on being grateful all your life."

Calvin got very red in the face. His mouth began to work. I stepped in and said, "Yessir." That was all. I had nothing else to say to a man who had so few objections to letting a woman get roughed up. And I sure didn't want Calvin to have to discuss with him the question of gratitude to kinfolk. To avoid exchanging more words with the brother-in-law, I asked Mr. Desmond if that dog belonged to him, and he looked firm and said, "Yes. He won't be any trouble."

"What's his name?" I said.

"Nemo."

"I never heard a dog called that. What kind of name is that?" I said.

"I don't know," Mr. Desmond said. "I didn't name him."

"He looks like an old dog," I said, trying to be nice and show no one minded having a dog along. "Shall I lift him up in the wagon, or can he jump?"

"He's not old," Mr. Desmond said. "He's in his prime. He could jump anywhere I wanted him to, but he's not to ride in the wagon. He can walk."

Well, Calvin and Gil got on the bench, and Mr. Desmond stayed on his horse, and the dog followed the horse, and Emma sat next to me on the spring seat. Her eyes were looking red after all the good-bye-saying to her sister and the children, but when I asked her if we could just follow this road on out, she said, "Drive through town."

We did. She sat like a queen on the seat of that faded blue What's-It Wagon. The town wasn't very crowded, but there were people enough for her to look in the eye. I guessed they had postponed the raffling off of the parlor set, or there might have been even more. We passed slowly down the main street, and she said, "The best road's the one that goes by the cemetery. I guess you know where that is."

"Yes ma'am," I said. We were past the last house, a white frame one with honeysuckle growing heavy on the front fence, before she sighed and her eyes got red again and three or four big tears rolled down each cheek, but she checked it and didn't really cry. It was a long time after that before I saw her really cry.

So there we were, heading a little southwest out of that little Texas town, with my responsibilities consisting of one ailing old-timer and one somewhat unladylike lady and one horse and one dog more than when we'd rolled in. But the thing foremost on my mind was the paper parcel full of food smells that Mr. Desmond had put in the wagon, and I guess he saw my nose

sniffing in that direction. He said, "It's spareribs. A man barbecues them every Saturday, and I bought all he had left. But I
didn't run across any bread."

"I can make bread," Emma said. For some reason she sounded
indignant when she said it.

"Biscuits are quicker," I said hopefully.

"I thought we might stop somewhere when we get clean out
of this place," Mr. Desmond said.

We were probably two or three miles farther along when Gil
said, "There are some big trees ahead. Perhaps we should stop
and eat something."

So in we pulled. There were two ruts going off and a gate,
which Gil sprang down and opened, then fastened behind us.
We cut off from the ruts and went into the trees. It was just
grass, with no crops, so we did no harm aside from disturbing
a half-dozen Herefords, which got up when they saw Mr. Desmond's dog and moseyed off from the shade they had been rest-
ing under. It was obvious other folks had stopped there before,
because there was a rusted Crosse & Blackwell tomato can and
a jam can and other bits of junk, to which Mr. Desmond gave a
disgusted look. There was even one of Gil's posters nailed to a
tree, but when Calvin asked, Gil said that Hamilcar B. Burr
must have had others out nailing up his reward notices, for he
hadn't put it there.

I needed to find a bush, so I took the bucket and said I'd look
around and see if there was water. Everyone hurried off in different directions, including Emma. Traveling with a woman was
going to pose certain problems. Up a gully the ground was soggy,
so after I did my business I followed it farther and sure enough
found a spring. A rusty red fox was drinking from it, and when
he saw me he sat still and I stood still. We watched each other
for the space of several heartbeats. Then he was off, so quickly
that he was stretched out and running hard before I was even
sure he'd moved. I filled the bucket and went back to the wagon.

Calvin had spread a quilt for Emma to sit upon. Gil was building a little fire. Mr. Desmond had unsaddled his horse. It looked
as if they were settling down for the night, although it was still
full afternoon, and we easily could have made Denton.

"There's water?" Gil said. "How far? I wouldn't mind a wash.
. . . Oh, sorry Miss Prosser. You first, of course."

"No thank you," she said tartly. It was the way she said it that
reminded all of us that she'd already had just about an all-over
bath that day getting the molasses off. Gil made it worse a minute later when I asked if we weren't to go any farther that day,
and he replied, "Oh, surely there's no hurry. And Miss Prosser
has had a fatiguing day."

"If you think I'm ashamed of what happened, you've got another think coming," Emma snapped at him.

"No indeed," Gil said. "I'm sure you were completely in the
right. If anyone need be ashamed, it's the town of Krum, Texas."

She looked at him suspiciously, as if she weren't sure whether
he was speaking his true opinion or just teasing her, and to tell
the truth I wasn't sure myself.

Mr. Desmond said, "I'll tell you this, it's a long, hard road
ahead, and it's not going to make much difference whether we
get a few more miles under our belts today. I say we stop here
and make our plans and start out fresh in the morning. Not that
I'm tired. I feel fine."

I didn't really like his taking charge that way. After all, whose
wagon did he think everyone but him and his dog were riding
in? I said, "This here is obviously a ranch. You folks might stay
here, after we eat of course, and Calvin and I will go take some
portraits while the light's still good. We've got our travel money
to make."

"Oh, not today, Pepper," Calvin said. That was his way, to
forget his own interests and try to keep other folks happy. "Mr.
Desmond's idea seems best, to make our plans. I know you're
keen on good plans."

That was true. I said so, and agreed we should just stay.
Emma said if we had a Dutch oven and the makings, she would
put on some biscuits to go with Mr. Desmond's spareribs. I un-
hitched the mules and took them and Mr. Desmond's horse to
water. Gil came too, stopping first to get soap and things from
his pack, and Mr. Desmond sent his dog along.

The animals drank first, then Gil stripped down and jumped
into the spring pond and began to wash. He didn't mind being
seen naked any more than the fox had minded being seen in its

rusty red coat. He told me I should come in too, but I declined.

"You make a better Englishman than I, Pepper," Gil said. "You're reticent, and you keep your mind on business, and you don't like to bathe."

"I wash often enough," I said. "I got washed off pretty good this morning, helping Miss Prosser."

"I confess I'd rather bathe her than myself," Gil said. My face steamed up, and he laughed and commenced trying to coax Mr. Desmond's old dog into the pond with him. Nemo whined anxiously, obviously wanting to please but hating water, as some dogs will. He came to me to get his ears scratched. I calmed him until Gil came leaping out and dried himself with his shirt. But he wasn't through yet. He soaped his face all over again and began to shave.

"I know why you're doing that," I said after a while.

"Do you now?"

"You're doing it so she'll look at you. But what if she likes beards? A lot of women do—beards and mustaches too."

"Why Pepper," he said, "I wouldn't have dreamed you knew so much about women."

I clamped my back teeth shut, and though I waited for him, I refused to talk to him any more, for all his cajoling and trying to make friends again.

We went back. We staked out the animals. We ate. The biscuits were bitter and a little green from too much saleratus that Emma had put in, but I was so hungry I didn't mind. It was Mr. Desmond who acted picky.

"I see you don't care for cooking, Emma," he said. By that time we were all calling her Emma. "Ever do much of it?"

Her face turned red. "I certainly have," she said. "I did all the cooking for my poppa after our mother died, and he never found anything to complain about."

"Maybe you're just out of practice," Mr. Desmond said. "I take it your sister did most of the cooking while you were in Krum?"

"In fact, my brother-in-law did it, while she was busy with the children and I was busy running the newspaper," Emma said.

"Well, if that's the kind of a man he was," Mr. Desmond said.

88

"Some men can cook, and some women can run newspapers," she said. "Now, what do you have to say about that?"

In jumped Calvin, saying the biscuits were good, which they weren't, and Emma snapped at him just as if he'd been the one doing the complaining. "I did make the biscuits, didn't I?" she said. "I knew you were all expecting me to. Well, I'm determined to do my share. I'll make biscuits all the way to San Francisco if that's what you want, but I'd think you'd be gentlemen enough not to complain about the way I make them."

"We're only going to San Diego, not San Francisco," I said, hoping to draw off her snappishness.

"As if I cared," she said.

Mr. Desmond looked firm. "Arizona Territory beats California," he said. "There's no sense in going any farther than that."

"You must be crazy," she said. "Why, Arizona Territory is where all those Apache Indians are. Indians and deserts and a rattlesnake under every bush. Why, you wouldn't catch me dead in Arizona Territory!"

Calvin tried again. "I imagine there are no end of newspapers in Arizona Territory," he said. "You might find just the niche you're looking for."

Mr. Desmond said, "No, it's gold. That's what's worth aiming for, enough gold to get up that stake for cattle. There's plenty of good cattle country in the territory, and cattle's about the only thing that's any good any more. It's too bad that the buffalo are just about gone, or I'll tell you this—we'd eat royally all the way west, and live royally once we got there."

"Did you ever see a buffalo?" I asked.

"See them?" He smiled his little smile, looking kind of puffed up, and I urged him to tell until he told: "I once shot two hundred and four of them from one stand in one day. That was in '74. We were two killers, with a cook and a reloader and a hide pegger and two wagon men and nine skinners. One thing's sure, we kept those skinners busy."

"Where was that?" I said. "Where were you then?"

"Horse Canyon," he said, "by a big rain-water lake. We were all through that country. Wait a minute, it may have been

'76. Granada, Colorado, that was track's end for the Santa Fe then, and we sold our hides there."

Gil said, "Did you have to fight Indians?"

"I've done that," Mr. Desmond said. "The last time, I guess that was '76, too. There were four of them, camped in a dry camp. We got all four."

"While they were camped?" Gil said, sounding peculiar.

Mr. Desmond shrugged. "They would have been after us the next day." But he must have noticed the way Gil sounded, for he wouldn't say anything more about those times. Instead, he asked Calvin and me about our plans. Calvin told how we were going to work our way, and he got so interested in what he was saying that he even told about hoping to sell photographs to *Harper's New Monthly Magazine* or *Frank Leslie's Illustrated Weekly* in New York and began glancing about as if hoping some marvelous view to be photographed would pop up before our very eyes.

Mr. Desmond gave the What's-It Wagon something of the same kind of look he had given the clutter of rusty cans. He said, "It'd be slow, stopping at every farm and ranch along the way."

"We don't stop at every one," I said. "Just the ones that look like they could pay."

"I'm thinking of Emma," he said. "A slow trip like that, and a long one. It would wear out a woman."

She said, "Don't worry about me. I can stand it as well as anyone else."

"It comes down to money," Mr. Desmond said, ignoring her. "Nowadays it looks like everything comes down to money."

I stiffened. I didn't know what working in a slaughterhouse in Krum paid, but I couldn't see how it would be enough for some old fellow we'd just met that day to be looking down on us.

Gil may have felt the same way, for he said, "Desmond has money on his mind at the moment. He lost a packet on something called Red River City. Isn't that what you told me, Desmond?"

"No need to talk about that," Mr. Desmond said.

"Oh, but it's interesting. Red River City is a clearing in the jungle near the Indian Territory. It's the future Chicago of the Southwest. The future London. Tell them about it, Desmond."

Mr. Desmond stirred uneasily. "There's nothing to tell," he said. "I took the wrong advice. A man's a fool if he takes other people's advice."

Gil eyed him as if to see just how far he could go. He must have seen some leeway, for he told us, "Desmond here owns eight choice corner lots in that future queen city. The land speculators sold them by mail. They might be worth a fortune someday. Of course, at the moment Red River City is just a name printed on the local maps. There's not a single shanty, or even a ticket office, or a landing stage, or a drinking crib has yet been built. You know, it's a pity I didn't accept the A.C.M. Company's offer to sell stocks. I would have been delighted to sell you some solid mining stock instead, Desmond. Then you'd have something to show for your money."

Mr. Desmond's face got grim. I expect what Gil was repeating was drinking conversation, which a man didn't expect to be blabbed to all the world once the last cup was swallowed. Mr. Desmond said, "I see no point in talking about that. The point is, I have less money now than I did once, or I'd buy a proper rig for Emma to travel in comfortably and quickly to the West."

"I certainly couldn't let you do a thing like that," Emma said.

"It's beyond arguing now," Mr. Desmond said.

"Really, Mr. Desmond," she said. She looked flushed and uncomfortable. "I'm quite capable of looking out for myself."

"It's hard to do without money," he said. "How much are you carrying?"

She blushed deeper at the direct question. "Enough," she said.

But he said, "How much?" He spoke in the firm, calm, even tone a man would use to an unbitted pony.

"Thirteen dollars," she said in a low voice. Then she raised her head and flashed her eyes angrily at all of us. "I know what you're thinking," she said. "You think I was just putting on in front of that mush-head my sister married. Well, I would have given her that thirteen dollars. And let me tell you, she'll need it! He'll have those poor little children living in a shack and hoeing cotton before the summer's over!"

Mr. Desmond said, "Well now, there's nothing to get excited about. You outdo Gil by about ten dollars, and I'm not too far ahead of you myself. I've got the horse and my rifle and twenty-eight dollars to my name. But I've started with less before."

Everyone was thoroughly uncomfortable by now. If he weren't so old and didn't go about it so rough-handedly, I could have sworn Mr. Desmond was courting her. Frankly, I couldn't see why. She had that ripe look, all right, but she must have been all of twenty-five, older than my stepmother, and she fancied unwomanly activities such as running newspapers. Calvin was as ill-at-ease as the rest of us, or perhaps more, for he had that way of always feeling right along with a person. His eyes fell on Hamilcar B. Burr's poster, and he said, "What we need to do is win that thousand-dollar reward, and then we could all travel to the West in style."

I blushed for him, having to say such a silly thing to get people thinking about something other than Mr. Desmond's possible intentions, but Gil sat up straighter and looked at the poster too and said, "How odd. I never thought of that before. I could surely use some money. Why, I could buy into the A.C.M. Company after all. We all could. Then we'd all be pleasantly rich when the stocks go up."

Mr. Desmond, too, regarded the poster, and so did Emma.

Emma said, "A thousand dollars. That would be two hundred dollars apiece."

Mr. Desmond looked at her calmly as if wondering what she could do to help catch a bunch of murderers, and the thought struck me that he might be wondering the same about me, me being only fifteen. Calvin winked at me, maybe saying he just wanted to keep them talking. He said, "It would take some kind of perfect plan. You couldn't do anything without investigating the facts carefully and figuring things out and then tailoring a plan just so. Pepper's good at planning. Tell them how it could work, Pepper."

He was giving me a chance to show off. I admit that I proceeded to do so, mainly to demonstrate to Mr. Desmond that, fifteen or not, I was a person to be reckoned with. I said, "Well, of course you do have to find out the facts first. Gil, you talked with Mr. Hamilcar B. Burr himself. How was it those three men were slain?"

"Ambushed, I believe," he said. He studied the poster some

more, then told us what he'd heard in Denton when he collected his money from Mr. Hamilcar B. Burr. The first murderee mentioned on the reward notice, Jason Waller, was the main robbery, they said, some thirty-six hundred dollars. I couldn't understand why he had so much money on him, but Gil said there had been some nervous chatter about the bank in Denton, and Jason Waller had pulled out his balance. He had been knifed right while he was sitting in his buggy.

Gil couldn't remember what they'd said about the second man, but the latest man to be killed, John Thomas Blanchard, had been robbed of more than five hundred dollars and killed not three weeks before. Stabbed in his quilts, they said, in his camp at a spot we would pass on our way to Jacksboro, where the old Military Road crossed Denton Creek.

No one knew who was doing the killings. People had gotten nervous about coming near Denton, and Hamilcar B. Burr, who was a big merchant, was trying to do anything he could to keep all the trade from going to other towns. That's why he put up the reward.

Well, I heard this through, then said, "The thing to do is obvious. Since no one seems to know anything about these robbers and murderers the trick would be not to go looking for them, but to make them come looking for you. You'd have to pretend you were rich as Croesus and draw the robbers to you, for I see no other way a stranger could single them out and track them down."

Calvin egged it on. He said, "A thousand dollars reward . . . why, Pepper, that would make a stack of money two feet high."

I turned to grin at him, but the grin fell right off my face. He was staring at that poster as if it were already money. Calvin wasn't just diverting the others; he was serious.

So were they. Gil cried, "I know. I know just how to work it." He pointed to Calvin. "You can be S. J. Boldini, World Famous Photographer, just returning from a successful tour. You've made fistfuls of money. The Prime Minister himself has given you a sitting, and you've sold absolutely everything to *Harper's*. Pepper can be your helper. I'll be your man. You're so rich, you see, that you travel with a valet. Only it's a pity one wouldn't travel with a butler. Butlers are much more impressive."

Calvin's hand crept up and covered his mouth. "Oh, I couldn't do that," he said. "I couldn't talk in front of a whole bunch of people."

"Nonsense," Gil said. "With a name like Boldini people will just think you have an Italian accent."

Emma chimed in, "I'll be Mrs. Boldini, touring with my world-famous husband."

"No need for you to mix in with this," Mr. Desmond said. "Someone from Krum might recognize you in the county seat anyway, and that would give the game away. You'd stay with me. I'd keep low and wait at the camp, where we'd spring the trap. Then they wouldn't know there's a man around to protect the outfit."

Gil shot Mr. Desmond a glance that I was glad Mr. Desmond didn't see, but he only said, "Oh, let her come with us. A beautiful woman always attracts attention, and attention is what we want to attract."

Emma looked properly modest and moved her hand as though to fend off the compliment. Calvin looked flustered, too, perhaps at the thought of being Mr. Boldini while Emma was Mrs. But Mr. Desmond said to Gil, "I'm not sure you could go dancing into the county seat either, without tipping our hand. You've already been there, haven't you, picking up your money from that Burr fellow?"

"But I spoke only with Mr. Burr and his agent. Besides, I've shaved off my beard since."

Mr. Desmond said, "Shaved? Yes, now that you mention it. But I've got to wonder how many five-and-a-half-foot-tall Britishers with a funny accent Denton has visiting it every week. People might recognize you as the same man."

"I'm considerably taller than just five and a half feet," Gil said stiffly, "and my accent is perfectly normal."

"How much taller?" Mr. Desmond asked.

Gil wouldn't answer him, but that didn't seem to bother Mr. Desmond at all. He just went on thoughtfully, "It'd take money to set it up right. Without money you couldn't act rich enough in the town for the robbers to get interested. And if the robbers happened not to be hanging around watching for victims that day, it'd just be money we'd be out."

That made my back get as stiff as Gil's, but Emma said, "It takes money to make money. I'll put in my part."

Mr. Desmond said, "No need for that. I guess I can bankroll the affair. I've got enough for that."

Gil, from the height of his whole two dollars, said huffily, "Certainly not. We'll all chip in. Won't we, Pepper?"

"With what?" I said. "Salt beef and blueberry preserves?"

Calvin said, "But we've made some cash, Pepper. Doesn't it come to near six dollars? Can't we put in that?" His face was pleading. I knew what he was thinking. He was thinking about San Diego and Mr. John Swiss Parker, and about having to take charity from family connections.

But I firmed myself. If we pitched in together, we'd have to pitch in equally. A Fairchild couldn't pitch in less than a woman and an old fellow who'd got rooked by land speculators on a patch of clearing called Red River City, and that meant that it would be a large part of what was left of my money sack that would have to hold up our end. And for what? Their hope to win that reward was speculation beyond the pale of any standards of practicality. I said:

"Hold on a minute, now. Planning's fun, but y'all haven't thought through the deep-down core of the matter, and once you do you have to give up all thought of things like big rewards."

Calvin said, "Pepper, doesn't it make you mad, too?"

"What makes me mad?"

"Those killings. And those robbers going scot-free."

"Well, sure it makes me mad, but—"

"Pepper, you wouldn't have to do anything but guard my back. I swear, I'll do all the rest."

"But that's what you haven't thought through," I said. "It's living bait we'd have to be. What about Mrs. S. J. Boldini? At best she'd be sitting there, waiting and waiting, and what would she be waiting for? Murderers with knives, that's what. No, I didn't mean for the plan to be taken seriously. I was just funning."

Mr. Desmond said, "You wouldn't be scared, would you?"

The words fell on me like a fist. My ruined Claiborne Parish past suddenly seemed to reach out, blackly, toward this new life I had begun so cockily to lead. I jumped to my feet, and I do believe my mouth worked just like Cousin Calvin's when he was trying to get out something hard. Mr. Desmond didn't say it nastily—nor sternly and contemptuously as I thought my father had—just thoughtfully, but how could anything like that sound nice to me? Calvin grabbed my arm. "We'll pick the perfect camp, Pepper," he said. "Maybe right on the very tip-edge of some bayou. Then nothing can come at us from that direction. And between the lot of us, watching the other sides will be easy as pie."

We'd left bayou country far behind, so you can see how clearly he was thinking.

"Let go my arm!" I said.

Mr. Desmond said, "Easy now."

Gil said, "Pepper wouldn't be frightened. He's just thinking about Emma."

I said, "That's right."

Gil said, "And I think he has an excellent point. Emma, you mustn't stay with us directly in the camp when we spring the trap. We'll stash you off somewhere safely on the side."

She said, "We'll see about that."

Mr. Desmond was still looking at me speculatively. I loosened my arm from Calvin's grasp and said, speaking directly to Mr. Desmond, "I haven't seen anything, anywhere, yet that scared me."

"I have," he said. "Maybe you just haven't seen a whole lot up till now."

"Maybe that's so," I said, "but if there's one thing in the whole world I'm not, it's a coward."

"I didn't mean that," he said calmly. "A man can be scared without being a coward. It don't matter what he feels, it matters how he acts."

"Well, you can see for yourself how I generally stand up," I said. "We'll do our share. You can count us in."

I walked off. The old dog, which had been lying next to Mr. Desmond, got up and followed me. Emma spoke softly to the rest and jumped up and followed me too, but I told her, "I'm looking for a bush, if you please."

She fell back. She said, "Don't be long. I'm going to make another pot of coffee."

"Yes ma'am," I said.

I went to the spring. The fox wasn't there. Nemo came along, nosing every bush, lively after lying down awhile. The sun was just setting, but there was no color because there were no clouds. Except in my thoughts. In one funny way, maybe I *was* a coward, for I was afraid not of robbers nor murderers nor acquitting myself poorly, but of what the folks back home would think. They'd have themselves something to whisper and laugh and condemn about for sure if they ever got the least hint that I was letting myself get mixed up in the world's most cockeyed scheme with the parish's second-most-talked-about fool, my Cousin Calvin, who I had edged out of first place ten days before on a hot May afternoon in a store loft.

I didn't think about it long. The ones down there by the wagon might think I was off sulking. Or, worse, feeling scared. I whistled to Nemo and started back down the gully. I should have carried the water bucket up with me. They'd be needing water, and I felt that I was surely the only one in this outfit with sense enough to get it.

Six

It took more than one bucket of water and all the sense I could
muster in figuring out the details for their risky scheme to get
us even where we were by Sunday-school time the next morning: a few miles from Denton, with Calvin sitting all stiff beside
me carrying the stake we'd finally decided upon. This was thirty-
nine dollars—ten from Mr. Desmond, and eight from Emma,
and half of everything Gil owned in the world, meaning one
dollar, and twenty from Calvin and me, meaning the silver dollar with the X mark I got for selling the barrow and all of my
greenbacks. So Calvin was stiff with responsibility and also because he was all dressed up in his good suit, with his boots polished, his last starched-before-we-left-home shirt glimmering
like whipped cream where it showed around the edges of his
coat and vest, and a blue silk cravat of Gil's that Gil insisted
matched the blue of the What's-It Wagon but which didn't.
From his pack Gil had pulled an even more astonishing outfit,
the high points of which were nankeen trousers and a brown
sack coat and a black bowler. He sat in it, not even looking uncomfortable, on the bench behind us, saying to a farmer he'd
insisted that I hail:

"Indeed, sir, we're very grateful for the information. An artiste
of Mr. Boldini's distinction cannot be too careful."

The farmer, a small, skinny man with a strapping wife sitting
beside him and two strapping girls sitting in chairs they'd put

in their wagon bed, glanced at me and Calvin. We had cautioned Gil about speaking slowly and clearly, but I wasn't sure how much was coming through, so I said, "Much obliged."

"No trouble," the farmer said, and he gave his reins a little shake and went on, his team laying into their collars to get up the hill before them. I'd told Gil we shouldn't stop them, that we'd make them lose the momentum the farmer was mustering coming down one little hill before going up the next, and now I told him, "Hell fire, Gil, we didn't have to pretend with those folks. They're just going to church, can't you tell that? They're not going to turn around and rush into Denton and tell everyone they see that Calvin isn't Mr. S. J. Boldini."

"We really can't be too careful," Gil said. "With the robbers' identity unknown, we can't be sure of anyone, now can we?"

I got a prickly feeling. What Gil had been so interested in stopping and asking someone was if there had been any talk of any more killings or of the robbers being caught. There wasn't, as far as the farmer knew, and the prickly feeling came only from what Gil had said: we couldn't be sure of anyone.

I admit that my world before then could be regarded as small, its outermost radius extending only as far from the center, Claiborne Parish, as Bay Tree, Arkansas, but I had thought it a fair sample of what the rest of the world was like. In terms of my father's profession, lawing, you could look at it as a world covered by a contract, in which the individual person agrees not to murder, buffet, set afire or otherwise molest others in his group, the co-signers to the contract, and they likewise agree not to mount violent, unpredictable attacks on him. You *could* be sure of the next fellow you met, because you were both signatory to the contract, and if he didn't live up to his agreement, well, then you could shoot him or have him hanged, or otherwise sic the law, which was merely the codification of the social agreement, on him. At least that's the way I looked at it until Otis Wasum shattered my illusions with his brother's rifle. Thinking that I now couldn't even trust some plain country farmer who I happened to meet on a roadside gave me a feeling that I had somehow moved into a changing world full of maniacs.

Mulling on that, I had left Calvin to answer Gil, which he was glad to do, for they'd been palavering like crows in a cornfield ever since we'd left camp that morning. In fact, they'd been palavering since the previous evening, only then Emma and Mr. Desmond had still been with us to palaver along with them. Now the newest members of our party were gone, off to wait for us at the site I had reluctantly suggested for the trap, the same site where the last murderee had been stabbed in his quilts at the crossing of the old Military Road and Denton Creek. They'd ridden on ahead at an easy Spanish trot, Emma riding double behind Mr. Desmond and looking a bit uncomfortable about it, and Mr. Desmond's hard face showing nothing about whatever he may have thought of the ripe curves that must have been quivering against his back.

Maybe because of me mulling so much and paying too little attention to the mules, we got into Denton a little later than we'd hoped. Right off, we saw one of our posters pasted to a fence, and another poster that said:

PUBLIC WARNING

The practice of discharging fire arms within the limits of Denton, contrary to an ordinance of said city, having become so frequent as to endanger life and greatly annoy the quiet and peace of orderly citizens; I have taken this method to inform every one that I intend to enforce the Ordinance against EACH AND EVERY VIOLATOR thereof; and if found necessary, will, by the authority of the Mayor, employ the secret police for the purpose of giving information against every one thus offending.

William D. Shockley
City Marshal

"Secret police?" Gil said. "In a town this size? What does that mean?"

"I've heard tell of it," I said. "Some marshals and sheriffs take on local men to act as undercover police, to help out the deputies."

"And inform on their neighbors?" Gil said. "That doesn't sound very admirable." He seemed shocked.

Calvin read the poster again and asked Gil if he had brought his little pistol, and Gil said yes, but if there were secret police about, he would keep it carefully in his pocket and bring it out only in case of emergency.

We were too late to be seen by the whole town as it got out of church, but at least in time to be seen by the late stragglers, the ones who always stayed behind on the porch steps to talk. We engaged in mutual staring.

I must say the town fooled me. I don't know exactly what I expected, but it was probably something gloomy, with dark clouds rolling overhead, and awful, sinful-looking people. I guess I was remembering pictures in a big book of Grandmother's called *The Bible Looking Glass*. In any of the pictures which dealt with dark deeds, and there were lots of them, the sky was always gloomy and everything had a terrible look.

But Denton was as fine a town as my own home town. Maybe it was even finer, for it was bigger. Downtown was very much the same, with the store buildings standing around a big square and the courthouse in the middle. There was plenty of sun, and boys just like me were cutting up, as much as you could on a Sunday.

I had thought we might begin by just letting ourselves be looked at and then investigate things carefully. But no. That wasn't Calvin's and Gil's approach. They started out right away making loud, noisy fools of themselves all over Denton. We did get to eat in a real restaurant on the square, but Gil and Cousin Calvin spoiled it the minute we got inside.

"Mr. Boldini's party," Gil announced loftily to a nicely dressed man holding some menus near the door. When the man just blinked at him, Gil said, "Signore Boldini? The New York photographer?"

"Oh, yes," said the man, and showed us to a table.

Well, it wouldn't do. Much too near the kitchen, Gil said. Surely the man didn't think an artiste of Mr. Boldini's distinction was accustomed to lunching with the sound of pots clattering in his ears. The next table wouldn't do either. It was near the front windows, and the sunshine coming in might disturb

Mr. Boldini. They settled on one in the middle of the room, but Gil wouldn't let Mr. Boldini sit down until he'd whipped out a black silk handkerchief and carefully dusted off the chair.

You'd think that Calvin would have been dying of shame during all of this, especially with him being as shy as he was around strangers. But no sir. His old mouth got to working and then words popped out everywhere and it was "This will do nicely," and "Thank you, my good man," and "Carmichael, a little something, please, to indicate my appreciation." And by God if Gil didn't lay a whole silver dollar, one I knew well that was marked with an X, in that man's open hand. As always, I could tell that the man didn't necessarily understand Calvin, but he sure understood that silver dollar.

And that was just the start of it. To me, the money part was bad enough, but even money wasn't quite, quite everything in life to me. There were also little things like decency and manners and self-respect, but Calvin loaded them all in the same boat and promptly sank it. Gil wouldn't sit at the same table with us. He told the man with the menus that he was Mr. Boldini's man and acted like the idea of sitting with his employer was the most improper thing he'd ever heard, but after the silver dollar went into the menu-man's palm the whole restaurant staff was quick to bustle around and move other people's tables, where they were sitting and trying to eat Sunday dinner after getting out of church, and put in a little table for Gil next to ours.

I wished I was sitting at it. Or farther away. As far away as the old Military Road, where Emma and Mr. Desmond were waiting for us, for Cousin Calvin barely glanced at the menu and instead opened his mouth and started calling me "My boy," and "My dear young assistant," and bragging about how much money he'd made on his recent tour through the western territories. To hear him tell it, he had the most money and the finest collection of views and portraits (no, not including England's Prime Minister; Calvin substituted Geronimo), and the most plates sold to the New York illustrated magazines, and the finest assistant (me!) in the whole of Louisiana and Texas combined. All this he said in a loud, silly way that beat any way I'd ever seen him act before. Gil kept jumping up and down to wait on Calvin, and he'd repeat bits after him in a flattering, marveling way, to be sure that none of this information was lost to anyone in the restaurant.

I was soon choking on the food, and I could barely get through it. As it was, Calvin had to tell me later what I'd eaten: corn soup, and tenderloin of ocean trout with tartar sauce, and roast pork with dressing, and string beans and potatoes and French peas, and apple sauce, and a hard-boiled egg and beet salad, and vanilla cream puffs (they were the one thing I think I really tasted and therefore remembered), and custard pie and coffee, all for the not-unreasonable price of sixty-five cents. But they managed to spend plenty more money than that, what with tipping anyone who came near no less than two bits, and some, like the girl who brought our plates and things, more than that. Though I expect all told it only came to about three or four dollars, it began to look to me like they'd get rid of all thirty-nine dollars right there in one spot.

Everybody in the restaurant was staring at us, the nicer people trying not to. I was forcing down the last bites of custard pie, which I didn't especially care for but didn't wish to see go to waste, when Gil pulled out what I could have sworn was a sterling-silver cigar case that I'd never seen before and offered Calvin a cigar that I had no idea how he'd come by. He lit it for Calvin.

"Was luncheon adequate, sir?" he said. "Would you care for anything more?"

"Naw, naw," said Mr. Boldini. "I'm full up to the brim. Ask back that head waiter and inquire what if anything of interest may be going on today in this pleasant little city."

That was according to my plan. Wherever the most people might be gathered, that's where we were to go, to give everyone a chance to watch us act rich. That's why I'd thought of getting-out-of-church time and a restaurant. So Gil summoned the man with the menus and put the question to him:

"Sir, Mr. Boldini has expressed interest in what events may be occurring today in your city. Perhaps you would be so kind as to tell us."

"Uh, public events?" said the man.

"That is correct, sir."

"Well, a Miss Elena Mancera from Mexico is in a theatrical

exhibition tonight at eight-thirty in the Cosmopolitan Hotel. She's to execute a dance called 'La Flor de la Canela.' That means 'The Cinnamon Flower.'"

"Hmm," said Gil. "Is nothing scheduled for this afternoon?"

"Oh yes sir. There's the base ball game between Denton and McKinney, and there's some Fiji Islanders performing at sundown. They say that the old chief will bring out the leg of a man and eat it before the audience, and that the princess will eat a whole baby, all by herself."

A lady sitting well within earshot started to strangle, and the man with the menus ran over to apologize to her.

Gil said to me, "What's base ball?"

I stopped chewing pie. "Why, don't you know?" I said. "It's a game. It's—"

"A sporting event? Fine, I thought so. Do men go? Do they bet?"

"Ladies can go too," I said. "At least at home they do. And some men bet, yes."

The man with the menus was coming back, and Gil said, "I believe you might consider the base ball match, Mr. Boldini. You might find it diverting."

"Is Mr. Boldini going to photograph the base ball game?" the man with the menus asked eagerly.

"Not on Sunday, my dear sir," Gil said.

"Well now, I might make an exception," Mr. Boldini said. "Let's us just drive my fine portable studio to wherever the game is to be, and we'll see how it looks."

So we found out where the game was being held, and Gil asked loud questions about how to get from there to our intended campsite out where the old Military Road crossed Denton Creek. This mention of our intended campsite was according to plan too. The robbers had to know where to come rob us in peace if we were to spring our trap.

We paid out, with as much fuss and throwing money around as they could manage. I went to get the wagon. We'd left it right on the square, and three or four little boys were hanging around, looking it over. They followed as I drove to the restaurant for Calvin and Gil. Calvin started making squares with his fingers at the courthouse and saying loudly that if it wasn't Sunday he was darned if he wouldn't take a view of that fine-looking courthouse, and the little boys started snickering. I'd have whammed them good if they hadn't been so little.

Calvin kept up his craziness, talking at the top of his voice and lifting his hat to people he'd never even met, all the way out to the base ball game. Gil poked me from time to time and told me to drive slow, drive slow, and we drove so slowly that the little boys who kept trailing us had an easy walk of it. We passed a big tent with signs all around it and a man standing out front shouting that at three o'clock Professor E. G. McDonald would lecture to ladies only on "How to Acquire Health, Retain Youth, Augment Beauty and Enhance Happiness," while at sundown King Tamehameha and Princess Malama of the Fiji Islands would give their exhibition. Denton was beginning to appear to me to be the liveliest town I'd ever be in, and I would willingly have driven slowly by the tent so I could look at all the signs, but Gil, poking me, insisted I drive fast at just that point.

"It's the one place I'd expect to encounter Hamilcar B. Burr," he whispered to me. "Not that he isn't too close-fisted to buy a ticket, but he's probably there right now, selling this evening's baby."

The little boys following us almost peeled off, as if attracted by the Fiji Islanders' tent, but then they kept coming. I guess King Tamehameha and Princess Malama had perhaps been in town longer than Mr. S. J. Boldini and the What's-It Wagon, so the newer spectacle won.

Denton had a real, permanent base ball diamond, with wooden bleachers and everything. In those times, or even earlier, starting about the time the war ended, the whole country had begun to be crazy over base ball, not just in the North, where the big professional teams played, but everywhere, and Denton had apparently caught the craze. I could see the teams warming up, and I was dying to get to a good spot where I could watch, but I let Calvin and Gil out of the wagon and went to find some place to tie the mules. There was a big crowd, and I looked quite a while for an unoccupied shade tree and finally had to tie them in the sun to the west of the diamond.

By the time I got back Calvin and Gil had gotten themselves

surrounded by a considerable group of men. I snaked through, feeling anxious, but my anxiety was misplaced. Calvin and Gil were in no danger; what was endangered was my hard-saved little collection of greenbacks.

They were clutched in Calvin's right hand, held high above him, and he was talking and laughing like a drunk man. "Naw, naw," he was saying, "two to one is the best odds I'd care to give. That McKinney team looks mighty good to me, but I only care to do a little wagering to add interest to the game. You boys go look up some McKinney folk if you want better odds than that."

"What did he say then?" one man near me asked another, and it was a sure-fire indication of how much Calvin had been running off at the mouth that the second man was able to repeat it all back to the first.

I shoved hard to get to Gil, who was standing by, smiling superciliously and watching the fun. "My God!" I said. "What are you doing!"

"Acting wealthy," he whispered. "Don't worry, we're not really taking many bets. It's just to make a show."

"Well my God!" I said. "Make him stop!"

Gil gave me his measuring look and stepped quickly over to Calvin. "Your assistant suggests that you might care for a refreshment, Mr. Boldini. Shall we take some seats? Shall I bring you something?"

"Sure, a lemonade might be fine," Mr. Boldini said with a half-dozen crazy pops and pauses.

"If you'll excuse us, gentlemen," Gil said to the circle of men.

"Have you decided to take pictures of the game, Mr. Boldini?" asked a plump, perspiring man in a banker's suit and a planter's hat.

"Maybe later," Mr. Boldini said grandly.

The plump man followed him a few steps, then turned back to me. "If he does decide, my wife and daughters just might be interested in having their portraits made by an artiste of Mr. Boldini's distinction. Why, he could make their portraits right here. Al fresco. Ladies do sometimes pose al fresco, don't they?"

I collected myself a little. I assured the man that lots of New York ladies posed al fresco, whatever that meant, and I asked him where he would be sitting in the event Mr. Boldini decided to take his camera out. The man's show of interest offered at least a faint possibility of making back part of the money Mr. Boldini and his valet had been running through.

The pair of them waited for me, a little farther on, and after I got through with the plump man I just looked at them and wouldn't go to them, and finally Calvin came to me.

"Pepper, what's the matter?" he said in a low voice, putting his hand on my shoulder.

I jerked loose and started walking.

Calvin came alongside me, talking. "You backing down on me, Pepper?"

"Go away and spend some more money. Personally, I am going to look through the crowd for criminals."

His mouth started working, and it was longer than ever before the words would stop sticking and come out. "Listen, Pepper, we're baiting 'em, don't you see? Listen, we're hunting now, partner. You wouldn't back down on me, would you?"

His voice wasn't silly any more. It was begging. I stopped walking. "Gee, Calvin," I said, "isn't there some way to act rich *dignified*? I tell you, my blood turns cold when I think of what any of our home folks would say."

"We can't take any chances that they'll miss the bait, Pepper. Going fishing up at Bodcau Bayou for jackfish, you don't just plop the bait in the water and sit there, do you? No, you wiggle that old strip of bacon or red flannel all around, and pretty soon here comes Mr. Jackfish, his back fin cutting the water, and wham! You jerk him out."

Well, there was no way to argue with that, no matter how much I hated looking like a fool in front of all those people. As if to make things easier for me, Calvin stopped being so loud and did little more than raise his hat to strangers and we stood by a lemonade stand and had some. Unlike back home, there was no liquor being sold on the sly, as far as I could see. Maybe Denton had been afflicted by the temperance movement.

The bleachers were all full, and although I expect Gil wouldn't have hesitated to try to shoo people out so the famous Mr. Boldini could be seated, Calvin said why didn't we just stand, as many other people were doing. The Denton Olympics and the McKinney Mutuals were still warming up, and I tried to watch them and watch the crowd at the same time. It seemed to me we were getting a lot of attention from a big man with a big, important-looking hat with the tip of a guinea feather in its band. Two or three other less imposing fellows seemed to be with him, wandering off from time to time and then returning to him, milling about. One was a black man carrying a bucket of hard-boiled eggs that he was trying to sell. They all kept their eyes pretty much on us, and I asked Gil and Calvin if this was a man they'd placed a bet with.

"Which one?" Gil said.

I didn't want to point, so I said, "The big one, with the guinea feather in his hat."

Looking, Gil said, "No."

But looking elsewhere, Calvin sucked in his breath and said, "That nervy little sonofabitch! It *is* him, Pepper! It's him!"

"Who?" said I.

"What?" said Gil.

"Otis Wasum!" Calvin said.

"Where?" I said.

Calvin grabbed me and whispered, "Are you sure, Pepper? Are you dead sure it was him who did it?"

"What?" said Gil again.

I said, "Course I'm sure. Where is he? I don't see him. Calvin, where is he?"

Calvin turned to Gil. "I guess you'd better give me that pistol in your pocket," he said, "for that little Wasum sonofabitch dealt our family a despicable blow, and I cannot now question but that he means us further harm, and I expect it's up to me to shoot him."

The crowd started to cheer and some to hiss, and in the madness I felt, I thought they were hissing and cheering at us. I whirled, my eyes going every which way in search of Otis Wasum, but I only saw some umpire walking out on the field. Gil looked confused, but he was holding his hand over his pocket to keep that little pistol away from Calvin.

"I don't see him," I said. "You imagined it. He ain't there."

"Yes he is," Calvin said. "He's there clear as day, over by that sandwich vendor."

Well, he was. Once Calvin succeeded in drawing my attention to it, the figure he was straining so hard to get at stood out in the crowd like a sore thumb. There, on a steaming June afternoon, skulked a man in a tatty buffalo coat, the collar turned up and the brim of a big floppy hat turned down. But the eyes that stared nervously out from under that hat were a familiar pale blue. No disguise could hide it. It was Otis Wasum, seventeen years old, from Claiborne Parish, Louisiana. He saw us gawking at him and ducked back.

"That boy in the coat?" said Gil. "You can't shoot a mere boy."

"He's no boy," Calvin said. "He gave up being a boy the day he took up killing men in the streets. Now give me that pistol and stay out of this, Gil. This is a family matter, and I'm the oldest, so I have to do it."

"But you can't do it here. You'll ruin everything," Gil said. "Wait, and if you feel you must we'll get him off to the side and you can shoot him later."

"Pepper?" Calvin said to me.

He was asking me to throw in with him. To throw in with a matter concerning the family. I could see that Calvin felt required to do it, but I could also see that he didn't fully like the idea. I had a funny mix of feelings myself: rage because Otis had caused me to leave my home under the blackest of clouds, and rage because apparently Uncle Raleigh was right and Otis had followed us all the way to Texas with blood in his crazy blue eyes, and rage because of poor Mr. Stein, provoking the call of family duty, but also a feeling of—yes, I admit it—fear, fear of just what family duty seemed to call for.

That cold gust of fear confused me. Too many things were coming at me at one time, and it was more than I had rules for or could handle. But what was it helped me make up my mind? It was my greenbacks. All the money we'd spent would go to waste if I let Calvin stop being the rich Mr. S. J. Boldini. And all the snickering and staring that I'd endured being Mr. Boldini's unwilling assistant would go for nothing if I let Calvin start being a regular Fairchild.

I said, "No, Calvin, no, no, no! We're just getting ourselves that nibble! The man with the guinea feather! My God, Calvin, are you going to ruin it all at the last minute?"

"I got to do it," Calvin said, and he tried to wrestle that gun out of Gil's pocket.

I helped grab him and said, "Calvin, you said we was partners!"

All this was conducted in hoarse whispers, but with the wrestling and the whispers sometimes louder than they should have been, we were attracting plenty of attention. The man with the guinea feather in his hat was looking at us in a funny way, and other men lounging about also didn't bother to keep their eyes to themselves. Why should they, when we'd worked ourselves to a frazzle to become the town's major freak show? Only Otis Wasum had stopped staring at us and had hurried to disappear in the crowd. Maybe he was loony, but he was smart enough to know that a Fairchild from Claiborne Parish might rise up, even in a public place with a thousand witnesses, to claim an eye for an eye.

Calvin was trembling. He didn't seem to want to look at me. But he straightened up and patted his cravat vaguely, and turned his eyes to the base ball field. I did too, in time to see a Denton player take first on balls. The game had started, but crazy as I was about base ball I couldn't very much care.

I kept looking for Otis, but he had flat vanished. After only about maybe two or three minutes of wondering where he was, I said I had to go under the bleachers to relieve myself. But what I did was, I went to the back of the bleachers and I climbed up on the scaffolding and I looked over the crowd trying to see where Otis could have gone. The man with the guinea feather watched me curiously, and I tried to look like someone who was just taking in the sights. I craned my neck to look out at all the trees and fields around the base ball diamond, as though that kind of thing interested me, and I got a little shock when I saw Otis's heavy buffalo coat wending its way through the wagons and buggies parked south of the diamond, kind of furtively, heading out toward a thicket of redbuds. I ducked down, not out of fright but just being careful, and stared at him as he hurried away. Then I looked out beyond him to see where he was going, and I got me another, far bigger shock. For out there, lingering in the edge of the thicket, holding two horses and waiting for his little brother, was Shirley Wasum.

Oh lord, I thought. Uncle Raleigh was right about both of them. There was not one but two Wasums, just as clear as could be, not back in Claiborne Parish where they belonged, but here, at a Sunday base ball game in Denton, Texas, with no other logical reason in the world for being here other than the presence of Calvin and myself.

I watched Otis hurry up to Shirley and I watched them talk with their heads bent together, like two thieves planning a bank robbery or something. Of course from that distance I couldn't hear, but I could look, and I looked anxiously while Shirley seemed to shake his head and move back a step or two from Otis, then shake his head again and gesture impatiently. But Otis kept right with him, like Mr. Desmond's old dog (and maybe me) with the parcel of spareribs. That drew my attention to the fact that there was a gaunt and ill-kept look to their horses, and Shirley didn't look like he'd just risen from a filling Sunday dinner or a refreshing Saturday night bath, either. As I watched, finally Shirley started nodding a little, and I saw Otis nod eagerly and turn and start back toward the base ball diamond. I jumped down to the ground and fairly jogged back through the crowd to Calvin and Gil.

"I saw Shirley," I said to Calvin, low, where no one else could hear.

His mouth worked briefly. "I feared this," he said. "Where?"

"Out by some trees. Him and Otis was talking."

"Was Shirley armed?"

"Not so as I could see."

Calvin scowled blackly over my news, but he shook his head twice and said, "Well, I guess there's not a thing we can do about it now. Our friends' money is riding on us, and we can't let them down. But be ready in case they make a move at us."

I blinked at him. Ready? How? As we only had one gun among us, and that in Gil's side pocket, I didn't see that the advice was worth much. Nevertheless, I kept moving my eyes back to the crowd, watching for Otis.

We kept on playing our rich Mr. Boldini game while the Olympics and the Mutuals played their base ball game. The man with the guinea feather kept watching us, and Otis Wasum, getting braver now that we had made no threatening gestures toward him, edged back into the open and watched us too. What's more, he saw us watching our watcher with the guinea feather. I could see those faded blue eyes of his go from us to the man with the guinea feather, then back again. Gil pointed out that we had another dedicated watcher as well—a middle-aged fellow with a sour-looking face, who kept meandering around in the crowd, and whom two or three fellows kept coming up to and then going away from, just like the man with the guinea feather. One of the fellows, Gil said, had tried to make a two-bit bet with Calvin and had seemed quite inquisitive. He was a little man, about Gil's height, and he scurried away from the sour-faced man when he saw us looking at him.

I tried to pay attention to the base ball game, but that only served to worry me more. It was beginning to look as though we had bet our money on the wrong team. Denton scored a run in the third inning when a hard-hit ball bounced off the McKinney second baseman's leg, and there was a lot of cheering and intense excitement. The McKinney players looked pretty good, at least four or five of them did. But others were not as active as I would have preferred, particularly for a team upon which Mr. S. J. Boldini had rashly bet so much money. I was especially disappointed in the second baseman, who looked feisty and fast, but who could not move well at the crack of the bat. Second base was the place I played back in Homer, and I really think I could have done better if I had been asked.

Things stayed quiet in both their game and ours until the fifth inning, when Denton made the second run of the game—McKinney was still scoreless—and the crowd went mad with joy. That's when our private game picked up, for Otis Wasum made a move.

Not at us. He moved to the man with the guinea feather in his hat, and they started talking. Gil gave a low groan.

"Goddamnit, that bloody well does it," he said.

"What?" said Calvin.

"Your little friend is telling the wolves to stay out of the trap."

Calvin looked at him so coldly that I said quickly, "Best call Otis Wasum no friend of ours. He isn't."

"Sorry," Gil said. "What I meant was, if he knows you, won't he tell who you really are? He'll give us away."

"Maybe so," said Calvin.

"Maybe that's not the right gang anyway," I said. "Maybe it's the man with the sour-pickle look. Or it could be anybody. That's what you said, Gil. It could be somebody we haven't even noticed yet. Or it could be that man who said he had a wife and daughters to take portraits of."

"I guess it doesn't matter," Calvin said. "We can't do more than hold up our own end."

And that's what we did. We played our game out all the way, which is more than the Olympics and the Mutuals did. McKinney finally scored a run in the next inning, due to some erratic fielding by the Olympics, but the umpire ruled that it didn't count because the McKinney runner had interfered with the Olympic short stop by pushing him down in the dirt as he ran past. At once, the president of the McKinney team rushed out onto the field and ordered his club to stack their bats.

The crowd was in an uproar. There were McKinney people there, that was for sure, for there was plenty of arguing going on amongst the spectators and against the umpire. The tumult grew and the crowd swept out onto the diamond. They surrounded that umpire, but he had plenty of sand. He climbed up on a chair and announced, "I decide the game in favor of the Denton Olympics because the Mutuals of McKinney refuse to continue it."

Then the Denton folks drowned out the McKinney ones with their cheering, and Gil said, his voice pitched low enough so that only Calvin and I could hear it, "I wonder if the time hasn't come for us to make a rapid departure. You'll recall that we placed our bets on the McKinney team."

Calvin sort of sighed, as if between Gil and me he was in danger of forgetting what a gentleman was like. "That's maybe not the best way to play rich," he said. "Do you reckon these folks believe the distinguished Mr. S. J. Boldini of New York City would welsh on a bet?"

"But—" said Gil.

"We'll finish what we've started," Calvin said.

Was it, in any part, deliberately to punish me? I mean, for putting greenbacks in front of family honor and not letting him try to shoot Otis the minute he saw him? I never knew for sure, but then I never asked. What happened was, we stayed right where we were, until the men Mr. S. J. Boldini had bet with made sure that the forfeiture was accepted as legal and would stick, and then they came to collect their money.

Calvin paid them as calmly as you please. Gil fell back into his role of the rich Mr. Boldini's valet, and took care to tell as many people as he could where Mr. Boldini planned to camp when he left Denton that night, just in case we overlooked anybody in paying off our bets. There wasn't much chance of that. Soon, the greenbacks had gone and Calvin was digging into his pockets for metal.

All this was hard for me to watch, and fortunately it wasn't necessary. There was still the man with the guinea feather and Otis who needed an eye kept on them. They were standing together, not talking now, but looking our way every once in a while.

Why had Otis Wasum and his brother Shirley tracked us to Denton, Texas, instead of staying home with their family in Claiborne Parish, Louisiana? Even if Shirley had broken out of jail and was on the run, why didn't they do something easy like heading up to Arkansas or the Indian territories to hide out? Why were they acting so funny and furtive? Involved as I was just then in lying and pretending and trying to win Mr. Hamilcar B. Burr's reward, an even livelier question in my mind was, had Otis told the man with the guinea feather that Calvin was far from being a rich photographer from New York City with an English valet and a young assistant? I stared and stared at Otis and the man, until Gil punched me and told me to stop, but I could tell nothing from their actions.

And then the crowd was leaving, and Otis and the man with the guinea feather and the two or three fellows who had been hanging around with them were leaving too, heading out behind the bleachers toward where Shirley was waiting, without ever coming very close to us.

"Shall we follow them?" I whispered to Gil.

"Good lord no," he said. "They're the ones who are supposed to do the following." His eyes changed direction. "Or perhaps him." He was looking at the pickle-faced man.

"Or him," I said, because the man with the wife and daughters was coming by, but there was no sign of any wife and daughters, and he just lifted his hat and called out, "I see Mr. Boldini decided not to bring out his camera. Pity," and went on past.

"Shall we leave, then, and let whoever it is start their following?" Gil said.

We both looked at Calvin and waited for him to decide.

"Yes," he said. "We're finished here."

But we weren't. Not quite. As we started for the What's-It Wagon, the pickle-faced man and two of his sidekicks, including the little man who had tried to place a twenty-five-cent bet, stopped us.

Gil's hand went to his pocket, as if to feel for the pistol he kept there, and Calvin's hand went to Gil's arm, as if to caution him not to rush. There were still plenty of people around, getting their buggies sorted out and all, and I, too, judged we were in no immediate danger.

I was wrong, in a way, for the pickle-faced man whipped out a city marshal's badge and introduced himself as William D. Shockley. He shifted a big chew of tobacco to the side of his mouth and spat, and started in on us with his tongue.

"There's been enough trouble around here, brother, without damned fools from New York City trying to bring on more," said he to Calvin. "Now you and these other two, speak right up and explain just who you are and exactly what you think you're doing here."

Gil said, perhaps trying not only to shut Calvin up but to take up for him, "We already told all that to one of your friends here, when he came begging Mr. Boldini before the game to take a tiny twenty-five-cent bet."

The marshal cocked a glance at the little man with him. "That right, George?" he asked.

George nodded. "Yes, they was acting funny, and I thought of the ruse to ask some questions of this man who calls hisself a valet."

"Next time you think up a ruse, think up one that don't involve betting," the marshal said.

"Betting's not illegal," George said.

"No, but there're plenty of Baptists in town as think it immoral," said the marshal. To us, he added the words of explanation, "New deputy," and then he really lit in on Calvin. He roasted him good for the way he had been acting, showing money around and things like that, and he said that if we didn't cut it out and put that money into safekeeping, he and his deputies would be seeing us again.

Calvin answered that he was going to go directly to his wagon and take leave of Denton right away.

And that's what we did. We kept our eyes peeled but we acted so ordinary going out of town that if it hadn't been for the What's-It Wagon, I don't believe anybody would have paid any attention to us at all.

King Tamehameha and Princess Malama of the Fiji Islands would have their chance after all. The town's other main attraction left, with about an hour to go until sundown.

Seven

We didn't see a trace of Emma and Mr. Desmond when I stopped the mules on the far side of the bridge at our agreed-upon camping site, but then suddenly Mr. Desmond was there, standing beside a red oak tree.

I caught my breath with a start. Mr. Desmond glanced at me, but he only said, "So you made it. We've been kind of looking for you." A long time later, it occurred to me that maybe he hadn't been looking very hard. In fact, he had something of a disgruntled look, as if he wouldn't have minded if we'd stayed over in Denton and he'd had Emma's company alone. But just that moment my head was buzzing with more pressing problems, some named Otis and Shirley Wasum, and some who were name-less and faceless but who were murderers and robbers whom we had idiotically invited to call on us that night. I must admit I found it downright nerve-racking to be in such an isolated spot.

Knowing that two Wasums were lurking around Denton County, Texas, worried Calvin, too, and we told Mr. Desmond we had a little problem he and Emma had better know about, and then, apologetically, told them. After all, if Otis and Shirley were to start shooting, our new cohorts might stumble into the line of fire. But no one seemed especially concerned with anything but winning that one-thousand-dollar reward. Emma just tsk-tsked that it was a pity those two young scoundrels had agitated us, and Mr. Desmond waved off the question of a traveling feud with a "Don't worry, if you hear from them again they'll find there's a man around to help protect the outfit," then started giving us orders about unhitching the wagon and setting up camp.

Mr. Desmond told Calvin and me to take the mules clear across the road to stake them out for the night where he had staked his horse. I couldn't understand the why for this until he said we wouldn't want anything up close around the camp, maybe stamping around, to make it hard for us to hear any other sounds. The idea of those sounds struck me jarringly, and I was glad to have Calvin's company when we went to give the mules a good big ration of corn and rub them down.

The others stayed back at the camp. Gil was getting up some extra firewood, and Emma was getting up some supper, and Mr. Desmond was generally masterminding the last touches of getting ready for the upcoming events of the night.

The events of the night. Thinking of that gave me the prickly feeling again, a feeling that seemed to have put down roots only that morning but was ready to bloom by evening. I didn't know what had come over me, but I certainly didn't intend to let it show by acting spooky and quiet, so, rubbing Old Jeb, I said to Calvin, "I told you it must have been Otis who wrote that note on our wagon. But what I can't figure is, how in hell did him and Shirley get here so fast?"

"Don't cuss," Calvin said. "Maybe they had to ride hard, but if they left Homer pretty soon after we did, I guess they had eight or nine days to catch up to us by the time we stopped to have our wheel fixed."

"But that's over three hundred miles."

"Yes, if you make it by train as we did. But a couple of men on horseback could just cut due west and a little north and make it in a little over two hundred."

I finished rubbing down Old Jeb, who liked it and held himself good and still for it, and went to help Calvin with Young Jeb. I said, "But why in hell are they acting so sneaky?"

"You're sure doing a lot of cussing," Calvin said. "And on a Sunday, too."

"You cussed this afternoon when you saw Otis," I said.

"I guess I did," Calvin said. He was quiet for a minute, then tried to answer my question. "Maybe they just plan on waiting until they catch us off guard."

"Then they're in for a long wait," I said. But I remembered that I didn't have a certain Greener 10-gauge with me now, and I said, "You about finished? Maybe we ought to be getting back to camp."

"In a minute," Calvin said. He stepped back from Young Jeb and shook his rag, and Young Jeb shied as if he was scared. It was just play. Young Jeb was young, but he was a mule, and mules are smart enough to know that what you've been rubbing them with is just a rag. A horse, now, is capable of getting confused, or of thinking that a rag at one moment can change to something else at another moment.

"Maybe it hasn't got anything to do with a feud," Calvin said. "Maybe they're just mad because we said it was Otis and not Shirley who shot Mr. Stein."

"It wasn't *us* that said it. It was me."

Calvin's mouth worked briefly. "It should have been both of us who said it. You wouldn't have told it false. If you said it was Otis you saw in the loft, then it was Otis you saw, and I should have backed you up. If I hadn't believed you, I guess I'd never have been fool enough to think about shooting him this afternoon. I'm glad you stopped me."

"Well, hell," I said. "Maybe I shouldn't have. That's been on my mind. It looks like I'm going to have to stop calling myself a Fairchild and think up some other name."

"No, you did right. Shooting Otis wouldn't have helped Mr. Stein, of course, even if I could aim well enough to have hit him. And Pepper, it wouldn't have helped the Fairchild name, either, if that's what you mean. I was wrong. Getting yourself thrown in some Texas jail for killing a young boy is not the way you keep your family's name clean. That's old-timey."

I said, "Another thing's been on my mind, Calvin, that I want to apologize for. It seems to me sometimes I spend all my life doing things that need apologizing."

"You haven't done a thing in the world," Calvin said.

"No, I did. You acted fine today, Calvin. You did just what we set out to do, and you did it fine, and I shouldn't have acted so thin-skinned and all."

It was getting dark, but I thought I saw him smile, and his hand came out and patted me on the arm. Then I knew he was smiling, because I could hear him chuckle. "You mean I did fine at making an ass of myself? You want to know something funny, Pepper? I enjoyed it. For once in my life it was fun, to talk big and brag and make folks look at you and make them laugh at you, and know that you were doing it on purpose this time for your own good reasons, and not give a damn if they was looking at you and laughing."

"Don't cuss," I said. Calvin's chuckle became a low, deep laugh. But we didn't laugh together long. A dark figure suddenly stood out from the trees, and once again I gasped and started.

Mr. Desmond said quietly, "What's keeping you? Emma's waiting supper."

We went back across the road with him. Mr. Desmond wanted to ask us if we knew exactly what we were supposed to do and had everything ready, which got my back up and led me to repeat to him that he needn't worry about Calvin and me, we knew what we were doing and we'd hold up our end. Mr. Desmond's hard face flickered with his little smile, and he went on about his business.

Gil and Emma had already started setting the trap. Only Gil was in sight by the fire, and Mr. Desmond stayed back out of the firelight. His dog wanted to come and greet us, but he spoke to it, low and sharp, and old Nemo stayed back. The dog couldn't figure out just what was expected of him, and seemed bewildered and troubled.

There was no talking. Emma, lurking in the deep shadows of the trees, gave us cold cornpone and some kind of hash made with salt beef, and we were allowed to sit by the fire with Gil and eat it while she and Mr. Desmond sneaked about in the rapidly gathering darkness. She seemed to enjoy it, but my vote was with Nemo.

Then Calvin yawned and stretched and said in Mr. Boldini's loud voice that he reckoned we'd better turn in. He went to the wagon and fiddled some inside the dark-box and locked it carefully. Then he climbed into the wagon bed, where most of our quilts and some of the corn sacks and things were rigged to look like people were sleeping there.

I retired as if I was visiting a bush. In truth, I did—a clump of blackberry bushes that grew near the creek. I felt my way behind them to the quilt we'd stashed there and picked up my shotgun, which I'd also put there to await me, and tried hard not to think about snakes. In a minute or so, the bushes whispered scratchily. Cousin Calvin came crawling on hands and knees to join me on the quilt.

Our trap was ready.

We settled ourselves back to back and pulled the quilt partway over us, although the night was warm. We began our watch, me with the shotgun and Calvin with a big stick of firewood that he had apparently picked up just for safety. In another station far to the other side of the fire, Gil was watching with his little pistol, and in still another was Emma with a big Smith & Wesson's D. A. Navy revolver of Mr. Desmond's, and Mr. Desmond's dog to help look after her, and Mr. Desmond himself sitting beside her with his rifle. From that point on we were forbidden to talk, and we had no urge to, so we said nothing. For a long time, sitting there, watching and listening, we heard nothing at all, either, but by and by there began to be some sounds.

Even in the stillest woods, on the stillest nights, there were always two kinds of sounds—the far-off ones, like the bawling of cows and barking of dogs at farms somewhere, and close-by sounds, like the sound of a tree rubbing against another tree, or a bird complaining in its sleep, or maybe a night-roaming squirrel.

So it wasn't long before I had plenty to cock my ears at and wonder about, feeling jumpier every time our cooking fire sputtered or a chunk fell down into it. After a long time, a pale, bloodless moon came up, but there was heavy cloud cover, so it stayed mostly dark. Way off I heard some dogs begin baying at each other.

Then there began some far-off singing. Colored church singing, I thought, since it was Sunday night. I did like to listen to colored church singing. We were so far off we couldn't hear the words or the tune, but that seemed to make it even better, for that made it a kind of lonesome, different music, now high, now low, but lonesome and sweet.

Cousin Calvin's hand shook my leg, and I raised my head with a jerk. I'd been dozing. I looked around, but I couldn't see anything. I couldn't hear anything at first, either.

Then it seemed to me a stick snapped out in the trees. And maybe some leaves rattled. The fire was low, but it still made a little light, and the cold, hard barrel of my gun felt good to my hand. The sound came slowly closer.

Finally, on the other side of the fire, I could see something, dark-colored and moving, and I reached back and punched Calvin's arm, to let him know that I was really awake now and watching. A burning chunk fell back in the fire and blazed up a little, and my mouth opened and got dry.

Two shadows seemed to float up slowly near the fire, and then they were still. I couldn't make out their faces, but they were both on tiptoes and trying their best to be quiet. They stood there a long time. Then one shadow seemed to point where Calvin and I were shivering and watching. I began to switch my gun around.

There was a change in the shadow nearest us as it stirred and seemed to be moving toward us. Calvin would give no sign when I touched his leg, shook it, even pinched it. He must have been watching pretty hard too. There was a last, soft blooming of that faraway singing. Leaves murmured, then there was a faint rustling closer to us. My hands were numb from gripping the shotgun so tight. I sucked in my breath and thumbed the hammers back and tried to take a steady aim as the shadow drew closer.

Then off in the darkness there was a muffled moan, like an animal sound. The sound was so startling that I almost pulled the trigger then and there. The shadowy figure, whoever it was, turned back toward the near-dead fire. After that there was a light rustling of leaves as the figure moved slowly back toward the wagon.

A soft, tired sigh came from Calvin, and his hand touched my shotgun, and then he sighed again, as if he couldn't help himself.

I twisted around to speak in his ear. "I would have shot," I whispered. "If it had come a step nearer, I would have shot."

"I know," he whispered back. "I never felt a bit worried. But

I did kind of wish I had a gun, instead of just a stick. I got me something else in my pocket, something I thought might come in handy, but when he came at us like that, I realized it wouldn't do any good out here. Only up there by the fire."

I started to ask him what, but suddenly a voice spoke up, out in the dark, near the wagon:

"I've got you, you bastards! One move, and I fire!"

"Oh good lord," said I, and I forgot myself so much as to jump up and take aim toward the voice.

"No!" Calvin said. "That's Gil!" He started running toward the wagon. I followed him.

"Who's that?" Gil snarled.

"Don't shoot," I said. "It's us, Pepper and Calvin."

"But . . . ?"

We rushed to the fire. Calvin threw wood on it. Gil held his pistol steadily on the two men. One I'd never seen before, a small man in a dark frock coat and flaming red hair, as red as mine, redder than mine, and a red beard. But the other man I knew: it was William D. Shockley, city marshal of the city of Denton, Texas.

Gil saw their faces in the firelight and his eyes bugged. "What are you doing here?" he asked. He seemed to be speaking to the red-bearded man, as though he knew him.

It was the marshal who answered. His voice was shaky, whether with fear or with rage I couldn't tell. He said, "You better put that gun down, and you better do it right now!"

Gil looked confused. Before he could decide what to do, Mr. Desmond popped up by the wagon wheel and whispered, "There's more of them out there. Get out of the firelight. Quick."

Gil didn't hesitate. He grabbed one of the two men and Mr. Desmond grabbed the other and they hustled them around the edge of the wagon, into the darkness. Calvin and I started to duck out of sight the other way. But there was a sudden rustling sound, and Calvin said, "No. This way."

I just stood there, rooted, my body refusing to stir but my thoughts a whirlwind. Who was that rustling out there in the trees? Who else was in the dark, sneaking up on us? Which way should we run?

Calvin tugged at my arm. "Pepper, come on!" he said.

And then as my feet finally started moving, the rustling out in the trees became a crashing, and a whole group of men broke through the brush and seemed to hang right in the edge of the firelight, between us and the darkness. I saw the man with the guinea feather in his hat and the black man who had been selling hard-boiled eggs and another man who was big and muscled-looking. And to my horror I also saw Otis and Shirley Wasum.

"That's them!" Otis yelled with his Claiborne Parish accent. "That's the ones with the money! Kill 'em!"

My tongue came up big in my mouth. I tried to bring the shotgun to my shoulder, but my fingers were so twitchy that I somehow yanked the triggers before I even started to aim. I heard my gun bust loose and felt it kick back in my hands while it was still pointed upwards. My fingers must have given the triggers a real jerk, because both barrels went off at once, blowing a hole in the top of a big hickory tree. Twigs and leaves and a couple of branches came falling down around us.

There was the damndest scared screech from one of the men, and a big, loud yell from Shirley Wasum, and then the man with the guinea feather came rushing toward us like a train, hollering and swinging something my eyes fastened to like glue. In the firelight I saw clearly that it was a big, long knife.

Calvin yelled, "Shoot! Shoot!" Then it must have sunk in on him that I already had, kind of prematurely, because he didn't wait for any more yelling. He clawed at his pocket and jerked something out with one hand and threw it on the fire, and yanked the shotgun out of my grasp with his other hand and swung it like a base ball bat. Light exploded like sudden summer lightning and Calvin slammed the shotgun hard against the leaping figure, and the man with the guinea feather stumbled, and then he rushed on past us. I was half blinded by the burst of light but I could smell fresh whiskey on the air as the man tumbled past us, which indicates how alert my senses had become, for the air as high as what was left of the treetops was filled with an even stronger element, the stench and rolling smoke of Calvin's flash powder, bought for his James Flash Lamp.

Well, the world went mad. There was a hideous, wolf-like growling and something flashing through the brush. There were gunshots. There was a cry of pain. There were confused yells and shouts. There were running feet. And through all of this I was still groping around, trying to see, until someone jerked me into the shadows and slammed me to the ground. Whoever it was jumped on top of me and I tried to fight back until Calvin said, "Be still, be still!"

And then there were angry men's voices and a woman's voice speaking up, and otherwise comparative silence.

After a while, Calvin got off me and took me by the arm and gave me a boost to help me to my feet. "If they start shooting wild again, drop," he said.

I looked toward the fire and found that I could see a little better now. The small man with the red beard was there arguing furiously at Gil. Emma was there, too, and Mr. Desmond. And there was a man I hadn't seen before, a tall rangy man with a carbine, glaring at Gil and Mr. Desmond. The marshal had disappeared. So had the others—Otis and Shirley and the man with the guinea feather and the black man and the other one who had come out of the trees at Calvin and me.

We went back to the fire. Calvin busied himself with my shotgun. He trotted to the wagon and unlocked the dark-box and came back with shotgun shells. He reloaded the gun. I stood by the fire watching him, and my face got hotter than a fire could ever have made it. He whispered to me that there was a dead man over by the wagon, but he never said a word about the way I had disgraced myself with the gun. I only hoped Mr. Desmond hadn't seen it. He had been right about me, after all. And a little thought whined in my brain: could all the folks back in the parish possibly have been right about me too? Because when it came right down to it, I had been completely, white-livered scared. With Otis and Shirley and those men yelling at us and wanting to kill us, all I had managed to do was to blow a hole in the top of a tree.

That was the first time I ever succeeded in staying up all night. Sleepy as I got, while we stayed by that fire for hours and hours until streaks began to show up in the darkness and then turned into trees taking form in the thinning blackness of the dawn, every time my eyes would begin to close I'd think of that gun and how I nearly got Calvin and me killed by my twitchy trigger finger, and I'd jerk awake and go back to helping our side argue.

Because yes, there was a hellish argument going on. Mr. Burr had started it with Gil long before the marshal and his other two secret policemen got back from chasing Otis and Shirley and the man with the feathered hat and losing them completely in the woods. And yes, the small man with the red hair and red beard was Mr. Hamilcar B. Burr.

This was Mr. Burr's testimony:

Having heard from the city marshal that there was a rich stranger in town who had made a dangerous display of his riches, he had talked the marshal into secretly bringing his corps of three secret policemen and Mr. Burr himself to keep watch at our camp and see if the heinous criminals who had been terrorizing Denton made a try for us. They intended to protect us, in spite of ourselves. They intended to catch, if they could, the heinous criminals who had been blackening the name of Denton, Texas. They had arrived late only because it took considerable police work to track down our intended sleeping spot (Gil and Calvin both growled at that), and once they found us Mr. Burr and Marshal Shockley approached our camp only to reconnoiter and assure themselves that we hadn't already been murdered.

This was Gil's testimony:

Having seen two shadowy figures come into our camp in the wee hours of the night, and having noted that their coming aroused no response from any of us, and having heard a moan from where Miss Prosser and Mr. Hap Desmond had been stationed, he had naturally concluded that the two intruders had murdered us all and had therefore taken them into custody.

This was Mr. Desmond's testimony:

The moan had come from his dog, while wanting to bark, but while having Mr. Desmond's hand over his muzzle, while Mr. Desmond carefully watched the two intruders.

When the marshal and his other two secret policemen came back and joined in, this was the marshal's threat:

We should all be in jail, not only for being responsible for allowing the robbers (the marshal and his secret policemen had recognized most of their faces in the firelight, including the man with the guinea feather in his hat, a well-known Denton man named Sidney Clinkscale, who sold butter and eggs door-to-door) to escape, but also for somehow causing the death of his new deputy, George McGowan (for it was his dead body that lay by the wagon).

This was Calvin's question:

Was George McGowan a new deputy marshal known as such to the world, or was he a member of the marshal's secret police, or was he both?

"Balls, son, you can't be both known to the world *and* secret," Marshal Shockley said. Then his face—it was getting to be good and light by then—turned red, and he spent two or three minutes apologizing to Emma and, for some reason, to Mr. Burr.

"So he was only a deputy marshal?" Calvin said, when the marshal finally ran down.

"Of course he was."

"And you brought him along as a deputy marshal?"

"No, of course not. I didn't bring him at all."

Emma was the first to see what Calvin was driving at. She said, "Then what was he doing here?"

"Why . . . why he was . . ." The marshal turned and looked at his three secret policemen and at Mr. Burr, but they all shook their heads, and the marshal's face got red all over again. He pulled out his plug of tobacco and bit off a chunk, then said that it didn't matter why, and the question was who, among all those rushing about and firing off guns, shot little George McGowan, because that was who was going to jail, and Mr. Desmond said:

"I might have done it. At least I tried, and I usually succeed at what I try at. I'll tell you this, I'd shoot any sonofabitch that tries to kill my dog. And he did. Excuse me, Emma, but some things need saying."

"Then you're the man who will hang," said the marshal.

"Tut," said Emma. "He's the man Mr. Burr will pay a one-thousand-dollar reward to, because any fool can see that little George was one of the robbers."

"Now wait a minute," the marshal said. "Mr. Burr isn't paying any reward to any stranger. For one thing, the robbers aren't caught yet, except for George. And we can't be sure he was one of them."

"But you will catch them," Emma said. "You told us you recognized them all by the firelight, and you wouldn't have done so if we hadn't set this scheme up."

"We recognized only three of them," the marshal said. "There was two strangers with them. A man and a boy. We got to catch the whole gang."

"That was Otis and Shirley," I said.

"Otis and Shirley? Who's them?"

"Uh," I said, and stopped.

But Gil said, "They're two young men from Louisiana who murdered a friend of my friends here not two weeks ago. Shot him dead in the street. Tell the marshal about them, Pepper."

Why didn't I want to? There was every good reason why I should, except for a lingering thought that Calvin might have been right and that the Wasums were something a Fairchild should attend to, or maybe it was that Otis was only two years older than I, and it was hard to feel it right to tell on another boy, even a boy who did what Otis had done. But the marshal insisted. I told. I maybe left some circumstances out and told it shortly, but I told it fairly, not only what I had seen back in Homer, but about its being Otis's brother Shirley who confessed and was jailed for the killings and had somehow succeeded in escaping.

"So there you are, Marshal," Emma said. "Now you know the identities of them all, so catching them should be easy enough, and I must say we will appreciate your jailing those two horrid young men from Louisiana who've been annoying our friends. I also say we've earned the reward."

"We're the ones have got to catch them," Marshal Shockley said. "And we're the ones as will collect the reward."

"Now just a moment," Mr. Burr said. "You'll only be doing your duty, Marshal. There's no reason a man following in his own profession should be given a reward for doing his normal day's work."

"I'm damned if you'll give the reward to these strangers," the marshal said. "Especially when it's me and my men as will have to go out and face the danger of catching them."

"I quite agree with that," Mr. Burr said. "These people have done nothing to earn the reward, but I don't see why I should give up hard-earned money to a man who's only doing his elected duty, either. I'd say the reward is canceled. It's only fair, now that they've all been identified."

Calvin made coffee, because Emma was too busy arguing with Mr. Burr that our party had too won the reward. The sun came up behind a still-heavy cloud cover, and we all sat there and drank coffee. Nemo came and put his nose in my hand. I let him lap the sugar that was left in the bottom of my cup.

The arguing raged for another hour or so, the confusion of the whole event adding fuel to its fire. The way it all turned out, Mr. Burr refused to pay us the reward because he said we hadn't really done anything but interfere with the working law. And he let it be known that he didn't intend to offer up any reward to the marshal and his men, either, particularly as one of the marshal's own men appeared to be one of the robbers.

And eventually they left.

By the time they did so, Marshal Shockley was talking thoughtfully and saying, "I never was too sure about George anyway. Why, Mr. Burr, I think I even commented on that once to you, didn't I? I don't see how anyone can hold a man of my record responsible for what some little weasel like that might have done."

Only the mules and Mr. Desmond's horse had gotten any sleep at all.

The heavy cloud cover lived up to its threat, and it started to rain.

We all felt pretty bad.

Calvin helped me get the mules harnessed up. We didn't talk about the shotgun, because the others were around, and I don't know if Mr. Desmond ever did know what I'd done. We got into the wagon.

"Come on, partner," Calvin said, "cluck up those mules. You and me and all of us, we're going West. That's where true opportunity lies."

I looked down at the reins in my hand for a moment. "It doesn't strike me right for a boy to be doing this when there's a man like you around, Cousin Calvin. You cluck them up." And I handed him the lines.

131

He handed them back. "No, Pepper," he said. "I'm just the man who's lost all our money for us on a fool scheme, but I swear to you all that I'll make it up to you."

Emma started jawing again, saying it was purely adverse circumstances and not Calvin's fault that had lost us our investment.

But Gil said, "Look here, all of you, I have the most marvelous idea. We'll simply ramble directly to Tombstone, and I'll pawn my aunt's allowance to Freddie's associates, and we'll use it to buy into good old Freddie's mine for all of us. Why, there's worlds of time. We'll get there long before August, and Freddie will speak for me, you see, about the allowance. There'll be nothing to it. England would have died off a few hundred years ago if one weren't able to find ready-money against one's allowance."

We all sort of looked at each other, and there was just the sound of the raindrops beating down on the canopy of the wagon, and it was Emma who finally spoke. She said, speaking very nicely, "That's generous of you, Gil, but you don't have to worry about us. We'll surely be happy to see you become well situated, though, and we'll expect you to buy us a dinner of pheasants and oysters and plovers' eggs so we can celebrate your good fortune."

"Why, why, why," Gil stammered, "why, that's nonsense. We're all in this together, and of course we'll all share. I absolutely insist on it. No, no, I won't listen to any arguing. Pepper, come now, it's on to Tombstone for all of us. Er, er, cluck up them mules, partner!"

I did so. But as we started on down the road, I think I never did see a sadder set of smiles.

Part Two

Eight

During many a hard, dusty day on the old Butterfield, we argued over Gil's open-hearted offer to buy into the A.C.M. Company for us. For the first week or so Mr. Desmond flatly said no, that he would manage on his own with the Big Bug and gold, but it hurt Gil's feelings so much that Mr. Desmond seemed to relent and started saying he'd be happy to consider accepting a loan from us rich stock owners. Emma and Calvin also seemed wishy-washy, which made me impatient, for although I spent hours pondering whether it was really right to impose that way on a friend, I was anxious to get well launched on my rich and respectable new life, and accepting a share in Gil's opportunity was a tempting starting place.

It maybe seems a queer pastime for us to have argued that way about our expectations, for they were definitely at odds with our circumstances. Our money was not what you could call plentiful, and we had to stretch it over a good many weeks. Gil sold his silver cigar case in Jacksboro for seven dollars, which helped, but Calvin and I were forced to buy more glass plates and photographic paper and chemicals in Abilene, which hurt. But at least we had the wagon and Calvin's profession and my business sense.

And that's mostly what we lived on, trying to find prospects who wanted their portraits made and piecing out the very last of our salt beef. Towns got farther apart. People had less and less that they could pay for photographs. Our assets dwindled. We didn't live very well, and June rolled by a lot faster than the money rolled in.

I never saw that black-haired girl from Missouri along the way, either. Nor did we see Otis and Shirley Wasum again until one day after we had passed a town built largely out of mud called San Angelo and were approaching the Pecos River.

Before that, we had twice more heard of the Wasums—once on a lawman's poster from Shackelford County listing four fellows wanted for sticking up a faro game, with tiny letters at the bottom stating, "Also wanted, Otis and Shirley Wasum," and the other time in a long letter from home which finally came to tell us what had happened. Uncle Raleigh sent the letter. It was not very strong on spelling, but he'd worked hard on the words. Here's what he had told us:

The *Rosa Bland*, a sternwheeler that made trips up the Dorcheat as far as Noles's Landing, brought up a boatload of fine mules, which, near the moment of docking, became frightened from some cause, rushed off the boat into the bayou, and all perished.

Grandmother was rallying after Mr. Stein's death and had allowed herself to be lured into making an expedition to Doyline, where the Fairchilds from Homer, the Leakes from Minden, and the Browns, Kirkleys, and Hutchinsons from Doyline all met and enjoyed a superb repast.

Shirley Wasum had broken out of jail, as Uncle Raleigh had alerted us in his telegram, and in the doing had smashed the head of Louis Jardine, a deputy constable, who was now paralyzed from the neck down and lingering on the edge of death.

Immediately, Shirley and Otis had disappeared from Claiborne Parish under circumstances that became clear only later. The whole parish was up in arms about the accidental assassination of Mr. Stein and the brutal assault upon Mr. Jardine (a family man with three children under school age), and consequently a crowd of Homer hotheads had gone by torchlight to the Wasum home place and had dragged Mr. Wasum from his quilts and had taken him out to beat him and do him other bodily harm. Only the arrival of my father, the judge, had saved Mr. Wasum from a crippling hiding, and the hotheads were soon dispelled, with more than a respectable number of younger Fairchilds among them.

Mr. Wasum was expectably upset, but declared that the judge had acted more than fairly, and stated he could only repay the judge's fairness with a warning. Looking shamefaced and feeling bad, Mr. Wasum confessed to the judge that, upon the occasion of Mr. Stein's death, he had felt it impossible to allow his boy Otis to be hanged, which is why he had signaled Shirley to take the blame for the shooting. His feeling was that he and his other boys could spirit Otis away to kin in Mississippi as soon as they could obtain a bankroll to send him with, then let Shirley own up to the fact that it was indeed not he who had shot Mr. Stein, so the Wasums could get Shirley out of jail.

Unfortunately Mr. Wasum had had no private opportunity to explain this plan to Shirley. While Mr. Wasum and his remaining older boys had been engaged in a hog drive to Milliken's Bend to get the money for Otis, Shirley Wasum, who was not known in the parish for patience or subtlety, took the matter of his release from jail in his own hands and had broken out, with the ensuing damage to the health of Constable Jardine.

When Shirley came running from jail to the Wasum home place to get a horse and supplies for his flight, he found the house deserted save for Otis. One of the Wasum's darky sharecroppers later reported that Otis followed Shirley out to the barn and talked a long time to him about the family honor and name and the damage done to it by the judge's son (me, Pepper Fairchild).

According to the darky, Otis had not come straight out and told Shirley that a feud had started and that Mr. Wasum had charged them both to pursue Calvin and me to the death, but he had hinted at it strongly, and by the time Otis finished talking, Shirley was all lathered up and strong with the call of duty. The two of them had charged back to the house and had nearly torn it apart looking for money and guns and, finding none, settled for packing their saddlebags with eats, and rode off in the darkness like men possessed.

To the judge, in gratitude, Mr. Wasum pointed out he did not hold with a blood feud for a number of reasons, chief among them the fact that, on a tit-for-tat basis, the judge had managed to restrain his tribe from giving Fairchild tit for what the whole parish knew was a Wasum tat in the death of Mr. Stein. His fair reckoning was that his littlest son, Otis, had lied to Shirley, and that trouble was in the wind for Calvin and me, if the two ever caught up with us.

Mr. Wasum was distressed about it, feeling that now, through his folly, he had lost both his boys. With Constable Jardine sure soon to pass from this vale of tears, Shirley would have a death on his head, just as Otis had blood on his hands. But there was no point in the Fairchilds losing two (us!) in return, so his suggestion was that the judge write his boy and young Calvin and tell them to give word to the two errant Wasums that they should straightaway telegraph their daddy. He would try to get word to them himself, to tell them to accept their exile and engage in no more killings, but it would be difficult with him not knowing where his two boys were.

In the meantime, Mr. Wasum would hold no grudges against my father, and there would be no resumption of the Fairchild–Wasum battling. God willing, that would make things right.

The letter, which closed with repeated warnings for us to be careful and keep our eyes peeled, had taken near two weeks to catch up with us, and it had come alone. I had to wonder why we had not heard from my father, if he had been charged with warning us as Uncle Raleigh had said. Of course the mails weren't too reliable, but still it made me wonder.

The poster was also of particular interest to us, partially because of one of the other names on it. It was a name we had heard from the marshal in Denton as attached to a man who wore a guinea feather in his hat and carried perhaps the world's biggest knife—Sidney Clinkscale. We couldn't figure out if the other three men on the poster were new or not, since we hadn't heard their names that night, but at least one—as the notice phrased it, "Jim Spoonts, a colored man"—we figured we had surely seen on the night of the trap. We worried about the other two names, Cass Hubbard and John W. Angle, and we worried because the poster was from Shackelford County, which we had passed through on our way West. I worried mostly about a couple of things that seemed pretty clear to me: first, that Marshal Shockley in Denton obviously had not succeeded in catching Otis and

Shirley and the others, and second, that Otis & Company still appeared to be following our same route.

But that was about all we could do just then—worry. The one thing about the poster that didn't cause me to fret was that nobody in our group had appeared the least bit interested in whether there was a reward being offered for these men, nor in trying to catch them. We seemed to have learned our lesson.

We had traveled for weeks through country like I'd never seen before. Flat? You could stand still and look around you and see nothing at all but dry brown land stretching out in all directions and dry blue sky above that. And if you stood still, looking, long enough, the land seemed to start to rock slowly, back and forth, like a single wave sloshing slowly across a sea, then slowly sloshing back again, tipping the shores a little when it touched. To our relief, we were now in an area of broken hills and grassy slopes, and Mr. Desmond thought that during the next day's travel we might be able to catch our first glimpse of a big cliff he called El Capitan, which he said was a landmark marking a pass through mountains on the other side of the Pecos crossing.

I looked forward to seeing that and woke up thinking about it, but then the day didn't get off to what I considered a very promising start. Gil came out of his blankets acting silly. He fell to his knees and started yodeling, "Praise, praise, praise to the morning."

Emma stirred in her own quilts and looked at him through tangled brown hair. "What's bitten you?" she said.

Gil said, "Morning has broken like the first morning."

Emma yawned and turned over.

Gil didn't mind. He only chanted, "O ye sun and moon . . . O ye stars . . . ye green things upon the earth . . . ye fowls of the air . . . beasts and cattle . . . children of men . . . bless ye the Lord, praise Him and magnify Him forever."

Mr. Desmond opened his eyes and looked at Gil with the kind of look that I tended to reserve for snakes, and I wasn't sure whether to attribute that to my strong suspicion that Gil's praising and chanting was just an effort to catch Emma's attention, which Mr. Desmond wouldn't care for, or to the bottle of bust-skull whiskey that Mr. Desmond had consumed the previous evening, and which he definitely did seem to care for.

Mr. Desmond had bought what looked like a saddlebagful of the whiskey back in San Angelo, where he spent a full day looking unsuccessfully for some old pal that nobody in San Angelo ever seemed to have heard of. For that matter, Mr. Desmond seemed not to have heard of San Angelo, either. What he was really looking for was a town named Ben Ficklin, near Camp Concho on the North Concho River, which I figured might be well patronized by soldiers from the fort who would make good photographic prospects. But Ben Ficklin had been wiped out by a flood in '82, and its survivors moved upstream to a settlement named Over-the-River, which was renamed Santa Angela, which then came to be called San Angelo. With all this confusion, I found it no wonder that we couldn't unearth Mr. Desmond's old pal. Worse, to me, we couldn't unearth much business, despite the town's being a busy place. As treasurer for Calvin and me, who were just about the only ones still solvent, I was holding two dollars and forty-three cents when we left San Angelo, and it didn't strike me as a particularly appropriate thing for Mr. Desmond to have blown the last of his ready-money on that whiskey. It didn't seem to have done his state of health much good, either.

At breakfast that morning, Mr. Desmond declined biscuits and drank coffee in silence, still giving Gil that snake-look, for Gil was still acting silly. Mr. Desmond had the suffering, red-eyed appearance Grandfather used to get after he and Mr. Stein would stay up late drinking and talking, but there seemed something more to it than that to me, and I asked, "How are you feeling, Mr. Desmond? Is your trouble bothering you again?"

"What trouble?" he said.

"Well, your lungs. You said once you'd had some trouble with your lungs."

"My lungs are fine and so am I," he said.

Gil was prattling nonsense at Emma, the essence of which was that rural life had it all over city life. He proposed to her three times while she made breakfast, offering her "a simple garden, with acres of sky," and Mr. Desmond was getting so tired of his joking that he looked ready to bite him.

"You can't appreciate all this until you've seen a city like London," Gil said to Emma with a sweeping gesture. His "all this" was the same old brown dirt and a mesquite thicket. He went on, "It is only to the Sabbath, when two hundred thousand factory chimneys have ceased belching smoke, that Londoners owe the knowledge that the sky is sometimes blue."

Emma just said, "Do tell." To me, she said, "We're almost out of water. You should have brought more than just one bucket last night."

"I'll go get more," Calvin said.

"It's Pepper's responsibility," Emma said.

"He was busy helping me take that view of the cattle at the water hole last evening," Calvin said.

"You don't have to make no excuses for me," I said.

Gil prattled, "Marry me, fair one, and the A.C.M. Company will provide endless water, and we'll raise dainty dairy cows and live on cakes and clotted cream."

"Marry you, indeed. I suppose you think you're being funny."

"Well, yes, I did rather think so."

"You'd do better to save your energy and go help Pepper bring up water. I'll need at least two buckets, one for the breakfast dishes and one to soak a gunny sack to wrap around those cheeses." In our biggest business deal of the week we had traded a portrait to a woman for two home-made cheeses, plus a second-hand wagon harness that I thought we could maybe get a dollar for at curb auction if we ever came to a town again, and Emma had worried ever since about keeping the cheeses cool and un-spoiled until we got through eating on them.

Well, Gil did bestir himself enough to go with me for water. The rangy, underfed-looking cattle that Calvin had found handsome enough to waste a plate on the previous evening were still hanging around the water hole, and they'd muddied it so that we had to wait awhile for the silt to settle. They were half wild, but bold, and didn't go far from the hole. They stood, watching us, and fighting flies that sat on their legs.

"Pepper, you know how to milk cows," Gil said. "Why not embezzle us a little cream for tonight's coffee. Emma likes cream."

"I guess you should start learning that some cows give milk, and some cows, range cows, I hear you got to knock down and sit on and take it away from," I said. "That is, if you really have any hopes of marrying Emma and raising dainty dairy cows."

"Hell, man, I was only trying to amuse her," he said.

I liked that, his calling me a man. I said, "I expect you did. I expect you helped her through the morning, diverting her, sort of. I expect you've helped her through a lot of days."

Gil made a little open-palmed gesture, as though he were trying to shoo away my words, although I hadn't meant to say anything unpleasant to him, but the reverse. He said, "Do you think Emma is pretty?"

"I don't have to think it," I said. "She is pretty."

"She might be if she'd take any kind of care of herself. I don't believe she's washed her hair once since we left Krum. Or bathed."

"Well, that's her business," I said.

"Do you think she likes Desmond?" he said.

That's how he confirmed my suspicion that his early-morning pranking had just been a way to try to get attention from Emma. The longer I traveled with her, the more thought I had been giving to her myself, so it came as no surprise. I said, "No. I think she likes him just the way she likes all of us. I don't think she likes him anything special. Hell, Gil, he's old."

"He's not that old. Some women like mature men. He's always touching her. Have you noticed that? He's always got his hand on her arm or her shoulder or someplace. Haven't you noticed that?"

I hadn't. But I started watching for it. And the day wasn't out before I saw it happen a half-dozen times. But first we finished bringing up the water and breaking camp, and we got the day's travel under way.

We nooned in a thorny tangle of dwarf mesquite and I think catclaw and almost surely some prickly pear, none of which threw much shade, which was what we were hoping for, but Calvin thought it was grand and picturesque and wanted to take a view of it. Our portrait business may have dwindled, but the dents Calvin kept making in the photographic supplies surely hadn't. About every other stand of trees or sweeping vista or towering bank of clouds we came across struck Calvin as just beautiful, and beautifully Western, and he had sent views to the New York magazines from Abilene and then San Angelo and would surely have one of the world's largest, heaviest collections of views to send along after them by the time we reached El Paso. I'm afraid Gil and Mr. Desmond both kept encouraging him, not in taking views, but in looking at all this dry, cactus-y stuff as something marvelous. Mr. Desmond was as proud of the West as if he'd been its personal creator, and Gil was eager to see and admire and try to learn the name of every little twig of greasewood or sage or salt cedar that we passed by.

We ate biscuits, again, and beans, again, and Mr. Desmond traded his Navy Colt for my shotgun and told us to start on without him, he and Nemo would catch up when they had some game to enliven our evening meal. Eventually they did, somewhat sooner than we expected. Mr. Desmond came riding up fast and dropped three prairie chickens and two big jack rabbits into the wagon.

Emma said, "How grand. Just look how fat they are."

Mr. Desmond smiled his little smile, but he said, "Pepper, quicken the mules a bit and ride on. We've got company."

"Company?" I said.

Mr. Desmond nodded his chin at the trail behind us. "Men on horseback," he said. "Maybe four or five of them."

I craned my neck. "Where?"

"A couple of miles behind us," he said. "I headed back for the wagon as soon as I saw them, but I fear they may have spotted me."

"Who are they?" Calvin said.

"I don't know," Mr. Desmond said. "I didn't get all that close." His leg, heavily muscled with the kind of muscles you get when you do a lot of riding, moved slightly as he nudged his horse with his heel and moved closer beside the slowly jouncing wagon to lay the shotgun in beside Emma and take back his pistol. "Whoever it was, I don't care for the idea of them trailing along after us, even if they do keep their distance. I'd suggest a little more speed, Pepper."

So I clucked up the mules and set them off at a faster pace. Mr. Desmond dropped back maybe ten yards behind the wagon, watching the trail. Nemo, as always, followed closely by his horse, trotting to keep up. It was hot, and poor old Nemo's tongue was hanging out half a foot.

And that was when we heard that day from Otis and Shirley Wasum.

Something whined rapidly past my cheek, and Emma said, "Oh! A bee!"

Gil said, "Fear not, frail little woman, I won't let it sting you."

It was that long before we heard the "Blam!" of the rifle shot. Then another bullet flew past us. By that time Mr. Desmond had come alive. "Whip up those mules!" he cried. "Run!"

The mules had heard the sound too, and don't ever let anyone tell you that mules aren't smart. Tired and thirsty as they were, they broke into a run before I'd much more than popped the whip once over their ears. Mr. Desmond's horse was galloping too, and he pulled up between the wagon and the direction the shots had come from.

I twisted my head to look. I caught a glimpse of perhaps five men on horses atop a little hill to the side of the road. Just then the wagon hit a jarring bump, and I had to turn my eyes back to the road, so that one glimpse was all I got. One of the men was black. That was the only thing I'd seen for sure.

Within two minutes we were abreast of a stand of chaparral, and Mr. Desmond fell back, pulling his rifle out of his saddle scabbard, as if he figured the chaparral would shield us from their view from now on, and he could turn his attention to other business. I heard him fire twice. If there were any more shots from the men on the hill, they didn't come close.

Somehow the wagon withstood our rapid flight without apparent damage, which is more than I could say for myself. I was too busy with the mules to do more than wish I was a grown man and had a horse and a rifle and was back with Mr. Desmond trying to help, but I wished it hard.

The mules didn't want to keep up a gallop for more than a couple of miles, and soon Mr. Desmond caught up with us again and signaled to me that it was all right to let Old and Young Jeb continue along in the fast trot they were trying to settle into. We stayed at that pace until he judged the men had been discouraged by the return fire and were no longer following us, then he waved us to a walk.

"Who was it?" I called to Mr. Desmond.

Gil had his little pistol out, and now he looked up at Mr. Desmond fiercely. "It was that pair from Louisiana," he said.

"Otis and Shirley?" I said. "Are you sure? Did you see them?"

Gil nodded, still looking angry and fierce and determined. "Them and three others. Desmond led them right to us. Desmond the great pioneer."

Mr. Desmond tightened his mouth and said, "All that can wait. We'll stop for the night in a couple of hours. I'm going to ride on ahead to look for a safe place for us to hole up." To me, he said, "You'll want to keep your shotgun handy."

Emma handed me the shotgun meekly, and Mr. Desmond rode off ahead of us at a trot. Gil kept his little gun in his lap and we creaked along in the ruts. Both Gil and Calvin kept watching behind us.

And that's the way it happened. I stayed on the road until Mr. Desmond came riding back for us later that afternoon and led us to a catch basin shielded by high rocks on three sides in a big patch of chaparral. He told me to pull the wagon in amongst the rocks, which I did.

Gil leapt out. "We shouldn't have run!" he said. "We shouldn't have run!"

I sympathized perfectly, but I didn't say anything.

Mr. Desmond only said, "I'm going to check around those rocks to make sure everything is all right. Gil, you take your pistol and look around the brush." He glanced at my shotgun. "You stay here with Emma, Pepper."

I knew he only wanted me to stay behind because I had the next-best weapon to his, the shotgun, and he wanted it available to defend Emma, but staying behind just added to my feeling of shame. Yes, shame. It was peculiar. I was ashamed because we had run, but it wasn't only that. I was mostly ashamed simply because we'd actually been shot at. Otis and Shirley Wasum had obviously found themselves guns by now, and had picked them up and aimed them at us and pulled the triggers, just as Mr. Desmond had shot at the three prairie chickens and two rabbits that were lying dead in the wagon. It seemed a queerly contemptuous act, as if we were of no more importance than those three dead birds and two dead rabbits. But that wasn't quite it, either. It seemed to diminish me, somehow, for someone to treat me that way, and that was all I knew, and that was what I was ashamed of. And, also, although I told myself that I'd wanted to stop and fight, I knew that I had once again been afraid. That made me so ashamed that I felt sick to my stomach.

Calvin helped Emma out of the wagon and stationed her between the dark-box and a thicket that looked too dense even for a lizard to get through. Mr. Desmond came back in five or ten minutes, and Gil came back five or ten minutes after that.

"Nothing," Gil reported.

"Me too," Mr. Desmond said. He took Emma's elbow and pulled her out from behind the wagon. "It's nothing to worry about now."

Calvin said, "It really was the Wasums. Gil saw them, and I did too. I also saw that Sidney Clinkscale. I couldn't be sure about the two other men."

"One was a nigger," Gil said. "He's surely one of the same group."

Mr. Desmond said to Emma, "Why don't you go have a look at the basin. It's not very clear, but it's drinkable."

"Anything you have to discuss you can discuss around me," she said.

"There's nothing to discuss," he said. "Why don't you go on. It might not be a bad place to wash. We've got plenty of dirty clothes stacked up."

She did what he told her. I was never so surprised. Mr. Desmond watched her a minute, then he said, "I guess I know from what you've told us why those boys from Louisiana are still on your trail and took those potshots at you, but you got any ideas why that gang is helping them?"

"No," said Calvin. "I've been wondering too."

"I've got to say I don't much like it," Mr. Desmond said. "People taking potshots could be mighty dangerous." He didn't say it unkindly, but I suppose he didn't say it kindly, either. He just said it quietly, his eyes bloodshot but thoughtful, his face hard but calm. I knew he was thinking about Emma and didn't really give a damn about the rest of us.

I mumbled, "We warned you at the very beginning there might be some kind of trouble."

"I know you did," he said.

"Well," I said, "I guess Calvin and me will just have to get out. I know we can't split up now, but maybe when we get to El Paso we can finally make some money and buy a train ticket or that rig for Emma, and the rest of you can travel on in style. We don't want you shot on our account."

He looked a little impatient. "No sense talking about splitting up," he said. Then he waited for a minute as if to see if Gil or Calvin or I had anything else to say, and said, "All right, we'll worry when the time comes to worry." He strolled away after Emma.

Well, there were animal tracks all around the catch basin, but just one set of fresh horse tracks, which Mr. Desmond said were his roan's. He looked over the rest and said deer and coyote and raccoon and civet cat. He said we'd have to keep our eyes on the dog that night, or old Nemo might be chasing and howling all night long. Emma didn't like the idea of camping where all sorts of wild animals came prowling around, but water wasn't easy to find in those parts, and Mr. Desmond was averse to moving on, so we stayed put. It was early. Neither Emma nor Mr. Desmond set me to rushing around doing chores as they often did. I went and got my portmanteau and took out Uncle Raleigh's letter that told about Otis and Shirley Wasum. Calvin came to sit beside me.

He'd heard the letter before a number of times. We all had, for getting a letter was an event, and since Calvin and I were the only two in our outfit whose family knew more or less where we expected to be and could send mail, we read our letters out loud and shared them.

I read the part again about Otis and Shirley Wasum coming after us, and old Mr. Wasum telling my father to warn us, although I already knew it practically by heart, and I said, "Goddammit, Calvin, why didn't the homefolks trust me enough to listen when I told them about Otis? Then they could have hanged him straight off, and we wouldn't be in this mess."

"Don't cuss," Calvin said.

"I'm beginning to think that if I'm old enough to get shot at, I'm old enough to cuss," I said.

That was one of the new things we said. We had sat and wondered many times before about Otis and Shirley, and what possible good Mr. Wasum's suggestion to my father would do, since Otis and Shirley were hardly likely to sit down and parley with Calvin and me long enough for us to tell them to write home and ask for news from their father. And we had wondered whether Otis and Shirley were now making a living robbing faro games and things like that, and whether Mr. Jardine had died and made a real murderer of Shirley, just as his brother Otis was a murderer. We had also wondered a few times whether they were actually trying to follow us as Uncle Raleigh's letter had said or whether it could possibly be by chance that their trail was leading them along in the same direction as us. But now that the Wasums had shot at us between San Angelo and the Pecos, that last question was decided in our minds and we had a new one to trouble us, that of their three companions and why they were also shooting at us.

"You think we ought to telegraph the family and tell them about seeing Otis and Shirley today and what they did?" I said.

"We already wrote the family about seeing them in Denton," Calvin said.

"But you know how uncertain letters can be."

"There's nothing they could do about it," Calvin said.

"Then what about us? What can we do?"

"Nothing," Calvin said. "Nothing but keep our eyes peeled better."

And that's what we did. Nothing.

To be more precise, we spent the late hours of the afternoon playing base ball with Gil. It was his idea. All I wanted to do was sit by myself and brood. But the moment I got to brooding good, here came Gil clamoring that he wanted a bath, and the catch basin was big enough to swim a stroke or two in, and I had best come in with him. Emma started right in on the washing, though, and Gil couldn't get close to the catch basin, so he prodded me to drag my dirty clothes for Emma out of my portmanteau, and as I did he discovered a base ball that I'd brought along.

To hear Gil tell it, base ball was a compound of rounders and cricket, played with an ash staff about the length of a cricket bat, but round and larger at the striking end than at the handle. I couldn't figure out what on earth he was talking about, but he'd worked out all sorts of explanations, such as that the batsman is called the batter and the wicket keeper the catcher and the bowler the pitcher and there was no slip field or off field or on field but just an outfield. He proclaimed that as he was adept at both cricket and rounders—which he said was a game and not a sport and played only at picnics or the beach—he thought he could do fairly well at base ball, and so we must all play.

And to tell the truth, he was very good. Mr. Desmond didn't play with us. He took his rifle and sat next to Emma by the catch basin and kept an eye on the open end of our campsite and simultaneously conversed with Emma while she scrubbed away at a pretty good pile of dirty clothes that we'd accumulated. But Calvin played, and Nemo helped chase, and for a while we had a good time, swinging away with a piece of mesquite branch we'd tried to trim to the proper size, and dodging thorns that were there waiting for us every time we got a pretty good connection with my ball.

Gil kept watching Emma, as if to see whether she was seeing how well he did, but when she wouldn't pay any attention to him and kept conversing with Mr. Desmond, he finally said that was enough exercise for one day, and why didn't he help me clean the prairie chickens and jack rabbits so we could start getting ready for supper. What he meant, of course, was that I'd clean and he'd watch. That was just like him. And just like Mr. Desmond, too. When it came to chores, like scrubbing dirty clothes or skinning slippery rabbits, they always thought of Emma and me. For more than one reason, I could hardly wait until I was a grown-up man.

I declined Gil's aid and he wandered off into the chaparral, and Nemo went to flop beside Mr. Desmond, and Calvin got out his camera. He came to the catch basin, where I was working on the rabbits, to beg Emma if she wouldn't consider sitting for a portrait.

"I wish you'd let me, Emma," he said, "and I think I could make a portrait of which I could be truly proud."

Emma laughed, looking flustered but nice, but she said, "Good heavens no. Can't you see I'm busy? Besides, I must look like something the cat dragged in."

"No you don't," Calvin said. "You look natural and busy and your hair gets curly as can be when it slips from its pins. You look like a nymph might look if she decided all her best tunics was dirty and she'd better do a little washing."

Emma laughed, but she kept saying no. "Who else do you suppose is going to finish the clothes?" she said. "I've heard from no volunteers." She had already done our shirts and drawers and was working on her own things now. She doused a set of long pink stays up and down in the catch basin, then began to wring them out, being careful not to bend the bones. Calvin looked away, and I looked down at the rabbit.

"I'll fix supper," I said. I looked up and discovered that Mr. Desmond was staring at me, but I stiffened my spine and went on stoutly, "I've fried chickens before, and I guess I can fry prairie chickens and rabbit."

"You don't know how to make biscuits," Emma said.

"No, but I can make pone, and we're near out of wheat flour anyway."

"Well," she said, "I consider that a very gentlemanly offer, Pepper."

"Pepper can't cook," Mr. Desmond said. I was looking straight at him, but he reached out and took Emma's bare arm and turned her toward him, and I was suddenly reminded of the way some men break horses, a way they learned in the old days from the Indians, some people said, in which you slowly, slowly acquaint the animal with the touch of its master, and when the time finally comes to ride the animal, it just lets you, without much fight at all. It was not that he was caressing her or anything like that. He just touched her, casually, like a man who unthinkingly touched whatever he was looking at, without meaning harm, but I saw that Emma seemed to breathe in a different way, and in a second or two she had slipped her arm out of his grasp and was reaching for the bar of yellow soap to suds a cotton petticoat.

I cleared my throat and said, "Sure I can cook, enough for a camp. It's the least I can do after Emma's doing my washing. You just let me take care of things."

Then we heard a wild whooping from Gil. Nemo began to bark furiously, and I cursed, I fear in Emma's hearing, and jumped up, thinking of my shotgun, which I had let get out of my vicinity and had left leaning up against the wagon. But Mr. Desmond wasn't as careless about his rifle and was on his feet and swinging it up toward the sound of Gil's voice before I could count to three. Gil came rushing out of the mesquite, grinning broadly. He was bare-chested, his naked breast showing scratches from a dozen thorns, and carefully cradling something in his shirt.

"Look, Emma! Look what I've found," he cried. "No, excuse me, don't look. Look the other way for a second."

"You almost found a bullet in your gut," Mr. Desmond said in a cold, quiet voice that you could barely hear over Nemo's continued barking.

"What's the matter with all of you? Give me your hat, Calvin. Look. I found a nest. They're eggs, and they look fresh. What are they, do you suppose? Are they prairie-chicken eggs?"

Emma didn't exactly look away from his bare skin, but she did keep her eyes on the eggs. "They're turkey eggs," she said. "Seven of them. There's an egg for everyone, and two left over."

Gil laughed jubilantly. "Lady and gentlemen, how will you have your eggs this evening? Rabbits. Prairie chickens. Cheeses. Fresh eggs. Who said a man needs money to get along in this world? Why, we haven't had to pay a penny, but we'll have an absolute feast."

Then his face suddenly went green-white, and he stared behind us, to the rocks atop the catch basin.

A strange voice roared:

"Stamumderimmer!"

Nine

The shock was like a sudden, soundless explosion. Across the catch basin I saw a tall, compact man, with a strong neck and well-set-up shoulders. He wore the oddest-looking pair of pants I had ever seen, made of leather and decorated on the sides with silver doodads. The leather pants hung from his belt and came down to his boot tops, where they were tied around his legs with thongs, and under them he wore another ordinary pair of britches. From what you could see of his face, it was bronzed and with angular features, but you couldn't see much. It was divided in two by the dark line of a chin strap and shadowed by the drooping brim of a big hat, which he wore at a rakish slant. The lower half of his face was covered by a dark kerchief.

All this I saw with peculiar vividness before a single second had ticked itself out, and it's strange that I saw even a smidgen of it, for the most riveting aspect of his rig was the enormous pistol he held in his hand.

We all stared at him. Sounding impatient, he said again, "Stamumderimmer!"

Gil looked at me as though, long accustomed as I was to translating for Calvin, I could provide an interpretation, but I shook my head. He took a step, I believe to try to move in front of Emma, and the man on the rocks ripped off his kerchief with an angry gesture and shouted, "I said stand and deliver!"

"Our money?" Gil said.

"What other? Are you all insane? Everyone will raise his hands. Someone will hold that dog if you do not wish him killed. You, you will drop that rifle and that pistol!" This last was to Mr. Desmond.

Gil said, "I beg your pardon, but are you alone?"

The man moved that big pistol in a tight circle. "This is all the assistance that I require," he said. "Now everyone will raise his hands. Quickly!"

Well, I did what he said, rabbit still in one hand and skinning knife in the other, and so did the others, including Calvin. But Calvin, helplessly, keeping his head down to hide his lip, let out the "Hppp . . ." of a suppressed but overpowering guffaw.

Gil was next to follow suit, but not having Calvin's habit of trying to conceal his mouth while laughing, he laughed out loud. It was as contagious as the smallpox, and there was no way in the world that I could keep myself from giggling, as did Emma. Lastly, Mr. Desmond's mouth twitched and I heard what I suppose I heard for the first and last time, the sound of Mr. Desmond roaring with laughter.

Trying to control himself, Gil gasped out, "Are . . . you . . . planning . . . to rob us?"

That set us to laughing even harder, until I noticed that the man's face was growing dark with rage. I tried to stop. I said, "We've got two dollars and forty-three cents, and if you'll wait just a moment I'll go and get it for you."

"No!" Emma said. "We worked too hard for that money." To the man on the rocks, she said, "You can't have the cheeses, either. If you feel it's worth your while to shoot five people for two dollars and two cheeses, you just go right ahead."

"Careful now," Mr. Desmond said quietly, for the stranger's face still looked angry. "Pocket change and cheese ain't worth getting shot for."

Emma looked at him with contempt. "That from you?" she said. "And you always acting like such a big, brave man?"

"Don't talk like a little fool," he said. "A man that's big enough chooses what he's going to be brave over."

The man on the rocks shouted, "Silence!" He gestured with the pistol. "Walk backward away from the water!"

I started backing toward the wagon, for leaning against it

was the shotgun, but I sometimes think it's wrong even to think things if you don't want other people to know about them. The man's eyes jumped to the wagon and he said, "No! Over there!"

We backed where he told us. He came down the rocks and around the basin, the pistol holding steady, and stooped to pick up Mr. Desmond's rifle and Navy Colt. He glanced at them, then strode to the wagon and scooped up my shotgun.

"Listen to me carefully," he said. His accent was very odd, but what with Gil and Calvin I was getting used to never being around people who spoke normally. "You have other arms. Where? You have money. Where? You have valuables. Where? I have no wish to kill you, but do not think that it would trouble me to do so."

I said, "I told you how much money we got, and otherwise we've got only a secondhand wagon harness that we hope to sell for a dollar. I don't think it's fair to take our arms, either. We're hard on the road to Tombstone, and we rely on them for game. We'll starve to death without them."

The man was beginning to look perplexed, but he said, "Do not lie to me. I will know instantly if you lie."

"Then you ought to know instantly if we're telling the truth. I'm sorry, mister, but you picked the wrong batch to rob."

Gil chimed in. "If you wanted to do things properly, you'd give us whatever money *you* have. It's a shame to disappoint you, but we're really on our uppers at the moment, old fellow."

But the man wasn't satisfied. He rattled the locked door to the dark-box. "Then what is locked away so carefully?"

I said, "Stuff that's no use to you unless you chance to be a photographic artiste. Glass and tin for making plates, and lots of chemicals that are poisonous as all get-out. Get a little bit on your hands and then forget and stick your finger in your mouth, and you could fall over dead." I didn't mention Calvin's fifty-dollar camera.

Well, the man refused to believe us and insisted on looking inside the dark-box, which Calvin unlocked and let him do, but clucking at him all the time not to rattle the chemical bottles or damage anything. Emma acted as if she was tired of all this and went back to the catch basin and got the clean clothes she'd finished and started draping them on the mesquite trees.

155

Next from the stranger it was questions: Who were we? Where were we coming from? I saw a chance to sneak in a question of my own as to whether he'd recently seen four or five men on horses who had maybe been doing some pretty careless shooting, and he answered, "No," then looked startled at himself for answering.

It was Gil—who else?—who invited him for supper. The man's perplexity was by then turning to bewilderment, and although I knew Gil was hiding his little pistol in his pocket, the stranger's ability to know a lie or the truth instantly seemed a little less certain than he had proclaimed, because it was Mr. Desmond on whom he kept a careful eye. I expect we were all feeling so crazy that we weren't thinking very practically or cautiously. Before all the questioning was over, we were wandering around pretty much as we pleased, except for Mr. Desmond, who still looked a bit edgy and who continued keeping an eye on the open end of our camp and on Emma.

Emma hollered to me to help her hang clothes. She was working mostly with our stuff, so I picked up hers. Corset covers and drawers with ribbons on them and petticoats with the same and that set of pink stays that I hung so slowly I finally feared she might notice it. My fingers felt funny when they touched the parts that curved where her breasts would be, and, sopping wet though the garment was, I could feel the palms of my hands sweating. What would it be like . . . ?

"Aren't you finished yet?" Emma said. "Pepper, you're going to grow up just like the rest, disdaining what you regard as women's work but not doing your own work half as well as a woman could."

"I volunteered to fix supper, didn't I?" I said.

"Then why aren't you doing it? It's getting late."

"I can't do everything at once."

Emma laughed. She was always surprising me like that. The minute I thought maybe I'd been uppity and she'd jump down my throat as likely as not would turn out to be the minute that she'd get tickled instead and give me a pretty smile that showed her short, white teeth.

"You're right," she said. Mr. Desmond had come over close to us, and she said to him, "And it would serve you right if Pepper ruined the food. You're not really letting that man stay, are you? Why, he's a bandit."

"Is he a Mexican?" I said. We'd encountered some coming through, meeting more and more as we got farther west, but I still hadn't learned to recognize them too well. Some were very dark and black-haired, but not all, and this man was just kind of in-between in coloring.

"Sure he is," Mr. Desmond said, "but that don't matter just now. The important thing, he's an extra gun, and that just might come in handy."

That seemed sensible. I asked, "What kind of funny pants are those he's wearing? I've never seen pants like those before."

"*Armas,* they call them," Mr. Desmond said, "or maybe *armitas.* It means like a shield or something. Mexes that work cattle in heavy brush sometimes wear them."

"He's no cowman, he's a bandit," Emma said.

Mr. Desmond smiled his little smile. "Don't let that trouble you," he said. "Some men sometimes don't like the law. It doesn't necessarily mean they aren't good men."

I guess maybe Mr. Desmond's talk was sounding sensible to Emma, too, because she said she'd fix supper after all. But I went with her to help, for she looked tired, and I'd made a bargain, and I believed a man lived up to the bargains he'd made.

I fetched wood to a circle of stones that showed where other people camping at the same watering place had made fires, but Mr. Desmond vetoed the site because he said we'd better keep the fire small and place it where it couldn't be seen easily by anyone else who might come prowling around. He set new stones. That was a way of his too: he never minded the hard work, the kind that took muscles, but he refused to touch the cooking and cleaning kind. Calvin and Gil, having finally finished overseeing the stranger's scrupulous inspection of our goods and possessions, drew near, and I went to work on scalding and plucking the prairie chickens. I felt foolish doing that in front of a stranger, but as I said, a bargain was a bargain. The pretty, mottled birds were limp in my hands, and blood had dried on one's beak. Like all dead things, birds looked smaller dead than when they were alive.

The evening was hot, and the fire, which was little but going good, didn't make it any cooler, but Calvin and Gil hunkered down around it. The stranger waited until Mr. Desmond also settled on his heels near Emma, then he sat a little apart from us. I hadn't noticed where he'd put our guns, but his own pistol, although holstered by now, was still very much in evidence. The bone handle was shiny and polished like the seat of a saddle that is in constant use. His gun belt held a thick row of shells, and the pistol hung at his side like something that had grown there and was part of the man.

"I guess you could all use a cup of coffee," Emma said. "Pepper, fill the pot for me."

The stranger cleared his throat and looked at us, and then looked down, and then he said, "I ask your pardon, but I have something perhaps we men would prefer. A bottle of tequila. It is good tequila." He rose and looked at Emma with a questioning look. "With your permission?"

"Feel free," she said. "We've got our quota of hard drinkers around here anyway, and they never bother to ask permission."

"I only wish to contribute some small thing, as you have been kind enough to . . ."

Emma said, "I told you, feel free. In fact, I'll join you. Pepper, do we have any sugar left? My daddy used to say liquor was better that way, in a toddy with hot water and sugar."

Gil said, "My dear Emma, ladies don't drink hard spirits."

"This lady is tired, and she's planning to do just that," Emma said.

Well, she'd washed her stays, and heaven knows what she had on underneath just at that moment, but it must not have been as much as usual. There was soft, swelling flesh showing in the V of her blouse, and just then a bead of sweat rolled slowly down from about the area of her collarbone and disappeared into the V. Gil watched as though mesmerized, and he jumped half a foot when Mr. Desmond said to him, "I thought you'd been belly-aching about a bath. There's plenty of time before supper."

"Uh, ladies first," Gil said. "Perhaps Emma would care to bathe. And wash her hair."

"While I'm right in the middle of cooking supper?" she said. "Maybe later, when it's dark. It's so hot, even that muddy water would feel good. Unless . . . are there snakes?"

158

Mr. Desmond said, "Not likely, but Pepper or Calvin could beat the water good for you before you go in."

So Gil requested Emma to keep her back turned, and by the time the newcomer got back with his tequila bottle and his horse, a hammer-headed black, Gil was already splashing in the catch basin. He began to sing. The newcomer looked startled, but Mr. Desmond explained laconically, "Washing. He's English, but he washes a lot." He turned and called in a low voice to Gil to stop that singing. Did Gil want everybody in the world to know where we'd made our camp? Gil stopped, and Mr. Desmond continued to the newcomer: "I don't suppose you saw any signs of strangers when you went after your horse?"

"No, no one," the newcomer said.

Mr. Desmond said, "And I don't suppose you can see your way clear to giving me back my rifle. We've had a little trouble today, and there may be some men looking for us. That could be bad, with a lady among us."

"Ah . . . perhaps . . . sir, you need have no fears for the lady. My pistol will be quite adequate to protect her," the newcomer said.

"Um," Mr. Desmond said.

The stranger pulled himself to his full height, which was pretty good sized, and said, "May I introduce myself? I am Jaime Cienfuegos Villarreal, *a sus órdenes.*"

Sounding a little rusty at it, Mr. Desmond trotted out some Spanish that began with, "*Mucho gusto,*" and ended, as I learned later, with what we "called ourselves," and then our names, Emma Prosser, and Hap Desmond, and Calvin and Pepper Fairchild, and one Gil Carmichael, who was splashing in what would be our drinking water the next morning. It all sounded very polite, and the newcomer bowed at each name and said things like "*Mucho gusto en conocerle*" and, to Emma, "*Encantado.*" He offered his hand to us males but not to Emma. We all shook. Life was becoming so unsettled for me that I didn't even find it particularly strange to shake hands with a man who had just recently tried to hold us up.

Calvin tried to get his tongue around the name, and asked, when all the bowing was done, "Hymie? It's a small world. I've heard that name in New York City."

"No, Jaime," the newcomer said. The sound was maybe a little different, but it was hard for my ear to catch.

"What kind of a name is that?" Emma said.

Jaime blinked and seemed undecided as to whether to be offended or merely puzzled, but Mr. Desmond said, "It's like James."

"Oh, Jamie," Emma said, and after that, that was what we called him.

This ceremonial was concluded by the making of a toddy for Emma, and Mr. Desmond decided for me that such was the manner that I'd better do my imbibing too. I didn't argue. I didn't even bother to tell him that Uncle Raleigh had started me out on peach brandy at home at about the age of four, for my family seemed to think that lessons in drinking were part of a boy's normal upbringing. When I got to school age, we had a Baptist schoolmaster who was strongly opposed to drinking and who used to tell us such things as "Drink drives men to unspeakable crimes, such as lust, lasciviousness, licentiousness, theft, and rapine," and "The terrible thing about people who drink is that their innocent children are often born with brain damage and sometimes go completely crazy as they grow older." But I was the child and grandchild of men who drank, and I certainly didn't have a weak brain, so I put my faith in practical experience rather than merely in something a teetotaling teacher had forced on us.

I have to admit, though, that I'd never sipped more than a few tablespoons of brandy or one glass of wine at a time, and Emma and I both were feeling pretty gay by the time the prairie chickens were popping and sizzling in the skillet and the pone was working in the Dutch oven. Gil rejoined us, wearing a damp shirt that he'd plucked off the mesquites. It wasn't time to put on the eggs yet. We fell to discussing the fact that now that we had Jamie as a supper guest there was only one egg left ownerless, and what should we do with it?

"It must go to the lady," Jamie said courteously. "For that matter, I need no egg, and she should have both of them."

Emma giggled a little. "How in the world could I eat three whole eggs, with rabbits and prairie chickens and cheeses?" she said.

Gil said, "You could whip them up and put them on your face."

"Whatever for?" she said.

Calvin said, "Some ladies at home do that. But I think they use just the egg white. They say it's good for the complexion. Or some use buttermilk. I wonder which is better?" I believe the tequila was beginning to tell on him.

Emma said, "Until I get someplace I can stay out of this horrid sun there's no sense worrying about my complexion. I'll tell you what let's do—let's play a hand of poker for the extra egg."

Gil said, very stiffly, "Ladies do not play poker."

"Maybe not where you come from," Emma said gaily. "My poppa loved poker, and toward the end there was no one but me to play with him. Pepper, set those pots back away from the fire. We've got to dispose of this speckled egg before we can finish up supper. What can we use for poker chips?"

I think Jamie must have been feeling his tequila too, for he said, "I will offer the bullets from my cartridge belt."

Mr. Desmond looked at him slyly. "If you start losing, will you include the cartridges in your gun?"

Jamie smiled and said, carefully and properly, "Poker is a science, and I must warn you that I have studied that science. I can assure you that there will still be bullets in my gun when we have finished."

Mr. Desmond said, "Where was this that you studied poker?"

"Originally, Piedras Negras."

"On the Texas border? Is that where you learned all that English?"

Jamie nodded.

Mr. Desmond nodded too. After a moment, he said, "Mind telling us how come you left Mexico?"

"A man of my convictions had to do what he did to require his leaving Mexico," Jamie said roundly.

Mr. Desmond just nodded. "Pepper, go fetch the cards."

Well, Gil still wasn't in favor of letting Emma play, but we all ragged him into it. Nemo came and sat between Mr. Desmond and the pots, but not too closely. He was a gentleman.

Jamie counted out the cartridges from his gun belt and we began. There were six players, good enough, though some think five is better for poker, and there was Jamie's tequila bottle, and for a long time the conversation stayed with "Ace bets one bullet, gentlemen," and "Draw two," and "Pass that bottle, if you please." My Uncle Raleigh had also given me lessons in poker, maybe from about age six on, but he always cheated on my behalf, and I was soon out of cartridges. Everyone laughed, the tequila talking louder by now. They said didn't I want to bet my own egg, but I said no and checked the rabbits and the chickens and the pone and went down to the pond and followed Gil's example by taking a bath.

By the time I got back, hair still wet but combed, and the tequila humming gently in my ears, Gil, Mr. Desmond, and Emma were out, and the game was between Calvin and Jamie. It looked about even, their bullet stacks I mean, and Emma was yawning with hunger. I saw it, and so did Calvin and Jamie.

"High card?" Jamie asked.

"Why not just call it a draw?" Calvin said.

"One cannot split an egg."

"Of course we can. If you win, you're going to make Emma take it. If I win, I'm going to do the same." Calvin laughed, sounding both wistful and wild. "Let's just both make her take it."

"No, no," Emma giggled. "I didn't win that egg, and I don't want it."

But that's the way it turned out.

Calvin fried them, saying he judged that of the possible cooks of the moment, he thought he was most capable of handling them.

And he fried them very nicely.

After which we settled down to eat.

After which Jamie's tequila was gone, and Mr. Desmond went to get another bottle—how many did he have left?—of his bust-skull whiskey.

We had spread quilts, the way we always did, to eat on. Those rabbits and prairie chickens were cooked so tender that they almost fell off the bone, and although the pone had gotten itself a little burned, even our would-be bandit and supper guest, Jamie, said it was delicious. And I'd never tasted anything like those fresh turkey eggs after weeks of not seeing an egg of any kind. I'm not saying the liquor didn't help, but I was clean, and tired, and although a couple of different people had maybe tried to kill me that day, nobody had succeeded, and I don't know if I've ever before or since relished a meal as much as that one.

Naturally, we got to looking at the stars, which were close enough to reach up and grab a handful of, and I found Jupiter, and we talked of what to do after Tombstone. I was so tipsy that I told of one of my new heart's dreams, which was to find new ground perfect for raising long-staple cotton, on which I figured I was certainly expert, and Gil told of a new heart's dream that it seemed he'd recently been thinking on, due, he said, to Emma and Calvin, who were both journalists of a sort. He was contemplating a travel diary, which he said the London newspapers constantly printed and were wild for, and what would we think if he got some book publisher friend to print his, which he would entitle *Hard on the Road to the Last Frontier*, by Gilmore Carmichael?

Even Mr. Desmond's grade of whiskey tasted good when mixed with sugar and hot water. I said Gil's idea sounded wonderful, and I was on the verge of forgetting that it was Calvin's secret and telling of Calvin's ambition to be free and independent, when Mr. Desmond spoke up:

"As for my ambition, I've not changed my mind, and it will be gold first around the Big Bug, where they've made many recent strikes, and after that I'll go back to cattle again. And then I'll want a wife, and to bring my boys out with me."

"What boys?" said Emma.

"I've got two sets," he said. "The first set is grown, and their mother is dead, but the second set is only eight and five, and they need a father's guidance. I've been meaning to speak about that. It was their mother's brothers who were so red-hot for me to sell out after the drought in '83 and throw money away on Red River City, Texas. When I did what she kept nagging me to do and the money was lost, she divorced me for a telegrapher in Temple, Texas. About her, I care nothing, because she was born a slut and lived one and I only married her by justice of the peace. But I care about the boys, and I'll be frank, once I'm on my feet again I'll be looking for a wife to help me take care of the pair of them when I go back and fetch them."

"Excuse me," Emma said, not giggling now, and lay back flat on her quilt.

"Naturally, I'd be willing to marry, legal and proper," Mr. Desmond said.

Emma said dreamily, "Do you know how I've spent my life? Taking care of my daddy. I worked like a slave for my daddy, and that was fine with him. That was only what he expected. I'll never marry. Oh, yes, I'll cook and wash for you all, but I'm going to be a lady editor in San Francisco. I'll never cook and wash for another man. I told you I'd pay my way. And that's what I'm doing. And that's all I'm going to do."

Gil said, "Naturally a woman needs to marry, but she may certainly choose whom she wishes to marry."

"Not me," Emma said. Now she giggled again.

"Have another toddy," Gil said.

"Maybe you've had enough," Mr. Desmond said.

"I don't mind if I do," Emma said.

Jamie seemed to be finding all this rather strange, and he looked so bumfuzzled that I took the occasion to say, "Jamie, perhaps you'd care to tell us if you're traveling our direction or if you plan to hang around here and hope for more prosperous travelers to rob."

Jamie winced, and Calvin punched me, and I realized that I hadn't put it in the nicest possible way.

Jamie said, "I am glad you are young, Pepper. In another event, one might require a conversation over the possibility of your having called me a thief."

"No, now wait," Calvin said.

But Mr. Desmond said, "I guess I would call you a thief. The only question that had come to my mind was just what kind of thief, and where you planned to do your thieving."

The two men looked at each other. Calmly, Mr. Desmond went on, "Also, it may be that you would care to continue on with us to Arizona Territory, or it may be that you wouldn't care to travel with us at all. To speak frankly, we got little money now for ammunition, and I intend to stop wasting it on small game. There used to be plenty of deer and antelope in this part of the world, and deer and antelope are all right. But if none come my way, the next fat heifer I see that has no owner hanging around watching it is going to be shot and beefed and riding along in that dark-box before you can snap your fingers."

Gil laughed, a mean laugh. "Then they'll hang you," he said. "Even I know how Westerners feel about cow thieves."

Mr. Desmond's hard face didn't change expression. "If that occurs," he said, "I'll tell them none of you had any part in it or any knowledge that I didn't come by the beef legal, and I recommend that Calvin take views of the hanging. If I've seen one view of a dead criminal, I'll bet I've seen a dozen. Folks seem to go for that kind of thing, and you'd make good money off me. I trust you'd use part of the money to help Emma get settled, because we're still a long way from the A.C.M. Company and Tombstone and sure-money now might be worth more to her than maybe-money then. The way things are any more there's no sense in being poor if you can help it."

Emma giggled.

Gil said, "You don't have to worry about Emma."

Emma giggled again.

Mr. Desmond continued, and he continued addressing himself to Jamie:

"One last thing you might be interested in knowing is that these two boys here"—he meant Calvin and me—"really do have some fellows trailing them and taking potshots at them. Maybe you wouldn't want to get mixed up in such as that."

Jamie shrugged. "If I can be of service, naturally . . ."

He trailed off, and Mr. Desmond let him and sat there scratching old Nemo's ears and watching him calmly. It was obviously Jamie's turn to speak. Finally he did:

"Do you know about Mexico? Do you know what is happening there, or are you like most gringos and care nothing for what happens to a few filthy greasers below your border?"

"I know a little, but I never cared, and I don't care," Mr. Desmond said.

I watched Jamie's right hand. I watched that big pistol in its holster. The two didn't even come close to getting together, but I thought the hand was trembling slightly. Jamie said, "You speak frankly."

Mr. Desmond raised his cup in a little toasting gesture. "I believe I noticed that trait in you too."

"It would be better if you could speak your frankness politely."

"Well, I'm a rough man who never had much time for polishing, but I'll try to speak politely if that's what you care for. You might even try the same."

Jamie took a deep breath or two. Then he said, "You know of don Porfirio?"

Mr. Desmond nodded. "Porfirio Díaz, the President of Mexico."

"The dictator of Mexico," Jamie said. "The man who has taken the land and given it to the foreign speculators and to the twenty-seven governors of the twenty-seven states and to the generals he sends to hamstring the governors and keep the governors from obtaining too much power."

"Did you try to kill him?" Mr. Desmond said.

"I?" Jamie said. He laughed a laugh almost as mean-sounding as Gil's. "How could such as I get close enough to such as him? He cowers in the capital, and in the country we have his *rurales*, his governors, his army, his Americans and Englishmen and Swiss to whom he throws land like a bone to keep them building railroads and keep the people on their faces in dirt they cannot even own. Since you've heard of don Porfirio, you may have heard of his method—*pan o palo*."

"I've only picked up a little Spanish from cowmen and an occasional passer-by," said Mr. Desmond. "What does that mean?"

"Bread or . . . a stick. A club. In Mexico, since don Porfirio resumed the presidency, the *caudillos* do as they are told and are given bread. The people are given the club."

Gil was beginning to look interested. "It sounds like Rome in reverse," he said.

Jamie glanced at Gil and started to look back to Mr. Desmond, but then his manner underwent a change. It was as if he had been reminded that there were other people around, and that a conversation could be more than just a duologue. He seemed to make a conscious effort to relax, and he said to Gil, "I regret that I know little of Rome. In my school days they taught us little but Father Guzmán's catechism and the multiplication tables. Father Guzmán could not tell the rear end of a horse from the front, but he was excellent with the tables."

166

"What a pity," Gil said, in what I guessed he thought was a kindly fashion. "I suppose that means you've been taught little of political theory, and you know what Mill said—action or practice not based solidly on theory is not only valueless but possibly dangerous. Or was it someone else who said that?"

Now Jamie was stiffening again. He said, "How interesting."

Mr. Desmond said, "To hell with theories. What was it you done?"

Jamie seemed to think for a moment. Then he nodded and said, "My state, my land, Coahuila, has been given by don Porfirio to the Cuevas family. There are those of us who feel that one family should not own all the land. We have raided their haciendas. You speak of stealing cattle. We have stolen their cattle."

Mr. Desmond said, "And you shot a Cuevas."

Jamie nodded.

"A big one, or a little one?" Mr. Desmond asked.

"Just a little one. But even a little Cuevas is enough."

"And you didn't even look in his pockets to see if he had any money on him. You just lammed for the border."

"Lammed?" said Jamie.

"Ran. Fled," said Mr. Desmond.

Jamie nodded. "It was at the border that it happened. Or I would have . . . lammed? . . . for the sierras."

Mr. Desmond said, "More whiskey?"

"Thank you," Jamie said, passing his cup.

"Now what?" Mr. Desmond said.

Jamie said thoughtfully, "My problem is much the same as yours. There is too little money among my friends for ammunition. I concluded that since I had to lam for a space of time, I would rob rich gringos and take money with me when I slipped back into Mexico."

Gil said enthusiastically, "I thought so! You're an idealist. I can spot a fellow idealist every time."

"I see," Jamie said.

Gil burbled on, "You want to help the people. So do I. That's my ideal in life—to help the hundreds of thousands of oppressed peoples."

Jamie put down his cup. "Hundreds of thousands?" he said.

"I could name for you three men who need help right now. There is Ramón Torres, who dared to object when a *jefe político* raised the taxes on his field for the third time in one year and who now is hiding in the mountains to avoid being drafted very quickly into the army. There is Marcos de la Cardena, who stated in his newspaper that perhaps Mexico could accomplish social reform without the benefits of a dictatorship and who has disappeared into the Belén Penitentiary. Or if you prefer, there is Juan Moreno, a Yaqui chieftain who is still objecting to the sale of his people to the henequen plantations in the Yucatan for seventy-five pesos a head. If you really believe what you say, get on my horse with me, and we will ride to Mexico tonight and help these three men."

"But what good would that do?" Gil said. "Three men, help them and they're immediately replaced by three others who need help just as badly. We accomplish nothing."

Jamie said, "And what have you done for your hundreds of thousands?"

There was a sudden silence.

Gil said, "Well."

Emma laughed and said, "I guess that's telling you. Even a stranger can read you like a book—all talk and no action."

"Not always," Gil said.

"Prove it," Emma said gaily.

"Perhaps I will," Gil said.

There was an uncomfortable silence again, into which Calvin, naturally, said, "Not to change the subject, Jamie, but there's a little thing you could do for five people right now, if you cared to, and that is consider returning our arms. We'd take it very kindly. Uh, we told you the truth about getting shot at, and, uh, I can't believe that being a gentleman you'd sup with us and still keep our arms."

"Oh," Jamie said, sounding rattled. "A thousand pardons. I meant to return them, naturally. Excuse me, I will just go look for them. It was a rifle and a pistol and a shotgun, no? I am sure I hid them . . . I must have put them . . ."

Gil said to Emma, "For instance, if you're ready for that bath, I'll go beat the pond for you. Unless you're afraid to go without a chaperon, of course."

"What do I need with a chaperon?" Emma said.

Calvin said to Jamie, "Of course you have nothing to worry about. We wouldn't dream of shooting a supper guest, for we're all gentlemen here."

"Are we?" I growled.

Gil was on his feet and holding his hand down to Emma to help her rise. She hesitated, and he reached down, and, small as he was, he picked her up bodily and stood her on her feet. "It's quite dark now," he said.

"I don't think I'd better," she said. Her voice sounded giggly and small.

I looked at Mr. Desmond, but he didn't say anything. He was just watching Emma, with a waiting, watchful look.

"Come on," Gil said to her. He was a little unsteady on his feet, but Emma was even less steady. He put out his hand, and in the dying firelight I saw her take it.

I looked again at Mr. Desmond, but his face seemed to have gone shut, like a curtain coming down over a window, and he raised his cup and drank from it. Nothing more.

Gil said, "Everybody keep away from the pond for a while. Miss Prosser needs privacy."

"Goddamn you!" I said. "She's drunk!"

"I'll talk to you later," Gil said.

He led her into the darkness.

Jamie said to Mr. Desmond, "I would like to discuss your suggestion . . . am I right? . . . did you make that suggestion? . . . that I travel some farther west with you."

"Goddamn all of you!" I said. "Are you just going to let her go?" I struggled up as far as my knees, but Jamie took my arm in what felt like an unbreakable grasp.

"Hush," Mr. Desmond told me. "This isn't your affair."

"But she's drunk."

"She's not that drunk. Probably not as drunk as you."

"Damn you—"

"Hush," Mr. Desmond said. "A woman's just a woman, but she's not a child or a dog. She knows enough to make choices."

"But he's not even a man!" I said. "Have you ever seen a real man hardly more than five feet tall? He's only half a man."

"Hush," Mr. Desmond said, for the last time.

Calvin said, "He's not really going to do anything. He wouldn't. She wouldn't."

I said, "It's wrong, Calvin. It's all wrong."

Jamie said, sounding sad somehow, "It isn't always the strongest man who takes."

There were splashing sounds in the catch basin. I tried to pull loose from Jamie, but I made no progress.

Jamie said, "I started to ask about your suggestion. Another small drink? There seem to be two inches left in the bottle."

Calvin said, "Maybe not tonight. Maybe we've all had about enough to drink." And he started asking Jamie if he needed extra blankets, and if his horse was staked good, and I listened to the splashing sounds.

Jamie loosened his grip on me. I jerked away and stalked into the darkness. I promptly ran head-on into mesquite thorns and had to stop and untangle myself. Together with the splashing sounds, there were now voices, low and barely discernible. Calvin found me. He said, "Come on to bed."

Both Jamie and Mr. Desmond bedded down near us. I could hear the thump of their saddles as they dropped them, and then sounds as if they were brushing stones and thorns out from under where they planned to put their blanket rolls, but all the time I was listening for the low voices, two of them, down by the catch basin, and for the splashing sounds, which slowly died away.

After a while, old Nemo came and nosed me out and flopped down against my back and snuffled awhile and finally was silent except for his doggy breathing. I was glad to have him there. I listened for a long, long time. Once I thought I heard a sigh, as deep as the catch basin turning in its sleep, and, if I strained my ears and imagined hard, the sporadic, low sound of a murmur, a whisper.

It seemed like hours, and finally I said, I don't know whether to Nemo on one side or Calvin on the other, in a whisper that was near a sob, "Oh! Why?"

"Shhhh," Calvin said. "You're too young, and I'm too ugly. Besides, nothing's really happening anyway."

"He's too short," I said.

"Would you rather he'd been too old, like your father?" Calvin whispered.

I had not realized before that he understood me so well.

We went to sleep.

No one new tried to murder us in the night, and none of us tried to murder one another, and Mr. Desmond called a council the next morning.

That Mr. Desmond could even speak or move was proof to me, if I needed it, that he was a man given over to occasional heavy drinking. I could barely raise my head off my quilt. It seemed to me that if my teacher had spoken frankly about hangovers, instead of stuff like producing idiot children, he might have been a good deal more persuasive in his temperance teaching.

But Mr. Desmond, short of having those reddened eyes, acted the way he always did. Well, not quite. He seemed even quieter than usual, and he called Emma, when he spoke to her that day, Miss Prosser instead of Emma. But he hadn't stopped speaking to her, and he didn't even act particularly funny around her, although she acted funny enough for all of us, hardly saying a word, especially not to Gil, and her eyes acting as though she couldn't decide between keeping them down so she wouldn't have to look at anyone, or keeping them up so she could stare us in the eye. Gil acted strangest of all, color coming into his face any time anybody glanced at him, and generally acting hangdog. Emma's quilts that morning were just about where she always placed them, near the side of the wagon, and Gil's blankets were in their customary locale near Calvin's. Both sets of bedding looked slept on. So I didn't know exactly what all had gone on, except that Emma's hair was clean, which might have accounted for at least some of the splashing in the catch basin. The way I felt after those tequila toddies, I wasn't sure just then that I cared.

I managed to sip a little coffee and listen, at first apprehensively, to Mr. Desmond when he made his speech. But this is all he said:

We were moving too slow. At the rate we were going, it would take us ten or twelve more days even to reach El Paso, and the thing for us to do was to stop piddling around with penny-ante photographs and start traveling fast.

I thought of Otis and Shirley Wasum behind us and Gil's August tenth deadline in Tombstone ahead of us, but aloud I objected feebly, "We got no travel funds to speak of as is, and how are we going to eat if we stop trying to make money with Calvin's photography?"

"We'll live off the land," Mr. Desmond said. "Boy, you don't seem to realize what we're up against. There's hardly a town anyway, except for El Paso, between here and where we're going, and hardly no people except those you got following you."

Emma seemed to rouse herself. She said quietly, "If you're worrying about me getting shot at, you can stop. I can take my chances as well as anybody else, and better than some. Don't think you have to start us galloping through the countryside just for my benefit."

Mr. Desmond poured himself another cup of coffee. It was Arbuckle's and should have been good, but none of us had been operating at top efficiency that morning, and Mr. Desmond gave Emma a sideways look.

"Well, I wasn't exactly thinking on you," he said. "There's Pepper to think about too, as fifteen is no age to get shot and have to stop living your life before you've even got started good. I was thinking about everyone." He turned his eyes to Jamie. "What do you think?" he said. "Doesn't it make sense to speed up if we're ever going to get through New Mexico and into Arizona Territory?"

Jamie nodded and said, "I would have to leave you before you go into El Paso, I think, as there are Cuevas connections there, but I could meet you again on the other side."

I was beginning to come to life a little. I said, "Are you coming with us?"

Jamie said, "Perhaps you would rather I did not?"

Mr. Desmond said, "No indeed, if you want to make a lot of money, then Arizona Territory is the place you ought to head with us. From what I hear, there's not a train or a stage or a shipment of bullion that goes out without there being some gang on hand to rob it. If you're really good with that gun, I'd think any gang would be glad to take you on."

I said, "Oh, no, not a gang."

"Why not?" Mr. Desmond said. "That seems the way they do it. One man by himself couldn't take a whole train. A man by himself can only rob some ragtag outfit that's only got two dollars and forty-three cents."

"But a gang—" I said.

Calvin said, "If you're thinking about the Wasums, Jamie wouldn't tie up with the likes of them. They're small potatoes, if all they can do is rob some faro game. He'd want a proper gang, wouldn't you, Jamie?"

I said, maybe thinking of my teacher's opinion on alcohol, "I believe I must be going crazy."

Mr. Desmond said, "I believe what you need is a hair of the dog."

But I declined. And that was all that was said. Nothing else happened that day except that Gil offered, for the first time, to help Emma with the dishes, and then to help her get the cooking stuff packed up, and then to help her carry water to douse the fire. She turned him down cold every time.

We all traveled on together, and we traveled fast, too, trying for thirty miles a day or better, all according to Mr. Desmond's plan. True to his prediction, we encountered hardly another living soul except at the Pecos crossing, and even there he wouldn't let us stop to try to do photographic business. He wouldn't let Calvin stop every other mile to take views, either. I must say I was in harmony with any scheme that would prevent Calvin from using up so many photographic supplies, but, on the other hand, it seemed to me that Mr. Desmond's concern for the group was somehow infringing on Calvin's individual rights. Naturally, Calvin, as always, refused to take up for himself, and that made me cranky. In fact, the way things went until we next encountered Otis and Shirley Wasum, I was feeling crankier by the mile, but I wasn't sure just who I should be mad at. Mr. Desmond? Calvin? And God knows I was far from happy with either Emma or Gil, after the way they had acted. Even Jamie could get on my nerves without half trying, because he seemed to have accepted Mr. Desmond as our personal *presidente*, and no one ever bothered to consult me any more when it came to when we should start and when we should stop and what places we should choose to camp. It was almost a relief to meet Otis and Shirley again. With them, I at least knew who was the enemy, and who were my friends.

Ten

This time, Otis and Shirley and their traveling companions made no sloppy, ill-prepared attack: they seemed to have adopted one of my maxims and made a careful plan. It happened after we had forded the Pecos at Horsehead Crossing, then turned sharply up the west bank toward Pope's Camp, then west again to snake through the Guadalupe Mountains via a gap between the sheer cliff of the Capitan to the north and the Delaware Mountains to the south. Mr. Desmond was anxious for us to get off the Butterfield and try to shake the Wasums that way, but, considering where we were and where we wished to head, the rest of us voted that our best choice would be to continue on the Butterfield until it got us through the mountains. Jamie said he didn't know the area this side of the border and he refused to vote.

The foothills on the west side of the pass were where Otis and the others laid for us. This was dry country, sloping slowly down to a big salt flat, and the hills were dotted with little more than sparse bunches of bear grass and devil's-pencushion and what Jamie said was something called ocotillo and sotol. It was very hot. We were all in the wagon.

That was Jamie's idea. Or, as the rest of us shared the idea, it was his ruse to get Mr. Desmond there. Mr. Desmond had laid off the bust-skull since the night we met Jamie, but he still wasn't feeling well, and this was apparent to all of us. So what

Jamie did was to convince Mr. Desmond that they should pitch their saddles in the dark-box and rig their horses, his black and Mr. Desmond's roan, with the extra harness to help the mules get the wagon up the pass that morning, then switch them to the rear in the event we needed additional braking power coming down that afternoon. It shows how poorly Mr. Desmond felt that he fell for this, for the pass wasn't really a bad one, and the mules could have gotten us over it by themselves without much difficulty.

Mr. Desmond, sort of nodding what with the heat and his illness, was sitting in the spring seat beside Emma and me. Jamie and Calvin were doing their own drowsy nodding on the bench in back, Jamie perhaps regretting his kindly plan to let Mr. Desmond rest in the wagon because of Gil's droning. Gil was still hesitant about talking directly to Emma, but he'd taken up talking what sounded strangely big-mouth to me in her hearing. For instance, he currently talked not about himself but about the British all the time. For breakfast, he had told how the British were pouring surplus sons like Freddie Fassnidge into the New World through ports such as Galveston, and, he assumed, San Francisco, and opined that the surface of the earth was passing into Anglo-Saxon hands. At that moment, he was holding forth about California and how a white colonist there had three main ways of taking possession of California soil: first, marry an estate, in that dark women liked fair men, and if a half-breed girl was taken from her people young, she could be trained in English ways until she learned to be a decent wife. Second, lend money in small sums to any reckless native known to have good sheep-runs and extensive water rights, then take his land when he failed to repay those sums. Third, form an Anglo-Saxon Club with three or four other white squatters handy with bowie knives and rifles, and swear to stand by each other shoulder to shoulder and rifle to rifle, since an English hunter after an estate could seldom be foiled by an inferior race. That he was, as always now, talking for Emma's benefit was evident in the fact that he overlooked Jamie's being what he so casually classed as a "half-breed," a "native," and a member of "an inferior race."

Jamie said nothing. We crossed a little wash where there was a rare sight, some trees, and off to the side of the road in front of us a common sight, some high rocks. Then, suddenly, atop the dark-box, there was a loud thump.

I was supposed to be keeping my eyes open, but I had been half-drowsing myself. I was startled. I jerked the lines, and the mules stumbled and slowed. There was another thump, this time on the canopy, then a tearing sound, then suddenly a man's foot was dangling down through the canvas right by my ear.

"Good God almighty!" I said.

The shooting started then, from high in the rocks.

I wasted a precious second glancing at Mr. Desmond for instructions, but he was looking confused and had grabbed up neither his rifle nor the big Navy Colt that he wore at his side. I did the first thing that occurred to me. I slewed the mules around, almost toppling the wagon in the soft sand of the wash, and turned tail back the way we had come.

Simultaneously, Jamie seized the foot that was struggling and kicking, and hung on for dear life. The owner of the foot responded by beginning to rip at the canvas. A hand came through, which Jamie grabbed at but missed, then the hole in the canvas widened and a black face with white teeth clamped tight together appeared.

Three things happened in the next twitch of time. There was an abrupt, heavy tug from the rear, and we slowed down. The man on top of the canopy stuck a pistol not three inches from Jamie's nose. And in one smooth motion Calvin leaned forward and pulled Mr. Desmond's Navy Colt from his holster, raised it, and fired directly at the grimacing face above us.

The man fell through the hole in the canopy on top of me. He was bleeding copiously from a red wound on the side of his head. I yelled and tried to struggle out from under him, and I felt the lines yanked out of my hands.

"Oh God!" I cried and shoved hard. The man slithered down across my knees and lay bleeding all over my feet. There were still shots from the rocks, and shouts, and nearly busting my eardrums there began to be return fire from our wagon. Mr. Desmond leaned over the side of the wagon and fired rapidly with his rifle. Jamie was on his feet and with his head and shoulders through the hole in the canopy and firing over the top. Gil popped away with his little pistol. Calvin, trying hard to stay out of Mr. Desmond's way, cut loose methodically with Mr. Desmond's Colt. Nemo ran furiously in back of the wagon and managed to find breath from time to time to bark. Emma had the lines and was whipping the mules and cussing them on as though she had been born a mule skinner.

"Get off the road!" Mr. Desmond shouted to her. "Get us out of sight!"

She wheeled the mules and took off around the side of a hill. Glass plates and bottles shattering in the dark-box added to the din.

"They've shot your horse," Gil shouted at Mr. Desmond.

"I know," he shouted back, "and he's a dead weight. Can you clamber back and cut the lines?"

"I'll try," Gil said.

How he managed to hold on and scale around the side of the dark-box to where Jamie's black was helping drag Mr. Desmond's roan was something I'll never know, because Emma gave no consideration to rocks or cactus or anything else as she whipped the mules around the hill. But Gil did it. The wagon suddenly shot forward, relieved of the drag, and Jamie's horse ran beside us, trailing patchy bits of old wagon harness and the heavy ammoniac smell of a scared horse, and we careened on until we had the hill between us and the Wasums.

Emma spotted another rocky wash and headed us down to it. The black man was still bleeding on my feet, but when Emma said, "Pepper, can you take the reins now?" I took them immediately. She moved her skirts daintily aside from the blood, which meant away from me as well as from the man, for he'd bled so much that I could feel the sticky moisture seeping through my bootlaces. We clattered and bumped down the draw, the shooting ended at least for the moment, until Mr. Desmond saw an area filled with enough larger rocks and tall hedges of cactus to hide a whole fleet of What's-It Wagons and told me to snake our way into the middle of it.

We all jumped out, me quickest in order to get away from that blood, and Jamie ran to coax his horse to come to him, and Mr. Desmond and I ran to hold the nervous, panting mules.

"I never even fired a shot!" I said to Mr. Desmond.

"Never mind," he said. "You did fine." To Emma, shaking her skirts by the wagon, he said, "You too. I don't know where you learned to do it, but you drove those mules just fine."

She murmured a "Thank you," color rising on her dust-covered face.

And then we rapidly got down to work. Mr. Desmond, who had run out of rifle bullets, took back his Navy Colt from Calvin at the same time Jamie returned with his lathered horse.

"They may try to follow us," Jamie said.

"I know."

Gil said, "I'll stand guard on the top of the hill. If you hear me fire, you'll know they're coming."

"You might as well wait until they're in range, then, and fire directly at them," Mr. Desmond said.

"I intend to," Gil said.

Mr. Desmond nodded, not grudgingly. He and Gil hadn't had much to say to each other since Emma got her hair washed, and this perhaps was their longest conversation.

Mr. Desmond said, "I expect things were right busy for you back there, but did you have a chance to notice if my horse seemed dead, or just wounded?"

"Dead, I'm afraid," Gil said.

"That's good," Mr. Desmond said. "Better dead than sore wounded and left behind. I thank you."

"No thanks needed," Gil said. He paused a moment and looked at Emma, but she looked away from him, as she now had a way of doing. Gil gestured and said to Mr. Desmond, "That hill?" There were a half dozen to choose from.

"It looks best," Mr. Desmond said.

And Gil started off.

Mr. Desmond called after him, "Keep to cover. They may try to sneak up on us."

Gil waved in acknowledgment and kept going.

"I will watch at the head of the arroyo," Jamie said. "Have you still ammunition for the Colt?"

"Yes, enough. What about that colored man's gun? Did we lose it off the wagon?"

Leaving me to hold the animals, they went to see, quietly discussing guard positions and whether Gil could be relied upon to keep a cool head in an emergency, and who should stay with the wagon and who should attempt a watch to the south in the event Otis and the others tried to circle around that way. This was all done quickly. Probably not two minutes had elapsed since we had hidden the wagon in our cactus patch, and Nemo's and the mules' sides were still heaving hard from the running they'd had to do.

They lifted the man out of the wagon. He was alive. He groaned and spoke.

"Please hep a poor nigger," he said. "Dey made me do it. I jes a pore nigger, and dat Mist' Clinkscale, he allus save de worse work fo me."

The voice was halting but obsequious. Calvin said, "You don't have to talk that way around us unless that's just the way you're used to talking. We aren't going to do anything to you."

The voice changed. "Oh God, my head," he moaned. "Oh God, how it hurts."

Emma said, "I'd better take a look at him. Move over, Calvin."

"Help me," the black man said. "Oh God, missus, how my head does hurt. Help a poor man that never wanted to do you no harm."

She knelt beside him, and the voice subsided into wordless groans. Calvin came to me, looking sick.

"You couldn't help it," I said. "He'd have shot Jamie."

"He's in terrible pain," Calvin said, the sick look not diminishing.

"You'd best take my shotgun and go keep watch," I said.

That's the way we arranged things. The wounded man's gun had apparently bounced out of the wagon, so with no bullets for Mr. Desmond's rifle we were one gun short. Mr. Desmond and his Colt stayed behind with me and, more particularly, with Emma. I think Jamie and Mr. Desmond would have preferred that I, rather than Calvin, take the shotgun watch to the south, but, after all, Calvin had proved that day that he could hit what he aimed at when it was necessary, and Jamie spoke on that briefly before he went up the wash and Calvin went the other way through the cactus.

"I am indebted to you," Jamie said to Calvin.

"No, no," Calvin said.

"I will hope to have an opportunity to repay my debt," Jamie said in a quiet but determined fashion.

Mr. Desmond said, "Your opportunity might be waiting for you right this minute up that draw. You two had better get along now." You could never tell about Mr. Desmond, but I think he said it to save Calvin the embarrassment of being thanked any more. I was beginning to learn that the most unexpected people could be unexpectedly considerate at times.

Calvin went, looking glad to get away from the injured man's groans, and I couldn't blame him. Emma had jumped right into the task of tending the man. He moaned piteously when, at her insistence, we lifted him onto one of her quilts in the little bit of shade cast by the wagon. She bandaged his head, and the bleeding seemed to slow if not to stop. She gave him water, of which we didn't have very much, not enough for our winded and thirsty stock, and the man's suffering and the animals' lesser but still actual suffering bothered me more than I cared for Mr. Desmond to see.

But he saw. He said, "He won't last long. He's mostly bled out."

I looked at my boots and my bloody pants legs. Flies, finding us in the middle of nowhere as flies always will, were already beginning to buzz around the drying blood. "I guess so," I said.

"Come sit with me," he said. "I could use your young eyes to help me watch for any trouble that might succeed in slipping past our outposts."

"Shouldn't I try to help Emma?" I said. We both looked at her. Flies must have been after the wounded man, for she took the man's hat and knelt beside him and started rhythmically fanning him with it.

"No," Mr. Desmond said. "Seeing after the dying, that's one of the things women do best. And she's done it before. You know what she told us about her daddy."

So we went and sat together on a sloping chunk of rock maybe fifteen yards from the wagon. It was in the full sun, and sweat was dripping down Mr. Desmond's face and adding new contours to the sweat stain on his hat, but even though I thought perhaps he shouldn't be there, feeling ill and all, I didn't dare say it. He established himself on the rock, pistol held loosely in one hand and eyes roving the cactus hedges. Nemo came and lay down in about two inches of shade that the rock cast and within a few seconds was wheezy-snoring. I wished he wouldn't. I was watching and trying to listen, and Nemo's wheezing and the wounded man's sporadic moans made it harder.

After a while, Mr. Desmond said, "What're those boys like?"

"Otis and Shirley?" I said. "They're just as ordinary as the day is long. Shirley always had a kind of a wild hair, but I wouldn't have called him mean. Just hotheaded and stubborn. Once he makes up his mind to something, there isn't much way to go changing it."

"And that other boy?"

"Otis is the quiet one," I said. "I don't know where he found the gumption to keep coming at us this way."

"He got a daddy?" Mr. Desmond asked.

"Yessir. A mother, too. And four big brothers besides Shirley. He's got all the family anybody could use."

"That depends," Mr. Desmond said. "Do they pay any attention to him?"

"I think it's the other way around," I said. "I don't think he pays much attention to them. Except his momma. They say he stays around home all the time and helps her. They say he carves her little things. Not just whittling, but real little animals and people, carved out of cypress knees, each as perfect as can be."

"A momma's boy, that's not good," Mr. Desmond said.

"I wouldn't know," I said, "as my mother died when I wasn't much more than walking. I always thought it might be nice to have a mother around at least part of the time. A real mother, I mean."

"If you have to choose, a father's better," Mr. Desmond said. "A father can teach a boy things."

"Oh, Otis honors his father," I said. "All the Wasum boys do. Mr. Wasum, he's the one they all try to live up to."

"Did his momma and daddy get along?"

"Folks said not," I said. "Otis told me once they yelled at each other a lot. He said they threw things at each other."

Mr. Desmond nodded. His eyes roved over Emma and roved on to rocks and cactus. "I'll tell you this," he said. "It's better for a boy not to have a mother than to have the wrong kind."

"But Otis liked her," I said. "He always stayed home with her."

"He's not home with her now," Mr. Desmond said.

That was true. He might be out crawling on his belly through the cactus right now, scrunching along beside Shirley and trying to get a bead on us. I got my eyes busy again, helping Mr. Desmond, but I thought about Otis.

He had worked awhile at the store, until our fathers had their trouble and he quit. I think Uncle Dawkins would have fired him anyway, because the day-money kept coming up short. But while he was still there we'd talk sometimes, although he would never talk much. Sometimes he talked about how he might better himself and move away from the Wasum homestead to become a railroad engineer. But he never did anything about it. He wouldn't even go to school, which I figured was mandatory to become a railroad engineer. What he did was, he had apprenticed to a carpenter, Mr. Stakousky in Germantown, in our parish, but it didn't work out and he eventually came to Uncle Dawkins's store, which didn't work out. He talked some about those German people, especially Countess Von Leon, who was head of the colony, the count having died, and how she taught her daughters music on a board laid off as a piano, not having a piano, and how she had a set of Masonic regalia set with precious stones, left to her by her husband the count. Otis talked an unusual amount for him, now that I thought of it, about those precious stones.

I told that to Mr. Desmond and asked if he thought Otis was after Calvin's fifty-dollar camera, but Mr. Desmond said he couldn't figure it.

"I can see how that older boy got into trouble with the law," he said. "But what about that younger one? Has he ever been in trouble with the law?"

"Once," I said. "Once he threw a brick through the window of the school on awards night. He just stood outside and waited until they came and arrested him, and his father went and got him out. That Mr. Wasum, it looked like he never could decide between being too nice or too mean to Otis. They say that time he beat him with a buggy whip until Otis fell down. Do you hold with beating boys?"

"When they need it," Mr. Desmond said, "though I never took

a buggy whip to my own boys. Spanking's good enough. Was it a buggy whip caused the trouble between you and your daddy?"

"I never had trouble with my father," I said, looking away.

"Oh?" he said. "I guess I got the idea somehow that you did. I wondered if maybe he was being touchy because he was new-married. Men are like that. They get themselves a new woman, and it makes them touchy to have another man around."

Well, his speaking like I was a grown man was very pleasing to me, and his words certainly cast a new and interesting light on my father's behavior. I said, "When you got married the second time, did you get so touchy that you sent your first set of boys away?"

He smiled, that tiny movement at the corners of his mouth that showed he was tickled. "No," he said, "they went when they got grown up and restless, and they know they got a loving welcome with me anytime and anywhere, father to son and man to man. But you know, Pepper, if your daddy sent you off, well, I don't know the facts between the two of you, but have you ever thought he might just have been worried about that Wasum trouble you've mentioned, and used any old excuse he came by to get you out of harm's way for a while?"

Well, that was the second new and interesting thought that Mr. Desmond had given me, but before I could decide what to think of it, Emma called to us, "Come here!"

We went on the run, Mr. Desmond's pistol tight in his hand and his eyes searching around the cactus, and he got after Emma when she only said, "Tell them what you told me, Jim. This man is Jim Spoonts."

"Don't be yelling that way over nothing," Mr. Desmond said.

"It isn't nothing. Tell them, Jim."

Jim Spoonts looked up at us. One eye was heavily bloodshot now, and his breathing was very uneven. We knelt beside Emma and looked down at him.

"Tell them about the photograph," Emma coaxed.

Jim Spoonts seemed to work to get his breathing under control. He said, "Like I told miss, that little sonabitch, he lied to Mist' Clinkscale."

"Don't talk that way around a lady," Mr. Desmond said.

"I'm sorry, miss," Jim Spoonts said. "It's my head hurting so. I forgot."

"All right, go on telling," she said.

"God, it does hurt," Jim Spoonts said foggily.

Emma said to us, "Your Otis Wasum told the others that Calvin took a photograph of them. He said Calvin took it when he threw that flash powder in the fire that night. He's got them all scared that the law can track them down with that nonexistent photograph. That's why they're after us. If they can get us and what they think is the photograph, they think they can change their names and disappear West somewhere. Isn't that right, Jim?"

"Yes, miss," Jim Spoonts said.

"One's Sidney Clinkscale, and one's named Cass Hubbard. They're the ones that did that robbing and murdering in Denton County. They made Jim help them. Isn't that right, Jim?"

"Yes, yes, miss," he said. "I never wanted to hurt nobody. The worse thing I ever did was stealing chickens when Mist' Clinkscale caught me, and he made me help him or it would be the law. That big sonabitch. He always saved the worse work for me."

"Well, well," Mr. Desmond said musingly. I could tell that he hadn't even noticed the second "sonabitch."

"Lord God, my head," Jim Spoonts said. "Maybe it wouldn't feel so bad if I had a little drop of something. Mist', help a poor man. Give him a little drop of something."

Mr. Desmond started to rise, but Emma said, "No, a bad head wound, he doesn't need anything like that."

"It's not going to hurt him," Mr. Desmond said.

Jim Spoonts said, "Am I going to die, mist'?"

"Maybe not," Mr. Desmond said.

"Oh, oh," Jim Spoonts groaned. "This is some way to go. Help me pray, mist'. I did more than I told you. I did more than just stealing chickens."

"Look in the dark-box, Emma, and see if there's a whiskey bottle that didn't get broke," Mr. Desmond said. "There should have been two in my saddlebags." He maintained his kneeling position beside Jim Spoonts and said to him, "I'll help you."

"A little whiskey, that'll help more," Jim Spoonts said, sounding foggy again.

"You can have both," Mr. Desmond said. "Here, Pepper, take my Colt for a minute, and keep on the lookout."

"Wanted to get rich," Jim Spoonts said. "Helped kill three men, and all I was thinking about was calf-skin boots that lace to the knee."

"Tell God," Mr. Desmond said quietly. "Ask him to forgive you."

Well, back home I went to church with Grandmother every Sunday, but I couldn't have done what Mr. Desmond did. He helped Jim Spoonts pray, and Emma and I opened the dark-box and stared at the mess of broken glass inside.

"This will just about break Calvin's heart," I said, staring. Emma started to reach in and brush stuff off the two saddles that were on the floor of the dark-box, but I wouldn't let her. There were spilled chemicals everywhere. And some spilled whiskey. Only one of Mr. Desmond's bottles of bust-skull was intact.

"This stuff will kill that poor man," Emma whispered.

"I fear he's dying anyway," I whispered back. "God, but it's taking a long time."

"Not many rush to die," Emma said.

We took the whiskey and closed the dark-box. Emma wiped the bottle off on her skirts, already soiled with blood, and I didn't have the heart to tell her that some of those chemicals could eat holes in cast iron. Old Jim was muttering and not making much sense when we went back to him. Mr. Desmond rose and held out his hand to me for his pistol.

"How much shall I give him?" Emma said, indicating the whiskey bottle.

"As much as he wants," Mr. Desmond said. "It won't make no difference."

He went back and sat on his rock. I tagged along, feeling lost. Nemo's shade, in which he was still sleeping, had grown to maybe three inches by now. I leaned over and stroked his head.

Mr. Desmond said, "You like old Nemo, don't you."

"Sure," I said.

"He was my boys' dog," Mr. Desmond said. "The first set

186

that's grown now. The second set's mother didn't like him, so I kept him with me. But they liked him. They'll be glad to see him when I go back and fetch them."

"Mr. Desmond," I said, "do you really believe in God?"

His little smile flickered and then his face went grim. "Yes," he said, "I believe in God, and I believe in a man named Jesus. You couldn't go on unless you believed in a power greater than the stench of man."

As always, when things began to get quiet or I began to get interested in a conversation, shooting started.

It was from Gil's hill.

"Uh-oh," Mr. Desmond said. Sick or not, he came off his rock like the red fox way back in Denton County had come away from the spring at which I spotted it drinking, and like it he was running toward the hill before I could even be sure he had moved. I ran after him. He paused. "No," he said. "Stay with Emma."

"What for?" I said. "I got no gun."

He glanced up the hill and then at me, and something came into his eyes. He handed me the pistol. "Run," he said. "You're a good shot. Help him if you can, because if I must I can defend Emma with my bare hands."

I ran. I hit every last cactus plant on that hillside on my way up. Gil's little pistol popped three times as I scrambled upward, but there seemed to be little answering fire, and I didn't bother to keep my head down.

I arrived at the top of the hill, and Gil, red in the face as a banty rooster's comb, whirled and fiercely faced me with his pistol. Then he saw it was me and started dancing up and down. "I got one of them!" he said. "I got one, Pepper! Pepper, run back and tell Emma!"

There was dust on the side of the next hill, hanging in the air, and I thought I could hear horses' hooves pounding fast away. "Where is he?" I said, my eyes raking the hillside.

Gil settled down a bit. "Well, I just wounded him," he said. "At least I think I did. I saw him grab his leg."

"Which one?" I said.

"How would I know?" he said. "Well, at least I scared them off. You should have seen them scamper, Pepper. Run down and tell Emma. Oh hell, forget it, I'll go tell her. They won't be back, I'll bet my life on it. Just stay here and make sure."

It seemed to me that it was my life that he was betting, but away he ran before I could say boo, so I stood on the top of the hill and clutched Mr. Desmond's pistol and looked all around, except when I glanced at the cactus spines that peppered my flesh and my clothes and tried to remove two or three hundred of them.

I had that long before Gil came plodding back up the hill, looking morose. I took it that even running off a gang of murderers hadn't enticed Emma into changing her new manner of dignified indifference to him.

Gil took a position by my side and said, "Any fresh sign of them?"

"No," I said.

"I didn't think they'd be back," he said.

"What did Mr. Desmond think?" I asked.

His eyes flashed at me. "He agrees they may be frightened off for the day," he said. "But I decided it would be better to continue to keep watch. You can go back now. He wants his pistol, and he wants you as a runner to go report to Jamie and Calvin what happened."

"Did that Jim Spoonts die yet?" I said.

"You mean that nigger?" he said.

"Yes."

"Not yet," Gil said.

Jim Spoonts didn't, until nearly nightfall. It bothered Calvin terribly. Calvin wanted to stay and keep watch from a rise of rocks he had found to the south, I believe because of poor Jim Spoonts dying from the bullet Calvin had put in the side of his head, but as the afternoon wore on without anything further happening, Mr. Desmond decided it was best to bring our pickets in to watch the camp. Also, he said, we'd take turns standing guard that night, and he advised that now was a good time to get a little advance sleep. Jamie wouldn't. Calvin wouldn't. Gil wouldn't even budge off his hilltop.

It came down to sitting in a dry camp without water or much graze for the stock and listening to Jim Spoonts die. Sometimes he prayed. Sometimes he talked about calf-skin boots laced all the way to the knee. Once he talked about a girl called Ruby. And once he roused and asked us to write his old mother and tell her his fate.

When he did that, Emma called to Calvin and me to come, because she was an Ohio girl, and he was talking so foggily that she couldn't understand him.

Lyman, he said, north of Gulfport, Mississippi.

Calvin gulped, and it was I who spoke up:

"Your mother's named Lyman, and we write her in care of Gulfport, Mississippi?"

"Lyman?" he said. "No, her name Spoonts. Josie Spoonts. You write Miss Thea Spoonts in Lyman, and she'll ride out and tell my ma."

"All right," I said, "we will."

Emma said, "But what's her name? Josie or Thea?"

I said, "Josie's his ma, and Miss Thea's a white lady who'll ride out and read his ma our letter."

"Both named Spoonts?" Emma said.

"Sure," I said.

"Well I never," Emma said.

Jim Spoonts said, "My little old momma. I would have bought her Sunday shoes. Calf-skin too, if she wanted."

"That's all right," I said to him.

Calvin turned away, the sick look even stronger on his face, but Calvin was a man with a code of life, and although he turned his face away he stood still and kept listening.

"Hold on," Jim Spoonts said. "Hold on."

I thought he was admonishing himself to hold on to the little spark of life still left in him, but it turned out he wasn't. He was somewhere else, in some other time, and he said, "Hold on tight! She's running!" So I thought he was talking about jumping on top of our wagon and us running away with him stuck up there, but that wasn't it either. Because he said, "Let go my hair, Wyatt. Giddup. Giddup. Ooooowheeeeeeeeeee! Let go my hair, Wyatt, you not gonna fall."

A pasture? Near the town of Lyman, north of Gulfport, Mississippi? Clinging to a mare or a milk cow and kicking her hard in the sides to give some little black boy named Wyatt a fine, exhilarating scare? He lapsed into mumbling after that, and I didn't learn, and Calvin, listening unwillingly but listening, didn't learn either. By and by the mumbling stopped and there was just a struggle to breathe. It was pretty bad.

Well, Emma and Jamie and Mr. Desmond possibly all saw that it was bad for Calvin, for they all said Jim Spoonts was just about gone, and we should take tools and my shotgun and go off and find a clear spot in the cactus and rocks and start digging. They said it out loud, so I thought it was so, and I saw they all agreed that Jim Spoonts was too near dead to be able to hear our digging sound and anticipate what it would mean to him. But we went a good distance off. So far that Jamie maybe got nervous about Otis and Shirley and their gang, because he came and stood his guard where we were digging. We had only one shovel, carried along to dig the wagon out of loose sand when we hit it, and the ground must have been pure caliche, Jamie said, and it was hard work. Pretty soon he holstered his pistol and took up an old piece of wagon rim and started to help us.

Far, far to the south, puffs of black smoke appeared in the sky, spaced out from horizon to horizon. We all stopped and watched for a minute, maybe all hoping it was Otis and Shirley Wasum caught in a prairie fire and burning to a small, harmless crisp. Or perhaps it was just me, for Jamie looked questioningly at Calvin, and Calvin said, "The Texas & Pacific, maybe. It's supposed to dip south to join the Southern Pacific tracks somewhere around here."

Jamie looked a moment longer at the smoke, then spat and said, "Trains. Less land for the people."

Because of the tone in which he said it, Calvin said, "You sound like Gil. He calls progress the 'bitch-goddess of getting-on' and says we're sacrificing everything on her altar."

"I only know what is being done to my country in the name of progress," Jamie said. "In Mexico we pay the price of don Porfirio's progress with the coins of blood."

"Now you both sound sort of like Mr. Desmond," I said. "He hates progress, but I think he just means because the buffalo are mostly gone, which is queer because he helped kill them all."

"It is the *caudillos* who benefit from progress, and the people who pay," Jamie said absently. "I know nothing of buffaloes,

but about people I know." I thought he was just talking to keep
Calvin from thinking, but if so he forgot, for he nodded back
toward the wagon and said, "That black man there, what has he
gotten from your famous progress? Not even a pair of boots that
lace up to the knees."

"Well," I said, trying to get the subject back on unimportant
things and away from Jim Spoonts, "you and Gil and Mr. Desmond got more in common than you realize, for that's just the
kind of thing they'd say."

"Gil and I have nothing in common," Jamie said. "I realize
that he is your friend, but he insults me twenty times a day with
his bigotry. I was considering shooting him this morning when
the others almost succeeded in doing it for me."

"Oh, no, now," Calvin said, "Gil don't mean nothing by it.
That's just his way. He insults all of us, but he don't mean to.
He keeps calling us colonials all the time."

Jamie laughed. Against dark skin, teeth can look very white.
"Do not fear," he said. "I was only irritated. I had no real
thought of shooting him."

I said, "How much deeper shall we dig?"

"Much deeper," Jamie said. "The animals could reach the body
at this depth. Let us try for at least a half meter more, and then
if we must we can gather rocks to pile on the grave to protect
him. A man must be buried with dignity."

"The poor sonofabitch," Calvin said unhappily.

"Don't cuss," I said, but it did no good, because Calvin didn't
think to smile or let it distract him.

Jamie tried. He said, "My friend, it would be my grave whose
depth you were considering now if you had not shot him. I am
sorry that it troubles you. But I would much rather it be that
man than me."

I tried some more. I said, "Besides, Calvin, he's only a
nigger."

Jamie looked at me and dropped his piece of wagon rim and
backhanded me full in the face.

I toppled. There was that much force behind the blow. I fell
into the partly dug grave.

Groggily, I saw Calvin's face as he reached to help me to my
feet. He looked wide-eyed and startled, and he stared from Jamie

to me, and another reaction was waiting to flicker in his eyes, but Jamie forestalled it.

"No," he said. "I will listen to that from a poor ignorant foreigner like the Englishman. But not from this boy. He is one of us. He must learn better."

"Gil's one of us too," Calvin said.

Jamie looked rueful. "Ah," he said. "Perhaps you are right."

Calvin, still looking undecided, said, "Anyway, you didn't have to hit him so hard."

I staggered upright. "No," I said, "it's all right."

Jamie reached a hand to help hold me steady, and I didn't try to shake it off. He said, "Then you understand?"

"Maybe," I said. "I guess so."

But I didn't. It wasn't until near nightfall, and Mr. Desmond and Jamie coming carrying the mortal coils of Jim Spoonts, and I and Calvin helping them bury him, Emma standing quiet and with bloodstained skirts to the side. And then it seemed to me like spanking a boy when he needed it. I was near, but I wasn't quite grown up yet.

Eleven

The full casualties of the ambush were: Jim Spoonts; the Butterfield route, which we all agreed we must leave if we were to shake Otis and Shirley off our trail; El Paso, which would have been on the Butterfield; my right cheek, which was good and puffy for the several days it took us to struggle along on what was not much better than a goat trail up across the New Mexico line, where we were now; and just about all of Calvin's chemicals and plates to breakage, including most of the new views he had shot of Western scenes and hoped to send to the New York magazines.

Another type of casualty was Jamie, who was about to leave us that day and had only waited to see if Calvin had gotten yet another potential casualty, his big camera, fixed. He watched tensely as Calvin instructed Mr. Desmond, "Now be real still. Real . . . Good! You can move now!"

Mr. Desmond did, from the half-kneeling position he had held over the deer, our very first one, that he had just brought down with my shotgun, and Jamie asked Calvin anxiously, "Does it work? Have you repaired the breech?" This referred to a hairline split that had appeared in the mahogany frame of Calvin's camera after the bumpy flight from the ambush, and which Calvin had discovered was allowing extra light to seep in and ruin his plates. He had been working most of the morning, trying to mend the crack with sawdust and pitch.

"I won't know for sure until I develop the plate," Calvin said. He rushed into the dark-box and closed the door after him.

"Do you think it is repaired?" Jamie repeated to me, his angular face creased into a worried frown.

"I hope so," I said.

We had all been worried about the camera, which I expect was why Mr. Desmond, who ordinarily wouldn't have anything to do with Calvin's new-fangled photography, had agreed to hold still for Calvin's trial run before he started gutting out the white-tailed deer. But Jamie, who had adopted Calvin as his personal hero for saving his life, worried most of all. He didn't tell Calvin so. Twenty times a day I could see new "Thank you's" on the tip of his tongue, but Jamie had learned quickly that Calvin hated to be singled out for expressions of esteem and obligation, so Jamie told me instead. Jamie also worried because he had no money to contribute toward buying new photographic supplies, and I was convinced that was precisely why he had announced that he was going to ride ahead and meet us later in Mesilla, New Mexico Territory.

What he was going to do, as we all knew good and well, was to ride off ahead and rob some bank or stagecoach line or faro game between where we were sitting and Mesilla, New Mexico Territory. I don't know what had happened to us. Maybe it was being chased, and near-penniless, and all by ourselves in the wilds. But in my private thoughts it seemed perfectly all right, just as it was all right for Mr. Desmond to slay the young white-tailed buck, for Jamie to rob some outsider to help our group. We none of us talked about it, but I suspect the others felt the same.

We could hear Calvin making rattling sounds in the dark-box, and Emma drew near. Gil, as nearly always nowadays, tagged a few steps after her, and as nearly always she ignored him. Emma inspected us. To Mr. Desmond, she said, "Now you really look fine for having your portrait made. Couldn't you have cleaned up?"

He paused in his work and thoughtfully rasped the back of a bloody hand over his whiskers. "Well," he said, "Calvin said he wanted a view that just looked natural."

"He surely got that," Emma said. "Lord, lord, will we ever get anywhere again where there's plenty of water? Look at those flies already around the meat. And we can't even wash it before we eat it."

"The flies'll stay behind with the guts when we leave," Mr. Desmond said.

Mr. Desmond had attended to the musk sacks and was well on his way through the innards when we heard Calvin whoop triumphantly. The door of the dark-box flung open, and out he rushed with the wet plate.

"It is repaired?" Jamie said, hurrying to see.

"It is repaired," Calvin said happily. "Look, everybody. Come look, Hap. It's a fine portrait. This is one that I'm going to send to New York!"

We crowded around. There was a glass negative of Mr. Desmond, sweat-stained hat pushed back, and clothes dusty, and face lined and dusty and bearded, bending over that deer, and it looked just like him, only different. Except for the deer, I had seen him look like that a hundred times, but this was special. This was a moment of time caught forever by Calvin's camera, and not a moment that would flow into the next and be forgotten, and that made it special.

Gil said, "The mighty hunter."

"Kindly don't be snide," Emma said in her dignified, distant manner.

"No, I mean it," Gil said placatingly. "That's what it looks like. A hunter with his kill. It does look natural, Hap. It looks like something you've done many times before and will do many times again. I mean, you don't look conceited about it. Just natural. It ought to make a beautiful print."

"Well," said Mr. Desmond, "I guess if you start counting buffalo I've done it too many times to count."

Jamie said to Calvin, "I am so happy you were able to repair the camera. I am . . . that makes me very happy."

Then it was time for him to go. The only one who seemed especially happy about that was Jamie. You learn in time that it's always easier to be the one to say good-bye and go than it is to be the ones left behind. Jamie was in fine spirits, and the expressions of esteem and obligation to Calvin had a hard time staying behind his tongue. But Jamie was courteous, not only as all Mexicans tend to be but also in a special way of his own, and he kept the words back. He permitted himself the *abrazo*, a sort of manly hug, to all of us, including Emma, and we all said be careful, and don't get lost, and be sure to wait for us in Mesilla, and I got carried away and told him not to meet up with some Indian bride.

He saved Calvin for last. "I am so happy about the camera," he said for the umpteenth time.

The anxious look was on Calvin's face by now. He said, also for the umpteenth time, "Now you be careful, Jamie." This time he added, "There's all kind of chemicals left, and I can use window glass for plates, and I just know that we're going to make all kinds of money from now on out, so don't you . . . don't you . . ."

"Of course," Jamie said. "I will be waiting for you in Mesilla. I feel sure we will be able to buy new supplies there for your camera."

"Well, then, but don't you . . ." Calvin said.

"Of course," Jamie said. That's when he did the *abrazo* to Calvin. "Farewell, my friend," he said. "Until Mesilla."

"*Que te vaya bien,*" Calvin said awkwardly. He had asked some words from Mr. Desmond, and we had practiced him in secrecy.

So that made a big hit with Jamie, and he swung onto his wiry black and made it prance for us, and then he took off west. We waved. Even Mr. Desmond postponed finishing his deer and stood waving. Jamie waved back with his big hat, and then he seemed to square his well-set shoulders and point straight ahead, and he didn't look back after that, although we continued waving.

Finally we stopped. We looked at each other, maybe all feeling a little miserable, but all trying not to look it. It was Emma who said what we all felt. She looked up the trail after Jamie and said, "Well, hell."

Calvin said absently, "Don't cuss."

That was what helped us get started again, having something to laugh about. Even Mr. Desmond smiled his little smile as he squatted back to his deer.

Calvin asked him, a bit hesitantly, "Are we going to that

place? That Desgracia?" It was a mining town we had heard about from some tramps walking back east through the wilderness, all the way from California and heading back home, they said, because, in a leaf from Mr. Desmond's book, at least one had become discouraged with California after discovering that an orchard he'd invested in there was just Joshua trees to which the land speculators had tied oranges.

Mr. Desmond looked at his venison as if having it might alleviate the necessity of going through a town and trying afresh for photographic business, but then he looked at Calvin's hopeful face. "Why not?" he said. "At least it's not on the Butterfield." And as quickly as you please he finished up gutting the deer.

Now, Desgracia, Jamie had told us, was Spanish for "misfortune" or "bad luck," and you'd think we had already had plenty of that. I thought maybe we were in for more, because the first would-be photographic business we encountered just laughed at us, and the foreman's helper told us to move on. This was a bunch of drovers, mustachioed, dirty, some of them looking to be barely beyond my age, and they were heading a smallish herd of beeves northeast to pick up the Goodnight-Loving trail. Those who weren't sweating to keep the cattle moving, and even those who were, could hardly keep their eyes off of Emma. One hollered at us and asked if we were overnighting in Desgracia, and I hollered back maybe, and he laughed and did some fancy riding, perhaps to catch Emma's eye.

So all five of our group were less than happy. Gil looked fierce because the drovers looked at Emma. Mr. Desmond looked coldeyed and grim because he was a man sitting in a wagon and no longer had a horse of his own to do any fancy riding on. Emma looked miffed because of the *segundo*'s instructing us to ride on. Calvin looked wide-eyed and wistful because he had encountered some real drovers, and with all that dirt on them they were as natural-appearing as even he could desire, but even if they had let him photograph them he couldn't spare the supplies. As for me, I was just plain envious. I wanted to be one of those cowboys doing a real job and heading for glamorous places, instead of a plain boy driving a faded blue What's-It Wagon that had been run off the Butterfield by another once-plain boy and his big brother.

Then the little mining camp turned out to be just that, and not what you could call a town. It had a general store and a boarding house and three saloons that were just tents erected over a lumber framework. Calvin and I went into one to inquire when was payday for the mines. The bartender looked at us and replied, "What'll you have?"

Calvin and I exchanged glances. The man was going to make us pay for the information, and according to the posted signs even bar whiskey was twenty-five cents a drink. But we still had two dollars and forty-three cents, and I remembered that I was a practical-minded would-be businessman who knew that it takes money to make money, so I nodded, and Calvin said, "I'd like a shot of whiskey, please."

The bartender and five miners playing poker at a nearby table all burst into uproarious laughter. I didn't know what was the matter with them, until they started mocking Calvin. They did it better than the little boys used to back home in Claiborne Parish, and one caught Calvin's nasal speech almost perfectly: "Hi'd hlike a shont of whinskey, phlease," he told his friends, and they all nearly dropped their cards laughing.

"Hey, what's the matter with your friend?" the bartender said, pointing openly at Calvin.

"Nothing," I said angrily. Out in the wilds, I'd forgotten Calvin's speech impediment. It didn't matter there.

"Now don't get mad," the bartender said. "He's the most interesting thing to happen around here since a tent show went through a month ago with two freaks, a poet and an evangelist."

"He's not a thing," I said. "He's Mr. Calvin Fairchild from New York City and Homer, Louisiana, and he's a person and a photographic artiste."

"Is that so?" the bartender said with interest.

"Come on, Calvin," I said, and turned to stomp out.

"Stick around," the bartender said. "Here, his drink's on the house. What's yours, son? A beer?"

I'd never had beer before, and Calvin tugged my sleeve as if to remind me that he was long accustomed to accepting laughter from strangers, so we stayed. As if to apologize, the bartender told us everything useful he could think of about the camp: that payday was four days gone and wouldn't come again for three days, but that a party of drovers had been reported passing that day and would surely come into Desgracia that night and might provide us business. But I shook my head, so he asked one of the miners, "What about Corrine's?"

"What's Corrine's?" Calvin asked, and they all had another good laugh.

When they finished, the bartender again asked the miner, "No, really, how's business been for Corrine?"

"Bad," said the miner. "She always complains it's bad."

"Well, skip over and ask her if she doesn't want her girls' portraits made by a New York City photographic artiste."

I began to get the drift. I said, "A lady is traveling with us, so Corrine's maybe wouldn't be the best thing. Have you by any chance any hangings scheduled for today? I'm told folks always like to buy views of hangings."

"No," said the bartender, "the vigilance committee keeps things quiet here. We've got a good one now. The time was when you couldn't go out for a morning pee without stumbling over a dead man or two. I tell you, your best bet is Corrine's. If it's a real lady with you, she wouldn't know that it wasn't just a regular boarding house."

But Emma did. The miner obligingly went up the street to speak to Corrine and then reported she said come parley, and we went back to the wagon and tried to explain the situation. Emma caught on immediately.

"If there's any money in a town too small to have a bank, it's apt to have collected at a whorehouse," she said.

"Emma!" Gil said.

But looking disgusted, she said, "Oh! When will you learn I'm no ordinary woman? The things that shock me are mighty scarce in this world. Pepper, you just cluck up the mules and take us straight to that whorehouse. We've got a customer waiting."

Gil turned bright red, and said no, and Emma got red too and said yes, and our customer had to wait maybe fifteen minutes in all while they argued about it. Mr. Desmond just watched, amused. If Calvin hadn't finally gotten a word in and told Emma please, I don't know what would have happened.

So finally Calvin and Gil and I left Emma with Mr. Desmond and went on to this plain-looking two-story house and knocked, and this woman came to the door. To tell the truth, although she was younger, she reminded me of Mrs. Idabelle Sealy back in Homer. She had on a plain cotton housedress and an apron and looked as though she'd been doing housework. But she was Corrine.

She scrutinized us sharply, and said, "Which one is Mr. Fairchild?"

Gil said, "May I have the privilege? Mr. Calvin Fairchild, Miss Corrine . . ."

"Gertz," she said. "And it's Mrs. I'm a widow."

Then she got a busy housewife look and started questioning Calvin. Did he have samples of his work? Did he lower the rate for large orders of prints? Was he capable of producing quality *cartes de visite* "for advertising purposes," as well as full-sized portraits to put in an album in what she grandly called "the French style"?

Indeed yes, Calvin assured her, although he had to tell me later that a *carte de visite* was the little mounted print that people sometimes wanted and sometimes used as calling cards. And then we ran into two problems: Emma and eggs.

Emma came first. Calvin told Corrine his samples of his work were in our traveling studio, and Corrine said go get it, but Gil said, looking determined, "Madame, my wife is traveling with us. I wonder if you could inform me as to some comfortable and proper place for her to rest while Mr. Fairchild fills your photographic order."

Corrine started to laugh. "Good lord," she said. "Just about anywhere she goes in this settlement she's going to have a few hundred dirty, horny miners underfoot. You'd be better off to bring her here."

"Uh . . ." said Gil.

"All right," said Corrine, "take her to Mrs. Taft. She runs a bakery in the third tent north of the general store, and she's got two children, and she's as respectable as the sky is blue. I'll give you a note to her. No, don't look surprised. Of course I know her. I bake my own pies, but I buy bread from her. People have to get along in a little place like this."

Calvin said, "Pardon me, please, but . . . cream pies?"

"Now what?" Corrine said. "Are we talking about photographs for pies, or for hard money?"

"It's not pies," Calvin said. "It's eggs I need."

"What?" Corrine asked Gil.

So we worked that over for a while. Two women came and peeped at us. One had a big, square face, but one was younger and prettier. She was dark and looked a little like Emma, and Gil hesitated in the middle of explaining to Corrine, once he understood it, that Mr. Fairchild had, uh, had such a, uh, successful Western tour that he had run out of one of his standard chemicals for preparing photographic plates and wanted to substitute egg whites.

"You, I'm talking business," Corrine told the two girls peeping at us. "Get back upstairs." Then she said to us, "You expect me to pay hard money for photographs made with egg whites?"

But Calvin assured her that if she wasn't fully satisfied with his work, she need take none of it, and we left to get the samples. Calvin's face looked tense and pale. He said to me, "Pepper, run to the general store and buy some window glass, for this is our opportunity to make some money, and I must not fail us."

By the time I got back, Calvin had somehow coaxed Emma and Nemo into stopping off with Mrs. Taft, and the wagon was parked in the backyard of the whorehouse under some big cottonwood trees. Corrine had set her girls to getting ready and was instructing Calvin in her wants as businesslike as a banker.

The only thing Corrine wasn't especially businesslike about was Mr. Desmond. She saw his deer, tied to the back of the wagon, and said she liked a haunch of fresh venison now and again and would pay hard money for it. But, no, he said, he would trim it off for her after the deer had drained, and it would be a gift.

Corrine's face turned pink and almost pretty-looking. I swear, I don't know how that man did it. He was old, and he was often sick, but he sure could make a woman look at him. Maybe he had let Emma slip off the hook, but here was Corrine saying she might change her dress and have her own portrait made to go into the album as proprietress of the establishment.

"But not as a gift," she said of the deer. "You look my girls over and take your pick in exchange for the venison. Just don't get them tously until after the picture-taking. One, that Sissy, it takes her a full hour to do anything with her hair."

"I'll think on it," Mr. Desmond said. He smiled his little smile at her, and her face got pinker. She hurried into her house, her mind maybe already on what dress to wear.

Calvin didn't want me to help him with the pictures inside, and Gil also said I should go to Mrs. Taft's tent and see if Emma needed anything, but I said, "Look here, are we partners or are we not? This here is just a business endeavor, and you know I'm always right handy at those." Not wild horses nor even Otis & Company could have kept me out of that whorehouse. It was the closest I'd come to a thousand former thoughts that could be loosely categorized under "What if . . . ?"

The girls got fixed up. There were four of them. The square-faced one was Rose, and Sissy was a little, prim-faced woman who looked as if she would have been more at home in a school-house than a whorehouse. The young, pretty one who resembled Emma was Susanna, and the fourth, named Claudine, looked like a strapping, good-natured farm girl. Corrine lined them up in the whorehouse parlor, and they were all dressed fancily. Corrine herself had put her hair up in a big pouf and put on a lacy royal blue dress that would just look black in a photograph, but she called Mr. Desmond in from his deer to tell her if he thought the girls looked all right, so maybe her photograph wasn't her chief interest.

Corrine said to Calvin, "I thought a portrait in the parlor of all four girls, and then each one of them separate dressed, and then each one of them in their rooms not quite so dressed. What do you think?"

Calvin swallowed and looked things over. That parlor was dressed as fancily as the women were. Turkey carpets. Rose-patterned wallpaper and lace curtains. A picture of the Charge of the Light Brigade and one of what Gil said was a London street scene. Overstuffed furniture and shawls draped on all the tables and a big embroidered pillow saying "Forget Me Not" on the settee. The light was dim, and Calvin said so, but Corrine said, "Pooh, we can tie the curtains back, and besides, these girls will look better if it's not too bright."

Susanna, the pretty one, said, "You don't have to worry about me, Mrs. Gertz. I've had my portrait made before, and I turn out fine in bright light."

"Be still," Corrine said. To Calvin, she said, "Well?"

So Calvin, his color coming and going, arranged Rose and Sissy on the settee and stood Susanna and Claudine in back of them and put the big forget-me-not pillow in between Rose and Sissy, and Corrine said, "That looks just grand. What do you think, Mr. Desmond?"

Slouching in the doorway of the parlor, he said, "It looks fine to me."

And Calvin ran off with Corrine's egg whites and started preparing plates, and we worked like madmen for two hours. The most interesting part was in the bedrooms. Susanna went first. She undressed right in front of us, down to just her skirt and little chemise and a ribbon around her neck, and she laughed at us outright and said, "Like this?"

In a strangled voice, Calvin said, "That's just fine."

"What did he say?" Susanna said to me.

In my own strangled voice, I said, "He said that's just fine."

She ran to look at herself in the mirror. "No," she pouted, "it needs something. Flowers. I'll fetch some. You don't suppose that Mr. Desmond and Mr. Carmichael will look at me, do you?"

She ran out laughing. Dressed just as she was, she went all the way out in the yard. I saw her, watching from the window, and I was surely glad Emma was at Mrs. Taft's.

Calvin's mouth worked and popped and he said to me, "Pepper, if Grandmother ever hears I let you come into a place like this, there's no use in me ever going to Mr. John Swiss Parker in California or you ever going back home, because the family will disown the both of us."

"Well, who's going to tell Grandmother?" I said. "Not you. Not me."

Susanna ran back up the stairs with a handful of just plain zinnias, dusty ones at that, but she fussed around and put one in her hair and pinned four or five to the front of her chemise, which in the process slipped off one shoulder and halfway down one white breast. She took a stance with one knee on the side of her bed, with a hand stretched out languidly on the knee. "Now," she said.

It was not the easiest work in the world. We charged up and down the stairs, getting the plates ready and developing them, and that Susanna got us both so rattled that we had a hard time not dropping and breaking the window glass that I'd plunked down our last two dollars for. The other girls, being less pretty, were a little easier, but Calvin and I were both having difficulties with our breathing, and it wasn't just the stairs. Corrine looked at each plate as it was developed, but Mr. Desmond had stayed with her, and she approved every last one and said now let her see the prints.

So that was more work. Gil and I both did everything we could, but Calvin was the one who had to shut himself up in that hot little dark-box, and about all we could do was fetch bucket after bucket of water from Corrine's well and, for me, run the prints in for Corrine to see as they were finished.

She looked for a long time at the ones Calvin had taken of her, standing in front of the lacy parlor windows. I must say that Calvin was good at his profession. The focus was soft, and the shadows were just enough so you could see her features clearly, but you couldn't see the little wrinkles that years of living had left on her face. In one picture she was looking down with a pensive expression, and in the other Calvin had coaxed a little smile that showed like sun-spangles in her eyes. When I ran in to show the print of Susanna in her chemise, Corrine was looking again at her portraits and saying to Mr. Desmond, "Well, now. Well, now."

"Here's another," I said.

She ignored me, and looked up at Mr. Desmond. "Do I really look like that?" she said.

He said, "The way I hear it, a camera can't tell lies."

"Well, now," she said. Then she seemed to firm herself up and took the chemise picture of Susanna from me, and she said to Mr. Desmond, "You take this one. I've seen you looking at her. She's the one you like best."

"Oh, I wouldn't necessarily say that," Mr. Desmond said.

"I would," Corrine said. "You take her, she'll be all right. She's nothing special, but I know my work as proprietress of this establishment"—she came down hard on the "proprietress" part—"and she'll give you a good-enough time."

"I'm not sure," Mr. Desmond said.

"Well, I'm sure. Running this establishment, that's my job. That's my only job. I've never been a boarder, only a proprietress. This establishment makes good money too." This was all said very archly, and I stood there watching, feeling puzzled.

Mr. Desmond said, in his old firm way, "That all sounds fine, but personally, I'm planning to try for gold in Arizona Territory."

"There's mines galore all around here," Corrine said.

"And after that I'm going to go back into cattle again."

Corrine said, "Now that I think of it, there's some good grazing land here too."

Mr. Desmond said to me, "Well, Pepper, got your eyes full enough yet?"

"Oh," I said. "Beg pardon." I left the portrait of Susanna in her chemise and ran back outside to Gil and Calvin.

Well, what happens after that but Mr. Desmond comes strolling into the backyard looking calm-faced and maybe a little tired and smoothing his shirttail into his pants. I watched him so carefully, thinking of Susanna and my "What if's?" that I barely heard him say, "Gil, Pepper, you'd better pull Calvin out of that dark-box and tell him more business is knocking on the front door. Part of them drovers has hit town, and if I can believe my eyes, one's wearing a hard-boiled hat."

Corrine came out after him. There was laughter in her voice as she said, "Now this is a hell of a note. A bunch of drovers that you'd think would be looking for a woman, but what do they want except to have their pictures made."

Sounding rattled, Gil said, "I'm sorry, Mrs. Gertz, but you must be mistaken. We encountered those men earlier, and they hadn't the remotest interest in sitting for portraits."

"Cowboys," Corrine said scornfully. "There's nothing lower and nothing vainer, but they never like to let on in front of people that they're vain. They want pictures so they can think how handsome they are. Just see that Mr. Fairchild finishes my order first." To Mr. Desmond, she added, "I believe you owe me a haunch of venison."

"I was just going to get it," Mr. Desmond said lazily.

"Come on back in," she said. "I've got to keep an eye on those wild men, but I've got some brandy like you've never tasted."

"I'll be there in a little while," Mr. Desmond said.

"Then you come," Corrine said to Gil, "and talk business with a bunch of drovers who've pulled checkered suits with vests out of their war bags and look so clean and slicked up my girls can hardly believe it. You know, we might have something good working here. A photographic studio and my establishment combined. We could get them coming and going."

Off she went with Gil. Calvin called for more water. Calvin was looking a lot more tired than Mr. Desmond when he opened the dark-box, but his tired face was happy.

"Did you hear that about them drovers?" I asked.

"Indeedy I did," Calvin said enthusiastically. "Partner, we're really in business this time." He took the water and closed the dark-box door again.

Mr. Desmond was over under the trees neatly skinning the deer. I wasn't sure if he'd want me, but I went to see if I could help. He said to me, "Pepper, has Calvin ever had a girl?"

"I don't know," I said.

He said, "That Susanna might be worth his while. And a deer has two haunches."

I said, "I guess he's made enough money to pay."

Mr. Desmond just looked at me, and I turned red, and I said, "Mr. Desmond, you're not going to stay in Desgracia, are you?"

"What made you think I would?"

"The way Miss Corrine was talking to you."

He shook his head. "Miss Corrine's looking for a husband."

"Well, you're looking for a wife."

"Not that kind of a wife. Emma, now, she wouldn't be the best, she's too uppity. On the other hand a man my age can't be too choosy, and a woman like Emma might break in all right in time. But Corrine would never make a mother, and that's what I'm in the market for, a mother for my second set of boys. Hell, Pepper, a man don't need no wife otherwise."

"Because there are whores?"

"Yes, I guess so," he said. "Or enough women who act like one."

"You mean Emma," I said.

For a second, I thought I was going to get backhanded again. But then Mr. Desmond took a deep breath and went back to his skinning, working rapidly down to the haunch. He said, "If I was you and was only fifteen and didn't understand the difference between a woman and a public woman, I'd be careful what I said and thought."

I said, "But Mr. Desmond, then why is Emma so mad at Gil?"

Mr. Desmond studied me again, a long time, then he said lightly, "I expect she thinks he took advantage of her. Not the kind of advantage you've been thinking, but just the kissing and playing kind. Even that can make a woman mad as a mud-dauber. Gil didn't do himself any good that night. Any good at all."

"Then they didn't really do anything but kissing and the like?"

"That's right," Mr. Desmond said firmly. "Now scat and help Calvin, and if you're going to think bad thoughts about women you think them about women like Susanna."

I went. He called after me, "And mention Susanna to Calvin. I'm taking in both these haunches."

Calvin came out of the dark-box with the last of the *cartes de visite* and poured half a bucket of water over his head to cool off. I mentioned the extra haunch of venison that Mr. Desmond took in through Corrine's back door, and as Mr. Desmond had told me, I mentioned Susanna.

"Oh, no," Calvin said, and he looked down at his boots. They'd gotten water on them, and little dabs of chemicals that always spilled a bit when he was working.

"If you think I'd ever tell Grandmother, you just don't know how close-mouthed Pepper Fairchild can be," I said.

"It isn't that," Calvin said.

I said, "Calvin, the fee is paid, and an opportunity is an opportunity. I'll tell you frankly, I don't know if I'd be standing here talking if the opportunity had been offered to me."

Calvin absently straightened his clothes some and looked toward the house, but he said in a low voice, "Pepper, you and I are partners in just about everything in the world, but a man doesn't want his partner choosing a woman for him, and another man paying a haunch of venison for her. A man wants to make his choice by himself."

And Calvin chose to restrict his activities to taking portraits of the drovers, for which Corrine loaned her whorehouse parlor. I sat and thought for a long time, wondering what I would have done if the second haunch had come my way. Would I, like one member of our group, have gone upstairs with a girl because she looked like Emma, or would I, like another, have stayed downstairs, perhaps for the same reason? I couldn't decide, so I went back in and helped Calvin until he said he was ready to go make prints of the drovers, and then I ran off to find Mrs. Taft's tent and Emma. Nemo and Emma were glad to see me, and Emma and Mrs. Taft, who had previously penetrated only as far as Corrine's kitchen and learned only that Corrine preferred salt-rising bread, sent the children away and asked me several thousand questions. Until the rest of our outfit showed up, I kept Emma company all by myself all evening.

Twelve

In those times, in little places like that, it's hard to believe how hungry people were for entertainment. Everyone, including cowboys and miners, tended to go to bed early, because no one was well-heeled enough to spend all his time in saloons or bordellos, and there was simply nothing else to do. We stayed through the mines' payday. The miners prevailed upon us to do so, for sitting for a portrait became the craze of Desgracia. People, including respectable ones, came clamoring for photographs, especially after Calvin moved the What's-It Wagon from Corrine's to Mrs. Taft's.

Corrine sent word to Calvin that he ought to jack up his prices, but Calvin didn't. Then she sent word to Mr. Desmond to come advise her on some grazing land she said she was thinking of buying, and after Susanna came three times with notes and each time looked at Emma, and Emma looked at Susanna, Mr. Desmond went, his little smile almost permanently on his face.

Things went so well financially for us in Desgracia that we were able to afford a telegram home telling what Otis and Shirley Wasum had done, trying to ambush and kill us on the Butterfield. We also wrote Jim Spoonts's letter home, and we wrote El Paso and asked the post office to kindly forward any mail for us on to Mesilla, and we packed what was left of Calvin's Western views in cotton and cheesecloth and little wooden crates and sent them on to the New York magazines. And Gil sent a telegram to Freddie Fassnidge in Tombstone, telling him to hold onto some stock because we were on our way. With all that postage and telegraph money being spent, we were nevertheless able to stock the wagon with new ammunition and what food supplies we could find in Desgracia, and I had forty-one dollars as treasurer for us when we heard news of a hanging coming up in a big camp named Hagerstown on our route to Mesilla and then on to Tombstone. So we left.

That was my idea. I said we had pretty well worked out our personal vein of wealth from Desgracia's mines, so why didn't we go to this Hagerstown and make views of the hanging and make even more money? Mr. Desmond threw in with me, so I figured that Corrine's campaign was beginning to make things hot for him and that it was therefore time for him to depart.

We did, all in high spirits. I confided in them my half-held hope that if Otis and Shirley had tried to track us off the Butterfield, we would discover that they were to be the main attraction of Hagerstown's hanging, and although Calvin and Emma clucked, with Gil chiming in after Emma, that it would be a pity since Otis was only a boy, the hope surely didn't hurt my spirits any.

Hagerstown was over fifty rough miles away. Traveling hard, we made it in two days. We met a mule train on the way, and I asked about Hagerstown and what kind of prospect it might be for a traveling photographic artiste, and they said it was a booming little settlement. They had also heard about the hanging, and told us they thought it was to be one miner hung for killing another miner. But then we came across two men working a small claim, and they said no, they'd heard it was four men who had throwed down on the Little Jessie Mine pay wagon without considering that the Little Jessie always protected its pay with outriders, and yes, that Hagerstown was a booming place because of the big new strike. Silver, they'd heard, not gold, but then a little farther along a man and his wife and little boy in a wagon said gold, not silver. I thought that it didn't matter much one way or the other, just as long as Hagerstown was indeed booming, and I told Calvin I expected we could buy new plates and chemicals in such a big place and repeat our Desgracia success or even better it in Hagerstown.

Sure enough, it was a big camp, with numerous established businesses, and men on the streets everywhere, all eying our What's-It Wagon with considerable interest as we rolled in. On a building I saw a tattered poster advertising the same tent show with the poet and evangelist, but the date was weeks before, and I thought, ah ha, these people will have the money to spend and will not have had anything to spend it on.

Among the attention we were attracting was that from a man in shirt sleeves and town pants, and he came trotting up to the side of the wagon. He said, "I beg your pardon, but by chance might you have an overadequate supply of kerosene that a desperate man could buy?"

It turned out that he was the editor and publisher of the *Territorial Voice*, the camp's newspaper, and the camp was suffering a blackout that hampered his practice of setting every night the news that he gathered every day. Emma said to stop and I did.

"What size is your circulation?" Emma asked professionally after telling the man we had no extra kerosene.

"Well, it's one hundred and eighty-six at the moment, but the actual figures don't begin to indicate the influence of—"

"Daily?" she said.

"No, twice weekly, Miss . . . Mrs. . . . ?"

"Miss Emma Prosser," she said.

He took out a notebook and wrote that down. Then he asked the rest of us our names. We discovered that we were a news story. He wrote down that Calvin was from Homer, Louisiana, and New York City, and was in Hagerstown direct from a big success in Desgracia, New Mexico Territory, which Emma and I told him all about, ignoring Calvin's blushes. Emma didn't seem surprised that we were a story, nor did she seem surprised when the man started talking about the power of advertising, and how a notice in the *Territorial Voice* would draw business for us like nothing else, and if we took an advertising notice in his paper he could assure us of a good prominent position for the news story all about us.

"I go to press tonight," he said, "which is another reason I had hoped you might have some kerosene. With a little luck I can have an issue on the streets tomorrow, bearing your advertisement. I even have a brand-new font of type—that means a set of letters—that I've been saving to use for the first time on some special advertising notice, and it will really make people sit up and notice your notice." He laughed a little about his word play.

"What font is that?" said Emma.

"Why, Railroad Gothic," the editor said.

"Yes, I've worked with Railroad Gothic," Emma said somewhat snootily. "You mean you're just now getting it here?"

"Ah," said the editor, surprise struggling with a pleasant expression that he had plastered to his face, "do I detect a fellow journalist? I suppose you've set type somewhere."

"Not at all," Emma said, "although I know how to do it. I was last the editor of the *Krum Chronicle* in Texas, circulation two thousand four hundred and twenty-three, but I decided there was more opportunity farther west."

Now genuine excitement struggled with the editor's pleasant expression and won. He said, "The *Chronicle*, why I've heard of that paper! Isn't that the one that went from less circulation than I've got to over two thousand in under six months? I'd give my right eye to know how your paper accomplished that, Miss Prosser!"

Emma said smugly, "There were several things I did. For one, I offered a lottery ticket with each subscription, for premiums ranging from a smoked ham to forty acres of land. People will even agree to read news if they have a chance to win a prize."

She was showing off, and the editor was soaking up every brilliant ray of her, and Gil said, "We came here to photograph a hanging. Shouldn't we get on with it and find out where it's to be?"

The editor paused in his discussion with Emma and said, "I'm sorry to disappoint you, but the hanging has already taken place. Two hours ago in the blacksmith shop. But the body is still there for public viewing if you'd care to photograph it. I understand it isn't to be cut down until sunset."

Mr. Desmond said, "Yes, next best to a hanging is views of the bodies, Calvin. Maybe we'd best move on while the light's right."

"Oh, that's excellent copy for your advertising notice," the editor said. "I can mention that you have views of the hanging available and it should draw you considerable business. If you'll permit me, I'll show you the way to the blacksmith shop, and we can just talk over the wording of your notice. I'm sure Miss Prosser knows exactly what you want, but a little assistance . . ."

He made as if to get into the wagon, but Gil and Mr. Desmond looked at him hostilely, and he paused. He put the pleasant expression back on, and he said to Emma, "Ours is a flourishing operation, but still small, Miss Prosser, with just my wife to help me with the typesetting, but I've been contemplating hiring an assistant editor . . ."

I clucked up the mules. Unlike Gil and Mr. Desmond, I didn't really mind him admiring Emma a little, but I certainly wasn't going to just let her sit there while he offered her a job. What if she took it?

But the man, not even offended by my rudeness, walked by the side of our wagon, saying, "Miss Prosser, Miss Prosser, my wife and I would be delighted to have you and your associates dine with us, Miss Prosser." We picked up a little speed and he began to pant, but he didn't give up. "I'd love . . . know . . . more details . . . circulation scheme," he puffed.

"That would be it," said Mr. Desmond. A sign said "Levois & Jamison, Blacksmiths," so he was right. Gil jumped down and tied the mules, and the editor of the *Territorial Voice* arrived puffing in our wake.

The editor knew good and well we didn't want him around, but he was a persistent fellow. He rushed up to Emma and began to tell her how Hagerstown might be small now but had a glorious future ahead of it as the queen city of the West, and every so often he would remember his other interests and mention the advertisement, and I had to step around him to help Calvin get out the camera. Gil and Mr. Desmond weren't much help, so busy were they glowering at the audacity of the editor in trying to snatch Emma right from under their noses. Calvin's nose was a little out of joint too, but he got busy and inspected the front of the blacksmith shop, which was sort of an L-shaped shed, and he said, "An indoor hanging. It might be dark. I'd better get out the flash powder."

I said, in spite of the way I felt about the editor and his attentions to Emma, "Calvin, that man might be right about an advertisement. I can go talk to him about it later. Emma doesn't have to have a thing to do with it."

"If you think so," Calvin said. Then he said, "I'm ready. Let's go inside."

When she saw us starting in, Emma called, "Wait for me," and skipped to catch up with us.

"Get back in the wagon, Emma," Gil said. "Ladies don't view hangings."

Emma lowered her voice so the editor wouldn't hear her and she said, "You kept me out of the whorehouse, and you're not going to keep me out of this. I'm my own person, and I do as I please."

I could see that Gil wanted to argue, but not in front of his new rival, the editor, so he bowed so low as to be sarcastic and said, "As you wish, Miss Prosser."

We went inside.

The blacksmith shop was doing no business that day. A bunch of men were loafing against one wall. Hanging from the rafters of the shop, hands tied behind its back, was just one body, already beginning to attract flies.

Funny leather pants with doodads on the side and well-set shoulders, crooked now from the rope, and angular features swollen and blank in death.

There was no sign of his drooping big hat or his gun belt.

It was our Jamie.

Mr. Desmond wordlessly handed me his Navy Colt and took out the knife he used for cleaning game. He cut Jamie down. There was a hubbub from the men in the shop, but although I was looking straight at them with the Colt in my hand, I didn't hear a word that they said. I didn't come to until one of the men said, "What the hell did you do that for? That was the man who tried to rob the Little Jessie payroll single-handed."

The editor of the *Territorial Voice* shushed them, saying that we had come to make a photograph of the hanged man.

Gil said, "We make no photographs here."

The editor looked surprised, but this time because he scented journalism instead of a fellow journalist.

One of the men said, "Hell, if you're not going to make a photograph, why is that fellow carrying a camera?"

"We've changed our minds," Gil said. "Now what are you going to do about it?"

Mr. Desmond got Jamie stretched out, and he stood to join Gil in belligerence. "Where's his hat?" he growled. "What did you bastards do, steal his hat for a souvenir?"

"Now see here . . ." one of the men said.

The resident editor stepped in to soothe things. "I may be wrong," he said, "but I believe these people may know the hanged man."

"Is that right?" a man said.

"That's right," Gil said. The what-are-you-going-to-do-about-it expression was still there.

One of the men slipped out of the shop. I knew why. He was going for the law. Knowing a criminal made us suspect as criminals too. There was uneasy shifting among the men in the shop, and I thought I could read both repugnance and fear of us in their expressions, but they left us alone. Mr. Desmond took off his own hat and put it over Jamie's face.

The editor asked Emma, "I'm right? You do know him?"

"Yes," Emma said. "He was a good friend of ours."

The editor's notebook was out in a flash. "What was his name?" he asked.

"Don't you know?" she said.

"Well, Miss Prosser, the man was a stranger in these parts and refused to reveal his identity, so the committee hung him unidentified. His name . . . ?"

Emma thought for a minute. "We don't know either," she said.

"He was a good friend, and you don't even know his name?"

"That's right," she said.

"But Miss Prosser—"

"We met him on the trail," she said. "We all helped each other. So he was our friend, but he never said his name."

Finally, she looked at the rest of us, as if for confirmation, and she found it and the next step in our faces. If Jaime Cienfuegos Villarreal of Piedras Negras, Coahuila, Mexico, had not wished to tell the name under which he would be hanged for trying to rob a pay wagon single-handed for our benefit, we wouldn't tell it. New Mexico Territory was not that far from Mexico, and I guessed he hadn't wanted that kind of news to travel homeward. Emma said, "Is there an undertaker in this town?"

"Yes ma'am," said the editor, "but—"

"And a priest? A Catholic priest?"

"Oh, yes," the editor said, "the priest came to see him. Father Polinsky has to leave today for San Augustine Springs, but he took time out this morning to, er, do whatever Catholics do for a condemned criminal."

Gil said, "Where do we find him? This Father Polinsky?"

"But he's leaving today for San Augustine Springs," the editor said.

"He's going to have to take more time out before he does," I said. "Jamie believed in decent burials."

"Was that his name?" the editor said craftily. "Jamie?"

"No," I said. "That was just what we called him."

And that was the name we buried him under. Father Polinsky didn't like it, but not being Catholics ourselves we lied to him most sinfully and swore up and down that the unlikely sounding name of Jamie was all we knew him by. Father Polinsky was anxious to get off for San Augustine Springs and didn't really like the whole thing, but the undertaker liked it. He charged us ten dollars for a coffin and twenty-five dollars for a hasty, half-hour job of "embalming," and we only had six dollars left over that we could pay for space in the Catholic cemetery. I tried to give Father Polinsky my shotgun to help make up for it, but he wouldn't take it, and Mr. Desmond said later that it was just as well, for with no money left we needed it again for small game.

The padre, a Pole, I thought, by his name, stayed long enough to run through a funeral mass in the little church the town had built for him, for when he could get there from other camps and towns in what he said wearily was an overlarge parish. Then he left on horseback, and we took the bench out of the What's-It Wagon and put in Jamie's ten-dollar coffin, with Jamie inside it, and drove up to a patch of weedy hillside with a four-foot stone wall around it that was the Catholic cemetery.

No one went with us.

We were just as glad, for if the townspeople didn't like us for being friends of a hanged criminal, we didn't like them for hanging a criminal who was our friend.

So it was just we five and Nemo and the mules, and the hot sun baking a weedy hillside.

Emma started sighing heavily when she saw the place, but she didn't cry. She said, looking about her, "Nothing grows. And we don't even have a flower to put on the grave."

"Who's got the key to that gate?" Mr. Desmond said.

"Not me," Gil said, sounding placating.

"Not me," Calvin said, sounding sad.

No one did. Father Polinsky had forgotten to leave it for us. We wrestled the coffin over the four-foot stone wall, all five of us, and Gil or Mr. Desmond for once had nothing to say about Emma doing improper work for a woman.

Father Polinsky and the camp's vigilance committee had arranged for gravediggers, but the gravediggers, who were nowhere in sight, had done poorly. The grave was deep enough but nearly a foot too short. I skinned back over the wall for the shovel.

"Ah, God," Gil said when I brought it back, "what else can go wrong?"

"Dig," Mr. Desmond said, handing him the shovel.

He did. Nemo had to make several tries, from the scrabbling sounds his claws made, but he succeeded in jumping over the wall and joined us. I was glad. It was lonesome there.

Finally the coffin would fit, and I said to Calvin hesitantly, "Shall we take the lid off, and you make a photograph? Just for us, I mean. To remember him by."

"Nobody's going to forget him," Calvin said.

We put the coffin in the grave. We all stood back. Emma's eyes were awfully red, but she was doing her level best not to cry, which I think would have broken us all down, and her level best was good.

Calvin came close to shaking her resolve, though, when he said, "If he'd just waited. If he'd just come with us to Desgracia. Then he'd never had to have—"

Mr. Desmond interrupted him. "We got to say the words, I guess," he said. He kneeled down.

We all kneeled with him, and Mr. Desmond seemed to think

for a long time, then he said simply, "Lord, here is a man that was our friend. We leave him in your hands."

Then he got to his feet and said to us, "Git. I'll finish up here."

We got. I helped Nemo over the wall. It felt so strange, sitting there listening to the clods fall on the coffin. For a short while but a strong while, we had been six, and now we were only five. We were lessened, and not just numerically. Maybe it was no worse than a person feels if he loses an arm or a couple of legs, but I also felt as if I'd lost something vital inside.

Part Three

Thirteen

We limped westward.

No one wanted to, but we went by Mesilla. Calvin was hoping for checks from the New York magazines to help our no-money situation, but all we found was a letter from home and a letter from *Harper's New Monthly Magazine* saying two batches of broken plates had arrived. Calvin got very depressed. The photographic artist in New York under whom he had studied had instructed him to submit plates, not just paper prints, because the magazines were picky, but perhaps he had overlooked the fact that a New York photographic artist could run down to the magazines with his plates in his hand, whereas a photographic artist roaming through the western territories had to ship the fragile things two thousand miles. We all kept telling Calvin it wasn't his fault, but he felt so bad that he gave up even looking at spectacular scenery and wishing he had photographic supplies.

The letter from home wasn't much better. It was from Grandmother, saying that even though Uncle Raleigh wouldn't let her look at it she had heard of our letter reporting Otis and Shirley had followed us to Denton, and surely we were mistaken, but she didn't like the sound of things, so we should turn around and come home. My father had censored it, marking through the last part, but not so much that we couldn't read it. In the margin, in his fine, flowing hand, he had written that he trusted we were well and had taken care of the Otis–Shirley situation. He also added that fall and schooltime for me would shortly be approaching, and he hoped we would soon be able to send Grandmother word that we had reached California successfully.

The way things were, we did well even to get to each night's camping spot as we wandered through the dry lands of southern New Mexico Territory and finally made Arizona Territory, which looked just like New Mexico, only more so. Their rainy season should have started by now, Mr. Desmond said, but it hadn't, and such vegetation as there was, greasewood and desert broom and grama grass, looked far more brown than green. Mr. Desmond never complained and generally denied it, but he had more bad days now than good. Emma was also feeling queer, and Gil was so worried about her that he never laughed any more, and Calvin had a worried look that never left his face.

We did our best. Mr. Desmond, after going off by himself and staring at the ground for a long time, sold his saddle, and that helped us get farther along. Mr. Desmond also asked in every settlement after old friends who he said owed him favors and who he hoped might be in these parts, but we never found a one. Worse, at a camp named Paradise, a tall, grinning fellow named Howard waved us down and told us four men had been through asking about a traveling photographer not a week or so past, and he was puzzled as could be when we looked so unhappy to hear about these particular "friends." After that, Mr. Desmond took over the mules, because I couldn't bear to whip the poor things, so gaunted they were by drought, yet he urged that we must hurry on to Tombstone, where Gil's opportunity and aid awaited us.

As close as we could figure, it was August fourth when we saw the town, lying on a windswept plateau amidst arid hills dotted with mines named West Side and Grand Central and Contention and Lucky Cuss, and, somewhere among them we assumed, the A.C.M. Company's own Sulphuret. But despite the fact that millions in silver lay in the hills, my eyes were all for the town, and I guess we crawled into Tombstone like you read about people lost in a desert crawling on their bellies to some oasis they finally find. Certainly we didn't roll in bravely; the mules were as skinny as the grama grass that had been all they'd had to eat in the past weeks, and I maybe wasn't a whole lot fatter. Mr. Desmond made me take the reins, saying he wasn't used to town traffic, and I felt like some little country cousin as I coaxed our wagon in, looking for Fremont Street, where Gil said good old Freddie's mine office was supposed to be located.

For Tombstone, Arizona, was a famous town. Gil told us he had even seen notices in European newspapers saying, "Ho for Tombstone! The place to make a fortune!" It claimed ten thousand population and regarded itself as second in size and grandeur only to San Francisco in the West.

And it was a gay, gaudy town all right, the streets ground to powdery dust by the heavy ore wagons that rumbled through day and night, and by the mule trains and flat wagons that carried the smeltered silver on to Benson, the nearest railhead. We'd gotten up in pitch dark in our anxiety to get there, and it was still early, but there was buggy and wagon and horse traffic enough for high noon. Folks were everywhere bustling around, some still swamping out their places of business and others running about on errands, and all so cosmopolitan that our dusty old wagon hardly caused a single head to turn. It turned out they were used to photographic artistes, having a well-regarded local one of their own named C. S. Fly, whose photograph gallery we saw when we asked our way to Fremont Street. The gallery was built on the back of a boarding house next door to the O.K. Corral Livery and Feed Stable, which it seemed to me I had heard of in connection with some city marshal coming up against a gang of what the local people dubbed "Cow-boys," not meaning cowmen but bad men. But that had been three or four years before.

In that very same block, a few doors down from the city hall, we spotted our objective, a big sign that proclaimed "Arizona Consolidated Mining Company Sales Office."

"Eureka!" whooped Gil, and he jumped out of the wagon while it was still moving and ran to it. We held back a little, not wanting to horn in on his reunion with good old Freddie, but Gil just kept standing outside and soon we all piled out.

Gil was peering through a window, which also announced, in real gold-leaf letters, "Arizona Consolidated Mining Company Sales Office." He tapped on it and called out, "Freddie? Freddie?"

"Maybe it isn't his business hours yet," Calvin said.

"Well it should be," Gil said worriedly. "I can't imagine why Freddie wouldn't have opened up the office by now. Wait here, and I'll pop around to the alley and check the back door."

Off he popped. We all peeped through the window. We could see a big desk, for someone important to sit at, and benches, for less important people to sit on and wait, and tables stacked high with papers. But the front door was locked tight, and there was no one in the front office, and Emma said apprehensively, "I don't like the looks of this."

Nor did I. Spotting a boy about my age washing the windows of some establishment across the street called the Gird Building, I skipped across, dodging wagons, to speak to him.

"Say," I said, "me and my friends just hit this town, and we're looking for Mr. Frederick Fassnidge. I suppose you know Mr. Frederick Fassnidge, don't you?"

"Nope," the boy said. He kept washing.

"Well look here," I said, taking a chance, "you must know this Fassnidge fellow, for he would stand out in any crowd. He's British, and that usually means you can't understand a word he'd say."

"Oh," said the boy, "you mean the one who sold the stocks right over there?"

"That's the one," I said, "although I understand there was lots of others selling it with him."

"Nope," the boy said.

He was beginning to rub me the wrong way. "Well," said I, "the one you know is the only one we're looking for, so mayhap you can tell me where he is."

"I didn't say I know him," the boy said, still washing. "Heard him speak one morning to some other fellow, and the other fellow like to've hit him before he decided the English fellow just said good morning. Not that anything like that means much. Half the people in this town can't talk anything but Mexican. The other half talks Chinese. And the half after that talks Papago. If you ask me, you sound funny too."

"Never mind how I sound," I said. "Where is Mr. Fassnidge?"

The boy turned on me. "Can't you see I'm busy?" he demanded. "Can't you see I'm washing these windows?"

"But you can tell me just that much," I said. "Just one word."

"Nope," he said.

Oh, but I was riled. He was my size and fair game, and the only thing that kept me from calling him out to the street to fight was Emma and Mr. Desmond and Calvin standing over across the way. I turned on my heel.

The boy said, "Takes two words. County jail."

I whirled. But he was already turned back to washing the windows.

Now, when it comes to talking about courage, here's something that really requires same: having to give sinister news to people you care for, particularly when they're already worn to the bone by misfortune. Over in front of the A.C.M. Company, I could see that Gil had rejoined the outfit, and all their faces had raw fear in them.

Before I could lose my own nerve, I scooted back across the street and told them all in a rush what I had learned. Gil just couldn't understand it. He kept asking me, "But why on earth is Freddie in jail?"

As mean as my informant had been, I wasn't even sure it was true. But Emma said we must find out and a passing lady told us where to find the jail, and we climbed into the wagon and started off. All the way Gil kept saying over and over, "I simply cannot believe that anyone would put good old Freddie Fassnidge in a jail."

But someone had. We tied the mules in front of a lumberyard on Toughnut Street and all started across to the courthouse together. A voice that was unmistakably British called jubilantly, "Gilmore! Gilmore Carmichael, you old put! What took you so long?"

Gil sucked in his breath. His head swiveled. "Where are you, Freddie?"

An arm beckoned awkwardly from a window, impeded by bars. "Here," Freddie called. "I got your telegram, old put, and I've been expecting you for a month. I should be much obliged if you'd get me out of this disgusting place immediately. There's a crowd of Mexican fellows in the next cell, and they're driving me batty. They sing all the time, you know."

Gil went toward the bars. Emma started to follow, but Mr. Desmond took her arm and said, "No, I guess they won't want company now."

"Freddie, is it really you?" Gil said. "What are you doing in there?"

We couldn't really see much of Freddie from where we were standing. The arm through the bars wore a white shirt sleeve, not very clean, and the hand at the end of it, while white and soft-looking underneath the dirt, had slightly grimy fingernails. A face as round as the moon and almost as pale loomed behind the bars, and an embarrassed voice answered, "Well, it's all rather shocking, but it seems I've been swindled."

"But . . . you mean there's no mine?"

"Of course there's a mine, old put. It's just got all that disgusting water in it. They ran away, you know. They didn't even have the decency to tell me they were running a swindle, just left me there selling their disgusting stocks."

"But . . . what about the pumps? You mean they never ordered the pumps?"

"Really, Gilmore, what have you been doing with yourself? You could do with a wash, old put."

"The pumps!" Gil said. "Are you trying to tell me there aren't any pumps?"

"No, of course not. Haven't I just been saying that the Sulphuret is five hundred feet deep in water? Perhaps a thousand, for all I know. I tell you, Gilmore, there I sat, doing my duty, selling the very devil out of my stocks, and these disgusting Westerners came and put me in this disgusting jail. You *have* come to get me out, haven't you? They can't keep me here. I'm a British subject."

Gil turned and looked at us with a face from which all hope and any hope of happiness seemed drained. He walked slowly away from Freddie's waggling arm, toward us.

"Gilmore," Freddie's voice called. "Gilmore, I say, you are going to help me get out, aren't you?"

I said anxiously, "Gil, your friend is still talking to you."

He blinked as if the hot August sunshine was blinding him

and kept walking, heading on back toward the wagon. We all followed him fearfully.

At the wagon, even Nemo acted quiet and hangdog, as if he were embarrassed, as we humans also were so deeply, in the face of the fortune that had come to Gil and his friend, good old devilishly clever Freddie. I rattled the lines at Old Jeb and Young Jeb, and we started down Toughnut Street like a one-wagon funeral procession. We passed the jail, and a British voice called to us indignantly, "Really, old put, you might at least have introduced me to your friends!"

That seemed to break through to Gil and he looked at us, kind of shame-faced and miserable. He opened his mouth, but he couldn't seem to find anything to say, and we passed on across the intersection of Third Street and Toughnut before he roused himself enough to speak.

"It's all my fault," he said. "I led you here. And now it appears I've led you to nothing."

Calvin said, "Pepper, we got to hunt us someplace where we can put the wagon and stop. I'm calling a council."

We found a place farther down on Toughnut behind a miner's cabin. The miner was a fine young fellow, a lean and hard six-footer with a dignified demeanor and a luxuriant mustache sweeping above a firm mouth. His name was Dugal Stewart, and when Emma volunteered to clean his cabin for him in return for letting us put the wagon on his lot, he said no, he was a tidy man for a bachelor and kept things up pretty well, but thank you anyway. He also said to me that I should put the mules in his shed, and showed it to me, and said wouldn't I do him a favor and let them eat on a load of hay he'd bought for his horse before losing that excellent animal in a poker game. There sat the hay, a fire hazard—so said he. I knew he was just taking pity on our poor, bony stock, but I couldn't find it in me to refuse them the food. I forked hay for them and then started pumping water from Dugal Stewart's pump to fill the water trough.

Mr. Desmond came to wash up, and before he went off, he said, "Pepper, I'll tell you this, next month I'll be fifty years old, and I'm glad I'm fifty. I wish I was seventy-five. No, I wish I wasn't nothing, because I wish I'd died that day we made our good killing near that rain-water lake. We brought down nine hundred buffalo, all told, in about eight days, but now this world's so changed that any man with eyes in his head can see it's going to sink into the sea."

Next Emma came for a bucket to take back to the privacy of the dark-box, and she said, "Pepper, we're all just going to have to straighten up and be cheerful. You don't really think we're licked, do you Pepper?"

Gil came out to wash and said, "Pepper, I've just got to do something. I've got to make it all up to you somehow. And Emma. I'm desperately worried about Emma. She's been sicking-up almost daily. I've got to do something to earn her decent food and care, and I suppose I must try to help poor old Freddie too. But my God, what am I fit to do?"

And Calvin came, practicing for his council, and said, "Pepper, Hap is ill and badly needs medical care, and Emma's got to have proper food, as do you and Gil, and we've got to think of the future. Pepper, we just can't go on this way."

"What can we do?" I said.

"I've been thinking it over," he said. "I've only got to find some kind of work to earn money for plates and chemicals, and then I'll make us fistfuls of money taking photographs. Enough for a doctor for Hap, and whiskey too, if the doctor says it's all right, and enough to take care of the others. My, Pepper, wouldn't it be nice to make so much money that Emma could have a new dress? I bet that would perk up her spirits in a twinkling. Don't you bet that?"

I bet that Calvin was trying to concoct a future, when we didn't even have a present, in the hope of perking up everyone's spirits—and possibly his own. But I said, "That sounds just fine, Calvin. We'll both look for work, for this is a big town and someone in it could surely use hands. I bet we can make a day's eating money by sundown."

"It's not just eating money we need," Calvin said. "We need to make forty dollars again. That would be enough to get a doctor for Hap. And maybe help him buy into some gold claim on the Big Bug. Well, no, I guess that wouldn't be enough. But maybe we can make more, and see him well and established before we have to leave."

228

"But Calvin," I said, "you don't *want* to leave. You wanted to stay West."

"Not any more, I guess," he said.

I said, "What is it exactly you have in mind for you and me?"

"Well, I've been thinking about that too. For us we only need enough money to feed the mules and get us on to San Diego, California, because you know and I know that Mr. John Swiss Parker will take care of everything. Listen, Pepper, I'm sure Gil will go all the way with us to San Diego if Emma goes, and she's always said she intends to end up in San Francisco, and I'll bet Mr. John Swiss Parker will take us all right in, and she can rest up and start feeling good again before we hand her a train ticket bought with money made by our photographs and send her off in her new dresses to make her big success as a lady editor."

"Calvin," I said hesitantly, "you're dreaming again, you're not planning. First off, even if we make enough money for photographic supplies, we can't count on making fine money here like we did in Desgracia, for they've already got a photographer."

"Then I'll just make better photographs than he does," Calvin said. He sounded so fierce that he reminded me of Gil.

"Well, then, but what about the Wasums?" I said. "If they were scouring little nowhere towns for us, what's to keep them from finding us if we hang around a big town like Tombstone?"

Calvin said, "Shirley and Otis are nothing but Wasums, and I'm a Fairchild. I can take care of them. I say to the devil with the Wasums!"

Then he went back to the wagon, and he said all this except about doctors and dresses to the others. He said about going to work to make money both for eating and for photographic supplies, so he could eventually practice his profession on our behalf. And that's what we did.

Fourteen

I was certain that the fine fellow whose hay Old Jeb and Young Jeb were contentedly munching would have helped us look for work if we had asked him, but we already felt beholden to him so we didn't. Emma only sent me to ask him if the town had a newspaper of which he might have an old copy or two lying around, and he brought us that day's copies of two, the *Tombstone Epitaph and Republican* and the *Daily Tombstone*. Emma was impressed, since both were dailies, and she started in helping us look for job notices.

What she found instead, in the *Daily Tombstone*, was a job for herself, via an advertisement that said:

> WANTED IMMEDIATELY, a young Lady between the ages of 10 and 15 years to learn the art of Type Setting. Must be Quick and Active, able to read common writing and not Afraid to Work. Steady employment guaranteed when Competence is gained.

"But Emma," I said, "you're some time past the ages of ten and fifteen."

"That's not important," she said. "What's important is that they need a typesetter and aren't scared to death of hiring a woman, and it beats taking in men or laundry."

"Emma!" Gil said.

"If you please," she said. "It's only sensible for all of us to find work to help Calvin buy photographic supplies, and that's precisely what I'm going to do."

Mr. Desmond said, "No, Emma. The way things are with you, what you need is rest. I'll rig a tent for you, and you'll stay with the wagon. There's bound to be a slaughterhouse in a town this size, and such places always need men, and I'll be bringing in money enough for us all before you can snap your fingers."

Her color came up. "What do you mean, the way things are with me?" she said. "If you mean my health, I'm feeling very well now, and I'll tell you the truth, it's your health I'm worried about."

Mr. Desmond, as always, said, "I'm fine. You don't have to worry about me."

They regarded each other. Emma's color was still high, and she finally looked away. "Hap Desmond," she said, "don't you dare—"

"I'm not saying anything," he said. "I'm just saying rest is what you need."

Gil said, "Hap is absolutely right, Emma. We'll all find jobs in no time, and you can rest here."

"Typesetting is the easiest thing in the world," she said. "You sit on a stool and don't move anything but your fingers. I tell you, it will be rest in itself."

"But—"

"No!" she said defiantly. It was meant for all of us, and to all of us she said, "There is an opportunity for me here. A daily newspaper that has to beg for ten-year-old girls to come set type is bound to be short on reporters and editors too, and I can fill that bill. I've told you time and time again I'm no ordinary woman. We need money, and I intend to do my share to earn it."

She did. None of us could talk her out of it. Something gave me the idea that perhaps Mr. Desmond could have, but after their first exchange he didn't try. He spruced up a little and put on his other shirt and tied Nemo to the wagon and went off to find the slaughterhouse. Gil went to try the saloons, having decided that since he knew all about the wine merchants' trade perhaps he could be a barman. Calvin wanted to try the mines and for me, who knew about them from Uncle Dawkins, to try a store, but Emma said to escort her to the *Daily Tombstone,* so when she was dressed in her best brown dress, Calvin and I did that first.

There was absolutely everything in that town. There were fancy hotels like the Cosmopolitan and the Occidental, and fancier saloons like the Alhambra and the Crystal Palace, and theaters like Schieffelin Hall and the Bird Cage. Reading issues of the paper while we helped Emma wait for the editor, we learned there was also a tennis court and a ladies' club and a hanging only the previous week, in which one Dennis W. Dobbs had been hanged for murder after a breakfast of breaded spring chicken, cream sauce, fried oysters, lamb chops, green peas, tenderloin steak with mushrooms, English pancakes and jelly, potatoes, bread and coffee. I liked reading about the breakfast, but I didn't like reading about the hanging.

The editor came in from selling advertisements and Emma tackled him without wasting more words than introducing herself and us, whom she introduced as her cousins.

"I note you need a typesetter," she said, "and I've come to apply. From the looks of this place you could also use another reporter, and while I'm a swift and no one can deliver more ems an hour than a swift of my caliber, I'm also one of the finest newspaper editors and reporters you'd ever care to meet. It was I who put the *Krum Chronicle* in Texas on its feet and raised its circulation from less than two hundred to over two thousand in a mere four months."

"The *Chronicle?*" the editor said, looking confused but defensive. "I'm sorry, but I've never heard of it."

"Then that shows how far behind the times you are, which surprises me," Emma said. "The *Chronicle* was even known in Hagerstown, New Mexico Territory, where the editor begged me for details of my circulation scheme and asked to hire me as assistant editor."

"I'm sorry, but you should have stayed there then," the editor said, still defensive but trying for firm ground. "We don't employ women editors in Tombstone. It's too tough a town for a woman."

"There's no tougher town anywhere than San Francisco, and lady editors are all the rage there," Emma said. "I'm afraid, sir, that Tombstone must not be very progressive."

Well, Emma soon had that man backed to the wall and had him apologizing for Tombstone's old-timeyness, but he remained

233

adamant about no lady editors or reporters, so she said all right, she'd start as a typesetter to prove her worth and would progress from there.

"I'm sorry, Miss Prosser," the editor said helplessly. "As my notice clearly stated, I just need a girl to begin as an apprentice, and the pay wouldn't be anywhere near enough for a swift, even a lady swift."

"What can an apprentice do for you but drop every tray and pi every last piece of type in the shop?" Emma said. "No, pay me a living wage, I'm not greedy, and I'll get right to work. Don't worry about not having enough around for me to set. I'll gather some news for you in my spare time, and I'm no novice at selling notices, either. And I can justify a line, lock up a form, ink it, and if called upon I can pull a perfect impression on a Liberty or a Ramage or any other kind of press I've ever met. Just what kind of a press do you use, sir?"

The editor, helplessly, still wanted to say no, and I think he would have said it, until Emma broke off her busybody talk and said, "Please, sir. I really need the work."

That full, moist lower lip of hers was trembling, and the editor gulped a few times, and of course he said yes. Who could have said no? I would have jumped into the deepest mine shaft in Tombstone if Emma had looked at me that way and said please.

So she whipped a big black apron and a set of black sleeve protectors out of a parcel she'd had me carry and bade us good-bye, her lower lip still trembling a little.

"Good luck," she said to us, "but don't worry. When he sees what I can do, he'll pay me what I'm worth, and we'll have the money in no time, Calvin, for photographic supplies."

She left us, with a busy rustle of her skirts. We didn't just want to stand on the boardwalk where she could see us, so we moved off a piece and discussed what to do next.

"Not the mines, Calvin," I said. "We've none of us been eating too good, and that work's too hard."

"Work don't come too hard when you need it," Calvin said in his new, resolute way. "I'll be going now, and Pepper, if you find a store, try to find it around here. Maybe you'll get off the same time Emma does and you can walk her home. This is no town for her to be walking alone."

I promised him I'd try, and he went, and I did. I tried two grocery stores and a hardware store and, thinking of Mr. Desmond as I did it, a butcher shop, then a gun shop. But no one needed a boy, so I decided to broaden out and include liveries, since shoveling manure didn't require any particular professional background. I saw Gil rushing up Allen Street, looking excited. I hailed him. He rushed over to me and said, "Thank God! I've been looking for you everywhere!"

I think I dropped into a half-crouch. My eyes swept that busy street like lighthouse beacons, and I said, "Where were they? Did they spot you?"

"Who? What are you talking about?"

"The Wasums! Where did you see them?"

"I didn't see anybody," Gil said. He pulled a poster from under his arm, and I thought for a dizzy minute that he'd gotten himself another job nailing up posters, for he said, "Look! Look at this!"

It was about a base ball game between Tombstone and Fort Huachuca, a nearby cavalry post. Gil tore the poster out of my hands before I could read all the way through it and said, "Sunday. Today is Tuesday, isn't it? God, I've lost track. But if it's Tuesday that leaves us five days."

"To do what?" I said.

"Practice," he said. "Pepper, you and I are going to play in that game."

Confused, I said, "I guess we could practice at night after work. Have you found your job yet?"

"This is it," Gil said, shaking the poster under my nose.

"But Gil," I said, "it's real work we need, to recoup our fortunes. No one but big stars in the professional teams get paid anything for playing base ball."

"We'll get paid," he said. "I've never known an amateur sport yet where money wasn't being handed around." He lowered his voice and said in a confidential tone, "Even cricket."

"But Gil . . ." I said.

He said, "Pepper, I've tried eight saloons already, and they've all turned me down for lack of experience. I've got to help us

235

earn money. Do you understand? I've *got* to. Well, here is something that I'm fit for. Past experience is no criterion in sports. All that counts is what you can do. They're not going to fire some barman just because I might be better than he is, but they're damned well not going to keep some clod on a sports team when there's a better man available. Come on. We're going to go and demonstrate what we can do."

I didn't like it. It wasn't right that we should be contemplating playing while the others of our group were all out working. But Gil gave me a look that told me he badly needed moral support, and I sort of nodded. That was all he needed. He grabbed me and hustled me along, chattering like I hadn't heard him chatter since before the Pecos crossing. He had asked questions and found out all sorts of things. The local nine was working out every afternoon. The game was a grudge match. It was to be the biggest event in Tombstone since Independence Day, when the Tombstoners had beat the Huachucas in a game that went twelve innings and thereby made everybody late for the horse races and comic mule races scheduled for the town's main street. Since, the Tombstoners had accepted a challenge from a town named Tucson and had played a series of three games there, losing every last one. Fort Huachuca's hopes had risen afresh, and its new challenge was the result. But what sounded best to me, there was to be two hundred dollars purse money, and I asked, beginning to pant with our pace, "Are they going to divide it among the players?"

"I'm sure they will," Gil said.

I tried to work it out. "That would be nine players and two hundred dollars, so it would be . . . well, there'd probably be a manager too, so make it a ten-way split. Why, Gil! That's twenty dollars. And if we both got on the team we'd stand to win forty whole dollars, all by ourselves!"

"That's right!" he said excitedly.

Then I stopped in my tracks. This all somehow had a familiar feeling about it. A poster. A chance to win big money. I said, "Uh-oh."

"What's the matter?" Gil said. Then he chattered on, without waiting for me to answer, saying, "Oh, and the fort gets paid two days before the game. So it's not only feeling that's running high, the betting will be running high."

"Dear Jesus," I said.

"Come on," Gil said, tugging at me.

"No," I said, tugging back. "Don't you see what we're doing? Haven't we learned our lesson about wild schemes? And didn't you and Calvin, when you were Mr. S. J. Boldini, learn your lesson about wild bets? We can't afford this sort of thing."

"But Pepper, we're not going to bet," Gil said. "We're just going to get jobs as athletes."

"Promise me," I said.

"I promise," he said facilely.

"No, I mean you also got to promise that if there's nothing in it but the chance of purse money, we turn right around and go back and look for real jobs some more. Fifty cents or a dollar a day that you can be sure of is going to buy a lot more decent food for Emma and photographic chemicals for Calvin than twenty dollars that's just a whisper in the wind."

"I promise," he said again. This time he looked sober and sincere. We were almost to the base ball diamond anyway, and I could see two men already practicing batting and a half-dozen other men standing around and more players drifting in, so I let Gil herd me the rest of the way.

As my grandmother knew, and as our preacher back home apparently knew, and as my father in his profession of lawing may have known, and as I was already beginning to learn all too well, it's easier to be stupid than it is to be wise. More opportunities for being stupid arise, and more little things for helping the stupid-being come along. So naturally the one citizen we knew in Tombstone, Dugal Stewart, the miner who had let us park on his lot, showed up at the base ball diamond as a member of the team.

Gil was maybe getting cold feet about how athletes only needed ability and no prior experience and was asking me the names of faraway teams that he might claim to have played on, and I was telling him the Milwaukee Hop Bitters or the New York Quicksteps or the Philadelphia Athletics, when Dugal hollered hello to us and waved to us to join him.

"Come to watch the workout?" he said good-naturedly. "Keep

your eye on me. I'm center fielder, and I only drop the ball ten times out of twelve."

The half-dozen fellows who were watching the players came drifting over. Gil glanced at them nervously, then steeled himself and said, "No, as a matter of fact we were thinking of playing ourselves."

"Is that so?" Dugal said. "What positions?"

"Bowler and second base," Gil said. "I mean, pitcher and second base."

"We could use a better second baseman," Dugal said. "The one we have drops the ball twelve times out of twelve."

I said, "It's pitcher that Gil plays. That's what we're most interested in."

Dugal passed to one of the men who were standing listening to us, a portly man in suspenders and no collar. The man said to Gil, "Ever play any base ball before?"

"I certainly have," Gil said. "For the Philadelphia Faststeps."

"Goddamn," I muttered under my breath.

"The Faststeps?" the portly man said. "I'm not familiar with that team."

"It's a brand-new team," I said, speaking up quickly.

"Hmmm, hmmm," the portly man said, nodding. "Well, throw us a pitch or two, and we'll have a look."

Out Gil ran to the field. The portly man turned to Dugal and started asking him about some mission Dugal had been commissioned to carry out, having to do with getting a Mexican band out of jail. The band practiced all day every day and played all night every night, and the city had jailed it as a public nuisance, but the portly man, who was Dugal's boss with the Mountain Maid Mining Company, wanted them out of jail in time to play for Sunday's game. I wondered if they might be Freddie's roommates, but mostly I was watching Gil.

First he forgot and took a running start at the pitcher's mound, which he had told me the evening we played base ball and met Jamie that fast bowlers did. Then he forgot and bounced the ball fifteen feet in front of the plate, shooting it off to one side. I crossed my fingers. I was considering praying when Gil settled down. He had an odd delivery, throwing with his elbow stiff and never bent at all, but once he got going good his control was great. And fast? The catcher was soon complaining and saying he wasn't going to catch any more of Gil's cannon balls, and the portly man, a Mr. Johnson, called that a couple of batters should see what they could do against Gil's fast ball. I was glad it wasn't me. To tell the truth, I prided myself on my batting almost as much as I did my fielding, but I wouldn't have looked like much up against Gil. Neither did the two batters Mr. Johnson sent to try him. Within five minutes, Mr. Johnson was calling Gil back to talk, and Gil came grinning and looking like old Nemo when he'd beaten up some other dog in a fight.

"We just might be able to use you Sunday for an inning or two," Mr. Johnson told Gil.

"Indeed," Gil said cockily. "Then we have a few things to discuss."

"Like what?" Mr. Johnson said.

"Like money. My young friend and I are looking for steady work."

"Is that right," Mr. Johnson said. He gestured at another portly member of his group and said, "It could be we could get you on at the brewery or mine office, but I don't know about the boy."

"I'm no boy," I said. "I'm eighteen years old."

"Oh," said Mr. Johnson. I didn't care for the way he said it, but at least he kept his face straight. "Then let's see what you can do on a base ball diamond."

So I went off, to my favorite spot, second base, and Dugal picked up a bat and popped some easy flies at me, until I hollered at him, "If you can't do better than that, Mr. Dugal Stewart, them Fort Huachuca soldiers are going to be saying 'Ha, Ha!' after a certain ball game come Sunday," and Dugal laughed and started playing base ball.

I admit it, I wasn't as good as Gil, but I held my own, and I didn't do too poorly when I tried out at bat, either. Eventually, Mr. Johnson called me to him. He and Gil had finished their conference. Mr. Johnson said to me, "You find you have to miss work at the brewery, you come and see me. But if you find you have to miss base ball practice, I don't want to see you for any reason at any time and suggest that you leave Tombstone fast."

I said, "I'm on?"

Mr. Johnson said, "Isn't that what I just said?" He and the brewery man walked away.

"Are we really on?" I said to Gil.

He gave me a big grin and a Jamie-type *abrazo*. "We're both on!" he said. "Didn't I tell you? You sweep a little at the brewery, and I hang around the mine office, and the rest of the time we practice base ball. We report for duty tomorrow."

"But is there money in it?"

"Didn't I tell you there'd be money? Ten dollars a week for you, and, um, fifteen for me."

Well, maybe he expected me to be mad because he was making half again as much as I, but ten dollars a week was not bad money for an eighteen-year-old man, much less a fifteen-year-old boy, and I said, "Yippeeeeeee!"

"There's purse money, too, if we win," Gil said. "That's going to make Emma sit up and open her eyes."

So we danced up and down, me a little distracted by trying to figure out how much ten and fifteen dollars a week would come to per day for the four days we'd be "working" until the game on Sunday, and Dugal came off the field looking very pleased and congratulated us.

"We can pay you now for squatting on your lot," I said.

But he said, "Save your money." He looked around to make sure none of the remaining loungers could hear him, and whispered, "Bet it on the game. Keep mum, because we don't want the sports to learn about it and mess up the odds, but Tombstone is a sure bet to win."

The chief target of his eyes seemed to be a man dressed in fawn-colored trousers and a matching vest and frock coat, which sounds fancy but wasn't because of the many grease spots that had collected, possibly over several years, on the fawn. I said, "Is he a gambler?"

"Shhhhh," Dugal said. "Now that you're one of us, I can tell you. We've clubbed together and bought ourselves the catcher of the Huachucas. Hell, that's what they did to us in Tucson. We're sure to win. Carmichael, if you can keep your arm under control, we're even surer."

"You've bribed the Huachuca catcher?" I said. "And nobody knows about it?" I couldn't keep my eyes from Gil. He was looking at me nervously. I stammered, "What odds are the local sports offering?"

Dugal laughed until his face went red. Then he said, "Shhhhh." He called out to the man in fawn, "Tebbel, what odds are you giving today on Tombstone?"

Mr. Tebbel came strolling over to us and presented his grease spots for closer inspection. "Oh, I might give two to one," he said.

Dugal laughed, but just for the show of it this time. "Thanks anyway," he said. "I guess I'll take my friends uptown and introduce them to the big boys. I hear they're offering three to one."

"My, my," the gambler said mildly. "You just can't keep some people from throwing away money." A mild, and I swear fawn-colored, gaze roved over us, and he added, "But maybe I could match the odds. Just how much were you thinking of betting?"

Reluctantly, Gil said, "I'm afraid we've misled you. We weren't thinking of betting at all."

"No," I said. "We have no cash just at the moment, although we might have before the game." My eyes went to Gil again. His were startled, and then I was startled myself. What had I said?

"I don't normally do it, but for friends of Dugal's I might consider kind instead of cash," the fawn-colored gambler said mildly.

"Sure," Dugal said. "You could put up that funny-looking wagon of yours."

"Oh? Just what kind of wagon would that be?" the gambler said.

"We couldn't put up the wagon," Gil said.

But I said, "It's a fully equipped traveling photographer's studio."

"Equipped," the gambler mused. "You mean with cameras and things like that?"

"That's right," I said. "A hundred-dollar camera. And two fine mules. The wagon itself is worth at least another hundred."

"I've never seen a hundred-dollar wagon before," the gambler said. "You know, that might just be worth going along and having a look at."

Dugal said cheerfully, "It's parked right on my lot."

"No, let's not be hasty," Gil said.

But I said, "If Mr. Tebbel would just like to look at it, it wouldn't be exactly polite to say no, would it?"

"But Pepper," Gil said. "Have you thought—"

"He's thinking about three-to-one odds," Dugal said.

I was. Figures were tumbling over and over in my mind. Like a hundred dollars for the wagon and forty dollars each for the mules and a hundred for Calvin's camera, if we could convince this man it was worth that, and, I finally got the per-day figures worked out, something like five dollars and seventy cents for my working Wednesday through Saturday at the brewery and eight dollars and fifty cents for Gil from the mine office, and I arrived at the staggering total of two hundred ninety-four dollars and twenty cents. At three to one . . . my heart almost stopped beating. That would be eight hundred and eighty-two dollars! And sixty cents! Dresses for Emma. The doctor and a stake in a gold claim for Mr. Desmond. Ready-money for Gil. Money to keep Calvin out of bondage to remote kin in San Diego, California, when he was right here where he belonged and with what he was in love with, by which I meant not only Emma, but the West.

As for me, to hell with it, for it wouldn't really hurt me to postpone becoming rich and successful and respectable for another little while. I swear to God I wasn't thinking about the money for myself. I was thinking about it for Emma and Mr. Desmond and Gil and Calvin. It swelled up before my eyes. I blinked, and we were walking along with Dugal and the fawn-colored gambler named Tebbel, and Gil was looking at me worriedly, and I blinked again and was looking at a royal blue lace dress for Emma and plenty of buttermilk to take the sun-brown off her skin, and I blinked again and knew that I wasn't even thinking straight, much less planning. I was dreaming. I was dreaming a wild, crazy, reckless dream. And I had let my dream out to feed.

I came back to earth a little when I heard Nemo half-barking at the stranger and half-whining eagerly at us, his friends, and I knew that we had reached the wagon. I said, "Now all we're here for, Mr. Tebbel, is to look."

"Certainly," the gambler said.

Gil looked relieved.

Dugal looked happy and enthusiastic.

And Mr. Tebbel made us an offer. Just to add a little zest to Sunday's game, of course, he was sure we understood that. He would offer only fifty dollars for the wagon, despite all of Dugal's enthusiastic talking, but he bought the lie about the hundred-dollar camera and accepted that, and he exceeded my expectations on the mules. Poor things, gaunt though they were with weary weeks of travel, he offered one hundred dollars apiece for them. He wanted to buy them outright from us, on the spot, providing we had titles, for there was great trouble in that part of the country in buying stock with titles, he said, as so much livestock was run over the line from Mexico lacking same, and if a man was not careful what kind of a title he had some fellow would jump him and claim his horse or mule right out from under him.

And, my God, it all came to three hundred sixty-four dollars and twenty cents, and three times that would make—

". . . final arrangements until we can talk with our companions. Isn't that right, Pepper?" Gil said.

"What?" I said.

Nearly eleven hundred dollars!

Gil looked at me queerly. "I said we couldn't even discuss Mr. Tebbel's offer without first talking it over with our companions. Pepper? Are you all right, Pepper?"

"Oh, yes," I said. "Oh, yes indeed." I was. Maybe I had picked a strange time to take up dreaming. But it was a splendid dream.

"I'm serious about those mules," Mr. Tebbel the gambler said.

"I quite understand," Gil said. "But you must understand that we can't sell them unless we decide to, er . . ."

"To bet the whole kit and caboodle," Mr. Tebbel said. "Yes, I understand. But you don't want to wait too long to decide. Someone decides to lay a big bet, why, the odds naturally might change."

"Yes, of course," Gil said.

"If your friends say yes, you can generally find me at Bob Hatch's saloon up on Allen Street," Mr. Tebbel the gambler said.

"Yes," Gil said. He probably said it ten more times before Mr. Tebbel left, and also said, "Of course." I didn't say anything.

My eyes were still wide open and staring at nearly eleven hundred dollars.

I thought about it during the whole time it took for afternoon to become evening. Dugal went back to practice some more, but we didn't. Gil finally gave up trying to talk sense into me and asked where Emma was, and he went off to check on her, then went back to the jail to apologize for his stupefaction to poor old Freddie, then went up again at getting-off time and escorted Emma home to our wagon, by which time Dugal had come back to his cabin, and then Mr. Desmond came dragging in.

Mr. Desmond looked bad. His face was so tired, and his clean shirt and his trousers were streaked here and there with caked blood. He had found the slaughterhouse.

"Oh!" said Emma.

"Now be quiet, I'm just fine," Mr. Desmond said. "You?"

"I'm just fine," she said. "Except . . ." She exhibited her hands, which were all black with ink around the fingernails. "Pull off that shirt this minute, and I'll try to get both of us a little cleaner by washing it."

"No, leave it," he said. "It'll just get dirty again tomorrow." He pulled a dollar and four bits from his pocket and handed it to her, along with a bloody package wrapped in newspaper. "I just drew pay for part-day," he said, "but I brought a little beef, and the bones for Nemo. We can have beef stew for supper." He leaned against the wagon, looking as though he needed a place to lean.

Well, Emma had made a dollar of her own for her afternoon's work of typesetting, and she told me to run ask Dugal where was a cheap place to buy potatoes and onions for the stew. I didn't have to run far. Dugal came out of his cabin, looking clean and healthily tired, unlike Mr. Desmond, who looked unhealthily tired, and said he was bringing some scraps for Nemo, although his eyes were all for Emma and not for the dog at all.

"There's a grocery right around the corner on Fifth Street," he said. "I'll be happy to show it to you."

"Not there," Emma said. "Gil and I asked prices of the centrally located stores as we came home, and they want four cents a pound for rice and two cents for plain old navy beans. Really, if the cost of living gets much higher, the human race is going to have to give up eating."

Gil said, "Now Emma, a few pennies for rice or potatoes aren't going to make any difference."

"How would you know?" Emma said. "Yes, I know, you never have any money, but you don't really know what it's like being poor. To be poor you have to *feel* poor."

"Maybe we won't have to be poor much longer," I said. "Gil and I were talking this afternoon, and we came up with a real great . . ." I caught him looking at me, horrified, and I let my eyes drop. "Scheme," I concluded.

"Another of Gil's schemes?" Emma said, sounding uninterested. "It can wait. Where is Calvin? Does anyone know when he's coming home?"

We'd none of us seen him since we parted to seek work. We decided that he must be working late, and without saying it we all knew we'd wait supper on him, and Emma said she would start the stew if Dugal could impart information on some reasonably priced grocery store.

"There's Hop Town," Dugal said, "but you don't want to go there. White people don't trade there."

"What's Hop Town?" I asked.

"The Chinese quarter," Dugal said. "You know, where the coolies live."

All of our group, even Gil, stiffened. I asked, "Do they sell reasonable food?"

"Yes, but . . ."

"Is it clean?" I said.

"I suppose so, but . . ."

I asked Emma, "How many potatoes and how many onions?"

"But . . ." Dugal said.

"Dugal," I said, as gently as I could, for he was a fine fellow, "we don't hold with holding against people what they happen to be. It don't make no difference to us."

"Oh," he said. "Naturally, I don't want you to think that I . . ."

"Of course," Gil said.

So I went to Hop Town and found that Chinese people sold potatoes that looked just like other people's potatoes, and I bought the vegetables for our stew and ran back to the wagon. Dugal had gone into his cabin, I hope just because he feared we would invite him to share our scanty supper, and Mr. Desmond was sitting bare-chested on his blanket roll and scratching Nemo's ears, and Emma was washing both his shirts, and Gil was trying to explain to Emma and Mr. Desmond that he had nothing to do with our betting scheme.

That's how I knew they'd been talking about it. They asked me quietly for more information and I told. Frankly, I think I half hoped they would throw up their hands in horror and tell me that I was a fool, had always been a fool, and was destined always to be a fool, but they both listened me out. They didn't even point out that they had brought home hard money and food, whereas I had brought home nothing but mad dreams. In an effort to make it sound better, I told them about the figures when it was all added up, about the three hundred sixty-four dollars and twenty cents, and how three times that was one thousand ninety-two dollars and sixty cents.

"That's a lot of money," Emma said.

"Nearly eleven hundred dollars," I said.

Emma said, "What do you think, Hap?"

Mr. Desmond thought. I sniffed the simmering stew meat. Finally Mr. Desmond said, "I think it's got to be Calvin's decision. After all, it's his livelihood that would be put up on a long shot."

"But you know Calvin," Emma said. Apparently by this time she did, and knew him well, for she continued, "Anything the rest of us wanted, Calvin would just go right along with it."

"I'll tell you this," Mr. Desmond said, "except for what it takes to eat, I'm willing to bet my pay. It's a chance to triple our money, and if ever money can prove useful, it will now. If we lose, well, I've lost nothing but four days' sweat, and I've sweated for nothing many a time before."

Emma said, "How much would it come to, Pepper, if we both bet?"

So I figured on it. Emma was making two dollars a day, which made Gil happy because he was getting paid fourteen cents a day more, and Mr. Desmond making three, which made Gil unhappy, but then we had a chance at a share in two hundred dollars of purse money. But their day-money would make twenty more that we could bet, which tripled would be sixty dollars more. I didn't take out for food. Hungry as I was, there was a deeper greediness either in my empty pocket book or my soul, and I figured we could get by for four more days without eating a whole lot.

"The thing I wonder," said Mr. Desmond, "is how come if Gil is so good and the cavalry team so bad, the local gamblers are still offering three-to-one odds?"

Gil said nervously, "Yes, I've thought of that too."

"But the local gamblers don't know the cavalry catcher has sold out," I said. "Besides, we won't bet anything until we check everything out real good, right, Gil? We'll even go watch the Huachuca team at practice and see how experienced they might be. Honest, we'll check everything very, very carefully. Won't we, Gil?"

"We'd have to," he said.

It got dark. We sat there waiting for Calvin and talking about what we ought to do. Gil had heard the Huachuca pitcher was weak, and I talked on about how we would carefully investigate that. Emma set the stew off the fire, it smelling so good that both Nemo and I moved to sit closer to it, and Dugal came wandering back out and sat with us and helped us contemplate the Fort Huachuca team, and we waited some more.

Coal-oil lamps had been blown out in neighboring cabins and a lot of folks gone to bed before we finally heard footsteps coming into Dugal's lot, and I called, "Calvin? Is that you, Calvin?"

"It's me," an exhausted voice called back.

And, oh, in our lantern light he was a sight. Dirt in his hair. Dirt and candle wax ground into his clothes. A weary smile on a face drooping with fatigue and four dirty dollars to give to Emma before Calvin collapsed slowly onto his quilts. He sat there a minute and then started slowly pulling off his boots. Mr. Desmond hurried to help him.

"Just sit there," Mr. Desmond said. "Pepper, bring him water."

I did. I said, "My God, Calvin, where have you been all evening? Have you been working all this time?"

He nodded a little. "They paid me for a full shift." There was weary pride in his voice. "I got myself on at the Silver Plume mine."

Dugal, who was still with us, said, "The Silver Plume? Where they had the accident?"

Calvin nodded.

"What accident?" Emma said.

"A man got killed. Shorty Holt. Part of a shaft caved in on him. It just caught his leg, but he bled to death. It wasn't even a bad wound. He just couldn't free himself, and he bled to death."

"Oh!" said Emma. "I set that story just today for the *Daily Tombstone!*"

Calvin said, "We're digging out the shaft." He finished washing his hands and face, with Mr. Desmond's help, and with a groan of weariness leaned back on his quilts. "I ought to get these dirty clothes off," he said vaguely. "Grandma would skin me alive if she saw all this dirt on a patchquilt she quilted with her own hands."

Dugal said, "Man, you don't want to work at a mine that doesn't even keep track of its own men and doesn't dig them out in time. You come with me tomorrow to the Mountain Maid Mining Company and I'll see if I can get you on there."

"No thank you," Calvin said. He closed his eyes. "They're paying me good pay, and I don't think I could better it."

I said, "But Calvin, you don't need to do such dangerous work. We're going to make absolute fistfuls of money. We . . ."

I broke off. Dugal was still there. And this business of risking everything we owned was a matter just for us. Dugal felt it. He said good night and left immediately.

I started in to tell Calvin about the base ball scheme, but Emma said let Calvin eat, but Calvin was too tired to eat. He seemed to have to struggle to understand us, weighed down with the dark clods of exhaustion from working beneath the dark and waiting earth. He fastened on Gil's telling him we were both to be paid for playing base ball and he said we must have his share of the stew, for athletes needed good, solid food. Emma coaxed until he sat up and sipped a little of the broth. He tried to listen to the scheme and to my telling that we were going to investigate everything very, very carefully before we made any decision, but I couldn't determine how much he understood. He was just plain tuckered out.

He lay back down. "It all sounds just fine," he said. "That'll be a fine lot of money, which is just what we need."

"But Calvin," Gil said, "do you really want to bet your wagon? Everything?"

"If y'all think we have a good chance," Calvin said vaguely. "It all sounds just fine." He rolled over and tucked his head in his arm and mumbled, "Be sure to wake me up in a little while. I have to be back at work at six in the morning."

Well, there was just no point in trying to talk to poor Calvin any more, or trying to see if he really understood what we had been telling him. I went off to Dugal's privy, and when I came out Gil was waiting for me, wanting to worry out loud about whether I meant what I'd only said a hundred times about us investigating everything carefully before we decided on the scheme.

The stars looked very near in Tombstone. The air was clear, and that desert country seemed perfectly designed for stars to swoop down upon, until you just knew if you climbed up on the nearest hill and reached up you could have one all for yourself.

I said to Gil, "All that is beside the point now. The point is, I've got to get Calvin out of that mine. Him, who thinks everything above ground is so beautiful he's got to take views of it all, working down in that dank, dirty dark? No sir. This scheme will pull him out."

"Will it, Pepper?"

"What do you mean?"

"I mean, maybe the rest of us are just betting a few days' work, but if we bet Calvin's wagon, we're betting everything he has in the world."

"Oh," I said.

"Yes," Gil said. "Remember, we could lose."

Fifteen

On the day of the game, when he finally woke up, we surprised Calvin with twenty glass plates and twice that much photographic paper and refills bought from Mr. C. S. Fly as replacements for his broken or used-up chemicals. That was Gil's idea. He traded our chances at the purse money to Mr. Johnson of the Mountain Maid Mining Company for the cash to buy Calvin's things, his rationale being that, if we won our bet, a mere forty dollars wasn't going to be of any particular interest to us, and if we lost, Calvin would at least have had one last chance to go out in the desert around Tombstone and take views. Personally, with a return of practicality, I didn't think Gil needed to have bought so much stuff, just in case Calvin didn't have a camera any more after Sunday. But when I saw Calvin's sleepy, dirty face light up, as his tired eyes drifted from the cup of coffee with which Emma awakened him to the photographic stuff that Gil and Mr. Desmond had almost buried him under while he was sleeping, my practicality fled to wherever it was skulking lately, and I was glad, glad.

So was Gil. He laughed nervously and said that Calvin could make the portrait of every last cactus growing around Tombstone, and he laughed nervously again when Mr. Desmond said why didn't Calvin start by taking a portrait of a certain prickly view closer to home, that is, Emma. But then Gil had been getting progressively paler and tenser as the day of the game came closer, and his nerves were strung as tight as catgut on a fiddle by the time of the actual day.

Yes, we had bet everything. Gil had even pawned his valet suit and derby to the Chinese grocer, a man called Sam Wah, I think because he wanted to show us he was as willing as Calvin to risk every last belonging he had in the world. And yes again, Calvin had nodded wearily when I kept explaining the scheme to him every night when he came home from the mines, and said it all sounded just fine, and his only objection was one I had lost sight of: Gil and I would be making ourselves plenty conspicuous playing in a base ball game that the whole of Tombstone and Fort Huachuca combined would be turning out to see, and although he was sure that if the Wasums were around anywhere they wouldn't have the nerve to attack us right in the middle of a big town, still we should all be alert and careful and not wander off anywhere alone.

That was why Mr. Desmond and Emma and Nemo went with Calvin and the wagon that morning to take views before they came back for the game. I believe Gil hoped until the last minute that they wouldn't come to the game at all, and I expect he was still hoping it when he and I and Dugal set off for the diamond.

We were good and early. The Mexican band hadn't even shown up, although there were several Mexican vendors around selling something Dugal identified as "tacos" and "birria," which looked like plain, everyday barbecue, and Dugal said we should try both, the treat was on him.

"No, no," Gil said. "I never eat much before a base ball game."

I wanted to ask him how would he know, as this was the first real game he would play in, but then we'd worked out for good long sessions daily for four days, so maybe Gil felt like a seasoned veteran because of that. I must say he played like one too. The first day of practice, like many good pitchers he could barely bat, but the second day he was doing better, and on the third and fourth days Mr. Johnson moved him up to fifth bat, after our team captain—a wiry little greengrocer—who was first, then a barber, and then me, with Dugal, a solid, heavy batsman, as fourth up. We had been late only for the second day's practice, by permission of Mr. Johnson, for we had taken him at his word and asked if we couldn't miss a few hours' work and go to Fort Huachuca west of Tombstone and scout out the Huachuca team while they practiced. It was that same evening that we placed our bet, and Gil was able on his nightly visit to the jail to tell poor old Freddie to hold on, help was on the way. The Huachucas were heartwarmingly bad, being both bumbling and weak, especially their pitcher, Gil told me repeatedly and happily, especially their pitcher.

Well, while we were talking to Dugal there on the field on the afternoon of the game, up rolled Mr. Johnson in a buggy and gave us our uniforms, which his wife had altered to fit us. Mine had had to be let out in the legs because it was too short, and I was very pleased. Despite that summer's poor diet, I was getting taller. The uniforms were nice, white flannel with red belts and red ties and a red "T" embroidered by Mrs. Johnson on every one of them. We changed behind Mr. Johnson's buggy, glad that there weren't many people around yet, and then my sponsor at the brewery came along in his buggy and looked me over good. He retied my tie for me. I didn't know whether to feel like his little boy or his slave.

Out we went to warm up. Gil was wild at first, then his pale face got a little color in it and his arm started working like a piston rod, and our team started chatting it up and calling insults and encouragement at one another, and we were all feeling feisty as can be when the first baseman, a miner like Dugal, called out, "Here come them pathetic sonsofbitches!"

It was army wagons, bringing the Fort Huachuca team. The whole town and the whole cavalry post seemed to be following along in back of them.

"Let's show them what they're up against!" Dugal cried, and we started a fast throw-about, whipping the ball over the field and no one dropping it a single time, and the Tombstone people who were flooding in all looked as happy and expectant as a tribe of cannibals sitting down to eat their favorite enemy.

So did Mr. Tebbel, our fawn-colored gambler, whose pockets were crammed with all of Calvin's title papers and all our money, which Mr. Johnson and Dugal had said we could trust him to hold. Miners were betting newly dug thousands in silver and gold, and our bet, although it was everything to us, was apparently only small potatoes anyway when compared to the sums Tombstone gamblers were accustomed to dealing in. Mr. Tebbel waved at me when he saw me looking at him, and smiled a mild and gentle smile.

I didn't know what he could find that hot, bright Sunday to smile about. Not until we cleared the field for the Huachucas to warm up, and an agile, brown-mustached giant of a man swung out of an army wagon and took up position as pitcher on the field.

"My God!" Gil said to me in a hoarse whisper. "Who is he?"

"He's not their regular pitcher!" I said.

"Hell no!" Gil said.

"Let's run tell Mr. Johnson," I said.

Gil wouldn't, but I had no such false pride, and I ran to tip off Mr. Johnson that those black-hearted connivers dressed in blue from Fort Huachuca were trying to slip a ringer in on us.

It was unnecessary. Mr. Johnson already knew. He button-holed a Huachuca captain, and we all gathered around. Mr. Johnson said, "What in hell are you trying to pull here, Forrester? That man's no soldier, you can tell by looking at him. Get him off the field."

But Captain Forrester was a bold one. He said, "There's nothing in the rules saying we're required to field only cavalrymen. Mr. Borden is a clerk at the post store. That makes him a legal resident of Fort Huachuca. He plays."

"Borden?" I said. "You don't mean Lon Borden?"

"That's right, young man," Captain Forrester said. "I see you've heard of him. Tell your teammates what you've heard."

I gazed steadily at the bold cavalry captain, hating him. He wanted to demoralize us Tombstoners. I was damned if I would be the one to tell them what I thought I knew from a youth spent on loving base ball and collecting base ball cards, that a Lon Borden had played two seasons for the New York Metropolitans before getting expelled for chronic tosspotting, then had drifted to the Buckeyes of Columbus, which was the last I had heard of him.

"No?" Captain Forrester said to me. "Well, but your team-mates might be very interested in knowing that Mr. Lon Borden played in the Eastern Championship League in both '81 and

'82. You'll want to study how he does it, boys. You might learn something about playing base ball."

A bitter argument ensued. Mr. Johnson claimed that anyone with eyes could see Lon Borden was no counter-jumper—meaning dry-goods salesman, an occupation in those times thought suitable only for the most effete of men, and, at that, men given to practices that nobody, not even other men, talked about. I wasn't sure. Lon Borden was posing and attitudinizing on the field like an Adonis, and I had heard a few things, even on a topic nobody in the world discussed, about those old Greeks. Captain Forrester counter-claimed that Lon Borden was indeed a bona-fide employee of the post store, and the records were available to anyone who cared to check them.

"Hell's bells, Forrester," Mr. Johnson raged, "you know you hired that man only for the game, and he's not a real citizen of Fort Huachuca at all!"

Dugal, red-faced and wide-eyed with listening, forgot himself and looked at Gil and me, and Gil put his hand over his face as though some fly might have bitten him there, and we both backed out of the crowd.

Gil pounded his fist into his open hand a few times and said to me privately, "A professional league player! I say it's despicable chicanery!"

"Then there's despicable chicanery on both sides," I whispered. "We claimed you were a professional league player too."

"We did?" he said.

"And don't forget our side has bought itself the Fort Huachuca catcher. Don't worry, Gil. It's going to be all right. We're not going to lose."

"God knows, we'd better not!" Gil said.

"Stop worrying," I whispered urgently. "All we got to do is play great base ball."

"Sure," he said.

"Besides," I said, "that Lon Borden's a drunk. He was never anywhere but in a saloon. Even on nights before games. Why do you think he got fired by the Metropolitans?"

"He doesn't look drunk now," Gil said.

We both turned and studied the big man posing out on the field. He would draw himself up and regard the sky and stand there for as much as a minute before he'd throw the ball, but it looked like whenever he could stop trying to make a mash by his elegant posture and remember he was supposed to be playing base ball, his pitches were both fast and tricky. The little bit of color slowly drained from Gil's face, and he looked downright greenish by the time the umpire, a man brought all the way from Benson hopefully to ensure his objectiveness, held court over Mr. Johnson and Captain Forrester and ruled, which shows you how hard objectivity is to come by, for Fort Huachuca. The final straw for Gil was seeing Emma. And Calvin. They had pushed their way to the front of the huge crowd that was now encircling the field. They'd even gotten the What's-It Wagon parked among the carriages and buggies at the edge of the outfield, and I figured Mr. Desmond, who was sitting in the wagon, had accomplished that. Nemo was beside the wagon, not tied but staying there and looking excited, and Emma and Calvin and Mr. Desmond all looked excited too. Emma waved.

"God help us," Gil said.

"Wave back," I said, doing so.

He wouldn't.

The umpire told the crowd to clear off the sidelines and summoned the captain of us Tombstoners and the captain of the cavalry team to toss.

My eyes wandered, preoccupied, over the crowd. Mr. Tebbel the gambler waved again, looking so stinking pleased with himself that this time it was I who wouldn't wave back. The Mexican band struck up something strong on brass. Whiskey and taco and barbecue and beer vendors snaked their way here and there through the crowd, and I wondered for an insane second if I could get ahold of a whiskey vendor and introduce him to Mr. Lon Borden, formerly of the New York Metropolitans, before I remembered that we had bet everything but Nemo's bones from the slaughterhouse, and that I had no money to buy or bribe whiskey for my opponent. Cavalry men in blue were everywhere, slapping their legs, happy, grinning about the umpire's ruling over their rung-in pitcher. And then the umpire cried, "Take the field! Play ball!"

"Ah Christ," Gil said in a low voice.

I grabbed him by both arms and shook him until he would

look at me. I said, "We can do it, Gil. And if we can't, we'll have done the best we can. That's all Emma or the rest expects of us, Gil. When you've done the best you can, what else is there?"

"All right," he said.

"I mean it," I said. "You're English, so you never got licked, but we got licked once, and it didn't matter. What matters is trying. Then you can hold your head up."

"Fight the good fight?" he said. He smiled a very small smile.

"Yes," I said.

"Be a man?" he said.

"Yes," I said.

Now Gil grinned at me. We took the field.

In the lines of both base ball and despicable chicanery, we did do our best. In fact, in the latter line, I have never seen anything like the way that ball game was played. The first fight, a private one, erupted after the third inning over on the Fort Huachuca bench. During the fourth inning, the crowd lost its collective head and descended upon the umpire and us ball players twice, once partially because of me and the next time because of me and Nemo. The pistol warning by Mr. Johnson, also private, occurred after the fifth inning. And after that things really picked up. This is the way it happened:

The game was still close by the third inning. Gil was good, and the Huachucas had only got one run off him, and although we hadn't managed a score yet, we were playing good ball in the field. But that Lon Borden, or, as I couldn't help thinking of him, Adonis, was a very fine pitcher. We Tombstoners just didn't get that many people on base, although it wasn't for lack of trying on the part of our bought-and-paid-for Fort Huachuca catcher.

The catcher was a hard-working thief. In the East, I had heard, just about all the players by then were using specially designed gloves to help them catch, but way out here our two teams were still catching bare-handed, all except Adonis, who had brought his own glove. The Huachuca catcher used this bare-handed catching as his excuse to stand well back from home plate and take Adonis's hard pitches on the bounce. This gave him plenty of opportunities to fumble the ball away.

Well, the catcher's fumblings in the third inning enabled the barber, who batted right in front of me, to steal to second when I—yes, I admit it—struck out. Then Dugal was up. On Adonis's first pitch, the catcher dropped the ball again, and it rolled forward. Dugal quick-thinkingly put his foot on it, while our barber got all the way to third.

That was our downfall. I said to Gil, as he stood nervously to the side of the field and swung two bats to get ready for being up after Dugal, "He didn't do it right."

"What?" Gil said distractedly.

"The catcher. He didn't put on a good enough show of trying to get the ball out from under Dugal's foot. Look. All his teammates are watching him."

"Don't bother me now, Pepper. God, if I only had a proper cricket bat instead of one of these ridiculous round sticks."

But I was right. Immediately, the catcher muffed the next catch, and our barber on third came roaring home and scored because the Huachuca catcher wasn't "fast enough" to retrieve the ball and tag him out.

It was too many mistakes in a row for the catcher to get away with. Captain Forrester was jumping up and down and waving his arms on the sidelines, and the minute Adonis struck Dugal out—yes, it can happen even to a heavy batsman like Dugal—the Huachuca players streamed in from the field and converged upon our—their—catcher.

Gil threw the two bats down, looking relieved because he wouldn't have to bat, but I said, "Look! Look!"

The Huachucas dragged the catcher over to their bench. White flannel backs with blue belts and blue trim, and Captain Forrester's blue-uniformed back, surrounded him. I couldn't really see what was going on, but there was a lot of shuffling and arms jabbing.

"We got to help him!" I said. "They're going to kill him!"

"We can't help him," Gil whispered. He was upset but steady.

"But . . ."

"It would be an open admission of guilt. If you want to help him, keep quiet."

"But . . ."

Calvin said happily, right at my elbow, "Oh but you're doing fine, partners." He and Emma and Nemo had all three come up without my even seeing them. "I want to take your portraits after the game. We'll want to remember this day forever!"

I tore my eyes away from the cluster of Huachuca backs and jabbing arms. I blurted out, "You'd better take your portraits fast, Calvin, for we're in trouble, and you may not have your camera long."

Calvin looked stunned and it was Emma who said, "What is it? What's happened?"

I said, "Not only have the Huachucas rung in a pitcher who once pitched for the New York Metropolitans, but they've just caught the catcher we'd bribed to throw the game to us."

"Why those dirty blackguards!" Emma said indignantly.

Now the circle around the catcher parted, and the catcher staggered over and slumped down on the Huachucas' bench. No blood was showing. I think the beating they gave him went unnoticed by most of the crowd. The umpire had gone to see what the delay was about, and the Huachucas, giving us hateful looks, thundered up to bat. We were waved away into the field.

Emma called after us, "Huzza for the Tombstoners! Huzza for the boys who are going to win! Huzza for Gil Carmichael!"

That got Gil so rattled that the first man up got a two-base hit off him.

All our team was rattled at having the catcher discovered. The next Huachucan made a hard hit to left field that whizzed right past our left fielder, and Dugal had to come racing over from center field to chase it. He nearly had it scooped up when it rolled under the edge of some lady's skirts. Poor Dugal danced to the right and to the left of that lady, wanting the ball but too flurried just to reach in amongst the petticoats and pick it up, while the two Huachuca runners made an easy run home and made the score three to one. I howled my grief, and the crowd was howling too, and Mr. Johnson came trotting at a portly, angry trot to the umpire and shouted, "He never touched third base! That second runner skipped third base by a good fifteen feet! By God, since when do you allow that kind of cheap and nasty base running?"

The Huachuca runner joined in. "Like hell I didn't touch it! Besides, what about that kid on second? He tried to trip me. By God that's a stale, worn-out trick!"

259

"I saw that," said the umpire. "He'll draw a ten-dollar fine."

He meant me. My stomach got tight. All the players gathered around the umpire, and so did Captain Forrester, and someone in the crowd shouted to me, "Go for the umpire, kid! Give him a licking! I'll pay your fine!"

Well, there had been a lot of drinking going on. The crowd came out of its wagons and seats and pressed onto the field. Women screamed. The Mexican band started playing. The police chief's men, who were among the crowd, drew no guns but did draw clubs and flailed them about. A series of drunken brawls broke out, with rings of spectators forming around the most active matches. In the midst of it all, Nemo came galloping up to Gil and me and barked and growled at all comers.

"Clear the grounds!" the umpire shouted. "Clear the grounds!"

It took the combined efforts of the Fort Huachuca post commander and the mayor of Tombstone to restore peace. It was an uneasy peace, for the umpire ruled that both runs were legal, including, since he hadn't seen the shortcut past third base, that of the second runner.

I said to Mr. Johnson, "But he didn't even come close to third base. I was looking straight at him."

"I know," Mr. Johnson said.

"And I didn't either try to trip him."

"Yes you did," Mr. Johnson said. "I was looking straight at *you*. Keep up the good work, boy. I'll pay your fine myself, and any more you chance to accumulate."

Well, with that sort of carte blanche, what would any rational person have done? Gil, by superhuman effort, kept the Huachucas to just those two runs the rest of the inning, and when our side came up for bat, old Nemo just happened still to be with me, and it will be remembered that Nemo had had some practice one day by a catch basin fetching base balls, and I had noticed how that business with the woman's skirts for the Huachucas had worked pretty well, so when one of our men got a little piece of Adonis's ball and sent it rolling gently out toward first base, where it was sure to reach before he did, I just leaned toward Nemo and told him softly, "Fetch!"

He did. Nemo was feeling titillated anyway by all the interesting barking he'd just done. He was on that field in a big black streak and racing Adonis and the first baseman for that ball. Nemo won hands down. Adonis drew back girlishly. The first baseman tried to snatch the ball from Nemo, and my, but that was good fun for a dog. Nemo leapt to the side, and the first baseman leapt after him. Our batter rounded first and headed for second. The first baseman cursed and shouted, "Drop that ball!" Nemo scampered back away from him and growled around the ball in his mouth. The Huachuca catcher—a new one, for our former friend was now spending his time on the bench holding his head—joined the first baseman in the pursuit, and Nemo dropped the ball to growl better. Our man made it to third before the first baseman decoyed Nemo's attention and the new catcher grabbed the ball and raced for home, with our man racing homeward and the crowd screaming its pleasure, and our man got there first.

That caused the second near-riot and the second surge of the crowd onto the field. Mr. Johnson screamed that he'd seen no dog and no dog had been on the field, and the umpire and Captain Forrester screamed back at him to the effect of how come the base ball was all wet with slobber if there hadn't been dog interference? The umpire ruled the run was no good and made our runner go back to third base, but Captain Forrester screamed some more and the umpire finally made our man go all the way back to second. That seemed to be a good compromise and everyone stopped arguing. When peace was more or less established again, Mr. Johnson came over to me and whispered that I'd done just fine in flustering our opponents, and perhaps I had, because we managed to bring our runner home to make the score legal before they finally settled down, and that brought us back into contention, being only one run behind at the end of the fourth inning.

No runs for either team occurred in the fifth, and the only relevant thing that I need report is that, when the Huachuca team started batting, I saw our third baseman miss an easy-as-pie roller that put one of the Huachucas on base. I'd watched that man handle much more difficult balls during practice, with nary a fluff. I groaned to myself, but it may have been out loud that I said, "Oh my God, can they have done it to us too?"

Mr. Johnson, ever alert, had also seen it. After the inning he called us over to the bench and said, "I have noticed some less-than-sterling play on the part of some of our team members. Now I'm making no accusations, but . . ."

Who can you trust? Not one man but two, our third baseman and our right outfielder, both went pale. The outfielder started protesting, "Now see here, Mr. Johnson . . ."

But Mr. Johnson waved him to silence. "I make no accusations," he said. "But boys, we're all here to play base ball, and that's what we're going to do. Most of you are doing just fine. Despite their big-league pitcher the score is close, and if we all play good ball we stand a chance to prove once and for all to Fort Huachuca that their methods are low and unworthy of an Arizonan."

That was when he pulled a big Colt Peacemaker out of his belt.

He looked at all of us, but his eyes were mainly for the third baseman and the right outfielder. He said, "Boys, I practice with this thing sometimes, and would you believe that it will shoot all over this base ball field? There's not a position anywhere that I can't hit from this distance. Boys, I just know you're going to do your best, and we're all going to go back out there to win."

There wasn't a word spoken.

Mr. Johnson sighed and put the Peacemaker back in his belt. The third baseman and the outfielder broke quickly out of our cluster. They didn't speak to each other. They stood quietly, looking something like Old Jeb and Young Jeb when time had come to hitch them to the wagon, not especially eager but wisely resigned.

Calvin approached and said, somewhat urgently I thought, "Pepper, I've got a photographic plate prepared, and it won't take more than a few seconds if you and Gil are ready."

"I sure hope your heart ain't set on us smiling for the camera, Calvin," I said.

He blinked and looked concerned. "New trouble?" he said.

"I'm not sure," I said. "But we may have two traitors of our own to deal with."

"Then I must make that photograph," Calvin said. "The camera is all set up and ready." He gestured. The big camera was sitting on its tripod not ten feet behind us, with Emma standing guard over it.

He looked so intense and resolute and . . . was it scared? . . . that I went to find Gil. I said, "Calvin wants to make our portraits now."

Gil glanced across my shoulder and said, "Is that what they're whispering about?"

I looked. Over by the camera, Emma and Calvin were whispering away. Out in the field taking his warm-up pitches, Adonis was watching them from the pitcher's plate and posing prettily for Emma. Or maybe it was the camera he was watching. He preened and flexed his muscles and smoothed his mustache, and he looked as if he had been doing it for some time.

Calvin called to us. But it wasn't really Calvin who called. It was Mr. S. J. Boldini, at his richest and loudest and silliest. "Come along, come along," he cackled. "I only got between innings here to shoot fine portraits of you fine base ball players to send to *Harper's New Monthly Magazine* and *Frank Leslie's Illustrated Weekly* in New York. I got to work fast, because I would dearly love to make the portrait of some fine member of the opposing team. Us journalists like to show both sides."

"Calvin, please," Gil said, pained.

"Shhhh," I said.

"What's wrong?" Gil said.

"Nothing," I said. Even then I thought I knew, knowing Calvin and Emma and what we had all been through together.

So Calvin made our portraits. He was quick, but he was loud, and it seemed like every set of eyes clustered around that base ball diamond was looking at us. Out on the field, Adonis wilted, especially as Emma fussed around us, as if to help pose us, and talked loudly with Calvin about how the New York magazines would surely be crazy about these up-to-the-minute base ball photographs. Calvin rushed off with the plate, leaving the camera in Emma's keeping, promising loudly that he'd be back instanter looking for more photographic subjects.

It seemed to do some good. Adonis was inattentive and gave both our first baseman and our catcher fair shots at his fast ball. But nothing came of it. Our first baseman got tagged out trying to steal third, and our team captain struck out. Then the barber ended the inning with a little pop fly to their short stop.

The Huachucas didn't do much better when they got their turn at bat. Gil was still holding steady, and our third baseman and outfielder didn't lose any more balls. Calvin came hurrying back while we were still out in the field, bearing another freshly prepared plate and something else. I watched him so hard that only the occasional thought of Mr. Johnson's Peacemaker turned my thoughts back to our base ball game.

Because Calvin and Emma walked right up to Adonis. Adonis jumped to his feet off the Huachucas' bench and did a lot of bowing and hand-shaking. Calvin ran back and picked up that heavy camera as though it were stuffed with baby chicken down and carried it over to the sidelines near the Huachuca team.

Adonis struck a pose.

Emma applauded.

Adonis changed his mind and his pose.

Emma applauded even more.

Calvin ducked under the focusing cloth and ducked back out and smiled encouragement to Adonis, then complained about the shadows from the strong sun and raised the something-else to compensate for the shadows.

It was the James Flash Lamp.

A fly ball went over my head as I stared, and our right outfielder came charging in to make a glorious catch on the dead run, and still I stared. I could hear Calvin call out to Adonis, "Now be real still. Look straight at the camera. Real still now."

The James Flash Lamp must have been loaded brimful of flash powder, because my eyeballs exploded as it went off.

I could hear Dugal call to me, "Come on, Pepper. We've got a ball game to win." I couldn't see him. In fact, I couldn't see anything straight ahead. If I concentrated on seeing just out of the corners of my eyes, I found I could make out something besides just the white glary spot that floated in front of me. It was from the corners of my eyes that I saw Adonis, still flexing his muscles, still posing, grope his way to Calvin's hand to shake it, having considerable difficulty in finding it. Adonis had been standing not five feet from that James Flash Lamp, while I was clear out on second base, and if I was partially blinded, what was he?

My pulse was beating loudly in my ears as Gil struck out the last Huachuca batter and we came in from the field.

Gil came to me. "What's the matter?" he said anxiously. "Are you ill?"

"No, no," I said. "I never felt better. That is . . ."

"What?"

"Never mind. We'll see."

But I was first up, and although I could see better minute by minute, I was still having trouble seeing Adonis's fast pitches. My heart was beating so I could barely hear, and I didn't know what was happening until I heard the umpire roar, "Ball six! The man walks!"

Oh lord, I thought. It's working.

It was. That fool Adonis couldn't see a thing, but even with his teammates yelling at him to bear down, he was trying not to let on. After me came Dugal at the bat, and Adonis walked him too. The second baseman scowled at me hatefully as I trotted to second base, and I grinned hatefully back. By the time I got there I could see better and better.

Captain Forrester was yelling at Adonis now and telling him to start throwing right or he would jerk him right out of the game. Gil, his face tense, took his position by home plate. Now the players on our bench were catcalling at Adonis and telling him his string was all raveled out.

Adonis tried. He tried so hard to throw strikes, not balls, in an area that he couldn't see clearly, that he sort of eased off a little on his fast ball. He offered Gil one of the fattest, prettiest, slowest, most dead-center balls I've ever seen.

And Gil connected. The ball went sailing, sailing, clean out over the head of the Huachuca outfielder and into the wagons and buggies.

I scored. So did Dugal. Gil might have scored too, if he'd started running right away. As it was, he just stood there at home plate, staring with slack-jawed surprise at that sailing ball that he'd managed to hit square and solid with a ridiculous rounded stick instead of a nice, workable cricket paddle. He didn't stop staring and start running until Dugal had already rounded third base and was heading home behind me.

Even with his slow start, Gil made third. And poor old Adonis had let down the pasture gates.

By the time the inning was over and Adonis was pulled out of the game and sitting on the Huachucas' bench, looking madder and madder and knowing he'd been hornswoggled, we were ahead eight to three. And we knew we had it made.

The final score was twenty-four to eleven. Our favor, of course. Or, better, make that Calvin's favor. The Huachucas wouldn't even have gotten eleven runs, but Gil took a hotly hit ball smack in the face, breaking his right cheekbone, and three doctors and one dentist rushed out of the crowd and set him and stitched him and bandaged him on the spot and dosed him down so heavily with laudanum that he was puff-eyed on one side and loop-eyed on the other and could barely stop grinning and laughing dreamily and finish pitching our game.

Gil and Dugal were the town heroes after the game, and members of the Turnverein Society wanted to drag both of them off for a huge feast to which all the town's leading lights were invited. But Gil, grinning, happy, loop-eyed on laudanum, said no, he had a previous engagement for a private victory celebration. He meant with us.

And so our moment had come. They all wanted me to do it, but I said no, Calvin, and we followed after Calvin and stood by while he collected the splendid, doctor-buying, dress-buying, out-of-bondage-buying sum of one thousand one hundred fifty-two dollars and sixty cents from Mr. Tebbel, the fawn-colored gambler.

Mr. Tebbel paid without a murmur of protest. He commented mildly, "That was a very interesting base ball game. The town will be talking about that until Christmas." He counted out all gold coins, except for the sixty cents in silver.

Mr. Johnson was certainly happy with Gil. Calvin had done a lot of it, but nobody really knew that except Calvin and Emma, who had thought up the plan to save our betting scheme, and me. And Adonis.

Mr. Johnson kept saying that Gil should take tomorrow off

but be sure to come to the Mountain Maid offices on Tuesday and they would discuss Tombstone's future base ball schedule and Gil's own future, and it took us forever to get rid of him and get back to the What's-It Wagon.

Mr. Desmond was waiting there with old Nemo. Nemo whined, happy as always to see us. Mr. Desmond just couldn't find words enough to congratulate Gil and me, and it was a good thing we had both Jamie's memory and the memory of Jamie's *abrazo*, for that is what Mr. Desmond used.

Then we made Calvin show Mr. Desmond the gold coins, and Mr. Desmond said, "Well now. Well now, it seems to me our fine athletes have earned more than just slaughterhouse beef for themselves tonight. What do you say we all go out on the town tonight and make them eat pheasants and oysters and plovers' eggs? How about it, Pepper? Gil?"

But Gil only giggled, so floaty on laudanum was he, and we decided maybe we'd better take him and the wagon back to Dugal's for our celebration, passing first by the jail to share the good news with Freddie.

As they all started to climb into the wagon, I said, "There's just one thing more in the world I'd like to have. I'd like to have five dollars of that money right now."

Emma said, "What are you up to, Pepper?"

I didn't want to tell, but Emma could get her way with anything in the end, and in the end she made me tell.

"I've read and read of champagne," I said, "and it seems to me that's what we should begin our celebration with. For five dollars I ought to be able to buy a couple of bottles."

Calvin gave me five dollars. Emma hollered after me, as I set off running, still in my white and red base ball suit, "Go to the Chinese grocery, and I'll bet five dollars will buy you three bottles."

I ran, laughing. I ran toward Hop Town to do as she said. People shouted at me cheerily as I ran, and the Chinese people certainly knew about that base ball game, for as I neared Hop Town and began meeting some, they shouted at me cheerily too. I tore through the darkening streets and around a corner, wondering what champagne would taste like, hurrying to get back with it to Calvin and Emma and Gil and Mr. Desmond.

Then rough hands seized me, and my feet went out from under me.

As two big men dragged me struggling to a stop, another, smaller figure came around to face me, and a voice with a Claiborne Parish accent grated, "Now we've got you, you little Fairchild sonofabitch!"

Sixteen

Otis Wasum was no bigger than I, for all that he was two years older, and it took his efforts combined with those of Cass Hubbard, a pug-nosed, curly-haired man with plenty of muscle, and Sidney Clinkscale, the man with the guinea feather and the knife, to keep ahold of me. Shirley Wasum didn't help them; he scanned our squirming bodies quickly with his Wasum-blue but lively eyes, as if assessing whether he was going to have to break down and touch the flesh of a foul Fairchild, then, as if seeing no need, kept those same eyes peeled for passers-by. They dragged me into the Gilstrap Livery & Feed Stables, just around the corner and in the same block as the Chinese section. They did it openly. They showed no guns, but Shirley stared hostilely at two or three startled Chinese people we met on the street, and they lowered their heads and hurried away. I was trying to yell, but Sidney Clinkscale had his dirty palm over my mouth. It tasted of tobacco and horse.

The livery was empty. I could hear movements from stalls, but nothing else. They jerked me inside and closed the door. My mouth free, I said, "Let me go. Otis Wasum, you let me go this minute."

He wouldn't. But Shirley spoke sharply: "Let's cut out this wrestling bout and get down to business." Cass Hubbard and Clinkscale took their hands away, and Otis had no choice but to follow suit.

"We'll see you all hanged for this!" I sputtered. "You can't get away with attacking a man right in the middle of a big, busy town!"

Clinkscale spoke. I had heard him shout drunkenly the night of the trap, but otherwise I'd never heard his voice before. It was deep and big, suitable to his big frame. He said, "I don't see no man, and I don't see no big, busy town. I just see a nasty little boy who's cost me a pile of money and sweat, and a bunch of chinks that won't want no trouble and therefore won't mix with white men's affairs."

Otis said in a voice as pale and cold and lifeless as his own particular set of Wasum eyes, "Shoot this one, and let's go after the others."

"Just hold your piss," Clinkscale said. "I'm thinking."

Shirley's face reddened and he looked furious, partly at me, but also partly at Otis and Clinkscale. He opened his mouth to say something, but whatever new quarrel he was about to start got stopped by a young Chinese man coming in through a back door of the livery with a lantern. The man said something surprised and Chinese-sounding, I think fussing at them for being in the livery stable after hours, and Clinkscale swore at him and charged him like a big, angry bull. He swung and hit the man on the side of the neck, and the young Chinese man crumpled, and the lantern fell to the floor, and Clinkscale began stomping out the little licking flames of spreading coal oil and cried to Cass Hubbard, "Help out, you bastard! Shirley, you check that back door and see if there's any more of them chinks out there!"

I broke for the front door. Otis was closer to it, but I figured I could bowl him over and get out before the others got back. But I heard a sound that stopped me cold, the click of a gun cocking. Then Clinkscale cried, "Otis, damn you! You shoot that kid, and I'll shoot you! We can use him!"

Otis had a real pistol, with a real holster and everything. I saw it clearly when Shirley Wasum reported there was nobody else outside the door and nothing but alley, and he and Clinkscale and Cass Hubbard retrieved the Chinese man's lantern and rushed back to us. The Chinese man lay sprawled on the manure-splattered dirt floor, breathing in such a way that, had the

Wasums and their gang been human beings, they would have fetched a doctor for him immediately.

"We're losing time," Otis said. "We got to kill this one and go after the rest."

"Otis!" Shirley said, sounding both shocked and warning.

"Didn't I tell everybody to shut up?" Clinkscale said. "Wait. Don't nobody say anything. I'm thinking."

He thought. Cass Hubbard stood by and watched him think, and Shirley Wasum watched Otis, and Otis watched me, his pale eyes gleaming at me like some animal's in the lantern light.

Finally Clinkscale began to nod, and Cass Hubbard nodded along with him amiably. Clinkscale said, "Sho now. Them people like traps, and here's one outside the common run. What are we going to do? We're going to hold this kid. What are them others going to do? Pretty soon they're going to miss him and get all worried about him. What are we going to do next? We're going to send mouthword that we got the kid, and we're not about to give him back until we've got that goddamned picture. There now. Shirley, what do you think of that?"

Shirley nodded tentatively, and of course Cass Hubbard nodded, but Otis shook his head. Otis said, "We don't need to hold him. I'll shoot him, and get him out of the way."

Shirley said tightly to his little brother, "Otis, you keep that mouth of yours shut."

"Damn right," Clinkscale said hotly, backing Shirley up. "Where's your head, anyway, Otis? We might have to show this kid. We'll march him up to that front door and you can hold that gun right up to his head, and we'll say, you bastards bring that picture and its plate and all its copies, or Otis here will shoot his head off." Otis wanted to interrupt, but Clinkscale fingered the handle of his big knife, which hung at his belt, and said, "No, damnit, it's a good idea. It's better than just charging up to their wagon and getting shot by that old bastard with the rifle."

Shirley said, "Yes, that'll get this damned underbrush out from underfoot, Otis."

Otis kept his voice quiet. It was so quiet you had to listen hard to hear him. He said, "But they're all witnesses. We got to shoot them all, or they can witness against you."

Clinkscale growled a curse.

Otis said appeasingly to the big man, "Listen, Mr. Clinkscale, it's a fine idea. But what we want to do is, we wait until they all miss him, like you said, and then they get worried, like you said. And they spread out looking for him. See? Then we catch them out by themselves. We can pick them off one at a time."

Now Shirley began to look blue-steel daggers at Otis, and Clinkscale said stubbornly, "I tell you, we got to get that picture first."

I said excitedly, "There ain't no picture. Otis lied to you. There wasn't never no—"

"Fore God!" Clinkscale thundered. "You hold your piss. You nasty, lying little sneak, I sure as hell don't have to listen to you. You just better watch yourself around me, kid. You're not in my good books. You and that goddamned photographing fellow, you know how much money I had to leave hid with that goddamned marshal on my tail? You know how much trouble it's going to be to slip back and get it once we gotten you all taken care of? No, by God, don't you be giving me mouth, or I'll cut your goddamned tongue out."

Otis was staring at me. I thought there was worry in his face, the worry that I'd stand up to Clinkscale and present evidence and expose Otis for a liar. But his eyes held something additional. Expectation? But . . .

And then I saw. I held my piss. Otis smiled a faint no-smile at me, the way he used to do when I'd go into Uncle Dawkins's store and say hello, how were things. Like those times, he now only looked at me and didn't say anything. For my own good reasons, neither did I.

They reconnoitered the stable, into which they'd apparently jerked me with only hasty preparation after trailing me from the base ball field. They found more coal oil for the Chinese man's lantern. Clinkscale made sure he was unconscious and carried no weapon, and after that he never paid the slightest attention to him. Cass Hubbard came, limping a little, and trussed my hands behind me, and I took what consolation I could find in thinking that maybe Gil was right and he had hit one of them in the leg on the day of the ambush. Then Clinkscale and Shirley Wasum chunked me in a corner, and the four of them drew away and argued some more about Clinkscale's plan.

I closed my eyes to keep from looking at them. The dimensions of my situation flooded chaotically into my mind.

As Clinkscale had said, there was a trap, as there had been a trap before. I was bait, as I had been bait before. But this time it was the others who planned to spring the trap, and we who were to get caught in it.

I tried to get a grasp on my alternatives, but they were not pleasant. I could keep my mouth shut and refrain from trying to convince Clinkscale and the others that Otis was a snaky little liar and there was no picture, and then I could sit there and be bait until Calvin and Mr. Desmond and probably Gil, loop-eyed and bousy as he was with laudanum, and even Emma, if they'd let her, came and offered themselves as targets for Otis & Company.

Or I could try to convince Clinkscale and the others that there never had been a picture of them shot by Calvin, and if I succeeded Clinkscale would let Otis shoot me out of hand, as Otis was so obviously interested in doing. And then Calvin and Mr. Desmond and probably Gil and even Emma would all go out looking for me, not knowing I was dead, and offer themselves as targets for Otis & Company.

I feared for my life. I feared for the lives of my friends. I frantically tried my knots, as prisoners must, and I was filled with fear and fury and despair.

Then Clinkscale sent Cass Hubbard out the front door and into the black night, and I jerked to attention, not that I could hear what they were saying, but hoping Otis had not won the argument and that Cass Hubbard was not being sent out to start shooting. Surely they hadn't waited long enough. Surely, especially with going by to see Freddie, Calvin and Mr. Desmond and Gil were not out already, alone, wandering dark streets, looking for me. Not a half-hour had passed since Otis and the others had grabbed me. I wanted to live, at least a little longer. I wanted my friends to live.

But Cass Hubbard came back directly, with a pint bottle of whiskey. Shirley and Clinkscale had cussed Otis quiet. They were apparently going to wait. The bottle began to pass around amongst them.

Otis came after a while and sat on a nearby bale of hay and

just looked at me with his pale blue eyes and that faint no-smile. He said to me softly, "Do you know what I'm going to do?"

"I don't care," I said. "Leave me alone." As Clinkscale had done, I was trying to think. Desperately.

"First I'm going to see you and Calvin Fairchild dead at my feet."

"Don't you try to scare me, Otis Wasum," I said.

"Then I'm going to go back home," he said. "I'm going to turn around and go straight back. I'll be home well before hog-killing time."

"A fine welcome you'll get," I said. "Your own daddy has already confessed to the whole parish you're a murderer and a dirty little liar, and he's not going to be very happy to see you again, that's for sure."

Now a little glow of heat kindled in Otis's eyes. He pulled his gun out of his holster and inspected it. But Shirley called, "Damn you, Otis, how many times do I have to tell you? That boy's a prisoner of war, and there's not going to be any messing with guns."

"That's right," Clinkscale chimed in. "Don't you go shooting that kid until I tell you you can." He reached the bottle out of Cass Hubbard's hands and said suspiciously, "What's all that gibber about anyway?"

Otis said quietly, "Nothing, Mr. Clinkscale. Just home-town talk. We told you, he's from the same place we're from."

"That's the town where this kid put up the lies about you and your brother and got you chased out of town?" Clinkscale said.

Otis glanced at me. But I didn't say a word, and Otis said to Clinkscale, "Yes sir, that's the place."

Clinkscale turned back to Shirley and Cass Hubbard, saying, "Fore God, we're going to have to get more whiskey before this night is over. That stuff I ate at the base ball game has give me the bellyache."

I whispered to Otis, "What does he mean, lies? I guess you've been telling him you and Shirley was innocent."

Otis's eyes went motionless. "It ain't none of your business."

"Like fire it ain't," I said. "It was my father you tried to shoot."

Otis smiled his no-smile. "Maybe somebody might have done it, too, if that old Jew fellow hadn't gone and got himself in the way. But it wasn't me. I wasn't nowhere near that loft, Pepper Fairchild. You was lying."

"What!" I said indignantly. "Damn your hide, Otis Wasum, I saw you, and you know it!"

"Ha ha, ha ha," he crooned softly. "Twas me saw *you*, stealing poor old Shirley's rifle and trying to get him in trouble, then shooting at your very own daddy, trying to shoot him dead, because he beat you that time till you couldn't sit or stand."

"What in the world are you thinking about?" I said, bewildered. "Not a word of that ever happened. The judge never beat me in his life. He just sentences me to the smokehouse when I make him mad."

"Lies, lies," Otis sang.

"Oh go away," I said. "Otis, you're just flat crazy."

Now he no-smiled and his hand pat-patted his pistol holster and he said, "You can call all the names you please, it don't bother me none. Some folks got themselves more important things to do. Guess what else somebody is going to do?"

I pressed my lips together and refused to answer such nonsense.

But Otis said softly, "Somebody's going to take himself a pistol, and he's going to go to town to the courthouse, and he's going to sit down and wait for your father to come out. This time that somebody's going to get him for sure. Kill him dead right where he stands. You Fairchilds, always thinking you're so much. What do you think of that?"

My eyes, that I'd been trying to keep closed so as not to have to look at him, flew open. I said, "You shoot at my father again, and Claiborne Parish will set a record for hanging somebody what's only seventeen."

"They won't catch the somebody," Otis said. "They couldn't even catch the somebody last time."

"Yes they will," I said. "You're going to run out of brothers to go to jail for you."

"Watch how you talk," Otis said. "You're a fine one to talk. I know what you've been doing. You and that other fine Fairchild, you've been traveling all over Texas and the territories with a whore. Just wait until I tell them that in Claiborne Parish."

And now my eyes opened even wider. No, not because of Otis

this time. There was movement by the back door of the livery. Not horse movement. It was too quiet. Just a flick of something. Otis saw me looking, and I jerked my gaze away. I began to shudder. I couldn't help it.

I said rapidly, "You'd better get your facts straight." I was too frantic to feel properly insulted for her. "That lady is Miss Emma Prosser, former editor of the *Krum Chronicle,* and that shows what you are, you can't even tell a lady from a whore." I saw the movement again. It was man movement. It wasn't from some Chinese person, either. As it had to be, as I knew the moment I caught the first flicker that it would be, the movement was Calvin.

I tried not to look. But I had to look, so I tried to look just out of the corners of my eyes the way I'd learned after Calvin and Emma had dazzled Adonis into oblivion that afternoon. I was looking for other movements. Where were the others? How had they gotten here so fast? But there was only the one movement, that of Calvin, creeping, silently creeping, trying to creep up with Mr. Desmond's rifle and get a bead on the pale-eyed, venomous boy who had just spat the word "whore" at me.

I kept babbling. "I'll tell you something else," I said. "They will too hang you if you shoot my father, because I know just what you'll do, you'll just sit there and let them take you, and you'll hang proud as pie because you'll think you've done something to make that old bayou rat you call your daddy proud of you after all this time. You think—"

I had gone too far. The fire went out, and the eyes went cold, cold, and the gun in Otis Wasum's hand was a real gun. I opened my mouth to cry, "Mr. Clinkscale!" But I couldn't. If I stirred them up, they might see Calvin. I said, my words tumbling over each other, trying to back up, "Well, I guess Mr. Wasum might be proud of you at that. I guess he might think you'd vindicated the family's honor. I guess—"

"All right, you two," Shirley Wasum demanded, "what's all this whispering?"

My breath, almost used up by my babbling, went out with a whoosh, so it was Otis who answered his older brother, whose approach I had been too crazed even to note.

"He's begging and pleading for his life," Otis said. "Now ain't that just like a Fairchild?"

Shirley shrugged uncomfortably. "What Fairchilds do is Fairchilds' problem," he said. "Ours is Wasums', and I'm telling you, Otis . . ."

Shirley trailed off, and in the silence a horse snorted softly, and its stomach gurgled sonorously back in some stall, and Shirley's head started to turn toward the sound. Fearing he would see Calvin, I squeaked, "He's lied, he's lied! There ain't no feud, and he got you to come off after us on false pretenses, and you're to telegraph your daddy, and he'll tell you so hisself!"

Shirley's face turned contemptuous. "Don't try to come between brothers," he said. "Anyway, there ain't nothing for you to be crying about and making up lies, little boy. Not now, at least. Otis, I've just been telling and telling the others, and now I'm telling you—the minute those ragtags this boy and Calvin has picked up with show up and we get that picture back, that's all she wrote. Clinkscale and Cass can go their own way, and them wagon riffraff had damn well better go theirs. Then we do things the Wasum way—me against Calvin, he's old enough. You can try your hand against this boy, since Daddy wanted it. But we do it open and proper, and no more of this talk of killing some trussed-up prisoner. Now that's not right, Otis, and I won't have you talking that way one more time in front of some pair of Texans and giving them wrong ideas about how Wasums act."

My, but Shirley was firm! I couldn't help listening to him myself, and, forgetting where Calvin was at that moment, I felt my face turn red with shame for the way I'd just spoken of his daddy.

Otis, he turned paler instead. His pale blue eyes went watery and dilated, and he said in a voice nearly as squeaky as mine had been, "But you're not saying we should just let him go! He's a Fairchild!"

"Of course not," Shirley said. "Untie him and give him a gun, if you want to. Or let 'em try to run for it again. It makes no nevermind, we'll get 'em one way or the other. But we do it right. Goddamnit, Otis, are you listening to me?"

"I never heard of such a thing," Otis said shrilly. "He's here, isn't he? He's a Fairchild, isn't he? So we shoot him, simple, neat."

Shirley looked at his little brother curiously, blue eyes examining blue eyes, and he said slowly, "But you couldn't be afraid to face him down open, could you? You couldn't be."

And Otis struggled to get his pistol out of his holster, and Shirley just stood there and watched him curiously, and listened curiously as Otis mumbled, "Ain't nobody *afraid*—afraid, for Christ's sake?—afraid, when it's just plain horse sense . . ."

And then Shirley took a deep breath. He spoke everyday profanity, but it sounded like praying. He said, softly and mournfully, "Goddamn it to hell, goddamn it to hell. You *are* afraid. Oh, Otis. Oh. Oh, you've been *lying*."

Otis stared at him. "Don't you keep picking on me all the time," he said.

Shirley sighed heavily. "It's easy enough to find out," he said. "We'll just go send a telegraph to Daddy and ask him."

"No!" Otis said.

Shirley inspected his brother as if he were some strange, rare animal, and his voice went steely. He pointed at Otis's gun and said, "All right, all right. I won't hold this against you, as you're my kin. But it ends now. I'm going to pack you up and take you back to the parish with me, and before they get around to hanging the both of us, we're both going to face up to Daddy."

He reached for Otis's gun.

It went off straight in his stomach. The report was a flat sound in the stable.

Clinkscale cried out, "Fore God!" and came running as Shirley sat down in the dirt hard, trembling all over and feeling with a shaky hand at the blood seeping from his lower abdomen.

"What the goddamned hell is going on?" Clinkscale said.

"Stay back," Shirley said in a little voice. "This is a family matter."

Clinkscale drew to a halt and watched. Shirley's blue eyes, filled with wonder, roamed over me and Otis and the stable, and I stared first at Shirley and then at Calvin in the back of the stable, and I swear to God that Shirley's roving gaze took in Calvin too.

Would Shirley have spoken? He was down and in shock from the impact, but his voice worked. I think his eyes did too, but I'll never know if he would have cried the warning on Calvin, because at that moment another voice called from outside: "Hello the stable."

The voice was alarmed, but firm and authoritative. It belonged to Mr. Desmond.

Well, that did stir them all up, but not in Calvin's direction. Old Otis just crouched back on his bale of hay, looking down at his wounded brother, but Clinkscale and Cass Hubbard rushed to the stable door. They threw their shoulders against it, then Clinkscale said, "Watch it! That damned rifle will shoot right through this door!" They backed to the side, fast, guns drawn but not very steady.

Mr. Desmond called again, "I've come to parley. Open up!"

"One shot, and we kill the kid!" Clinkscale called back.

"I've no arms. I've just come to parley. See for yourselves."

Clinkscale handed the whiskey bottle to Cass Hubbard, who dropped it. The top was off, and the whiskey soaked into the manure on the dirt floor, and Clinkscale looked as worked up as a man could get, not knowing what-all to be perturbed about.

"Damn your eyes!" he said to Cass Hubbard. "Jump. Open that door. No, just a little crack. Go ahead. I'll cover you."

Cass Hubbard did what he was told. Mr. Desmond walked in. Cass Hubbard leapt back and pointed his gun at Mr. Desmond. Mr. Desmond's eyes ranged quickly over me, and Shirley sitting on the floor bleeding, and Otis. Then Mr. Desmond said in a firm, calm, equable voice, "Don't get your bowels in an uproar. I'm here just to parley. You got a friend of ours here. We want him back."

Well, if I had misjudged how long it would take for word to get back to Calvin and Mr. Desmond and Gil and Emma at the wagon, Otis & Company had misjudged even more so, and they were off guard and not knowing, not having prepared for it yet, what to do first. They didn't know, and I hadn't thought of it, that various Chinese people knew me, and knew us, from our having bought groceries from them and pawned valets' suits with them, and since there weren't too many red-haired boys in base ball suits running around Tombstone that night, Mr. Sam Wah, when his people had told him of seeing such a boy yanked into a supposedly closed livery stable, had figured instantly it was me and had sent word to my people.

Now one of my people was standing boldly inside the front of the livery, and one was creeping deeper from the back, and a sickness, a new nausea of apprehension, blossomed blackly inside me. Clinkscale, seeing that Mr. Desmond was not wearing a gun belt, stood back and cursed him. Mr. Desmond cursed in return, hard and succinct, not moving.

"Goddamn you, I want those pictures!" Clinkscale said, getting down to specifics.

How could Mr. Desmond know the spot I was in? His eyes roved over me once again, taking in me and maybe Otis there beside me with his drawn gun, and Shirley holding his belly on the floor, but he never looked once to the back of the stable. I did. Calvin was only five stalls down now, ducked behind a stall door, and I could see the tip of the rifle poking out.

Mr. Desmond said, "There ain't no pictures. Don't tell me you were fool enough to believe that boy about there being some picture. There ain't. But I guess you were fool enough. That man of yours, Jim Spoonts, told us all about it."

"I tell you, I want those pictures," Clinkscale said.

"I tell you, I want my boy," Mr. Desmond said. "We're prepared to pay. Just stand back."

Mr. Desmond pulled a little pouch from his pocket, and Clinkscale tensed over his gun. Mr. Desmond poured out the pouch on the dirt floor. Gold coins picked up light and gleamed, gleamed, in that dim lantern light, and there was one hell of a pile of them. I felt my blood tickle in my veins and something hollow happen behind my cheekbones as Mr. Desmond said, "Count it, if you wish. There's something over eleven hundred dollars there."

And my God, it looked as though there was. All of it. I knew as sure as I was sitting there, lunging but trying not to look as if I were, at my knots, that they had sent absolutely all of it with Mr. Desmond, and my practicality, so off-and-on, wailed, why hadn't they saved back at least two or three hundred?

"Fore God!" breathed Clinkscale.

Even Shirley's eyes went toward the money, gleaming there, adding the golden light of stored, available, more-than-one-man-could-accumulate money light to the lantern light.

And Mr. Desmond backed up two or three steps to let Clinkscale approach it. Clinkscale did. Cass Hubbard limped after him, his eyes on that golden sum that was more than some men's lives. And Mr. Desmond raised his right hand, where, hidden in his big palm, or perhaps in his sleeve, apparently was Gil's little pistol. There was a loud pop. A little, black hole opened up right over Sidney Clinkscale's left eyebrow, beneath his big hat with the guinea feather.

I saw that. I saw that with my head turning, looking for Calvin, and I heard Calvin's rifle shot whizzing three feet from me but a half foot from Otis Wasum, and Calvin shouted out his dismay. He had missed.

As Clinkscale fell limp to the floor, Mr. Desmond turned Gil's little gun on Cass Hubbard, and Cass Hubbard bolted through the front door. Immediately, there were two shots outside, one that might have been from a certain Navy Colt, one that might have been from a certain shotgun, and Gil's besotted-with-laudanum voice howled, "God! Missed! Shoot again, Emma! Shoot again!"

Mr. Desmond paused, gun aligned, to exchange a look with Shirley Wasum, but he must have seen nothing there to warrant his immediate attention, and he turned instead to me.

By now Otis had me by a forearm crooked around my throat, and I discovered that his gun was at my head. Otis shouted to Calvin, who was still waving Mr. Desmond's rifle back and forth from his stall door, and to Mr. Desmond, who was trying to line him up in the sights of the small pistol, "Get back. Get back. Or I kill him where he stands!"

"Kill him, and you're dead," Mr. Desmond said.

But Otis said, and his voice was soft again, "Go ahead. I don't give a damn."

Mr. Desmond's pistol wavered, only a little, but Otis saw. He said to Calvin, "Stand aside. Hurry! Or I blow out his brains!"

"No, Otis!" Shirley said.

And Calvin said, "No! Take the money! Leave him be!"

"To hell with your Fairchild money," Otis Wasum said.

Calvin stood aside. But Mr. Desmond came a few steps forward. Otis edged me toward the back door. I stumbled over the young Chinaman, and Mr. Desmond's gun came up, but so did Otis's. We backed past Calvin. We were at the door.

"Stop!" Otis said to Mr. Desmond.

Mr. Desmond didn't. He came forward, slowly, testing Otis's bluff, Gil's pistol firm in his hand. It was raised, looking for a chink in Otis's shield, which was my body, at which to shoot.

Mr. Desmond almost got his chance. Otis shifted, because my body was slow and unco-operative, and shoved me to the alley door. Mr. Desmond fired, and, it seemed, simultaneously, Otis fired back, and Mr. Desmond staggered and shouted, "Calvin!" but Calvin didn't fire, he couldn't, Otis kept me between him and that rifle, and then the alley door slammed behind us and we were in the dark.

Otis hissed at me, "You whoremonger! You whiskey-drinking, card-playing whoremonger! This way! Get going!"

He shoved me hard, and I stumbled, bound, my brain on fire. He hustled me through the stinking puddles of nameless filth in the alley, his pistol jabbing variously at my head, my shoulders, my back. And my friends, who had tried to save me, were left behind and I was alone with a seventeen-year-old killer in a dark, reeking alley.

Only I wasn't. I had yet another, forgotten friend. This one didn't even growl, but charged silently, black, blackly invisible in the black alley. Otis screamed with fear. I'm afraid that, shaken as I was, so did I. It was Nemo.

Nemo's charge struck Otis in the back. The forearm crooked around my throat slackened. I jerked free. Then urgent growling from Nemo commenced. I ran. I ran down the alley. I hauled up by the side of a privy, holding my breath at its stench. I could see a light, a coal-oil lamp, with ten or twelve Chinese people clustered in a crowded backyard, drawn there I reckoned by the sound of shots, and I ran toward them.

"Help me!" I said. I turned half around to exhibit the ropes that tied me. "You gotta help me! They're trying to kill me!"

All ten or twelve of the Chinese people leapt apart and disappeared into the back doors of houses.

A black, silent shadow ran up to my side, wagging his tail. Nemo dropped a lolling wet tongue in my tied but cupped-behind-me hands. He seemed to say, hadn't he done well?

"Oh Nemo!" I whispered.

Lights went out in the nearest houses.

I half-whispered, half-cried, "Please. Please help me!"

A little woman, older than Grandmother, maybe older than any woman I'd ever seen, black-dressed so I could hardly make her out, came out of the third house down. Nemo growled at her.

I said again, "Please. I'm tied. I gotta get loose. They're trying to kill me."

The little woman said, "Hold the large dog."

"I can't," I said. "I'm tied. He won't hurt you. Please, can you untie me?"

"Speak to him," she said.

I did. Nemo wouldn't back up, but he stopped growling. The black-dressed little woman had a knife in her hand, and she sawed quickly and neatly, and I only lost a little skin on one wrist. She didn't wait for me to thank her. She scurried back to her house, and I called after her, "Ma'am? Ma'am! I got to have a gun!"

But she had done all the interfering that a Chinese person in a white man's town perhaps dared to do. The light in her house went out, and I was again in darkness. Nemo bumped against my leg and whined a little as if to say, what do we do next?

Yes, what? Somewhere in that dark, malodorous alley was Otis, but in what direction? Toward the street? Toward the livery stable? Or had he fled, his brother wounded by his own hand, another of his people dead and the last run out on him, realizing his vulnerability now that he was alone?

Then Nemo started trotting back toward the livery while I hesitated, and I whispered, "Nemo! Come back!"

He didn't. I followed after him.

Now, I was a country boy, not really a town boy, and that dark, stinking alley was not familiar ground. I crept along, keeping to the side, scraping past sheds and privies and stepping in garbage that town merchants and town residents threw wherever was handiest, my nose, my feet, my hands assaulted at every step. There was a light in some little shack, and a peculiar smoky odor, and I crept toward it, wanting light.

I tried to be careful and quiet, but Nemo didn't know any better, and I suddenly heard him growl low in his throat, and I stiffened, holding my breath, hanging back from the edge of the light.

"Keep that dog away from me!" Otis Wasum said.

Nemo barked, the bark of a hunting dog when it has found and cornered its prey. But my God, with me bare-handed and having no gun, Nemo had found not our prey but our preyer.

"I'll shoot him!" Otis said. "Call him off, or I'll shoot him!"

My voice was trembly, but I said loudly, "Like hell you will! Make one move and I'll shoot you!"

I couldn't see Otis. Nemo's fussing was directed across the pool of light, so that had to be where Otis was, but I could only hear him, and Otis said uncertainly, "You're tied. You couldn't have got loose."

"Oh, no?" I said. "I guess I just imagined my friend Sam Wah who cut me loose and gave me a gun and sent his eight big sons looking for you in this here alley and himself ran off for the law!"

"You're lying," Otis said uncertainly.

"You're the liar," I said. "You're the snake, the bayou rat, the trash. Step forward slow, I can see your every move. Lay your gun down, and maybe I'll give you a chance to get away so as not to blacken the name of my home town all over the West."

Why did I always go too far? I could hear Otis sigh, and then the sigh became a faint little laugh, and Otis said, "You ain't got no gun. *You're* the liar. *You're* the one that's going to step forward. Fast! This second, or I shoot!"

Some lies must be acceptable to heaven. Mine came true. Or at least part did. Suddenly, there were voices far up the alley, and lanterns, and Calvin's voice saying, "No, man, no, just let me go alone!"

I saw a shoulder jolt into the light. I saw the side of a head as it turned toward the sound. Before my mind knew what my body was doing, I jumped toward Otis, Nemo a half heartbeat behind me.

I got one arm. Otis stumbled, and I knew that Nemo had an ankle. I yanked hard, all my weight behind it, on Otis's arm, swinging him like the last one on the chain in pop-the-whip, and Otis went down in the filth of the alley, with me and Nemo both on top of him.

Nemo must have gotten kicked, for he moved away, and Otis's free arm stretched out, reaching. His gun had been knocked out of his hand by the fall. It was bare hands to bare hands.

He flopped, slippery as a fish, struggling to get out from under me, and me struggling to keep him there. "Damn you," I gasped. "Oh damn you."

Otis's fist swung up. He hit me solidly on the side of my nose. It would have brought tears to my eyes, but—yes, again, I admit it—I was already crying. I cried with black fear. I cried with black anger. I cried because I was wrestling with a plain boy who had managed to become a madman in a black alley. Otis arched his body strongly and got his legs free, and I slid up to his chest, then he flopped frantically, and he was getting loose, and I lifted my knee and rammed it square into his face.

He rolled over. I rolled off him. I grabbed up the gun from the filth in which it was lying. It was slippery, but I held onto it, and I jumped to my feet and held it on Otis, holding tight with both hands.

In our little pool of light, I could see Otis rise to one knee. "Now, Otis Wasum," I said. "Now."

"They're never going to hang me," Otis panted.

"No," I said.

Otis got the rest of the way to his feet. He glanced down the alley, toward the street.

"Keep that dog off me," he said.

"Yes," I said.

Otis was choosing where to run. He said, "I never hurt you."

"You tried," I said. The gun was so slippery. I wished I had something to wipe it with.

Otis tensed, wanting to take the first step but not quite ready to risk it yet. "I probably even missed that old man," he said.

I said, "You tried to hurt him. You tried to hurt all of us. You'll try again. You'll never stop trying."

"You won't shoot," Otis said. "You know what they already say about you in the parish, and you know that wouldn't be the half of it if you shot somebody wasn't even armed." He turned to run.

And I shot.

I shot him in the back. He never even got out of the pool of light before I did it. He crumpled like a dead bird, flat on his face, then he rolled over and tried to focus his pale blue eyes on me, the eyes wide and his mouth wide with surprise.

And then his mouth drooped slackly and his head rolled raggedly to one side. I wondered if I should shoot him again, to make sure, but the voices and the lanterns were coming down the alley, attracted by the shot, and I dropped the pistol in the filth and turned toward them.

At the last minute, I remembered, and took my shirttail and wiped my face. I didn't want them to see that I had been crying.

But, of course, I cried again. I couldn't help myself. Emma cried too, and we both started when Mr. Desmond whispered to us, "Don't let them, I can't stand it."

This was wrung from him as the doctors tried to place him on a stretcher, and Emma turned on them like a catamount and said, "Leave him alone! Don't touch him!" Then she cried, chokingly, awkwardly, as though she didn't know how to do it very well.

"Now now," Mr. Desmond said to her. Then, since I was crying, he said it again to me, "Now now." But hell, I wasn't ashamed. Calvin and Gil had tears in their eyes too, but since it seemed to bother Mr. Desmond I tried to stop.

The doctors, two of the same who had fixed up Gil at the base ball diamond that afternoon, used the stretcher for Shirley Wasum. They'd already tended him and the young Chinese man, and Mr. Desmond too, and had moved Mr. Desmond to a spread of clean hay that one of the police chief's men put on the floor.

Otis's bullet had entered the right side of Mr. Desmond's lungs, passing through the spinal column, completely shattering it, and emerging on the left side. Mr. Desmond lived only about one hour.

The doctors already knew how things were with him and knew there was nothing they could really do, so they didn't argue with Emma. One went off after Shirley Wasum and the young Chinese man, and the other withdrew with nice discretion. After a minute or so, Mr. Desmond must have felt a little easier, for he reached for my hand and said, "Did them scum hurt you, son?"

"Nossir," I said. "I'm not hurt, just dirty."

"You sure are that," he said. He smiled his old, familiar little smile and said to Emma, "You're going to have one mighty dirty base ball uniform to have to wash tomorrow."

"Oh Hap," she said. She sobbed it.

"Hush, now," he said. "It's all right. You know the way it was with my roan. Better dead than just sore wounded and left behind."

"No," she said.

"Hush," he said.

"Oh God," she said.

"Hush," he said. "When I'm still, I can't hardly feel it. But I'll tell you this, I'm shot through the lights." He tried to smile again, I believe not just for Emma or the rest of us, but because he felt like smiling. "I know what that means," he said. "God almighty, the buffalo I've brought down that way. If you shoot the outside herd bull through the lights, he'll buff and blow blood, and the others will mill around him while he dies, and you can get in the next clean shot without even disturbing the herd. Your gun will get so hot you have to carry a bottle of water to pour through the barrel when it gets too dirty to shoot straight."

Mr. Desmond said this earnestly, looking at all of us, and his eyes finally settling on me, as if this was a lesson, so I nodded and said, "I'll remember."

Then Mr. Desmond's eyes moved to Emma. He said, "There's things to get settled here. If it's thought I have a share of that prize money, it must go to you. The way things are with you, it'll be handy."

"No, Hap," she said, trying to stop crying. "It must go to your little boys. Things are all right with me."

"No they aren't," he said, "and that's something else we'd better get settled."

Now his eyes moved to Gil, and he sighed, maybe feeling the pain, but maybe only in regret. Because he said to Gil, "I would have married her. I like babies anyway, they don't have to be just mine. But it's up to you now. Can't none of you allow her to take some old women's medicine, that's dangerous, that's the kind of thing women die from."

Emma put her head down close. "No, Hap," she whispered. "No, I swear. I never thought that. You know I can make a good living. There's no need to go telling them."

"A living's one thing, but every child needs a daddy, and that's something else," Mr. Desmond said. "Gil might decide to grow up one of these days. And if he doesn't, well, he'll make a good playmate for the boy."

Gil said, "But my God!"

"Just be quiet," Emma said. "Besides, there's no telling if it will be a boy."

Mr. Desmond said, "Of course it will. I always wanted a little girl, myself, but they're always boys."

Gil said in a hard, strained voice, "Emma, are you pregnant?"

He said it straight out. Nobody used just that straight way of saying it in those days.

I was stunned. No, not at only the word. It couldn't have happened. Maybe it happened to my young stepmother with my father, but it couldn't have happened to Emma.

Emma said, "It's none of your business."

"Like blazes it isn't!" Gil said. His voice got harder. "Or is it? Are you telling me Hap is the father?"

Mr. Desmond said, "Oh hell, I don't diddle decent women. It takes a product like you to do that. The point is, are you or aren't you willing to marry her? If you're not, speak up! Right now! There still might be time for Pepper to run for a preacher, and if I can give her nothing else, I can give her my name!"

Emma said anxiously, "Be still, be still. If you go to thrashing around it'll go to hurting."

Calvin blurted, "Don't worry none. There's nothing to worry about. If she'll have me, I'd be proud to marry her."

Gil turned on him, and I was glad all the guns had been put away. "You will like blazes!" he said. "If it's my baby, I'll marry her."

"I refuse," Emma said.

"Well then," I said, "I can pass easy for eighteen, and I'm willing, Emma."

Now her tears started again, and she said, "Pepper, Pepper. Are you disappointed in me?"

"No ma'am," I lied.

"Will you all shut up?" Gil said. He looked at Mr. Desmond, then he looked at Emma, then he said, his voice a lot less certain, "Emma, will you do me the favor, the honor . . ."

"No," Emma said.

"Yes," Mr. Desmond said. "That's best."

"No," Emma said again.

Gil said, "Emma, you idiot! I love you!"

"No you don't," Emma said.

"I've been trying to propose to you for weeks!"

"Oh," she said.

"All right," Mr. Desmond said, "then that's settled."

He closed his eyes, and we all watched him, anguished, but pretty soon he opened them and said to Gil, "It is settled, isn't it? You'll marry her?"

"With the greatest of pleasure," Gil said.

"Teach her how to like being a woman," Mr. Desmond said. "Maybe you can do it if you'll be a man."

Then he closed his eyes again. It was a lot longer before he opened them. Then he smiled his little smile, and he said, "That rain-water lake. You remember that. We shot them through the lights there too. That lake must have covered a whole quarter section. Yes, it was in the fall of the year, and that lake was dotted all over with wild ducks and geese. All around that lake you could hardly see the grass for buffalo. There were ponies too. Amongst them buffalo you could see wild ponies running loose, and you could make out horses and mules with saddle marks on them. They'd broken free from somewhere. That was one of the prettiest things you could ever see in your life, that lake and the buffalo and the wild ducks and them wild ponies. We camped there about eight days. We brought down nine hundred buffalo. That was a good time. That was a good time to be."

Then he was quiet so long that the doctor came and tested his pulse, and although he nodded, Mr. Desmond didn't speak again. He breathed his last, surrounded by me and Calvin and Gil and Emma. Finally, the doctor shook his head, no, and

Emma got straight up, trying not to sob out loud, and she walked straight for the door, stumbling a little, but then she straightened up and made it almost to the door before Gil leapt up and ran after her. He got his arms around her, and she struggled for only a few seconds before she put her head next to his and wailed like a lost baby.

I bawled too. So did Calvin.

Gil took Emma out.

There was just Calvin and me.

Seventeen

Those last few days in Tombstone were not days a person likes most to remember. They were taken up mostly with arranging a fitting burial for Mr. Desmond, and then going to it, and arranging a wedding and going to that, as Gil, who had no head for figures, could at least count up nine months and apparently thought he had already wasted enough time. Then there were questions, questions, from the law about Otis and Sidney Clinkscale and eventually their burial in Tombstone's boot hill. I didn't bother to go to that, nor did we bother to do what the law also pestered us for, which was to file a complaint against Shirley Wasum. He'd live, the doctors told us, but Calvin and I knew he'd never live again with the Wasums of Claiborne Parish, Louisiana. I guess, having gotten to know Shirley as well as we did, we thought that was punishment enough for him.

Lastly, there was Gil and Emma's adamant wish that Mr. Desmond's share of the money go to his littlest boys in Temple, Texas, in spite of what Mr. Desmond had said, and Gil and Emma and Calvin and I and Freddie Fassnidge all sat together after dinner at their house and tried to write a letter that little boys eight and five years old could understand.

Yes, Gil and Emma had a house. It was on Sixth Street, next door to a female boarding house and not too far from the crib district, but Emma maintained her independence—no, perhaps that should be "secession"—of thought by deploring the nearness

of so many nosy boarders and apparently never gave consideration to any idea that the town's cypriotes were less desirable
neighbors. Mr. Johnson had arranged houses for them to choose
from, and all sorts of other things, including a lawyer and bail
for Freddie, who spent his days writing to England for money
and to Texas trying to get his ranch back, and his nights down
at our friend Dugal Stewart's place. He would cheerfully have
moved right into Gil and Emma's little house, until I pointed
out to him that newlyweds are best off spending their first time
together alone.

Gil was working at the mine office, and he concluded that he
might as well become an entrepreneur after all. Gil also concluded he would write his travel diary for the London publish-
ing houses but would retitle it *At Home in the Last Frontier*.
But I concluded that Gil would mostly play base ball in a white
and red uniform with a red "T" embroidered on it, and that if
anyone ever got around to writing the book about our travels it
would have to be me. I felt that Gil and Emma would succeed
in finding their lives, but Gil made me feel very grown up by
comparison. I strongly suspected Emma had married herself a
permanent boy.

As for Emma, she insisted that she would go on working for
a few months at the *Daily Tombstone,* and I figured the *Tombstone* would have itself a new lady editor inside a fortnight. For
one thing, Gil had made her write the news story about Otis and
Sidney Clinkscale, I think to get her mind working on something other than our poor Mr. Desmond, and the story attracted
no end of attention, not because Tombstone didn't stage plenty
of homicides to report, but because a lady had reported this one.
So that last night for the dinner, she had to rush home from the
newspaper to fix it, and the steak was tough, and the biscuits
had too much baking powder in them, and Calvin teased her so
about her cooking and Gil's chances of survival on it that we all
managed to laugh a little for the first time in a long time.

But no one was laughing when it came time to try to write
that letter to Mr. Desmond's little boys. Finally Calvin got up
and walked agitatedly through the litter of discarded paper on
the floor and said, "It's just no use. Some things got to be said,
not written. Pepper, you'll be going right near Temple, Texas,

on your way back home. Do you feel you'd be up to taking the money to their mother and telling them yourself?"

I looked at him, startled. Go home? What for? They had all insisted that I take my split, and Calvin had always insisted that the split be even, and I owned two hundred and thirty dollars and fifty-two cents. With a stake like that, if I couldn't manage to become successful and respected and quite probably famous after five or ten years on my own, well, then I deserved whatever disparaging word that might get back to Claiborne Parish about me.

Gil said, "Temple is an easy little ramble from your home, Pepper. Perhaps you could go by there every six months or so and see the little boys. You could help them remember Hap. You could help guide them. Don't you think he'd like for you to do that?"

It was blackmail, of the most blatant kind. Freddie may have seen it, because he tucked his good-natured moon face into his collar and said, "No, really, upon my word. That is, really, perhaps it would be too painful for Pepper. Some things are too painful to remember, old puts."

Calvin sighed. "Well, it's well known that I never seem to get things straight." I thought he was blackmailing some more, but he went on, "Is it wrong, to remember? Me, I don't want to forget Mr. Desmond or Jamie all the days of my life."

Emma said, "You know that none of us will forget, Calvin."

"Well, but Pepper could write us letters and tell us how Mr. Desmond's little boys are, and whether they look like him, and things like that. He could write you here in Tombstone and me in San Diego." Calvin looked straight at me. He was trading.

Emma said, "I wonder if there's a photographer in Temple. I'd love to see their portrait." She blushed, because her condition made it certain that by early spring there would be another candidate for our consideration, and she said, "It's strange, but since the little boys belonged to Hap, it seems like they belong to all of us. I wonder what their mother's like? Maybe she'd even let them come out here sometime. Hap would like that. He so loved the West."

So it was more blackmail, with only Freddie refraining, and it got me to thinking, as much as anybody could do much thinking with Calvin and Emma and Gil keeping it up until I finally said we'd put the money in a cashier's check, which I knew all about and knew how to deal with, and they must rely on me to inform the little boys in the way that I thought best for them and for myself. I guess I said it firmly, for they hushed. Freddie announced that he would now entertain us with the Mexican songs that he had, willy-nilly, learned in jail, and he sang so comically that we settled down and got to laugh some more during the last part of our last evening.

But Emma wasn't laughing when it came time for us to leave the next morning. Her eyes were red again, and her face was anxious, and it just got more anxious when Freddie and our friend Dugal dropped around for a minute to say good-bye and shake our hands. Then they left us alone for our own good-byes, due to Dugal's diplomacy I knew, and Emma tried at the last minute to persuade us to let old Nemo stay with her and Gil.

This disturbed Calvin, for he hated so to say no to her, and Gil finally settled it by saying, "No, Emma. If you weren't so idiotically stubborn about wanting to work at the newspaper, I'd say yes, but with you there and me at the mine office, poor Nemo would be left by himself all day. He isn't used to that. He'd be lonely."

"But how do we know Calvin will have a place to keep him in San Diego?" Emma said anxiously.

"I'll have a fine place," Calvin said. "And he can go right with me when I make my rounds for Phemister's Photographs and all."

"But all those photographic poisons might drop on him."

"Don't worry so, Emma," I said. "Nemo'll be just fine."

She was distracted and unhappy. She got more so when I brought the What's-It Wagon around from their side yard, where Calvin and I had been snugly camping. She said, "You must both write all along the way. I won't have a quiet minute until I know you're safely settled."

"We'll write," Calvin assured her.

Emma *abrazo*-ed us both, and so did Gil, but Emma kissed us, too. When she came to me, she whispered, "We'll take care of Hap's grave. Don't you have a moment's unease thinking that Gil won't want to. He's already said he's going to have some bottom dirt hauled into the yard and dig me a garden. There'll be flowers to take. Maybe roses."

So my eyes got red, but so were everyone else's, and Calvin and I climbed into the What's-It Wagon, and Calvin whistled old Nemo off Emma's front porch, where he'd been wheezy-snoring, and I clucked up the mules.

Emma ran a little way after the wagon. She called, "Write right away! Be sure to! Be sure!"

Gil made her stop running. They stood there and waved. Nemo hesitated, looking at them and looking at the What's-It Wagon and perhaps wondering where his master was, although we'd taken care to tie him and never let him know where was the grave, and then Calvin whistled to him again, and he trotted after us, being used to trotting after the wagon and maybe deciding in his doggy brain that this was just another temporary outing. And he always liked outings.

So he followed the wagon, looking rested and feisty, until we got a long ways out of town, heading west, the trace chains jangling and the mules' ears bobbing, and neither Calvin nor I saying much until we neared the San Pedro River, where the road split, one arm heading north up the Pedro, and one crooking a little south, I think to some town named Tubac, then the one called Tucson, and on to San Diego, California.

I stopped the mules to check the road directions Gil's boss, Mr. Johnson, had written out for me. Nemo paused a little way behind the wagon and looked back the way we had come, but Calvin whistled, and Nemo came a little closer.

"Reckon he's tired?" I said.

"No dog that's walked all across Texas to the territories is going to get tired so easy," Calvin said.

I looked around. Overhead, white puffy clouds were mounting, and I said, "Reckon it might rain?"

"This poor old desert sure could use it," Calvin said.

I said, "Them clouds are right pretty. They might make a pretty view. There's plenty of time, if you'd care to stop and take one."

"No," Calvin said, "I guess not."

"Hell," I said.

"Don't cuss," Calvin said.

"I think it's all right for me to do it now," I said.

"Well, maybe you're right," he said.

We sat and looked around. On the road behind us, Nemo sat and looked around.

I said, "Calvin, would you really have married Emma if she'd said yes?"

"Of course," he said simply. After a minute, he added, "I sort of had the idea that you would really have lied you were eighteen and married her too."

It made my throat feel chokey, when I thought of what I perhaps had lost before I had even had a fair shot at winning it, her being born so long before me, me being born so late, too late. But I just said, "Yes."

Calvin whistled some more at Nemo, but Nemo went down on his belly and lay there, sort of cringing as dogs sometimes will when they're instructed to do one thing but have some thought to do another.

But I still couldn't quite let it go. I said, "Calvin, maybe you think you're too ugly, and maybe she thought I was too young, but maybe not, and I can't help but wonder if she wouldn't have been better off with us than with Gil."

He didn't say anything.

"Haven't you wondered that?" I insisted.

Calvin sighed. "Yes," he said. "But on the other hand, I think Emma might sort of like having someone she has to look after, and you and I don't need looking after as much as Gil does. We're more like Hap. We're independent."

"That's true," I said.

Now, finally, we looked at the road where it split in front of us. "I wonder what a buffalo lake looks like," I said. "I ain't never heard of buffaloes being in California."

Calvin said, "I never heard of any in Arizona either. Besides, those times are gone now."

I said, "Calvin, maybe it's not for me to say it, since it was for me that he gave up his gold mine and his new ranch, but I've been thinking, and I think maybe Mr. Desmond did have his times. I'll bet he had himself plenty of fine things to know and see, and they're not gone as long as we remember them for him."

Calvin looked at me quickly.

"Then you'll go see his little boys in Temple, Texas?" he said. "You'll go home?"

"There's a condition," I said.

"Pepper, I'm your partner. Don't bargain with your very own partner."

"I'm just trying to be practical," I said. I gestured. In front of us there was . . . nothing. There was only land, unoccupied, uncluttered, incomplete. And this was the last of it. I said, "It just seems a shame to me for some fine photographic artiste not to be out roaming around taking views of all this. They say there's a giant canyon up north somewhere. I wonder what that would look like through a view camera?"

"Upside down," Calvin said shortly. "Pepper, you got to go back home. I can't let you ruin your fine young life just rambling around with me."

"Well, we're not litigating about that," I said. "You've been trying to make a case swapping me going back home for you giving in and going on to San Diego, California. But the case is, what if I go on back home for a year or two, and you go rambling, and I'll buy all the New York magazines and look at your photographs, and by and by I'll be all through with school, and I'll have me plenty of capital to look for some fine business opportunity and someplace nice to be, and I'll come back out and have a look around. With you."

Calvin stared at me, as if he wasn't quite sure he'd heard right. "You mean just forget about San Diego and Mr. John Swiss Parker? You'd do that? You'd go home and not hold me to my half of the bargain?"

"I don't remember ever agreeing to any such bargain."

His hazel eyes, rayed with gold, suddenly looked joyous, but his mouth worked, and he said, "Are you sure, Pepper? Are you real sure? It don't seem right for me to make you give up your heart's dream unless I'm willing to do the same. I'll go on to San Diego if you want me to. I wouldn't mind it. I really wouldn't."

"I don't see that's necessary," I said.

"But you don't want to go back," he said.

"I never said I would enjoy it. But, hell, Calvin, you've got to remember that I've invested in you. I've got me a financial interest in you taking all kinds of pretty portraits of the West. Then before you know it, I'll be back to join you."

"You couldn't come back until you finished your schooling. The judge might even want you to go into the law, and he'd skin me alive if I let you come out with me before you finished your education."

To tell the truth, I felt very educated already. Our trip had done that for me. But I only said, "Maybe. Although I think that's something I'll decide for myself."

"But holy God," Calvin said, now suddenly shy and fearful, "what would the home folks say if I didn't go on to San Diego?"

"I guess it depends on which home folks," I said.

Calvin's gold-rayed eyes searched mine, and then I saw that he understood. Maybe our world had indeed turned somewhat upside down, in that not those other nice people back in Claiborne Parish, but a Mexican bandit, an English remittance man, a fallen lady editor, and a sick buffalo hunter whose real days had maybe left him behind, had become the folks in our hearts' true home.

And we both knew what our true home folks would think.

I said, "There's probably three weeks or more yet before school starts, and I can afford my own train ticket. I sure would like to see that big old canyon before I have to start back. Of course there's not just a whole world of time, for I must route back through Temple, Texas, so maybe I'd best cluck up these mules, partner."

"Are you really, really sure, Pepper?" Calvin said.

"Aren't you?" I said.

He whistled to Nemo.

Nemo crawled a couple of inches closer on his belly, but he kept looking back, and he still wouldn't come.

"Wait a minute," said Calvin, and he jumped out of the wagon, as lithely and as boyishly as Gil had ever done. He squatted by Nemo and stroked him and spoke to him, and finally he lifted that big, old, black dog in his arms and carried him to the wagon.

"I think Nemo'd better ride from now on," Calvin said.

Nemo looked confused and uncertain when Calvin put him

on the spring seat. He was supposed to walk, not ride. He shifted and strained to get down, but I held him beside me in the seat. He kept looking as if he wanted to jump back out of the What's-It Wagon until Calvin climbed in and scratched his ears and calmed him and assured him that it was all right. Then Nemo relaxed and flopped down on the seat between us, and his tongue lolled out, and he started to pant wheezily, and he settled his shaggy rump against me and rested his front paws on Calvin.

I clucked up the mules. At the split of the road, I turned north. Calvin looked up at the clouds, gold-rayed eyes beaming as bright as the beaming desert sun, and he said, "You know, them clouds *are* right pretty. Maybe we can stop after a while and take a view."

And we continued on, at least for that time. And at least in my mind, we all went on together.